THE MURDERER NEXT DOOR

THE
MURDERER
NEXT
DOOR

RAFAEL YGLESIAS

CROWN PUBLISHERS, INC.
NEW YORK

This is a work of fiction. All the characters are fictitious, and any resemblance to persons living or dead is coincidence.

Quality Printing and Binding by:
ARCATA Graphics/Kingsport
Press and Roller Streets
Kingsport, TN 37662 U.S.A.

FOR LEWIS

———

THE
MURDER

B efore the murder I was grateful to live where I live, to work where I work—for all the happy facts. My only fear, besides the timeless one, was that it might change. Count your blessings, I told myself, don't be smug because everything is as it should be.

The happy facts—what were they? Nothing extraordinary. I was married, a partner in an excellent New York law firm; I had successful, interesting friends. Not taken for granted: I was proud, even vain, of my life.

Why should I have been so glad to be respectable? You know, of course. I was born poor. Born poor in the town of Sargentville, Maine, the daughter of a failed lobsterman, Sherman Gray. My mother too. And his mother, for that matter. All the way back into the gray mist of Maine history, my people have lost their boats to the banks, their traps to rivals. I've tried to pinpoint the first luckless Gray without success. Precision isn't required, however. All the early settlers were descendants of criminals, exiled or escaped or indentured to America. Generations of Grays have lived as if imprisoned in Sargentville, paying penalty for unremembered sins.

"Bullshit," Naomi used to answer, "the Grays aren't especially degenerate. Look at the Boston Brahmins. They're the children of pirates. And they haven't moved for three hundred years either."

I was paroled at age eight by Naomi Perlman. She had come to our front yard to buy crabmeat. The crabs were caught inadvertently in Father's lobster traps, and picked clean each morning by my mother's reddened and scratched hands. I peeked around one of several rotting cars in my father's front yard to get an eyeful of her—a new rich summer person. Naomi saw my straight and yellow hair first, so bright that even my filthy condition—there was grime embedded in every pore—couldn't dim it.

3

"Whose beautiful blond hair is that?" she asked. Naomi's tone wasn't prim and reedy, the usual Boston Brahmin voice; she squawked her question, an aggressive goose, neck extended, chin forward. She had a big animated face, a thick brow, long nose, strong jaw, knobby chin—and her hair was a wild bush, electrified by her brain, sizzling up from her scalp. "My daughter," Mother answered her in a mumble, eyes cast down—the ashamed, unworthy look of the poor.

"What did you say!" Naomi barked at Mother.

That startled Mother into a normal volume. "She's Molly, my little girl."

"Molly!" Naomi walked toward me in her peasant stride, each foot going as wide as it did forward, a three-year-old's gait.

I was drawn out to Naomi from my hiding place without being aware of it, mesmerized by her brown eyes, big and gentle, curious and willing to love.

"I'm Naomi," she said, and offered her hand. "Would you like to earn some extra money this summer? I need a mother's helper." Tall for my age, she mistook me for ten or eleven. I wanted to go with her anyway, and Mother was glad to have me out of the way, especially if it meant I could earn a few dollars.

Poor Naomi, I wasn't much help that summer. She did most of the work, not teaching me to care for her one-year-old son, Joshua, but telling me of the world, especially her startling (to me) statement that women were every bit as smart and strong as men. She handed me books to read aloud while she amused her baby boy, defining the difficult words, explaining their amazing ideas. She told me what I should love, what I should hate—and that I should always think for myself.

Her husband was Sam Perlman, an ex-movie-studio president, rich from the script he was given to produce as part of his termination package. The picture had been one of the highest grossing movies of the 1950s, and although he had no other successes, those profits were enough to live on for the rest of his life, even if he turned out to be immortal. Sam was twenty years older than Naomi: she was the adventure of his middle age, a youthful tonic, vigorous, brash, and fertile. An apparently independent wife, she gathered ideological causes for him to support, and netted lost souls, such as me, to help her redeem. I don't mean to make fun of Naomi. Although she was loud and angry and spoiled, she had the bursting, generous heart of a puppy scrambling after you for your attention and love.

I spent my days and most evenings at her house that summer. From the beginning I was made equal: freer, more respected, more loved than I was at home. I sat pretty, not serving, at her elegant dinners. After a month, Naomi became obsessed with the notion that I should go to a better school than the local one. By Labor Day Sam offered to send me to a boarding school.

Naomi and I went together to discuss the idea with my parents. Sam had objected: "You don't know how they'll react. You'd better—"

"Shut up, Sam." Naomi put the flat of her hand on his bald spot whenever dismissing him good-naturedly. "We don't need Big Daddy."

I thought we did. I was scared. My stomach gurgled in the passenger seat of Naomi's Volvo while we drove to my parents' trailer. The afternoon sun—we timed ourselves to arrive after their dinner at four—flashed across Naomi's deeply tanned, thick legs. In an effort not to intimidate my parents, she was dressed casually in shorts and a T-shirt. I guess she hadn't waxed recently because I remember her legs were hairy; usually black, the hairs were tinted red and brown by the sun, flashing as the light penetrated roadside maples, pines, and birches. We passed one yellow leafed birch, an early victim to fall, standing alone among still-green brothers.

"Look at that!" I pointed to the birch. "She's turned."

"Beautiful," Naomi said dully. She never noticed scenery, she seemed only to see people.

"Why do you think one of them turns before all the others? Is it sick? What makes it different?" I asked.

"That's clever." She smiled as if I'd made a joke, glancing away from the road to look at me. Her smile faded at my puzzled expression. She returned to her driving and frowned, worried.

"What's wrong?" I asked, knowing I had missed a chance to be clever.

"Do you really want me to ask your parents to let us send you to school?"

"I told you so already!"

"It might hurt their feelings."

"They won't like it," I agreed, and my stomach hurt, twisting. She stopped the car. "Should I turn back?"

I remember staring at the black dashboard. The ashtray was pulled out in the middle, filled with butts, its metal smudged gray. My eyes trailed to her toasted legs, flesh squashed out on the seat, red and brown hairs curled on top. Naomi did something shocking to the locals: she sunbathed topless on her beach, unconcerned if someone happened by. She had big breasts, much larger than my mother's, and I thought about them then, sitting in the car, although of course they were covered. I wondered how big mine would be. I worried they wouldn't be nice. "Let's go back," I said, giving up.

We returned in silent defeat. Again, Sam offered to go with us. For an answer, I burst into tears, upset by the confusion in my heart, a strong desire to be free of my dreary poverty, and the equally strong fear of a world I didn't know. Naomi hugged me. I cried into her T-shirt, and then sneezed from her perfume. When I had calmed down, they wrapped me in a blanket and I sat on the floor in front of their huge stone fireplace, big enough for me stand in if I crouched a bit, watching a birch log burn. I thought back to the yellow-leafed tree that had somehow puzzled my will. Naomi brought me a cup of hot chocolate and stared through the fire, unresponsive to the noisy crackling bark, pensive as she knitted one thick eyebrow with her fingers. I thought the oddness of her features was beautiful: long nose, black eyebrows, protruding forehead, argumentative chin—an angry storm of flesh—while her gentle brown eyes were calm and loving at the center. She seemed nervous, twisting her eyebrow hairs, her right foot jiggling.

I've let her down, I thought, and felt cold in the warmth of the blanket, shivering from the hot fire. "I want to go. I'm sorry. I changed again."

Naomi's foot calmed, she raised her head from the fire and stared at me, the brown eyes quizzical. But she didn't speak. The birch in the fireplace began to whistle. Father used to say wood made that noise when it was about to be split open by the heat.

Sam answered. He was behind me on the couch. "Take your time. I can call your folks, tell them you're sleeping here—"

"I want to ask them. I'm not scared anymore." Sure enough, the log cracked and flames appeared from its middle.

"I scared you the last time," Naomi whispered.

As soon as she said that, I knew she was right. She had weakened my resolve. Somehow, my inspiration had also been my nemesis. "Yes," I answered. "I want to go to that school. Let's go ask them."

"You're the bravest girl in the world," Naomi said.

We got back into the Volvo. This time I covered my eyes when we passed the prematurely yellow birch.

My mother and father were unsettled by Naomi's appearance. They both came out of the house to meet us in the yard, and they didn't ask her in, as if there were something horrible inside she couldn't be allowed to see. Mother nervously pushed down on the legs of her jeans while Naomi talked, the way a girl might if her skirt was too short. Father held the brochure about the school in his hand without opening it, without grasping it in his fingers, without a glance at its contents. To me it described a paradise.

"You'll pay?" were the first words my father said.

"Of course," Naomi said. "We'll pay for the extras too, clothes, books."

"They'll take her?" my mother asked.

"I'm sure they will," Naomi said. She was scared of them, or their reaction: I could tell from her formal tone. Her lack of nerve surprised me again.

"Do her good," my mother mumbled to Father, glancing shyly, fearfully, at him.

I felt no worry now. I was happy. The decision had been made and I knew that it was right. Father wouldn't have to worry about paying for me, Mother would have less work, and I could be part of the other world, where it didn't freeze for seven months, where you could become anything you wanted.

"Molly," my father said, moving to stand in front of me, the brochure pointed at my chin. "Don't you mind being so far from home? We can't come get you if you're homesick, you know. Can't afford to, anyways—"

"If she needs to come back, that'll be—"

"I have to hear you say it, Molly." What should have been my father's soft fair skin had been enameled by the ocean's shadeless sun, browned and hardened, a dark setting for his blue, blue eyes.

They shined bold and clear, looking at me without love or pity or worry or anger. Merely curiosity.

"I don't mind," I said, and then my stomach fell, knowing I had made a mistake. I hadn't understood his question until after I answered: he'd meant, didn't I mind not being his daughter anymore?

He hit me. Naomi told the story to anyone who expressed the slightest doubt that she had done the right thing. On many a summer evening I lay awake upstairs, furious because I overheard Naomi whisper it to an amazed houseguest.

Every thought in my head exploded from the blow. He used his fat callused hand, the same hand that held the brochure, stuck to his open palm. Its slick paper slid across my jaw. My plummeting face hit first. I stayed down, tasting the smelly ground between my teeth, mashing my mouth in even farther to eat the soil as it mixed with the blood on my lips, wanting to burrow into the shitty earth. Mother, of course, said nothing. Naomi screeched at Father. He ignored her. Instead, he stared down at me with blue, blue eyes, glowing in their sockets.

"Take her," he said, watching me writhe. "But she don't come with a money-back guarantee." He silenced Naomi with a turn of his head. "She changes her mind, you're stuck with the bitch."

⚜

I never changed my mind. I visited my parents on holidays and, of course, saw them summers. Mother wanted me to spend more time, or so she said. I'll be blunt: once you live without the smell of fish, the headache of black flies, the beery thick-mouthed jokes of drag-racing heroes, you're happy to face a panhandler, a cockroach, and hear a construction worker's smooching call. Without a defense against the outdoors, the country is filthy: a seasonal parade of mushy snow, chunks of mud, pillars of sand, smears of grass, whittles of bark, windowsill graves of dead bugs, and the agonized noise of trapped living insects. Then there's the live-in relationship with weather: cold knifing at the border of every window, sneaking up your legs from a floorboard, blasting your back at every exit and entry; or the ripe smell of chest-heavy humidity, the bone-aching damp of mist and fog. When you're poor, the first thing you notice about a wealthy home, whether it's an apartment on Fifth Avenue or a weekend house in Vermont, is the tight vacuum seal against Nature, the absolute control of environment. I never really looked back to that trailer or my sad parents. I'm not proud of my flight, I don't say that my father's slap gave me a right to leave. I had to take my chance at freedom: the pursuit of happiness is ruthless.

I'm concerned that you not think Naomi was capricious or thoughtless or inconstant. She tried hard to repair the damage done to my family's feelings. She nagged me to write them, spend my holidays there (at least for a few years), invited them to dinner (Father said no), and squashed the terrible snobbishness I exhibited as a teenager.

I wince at the memory of me at fifteen, dressed in preppie clothes, the caw of my Maine accent yawned into a lockjawed drawl, parading about Naomi's glassed-in dining room among her startled guests. I had had a glass of wine with dinner—and another secretly in the kitchen—before Naomi stopped me from pouring more at the table. Over dessert, a middle-aged woman began an anecdote about driving on an inland road, passing shacks and trailers, yards full of wrecked cars, describing the routine sloppiness of the poor with a kind of thrilled horror, a pleased superiority disguised as compassion. "Those poor people," she concluded.

"Why do they sit in their cars?" her husband said. "Have you noticed? They sit—"

"There's nothing to do." Naomi talked over him. She didn't return my look, so I knew she thought the conversation was hurting my feelings and that confirmed my belief I had something to be ashamed of. "The government has completely failed to—"

"It's like their porch." The husband ignored Naomi. His wife caught my eye. She smiled at me and nudged him. But he didn't take the hint to be quiet. "They have the highest retardation rate in the country, did you know that?"

"That's on the islands!" Naomi waved her ornate antique silver serving fork at him. "You don't know what you're talking about! During the winters, those islands used to be cut off and there was a lot of inbreeding—"

"They're boneless!" he went on, and most of the company

laughed. "Have you seen them in the malls? Boneless people, waddling through the aisles." Now they were all laughing, except for Naomi. What did he mean? I wondered, feeling the heat of shame gather about my face.

"That's disgusting!" Naomi shouted, and flicked the fork in his direction, spotting him with a fleck of blueberry pie juice. "You're being incredibly insensitive! It makes me sick. Who the fuck do you think you are? What do your people on the Lower East Side look like?"

While Naomi ranted at him, the man finally looked at me, and obviously remembered who I was. I couldn't meet his eyes. Boneless People, I repeated in my head, the words worrying me. They made me feel I came from creatures—science-fiction aliens—and that I would never be normal. I Am a Teenage Boneless Person.

"You would know," he said to me, a bold look in his eye. He must have decided that if he pretended to be unashamed, we would all assume he meant no insult. "Why do they sit in their cars in their driveways?"

"Don't be a schmuck," Sam said, wearily.

"They drink," I said. I had a part to play, I realized with relief. I could be the Boneless Person Expert. "They can roll up the windows, smash a couple of mosquitos, and know that no more will get in. They can neck. It's like an extra room."

"I see." He nodded. Everyone seemed to relax. I looked at Naomi for applause. She smiled gently.

"Anyone want more pie?" she asked.

"They're trash," I added, greedy for their attention and approval. "Can't read. Don't know any better. Drunks. Trash." I nodded sagely. "They act pretty retarded, so maybe they are—"

I don't remember how Naomi began, I don't really remember her whole speech. She shamed me, said I knew better than anyone that Maine's poor were victims, suffering from lack of opportunity. While she talked I sensed that every eye was on me, every mouth shut to restrain either amusement or pity. The lecture was painful. I had no real family, only Naomi. She meant to teach me the same compassion she had felt for me, but when she said, "You were one of them, you know how hard their life is," I heard only her separation from me, that I was different from her, from her smart guests, from the world

I now inhabited. I gripped my chair on the sides, pressed my finger-tips against the wood, wishing to shut my eyes and disappear, yet also not wanting to show any of them that I was bothered. I didn't feel angry, or sorry for myself. I felt unworthy.

"Molly's not one of them," the troublemaker said. I guess he meant to be charming. "She's got plenty of bones! She's got great bones." The table laughed with pleasure and relief.

I tried to, but a sob came out, and I swallowed it quickly before they heard. "I'd better clear," I said, and stood, grabbing two pie plates before rushing out to the kitchen. It's over, I thought with relief, glad to have a chore to distract me.

Naomi appeared with more plates. She leaned against the sink, studying me. "Did you understand what I was saying?"

I nodded, prayed she would stop.

"Don't become one of those people who despises what they are and where they came from. You have nothing to be ashamed of. In fact, it should make you even prouder. And—this is important—it should make you want to help others. Because you know, *you* of all people know that if given the chance, any of those kids could lead better lives. Understand?"

Naomi couldn't have guessed what that meant to a nervous fif-teen-year-old, a lonely girl who worried she didn't belong at the school she attended, or with the adults who cared for her. It meant to me that I wasn't special to Naomi—one in million she had chosen out of love and admiration—but merely a social experiment, a labo-ratory mouse. I lied, said I understood. She hugged me, said, "I love you," and went back to her guests.

Why didn't I ask her? Why didn't I say, am I no different from the others? Could you have gone into the next driveway and found another Molly Gray just as good? Because I thought she would routinely reassure me, that she was too kindhearted to tell the truth except by accident.

I was uneasy in the kitchen. Their voices intruded and I worried there would be more lectures, more hammering on my heart. The house was stuffy with their talk, smart talk that I had flattered myself before dinner I was equal to, and I now hated, thinking it was what disconnected me from Naomi, what had made me feel so miserable and alone.

I stepped outside into the cool air. Naomi and Sam owned a long stretch of private beach on the bay, dark and still that night. Above, there was a bright cloudless sky, exploded with stars, not vast, but crowded with life, a Manhattan skyline of the cosmos, far away, yet beckoning, knowable.

Walking down to the shore, I fought my feelings, tried to swallow their bulk. I told myself—and this was the only time I considered going back—that I should return home. I could drive there myself in a Volvo not too different from the one that had taken me away.

Go now and in a few years you'll forget all the nice things, I told myself. Be strong—go now or you'll always feel this sad and unsure. I thought of all my so-called friends at school and admitted that though they were polite, they were not comfortable with me. Somewhat precociously, I knew that soon I would be too old, too different, too spoiled to go back. If I returned right away, the beautiful things, the marvelous ideas, the grand ambitions might become nothing more than a fantasy, something to hug at night while I slept next to my drunk and snoring husband, also dreaming of some other life.

Giving up the struggle to pull even with all the bright rich kids, dropping my oars to drift with the current in an aimless boat appealed to me. I wanted to be defeated, to lose, to be free of freedom. I'm weak, I decided, surprised, because I thought that's why I had been chosen, for my strength.

"You made a mistake," I said out loud to Naomi, staring back at the glassed-in porch where she and her guests lingered over coffee, free now to openly scare themselves with stories of the weird Boneless People. "I'm not strong enough," I bawled, overflowing with self-pity.

The bay can amplify a voice and carry it for miles: mine seemed to echo among the pines. Ashamed that I might have been heard, I covered my mouth and panted through my fingers.

"Shut your trap, you stupid girl," I said to myself, imitating how my father scolded when he came home tired. "I'm sick of your bawling." My Maine accent had returned; I had flattered myself it was gone. "Don't you put your ugly red face in my food. Shut up!" I snapped my head back as if I'd just been slapped. "Now go to your room and shut your ugly mouth!"

You've gone mad, I thought. I spooked myself. Scared, I ran to the freezing water, knelt on the rocks, ignoring the sharp biting circles of the barnacles, and put my hot face in the bay, hoping its ice cold would shock me out of lunacy.

When I returned to the house, after all the guests were gone, to face Naomi's nosy, worried, even guilty questions, I had wrought a change. I was no longer a soft and willing clay for her gentle, and sometimes cruel hands. I had been fired, too hard for any more shaping.

❧

Since I am telling the story of the people I've lost or fought hard to keep, then our next stop is New York. I am a brand-new associate in the law firm where I eventually made partner. After two years in the city—as was the case in boarding school, college, and graduate school—I had few friends, although I had many acquaintances, dated a lot, and went to my favorite kind of social gathering, namely large, loud, anonymous parties. I had no close friend, no best friend, until I met Wendy Sonnenfeld.

That happened in SoHo, in a dark loft, blaring with music and quaking with dancers. Our dates knew each other and introduced us. Later we went out to breakfast at an all-night diner on Canal Street. Over pancakes, Wendy told me she had gone to Hunter Elementary, a school for bright children. It ruined me, she said. She claimed she suffered from a self-imposed pressure; that unless she was busy with an extraordinary endeavor, she felt she was squandering her time. That was her story. She presented it, a calling card, to the people we knew in those days, a gang of writers, actors, and painters every generation seems to see when they're young and then lose touch with by middle age. Maybe the gang are all Peter Pans and can be known only by the young. Wendy had reason to expect a lot of herself. She was talented. She played the flute so well I was amazed she hadn't pursued music professionally. On her walls she had preserved two paintings from that phase of her artistic wanderings, each stunning and quite different. Often people mistook them for the work of an established artist. There were several etchings, a sculpture, a notebook of poems, and so on, a restless dissatisfied trail, the tracks of a search party. It's not that she didn't have an identity—she had no conviction her talent was worth the effort.

"I'm not a genius," she'd say.

"So what?"

"I'm not even that good."

"So what?" I was pushing Zen those days. Process, not results.

"I don't have a vision."

"So . . . ?" I wavered. Even I thought a vision might be essential.

"Artists have vision," Wendy assured me.

I got wise to her eventually. She secretly thought she was an ordinary person, a quiet stream accidentally diverted into this babbling brook of so-called artists. Ashamed to be a regular person, she was creative out of obligation.

In time, I told her my story. Not the dinner table version, but the details of Maine's cold grubby poverty, my unhappy parents, and the sediment of gritty humiliation that must be swallowed at the bottom of even the clearest broth of charity. I took the risk she would think I was ungrateful to Naomi.

She didn't. She understood. From then on she was my best friend because I knew I could be myself with her. But I didn't think the reverse was true, no matter how frank she was with me, because it seemed that everyone was her closest friend. Wendy was totally open in those days, expressing her feelings with reckless ease—a bird singing in the public park, unconcerned by who might overhear, laugh, or be moved. In fact, she did have an unusually appealing voice, warm and melodic and inviting. She worked the phones at the real-estate office of a friend when she needed extra cash, and men often asked her out without having seen her, excited and in love, just with her conversation. You see why I liked her so, she was everything I'm not: emotional, friendly, trusting, charming, comfortable with humanity.

I don't know why she liked me. I really don't. I *do* know when I realized my primacy among her one million friends. She appeared at my door one Saturday morning, holding up a bag of take-out coffee and artery-stopping jelly doughnuts. "Are you alone?" she asked.

I don't wake up quickly, but I forced myself to fight against grumpiness. "Yeah, sure, come in. I can make you good coffee."

"I don't want good coffee. I've made a life choice, and I can only drink Greek-coffee-shop coffee on momentous occasions." She glanced at my bed—I lived in a studio apartment and the dining table was within view—and said, "Looks too messy to have been just one person sleeping."

"I kicked him out in the middle of the night."

She laughed. "Did you really?"

"He was moving around too much."

"Wonder Woman," she commented, a nickname she used for me. I had objected the first time, protesting that it was derisive. No, she had answered, I mean it admiringly. But from then on she called me Wonder Woman only when we were alone, presumably so that I couldn't claim strangers might misinterpret. Wendy took out a doughnut, a snowball of sugar, and bit down hard, with exaggerated appetite. There was a puff of white smoke, a confectionary explosion, flakes falling on her jeans. A dot stuck, clownish, on the tip of her nose; jelly oozed at the corners of her mouth. "Hmmm," she hummed, orgasmically.

The thought of that much sugar turned my stomach. I winced and looked away.

"I'm gibbon ub bart," she mumbled.

"What!"

Wendy opened one of the coffees, raised it greedily to her mouth, the steam arching in ahead of the liquid. "I've given up art!" she said after a swallow. "Fuck it," she said. "Fuck creativity. It's time to do something useful, something that works. So you'll be my only friend from now on." She opened the other coffee and brought it to me. "I'm going to become a teacher."

"A teacher?"

" 'Those who can, do,' " she said. "I'm gonna teach retarded children."

"Yeech," I said, not about the coffee, although the taste reminded me of burned wood.

She stared at me for a moment, surprised. "Aren't you impressed with my compassion, my self-sacrifice, my worthiness?"

"No," I said. "What a depressing job."

From the way she beamed at me you would have thought I had been supportive. "They can really be helped," Wendy insisted. "The earlier, the better. A lot can be done, they can function. Really."

"I believe you. But why am I going to be your only friend?"

"Oh. Well, you are already. Everybody else I know is only interested in people who are artists, actors, writers—something pretentious. You'll see. Besides, I won't be able to stay up late. I'll be in school getting my degree. Working hard."

I didn't believe her, although we spent the day filling out her application to a graduate program in special education. Even when she did begin her training, I expected her to quit any day. And I was absolutely sure she was wrong about her circle of friends. But they did recede gradually, a steady, barely perceptible evaporation. She replaced them with an equally large number of new friends and acquaintances. I was, however, the only survivor of the past, the bridge from one Wendy to another.

Perhaps our intimacy was intensified because we had no real families. Wendy was orphaned while in high school; her parents were killed in a head-on crash with a drunk driver on New Year's Eve. Her only close relative was an uncle who lived in Florida and she disliked him, although he had performed his duty to her: seen her through college and administered the insurance money wisely so that there was a slight income, enough for her to be bohemian, enough for her to pursue the teaching degree with the help of a loan or two and some part-time work.

As for me, after Sam's death, Naomi lost interest in everything except for her endowment of Stanford to collect feminist literature. She moved out there, and I rarely saw her. Besides, she disapproved of my choice to enter corporate law, wishing me to be a legal aid lawyer or something in the public interest. Naomi never said so, but I suspect she hoped I would return to Maine, to defend battered women or other worthy causes. I have to confess I believed she was right, that it was my duty to return something—and I took more than my share of pro bono cases to salve my conscience. Yet any attempt to force myself to go back was as hopeless as coaxing a child to eat spinach. My muscles fought it, my throat closed up, I was revolted.

Wendy and I became each other's family. We made Thanksgiving meals for ourselves, and later for friends who were apart or without homes to visit. I bought her a dreidel and lit candles on Hanukkah; she helped me drag the Christmas tree from Sixth Avenue to my apartment.

While I worked seventy hours a week in order to impress to make partner, Wendy's load of studies, clinic work, and her part-time job left her equally drained. She'd bring pizza, Chinese, deli, terrifying desserts on her way home (her apartment was only two blocks from mine), and the hour or two we spent consuming and debriefing was my only joy. We were so different in our backgrounds—the hard and sad yellow-haired lobster girl, the lively and nervous Jewish girl—the oneness surprised me, sometimes even bothered me. I couldn't imagine being so at ease with any man. I don't know how to describe those thousands of hours: intimacy and comfort, knowledge and forgiveness.

Twelve years ago Wendy got her degree. She was very proud. With the certificate of completion in her hand, she felt she could shake off the worrisome self-imposed label of dilettante that had dogged her since college. She already had a job in a children's city program that would begin in the fall, and she had worked three evenings a week in a halfway house for retarded adults.

"What do we do to celebrate?" I asked.

"We don't have to celebrate," she said.

"It's not fair. There's no cap and gown, no graduation picture with ten thousand people in it." Her eyes were shimmering with feeling. I wanted to make a fuss, to show her I was proud too. I didn't know how.

"Would you do me a favor?" she asked. She looked shy, which wasn't like her. "Would you take me to the cemetery where my parents are?"

They were buried in New Jersey, about a forty-minute drive from Manhattan. Wendy had gotten directions from her uncle in Florida. She hadn't been to the grave in years; in fact, she had never mentioned its existence to me. We went right away, that afternoon, in the beat-up red VW bug I drove in those days. I decided it was time to get a real car after listening to it struggle to keep up on the turnpike. The skies were threatening rain. With uncharacteristic caution, I had brought an umbrella, but when we arrived at the gate and stopped to ask directions to block 6, the sun came out.

I drove slowly on the narrow road between the dead. They were all Jewish. We had passed a temple for ceremonies near the entrance. "It's weird," I whispered, "to look at their names."

Wendy nodded. "My mother's family bought their lot here forty years ago. Uncle Manny was really glad I was gonna visit. You know what he said? That there's room for me and my husband and children."

"Brrrrr!" I shook off the creepiness.

We had driven on a suburban road to get to the cemetery, passing the usual houses, supermarkets, gas stations. When we found block 6 and got out, I looked around and all that was gone. Nothing to see but headstones, gray and silent. Off at the perimeter, to be sure, I could find the edges of the commercial world; and among the graves moved the living world, a few crews digging new holes, cutting grass. A block away a ceremony was in progress: someone was sobbing.

"Here," Wendy said. She had dressed up for this, I realized. Nothing dramatic, which is why I hadn't noticed earlier. She was in a gray skirt and white blouse, not formal but neat, a schoolgirl's uniform. Perhaps the way she dressed when they died.

There was a large rectangular granite slab in the middle of block 6, near the edge of a footpath that intersected it. KLEIN was carved along the top. Then six names beneath, along with dates of birth and death. Klein, Wendy explained, was her mother's maiden name, and those names were her grandparents and great-grandparents.

"Here's Mom and Dad." Wendy moved to a stone buried flush with the ground, below the upright slab, placed at the edge of the path. SONNENFELD was crammed onto it, with her mother's and father's first names below. Of course, the dates of their deaths were identical, a clue to their accident. BELOVED DAUGHTER & SON, it read on one line, and then beneath that, the oblique reference to Wendy: CHERISHED MOTHER & FATHER.

I started to cry. Embarrassed, I squeezed my eyes together and put my arm around Wendy's shoulder to remind myself that she was the one who needed comforting.

Her head was bowed, studying the carved symbols, the letters that represented her parents. Her cheeks were flushed, but her eyes were clear, not teary. She didn't move or speak for quite a while.

The burial in the other block ended. The doors of the limousines and cars opened and slammed together, a chorus of departure.

"You know why the rocks are there?" she asked me, pointing to other headstones. I noticed for the first time there were small rocks placed on the top rim. "You do that to show you've come and visited," she explained.

Out of guilt? Wanting credit? Or better things: wishing the love and grief could be as obvious and as permanent as death?

"Do you believe in God?" she asked.

"No," I said.

Another long silence. She closed her eyes for a while, but still no tears. When she opened them, I said, "Do you?"

"Yes," she answered. "Will you put a rock there?"

I bent down, searched in the grass, and found a small brown rock, half-covered with moss. I put it next to her mother's name.

"I'm ready to go," Wendy said, "but I need you to hold my hand while I say something."

I took her right hand in my left. She brought her feet together in a dutiful pose and looked down at the stone. "Ma," she said, and her voice broke on the word. "Dad," she struggled on, and at last there were tears in her eyes. "This is my sister, Molly. You don't have to worry about me. I'm not lonely because I know her."

※

When my mother was found frozen to death outside the family trailer I had a severe reaction, worse than might be expected, even after such a gruesome end. I hadn't seen her for several years and I felt guilty that I had transferred my daughterly feelings to Naomi. To my surprise, Naomi herself was uninterested in—and almost hostile to—this problem. I became depressed, sufficiently gloomy for Wendy to insist I go to a shrink. As a favor to one of the successful painters we knew, Stefan Weinstein (described to me as the "shrink to the stars") agreed to see me.

Stefan was small and very dark, a browned nut covered almost everywhere with silky black hair, even in spots you wouldn't think could grow hair. But the effect was fine and soft, a soothing fur, not an apelike coarseness. He was full of energy, cheerful and alert, the way an animated forest creature in a Disney movie is: eyes big and gleaming, teeth flashing while he laughs his deep, stomach-holding chuckle.

Stefan bounded out of his black leather Eames chair only five minutes into my story.

"Excuse me," he said, going to his desk and writing on a pad. "I'm going to give you the name of an excellent psychiatrist who will see you. I'll call him now and arrange a time—"

"What's wrong?"

"Nothing, not at all, don't be concerned, has nothing to with you—"

Stopping him required that I wave my hand in front of the onrushing words, flagging down a runaway car. "I'm not sick enough for you?" I demanded, trying to be light. My anger at his rejection was unmistakable, however. I had come reluctantly. Even phoning to make the appointment required effort, pumping a bicycle uphill.

"Do you think I want you to be sick—oh, this is ridiculous!" he interrupted his Socratic question. "I'm attracted to you. I can't treat you. It's unethical. And besides, it would make me unhappy in my work. Dr. Reynolds is superb—not as good as me"— he flashed his teeth happily between the night of his mustache and beard—"but he won't be having fantasies—" He lowered his head, shaking it, silently scolding. "Do you understand?" he mumbled.

"No," I told him, furious at his coy desires. "I came here for help. Not to be propositioned."

"Of course, that's why I'm sending you to Dr. Reynolds. Here you'll get propositioned."

I was shocked by Stefan's odd frivolity and wasted three sessions with Dr. Reynolds discussing it. I adjusted to my guilt feelings after four months. Although Dr. Reynolds wanted me to continue to resolve other conflicts (so would I if I were being paid a hundred and twenty-five dollars for a forty-five-minute hour), I stopped the analysis. Six months later, Stefan called.

"Thank God you didn't change your phone number," he said after establishing it was me. "I wouldn't have wanted to test Jim Reynolds's medical ethics."

I resisted Stefan's charm for weeks, refusing to date. Frankly, because he was a psychiatrist, I couldn't shake the suspicion that he was unbalanced. Goes to show you, you can take the country out of the girl, but—

I married him. I think he was the first man who was my friend.

To be honest, I had had many one-night adventures and several passionate suitors, a stormy on-again, off-again year-long relationship, but until Stefan, no male friends. He was just there, seemed always to have been part of my life, as if he were a relative that had returned from a long journey.

Naturally, this changed my friendship with Wendy. She had worried about marriage and children in the way we all do as our twenties seem to grind on endlessly, but once Stefan was on the scene and she turned thirty, she seemed desperate, talking obsessively, using phrases such as "old maid" and "biological clock."

I discussed this with Stefan. He said, "I think teaching the retarded is an expression of maternal—"

"Shut up, Doctor, you're not on call." Thus I reminded Stefan of my rule for our life together—no textbook language about us or the people we know.

"Okay." He gleamed, a merry chipmunk. "I think she's always wanted to have kids."

Stefan was right. She did. I don't. And thus I must have willfully ignored Wendy's desires. Once she began to work regularly with "special children" (as they were called at the clinic), Wendy, although she never complained, seemed sad, and began to talk more openly of her longing for kids.

"Is it hard?" I asked carefully.

"Just tiring," she said. "Sometimes it's great. I get excited. Joey's learned how to zip up his coat or bounce the ball, and then, two days later, he can't. Or worse, he still can and nothing else has changed and I think, so what?"

"They're always going to be retarded. You knew that."

"Yes, that's true," she said, her lips thinning, irritated. "I wish I had a child, a healthy child. Then it wouldn't be so depressing."

I haven't described Wendy. I wonder if that's because—well, she was plain. She had wide, maternal hips, narrow shoulders, small breasts. Her face was as round as a human's could be, her skin unblemished, but always a bit yellowish, unhealthy. She had small blue eyes, very pale in color, and overshadowed by her thick brow. Her hair was a dull brown, halfheartedly curly, sitting uncertainly on her head. There didn't seem to be enough of it, yet when she allowed her hair to grow long, the effect was merely sloppy, not full. Maybe

I should have taken her to expensive make-overs; I thought that would hurt her feelings. Although I usually don't tread lightly, I did about Wendy's looks. "You're so beautiful, and I'm bland," she would say, her shoulders sagging in despair while she checked herself at the mirror in my hall before we would go out manhunting—pre-Stefan, of course.

How could I answer that, except with reassurances she wouldn't believe?

"I hope I have a healthy child," she said so often during her first year at the clinic that I finally told her to quit if it preyed so on her imagination.

"I have to get married and have kids!" she yelled, frantic, the morning after she attended a high school reunion full of women with husbands on their arms and hands flipping photos of babies.

I understood her loneliness, her wish for a male companion. But pregnancy, birth, the abnegation of self to another for years, years of youth and strength that could never be recovered?

"That's because you've always been the adored child watching your various mothers wither, beaten and frustrated," Stefan said.

Shut up, I answered.

That summer, Wendy was . . . well, I can't help but use the term *man-crazy.* Wendy, once timid, almost squeamish, went to every party, every singles scene, and did it with any guy who even glanced down her unbuttoned blouse. She pursued one big blond hunk, the kind she used to long for fearfully, as a fantasy, and got him into bed.

"How was it?" I asked. "Disappointing?"

She dropped her head down low, looked up from beneath her heavy eyebrows, grinning. "It was great! What a body! I loved every minute of it!"

She astounded me. My little mouse of a friend, who had to be pushed from behind to approach the nerdiest of men, had become a ferocious tigress.

"Her womb calls," Stefan explained that night, and rushed into the bathroom to evade the shoe I threw at him.

I'm not complete, I decided. I'm not all female. Naomi had ruined me with her talk of strong women: I imagined strength to be lack of emotion. I wasn't brave, you see. Wendy was. Wendy was human, fully baked, willing to risk weakness and defeat. I loved her and wanted her to be happy, so I cheered on this dismal hunt until she succeeded, until she found her boxed set of gonads.

"I've met this guy," Wendy called one morning, much earlier than usual. "I like him. He's . . ." She grunted, an amused noise. "He's from the old neighborhood."

He wasn't, not exactly. Ben Fliess was a working-class Jew from Brooklyn, a similar but different enough population from Wendy's Manhattanite, more professional class. Ben's father was a rare example of an unsuccessful businessman in post–World War II New York. But his son had done well: Ben earned a scholarship to Cornell, majored in economics, and ended up on Wall Street as a securities analyst. He should have been living in the suburbs, I suppose, already married, but he had been detoured—like the rest of us—by the sixties, by drugs, and thus become hopelessly trendy in an effort to avoid his parent's trends. He lived downtown, near his office, one of the first to resettle Battery Park. Those were the facts I knew before I met him.

That happened in front of John's Pizzeria on Bleecker Street, a casual double date: a quick bite, a movie, coffee after. It was an oven-hot night in July. I arrived separately and ahead of Stefan, who was seeing patients late. Ben came forward, stepping in front of Wendy. He was big, six four, a thick body, not muscled, yet not fat either. The strong lenses on his black-framed glasses diminished his eyes, and he had lost all his hair but for a laurel around his head, exposing an elongated and large skull. The baldness aged him. I was surprised he was only thirty-five. His features were gross: a wide oppressive brow; big ears, drooping heavy lobes; thick white skin, heavy as an animal's hide—except for his mouth and lips. They were comically small compared to the rest, bright red, as if he'd just finished sucking on a red lollipop. I took one look at him, shocked by his plainness, and decided she would never marry him.

"Hello." He spoke thickly, like his body, the words stuck behind his tongue. "Wendy said you were beautiful, and you certainly are—"

Wendy quivered with excitement, shivering like a toy poodle from its pedigree nerves. She interrupted with a bark: "I didn't tell you to say it!"

"Well you told me not to faint when I got my first look! I thought she was exaggerating. She wasn't." Ben gestured at Wendy with his hands; they were big, of course, but once again there was an out-of-place bit of finery—the fingers. Slender, tapered, the nails longish for a man, and very clean for any New Yorker at the end of the work day. "There's no point in keeping secrets between us. You two have a great friendship. I don't want to mess it up."

"Good. Don't," I said sharply, and surprised him. I knew his type. He asserted himself at every opportunity, assuming boldness would compensate for his other defects. And I especially didn't trust his immediate declaration that he wouldn't mess up the friendship. It has been my experience, particularly as a lawyer who often has to negotiate contracts, that what people announce they *don't* intend is their real objective. Stefan calls that unintentional truth telling, the subconscious peeking out from behind the curtain. I call it lying.

Ben chafed my nerves all night: he bragged about his correct stock recommendations, teased Wendy whenever she spoke, was flirtatious to me and obsequious to Stefan.

"Wendy says you're the psychiatrist to the stars," he said, embarrassing her again when Stefan arrived. Indeed, Ben accurately guessed the more famous of Stefan's patients, and asked for confirmation that he was right. I accused Wendy with my eyes: I had told her the names in confidence after she complained that I didn't trust her, thereby violating a promise of silence I had made to Stefan. For a moment, there was a silent ring-around-the-rosy of betrayed glances. Of course Stefan refused to say. I suspect he was flattered by Ben's awe and that's why Stefan defended him.

"He's insecure," Stefan argued when we got home. "Ben wanted to impress you and so he bragged a lot, talked too much. I have to know him better before I can judge." So fucking reasonable. Sometimes I imagine how Stefan might respond to the news of nuclear attack: "Partly, I'm sad. So many people I know and love will die. But it does give me a chance to review case histories and work on my book."

The next morning, just as I was ready to leave for my office, again Wendy phoned uncharacteristically early. Ben had changed her rhythms. "I've been up all night. We have to talk."

"Why don't we have lunch?" I knew her, that quavering voice was a warning, and I wanted her to face me if she was angry. Wendy feared confrontation, liked to write letters when she should phone, phone when she should see.

"Uh . . . uh . . . I don't think I can wait that long. I'm so upset."

I gave up. "Go ahead."

"When you met Stefan, I feel I welcomed him."

"You liked him," I said, smart enough to be preparing my defense. Or was it smart? I wanted her to acknowledge that she liked Stefan, not out of duty to me, but approved of my choice.

"Yes, I did. So what does that mean?"

"Nothing."

"I think it means something."

"It doesn't."

"Well . . ." She sighed. "I felt you were hostile last night."

"You mean to Ben?"

"Yes." She spoke in a tense monotone, paused, ready to pounce on a denial.

I thought it through. Wendy had many acquaintances, but no one else would tell her the truth. We were true sisters, after all. The time to object was now. "I didn't like that he told me how beautiful I was, that he embarrassed you—"

"He didn't embarrass me!"

"Wendy," I implored softly. I had been honest. "Come on."

"He's open. He likes to be open with people. Especially people he wants to like him."

"I see."

"What do you mean, you see?"

"You're kidding yourself." I couldn't contain my irritation. "He was putting both of us in our place."

"That's ridiculous!" Her voice squeaked.

"And what was all that teasing about you crying at commercials and eating in bed?"

"Oh, you're just picking—"

"He seemed bent on embarrassing you, diminishing you in our eyes."

"*Did* that diminish me in your—?"

"Don't be silly! Of course not!"

"I think it did! I think it must have! Everybody knows you're more beautiful. Is that so embarrassing to me it can't even be mentioned? Am I so ugly that—"

"Stop it! Don't turn this around on me! That pisses me off! How long have you known this man? Two weeks? We've been friends for seven years!"

"So that's what this is about! You've always been possessive of me, but this is insane! What do you expect me to do, always be the third wheel? Dragged along like some maiden aunt?"

"Hardly maiden," I said, as if I were playing the bitch in a soap opera. The remark surprised even me.

"What!" Wendy breathed heavily into the phone. "What does that mean? Since when are you Jerry Fallwell? You made the rounds too—"

"Okay, okay, I don't know. I don't want to have this fight—"

"Oh, of course, just as we're getting to it, really getting down to—"

"Okay! Fine. We'll agree: I'm possessive of you, I can't handle you falling in love with me. I mean, with some—"

"Falling in love with *you?*"

"I mean, with someone—"

"I think that's a very revealing slip, I really—"

"Fuck off!" I hung up. I was panting, my heart was pounding. I thought, maybe I'm crazy, maybe I don't understand my own feelings.

Stefan had come into the room, presumably to find out what the shouting was about, dripping from the shower, dark little head cocked, the long semicircles of his eyebrows pasted up high on his forehead, questioningly: "You didn't tell her your opinion?"

The phone rang. Wendy disliked confrontation, but once the battle was on, she would fight to the last feeling.

"Do I want Wendy to be in love with me?" I spoke rapidly to Stefan, and in so low a tone, I could have been the subway, rumbling underneath the sidewalk, a distant tremor.

"Of course."

The phone was ringing.

"Then that means I'm a lesbian."

"No. It means you want people you love to love you back."

I picked up the phone. "I can't talk—"

"How dare you hang up on me! Don't you ever do that again!"

"I have to go to work!"

"That's bullshit! That's such bullshit!"

"Listen to me!" I was screaming. "Listen to me!" My throat filled with the sound and blocked my breathing. "Listen to me!" I yelled this last one so hard my ears rang, a blue spot appeared in my vision, and my veins seemed to expand, ballooning dangerously.

I had silenced Wendy. She waited, panting into the receiver.

"I love you," I said. "I don't care whom you love or what you do, I'm with you. I'm on your side. You want me to lie to you about my reactions, I'll lie—"

"I don't want you to—"

"Just tell me how you want me to behave and I'll follow your instructions. I can't lose your friendship."

"I don't—" She sighed. "Can't you hear yourself? I don't want to *have* to instruct you."

"I'm sorry. It won't happen again." Tears were flooding out of my eyes. Stefan appeared with a box of tissues (a psychiatrist's antibiotic, he called them) and discreetly left. "Okay?" I was begging her. Arguing with her hurt too much. I was scared by my tears, rolling from me, a river of me flowing out. "Please? Can't we forget about it?"

"I don't—look, I don't want to drag it out—"

"I really have to go. I'm sorry. I have to go. I have to hang up now. Okay? You understand. I'm not angry. I have to get to a meeting. Okay?"

"I think we have to talk later," Wendy insisted, primness in her tone, a teacher scolding. "I think we have more to talk about."

There was a bit of sadism in her self-righteousness. She had to hear at length that she was right. I resented her for wanting to drag it out, but I wrote that off as my being a strange person, a poor girl from Maine, desensitized to real feelings, a Wasp, used to preserving emotion in jars and storing them in cellars. I knew that's what they thought, my husband and my best friend. I couldn't help myself: I suspected there was cruelty in all the churning of emotion.

We met that afternoon for a drink at Bradley's, a bar on University Place near where we both lived. I listened and dutifully admitted I had done wrong. She didn't forgive me wholeheartedly for months:

we socialized only as a foursome and in ritualized dinners, as though we were getting together out of obligation. Privately, no matter how much I disliked Ben, I swore that I would never show or express it.

Six months after the fight she truly forgave me. She called in the middle of the day to gossip, and that weekend she and Ben dropped by without warning to suggest we go to a movie. Everything was back to normal. Only she never told me the inner world of her relationship with Ben, presumably out of pride, and I didn't probe, out of fear.

❧

Obviously I don't believe what people tell me, especially when it's Stefan showing off his proudest possession: the ability to see the true motives behind the actions of others. Stefan—and Wendy for that matter—had declared that she had a desperate need to be married and have children. Sure enough, within seven months of meeting Ben, they had set a date, and within three months of their marriage, Wendy said, "Ooops," over brunch, to announce she was accidentally pregnant and they were going to have the baby. Nevertheless, despite all the warnings and observations, I was surprised that she married Ben, and stunned that she was pregnant.

We were in the formal dining room of our new co-op when she told us the news. I had made partner, Stefan was already successful, so we had splurged and bought a three bedroom in an elegant building on Fifth and Eleventh—far more space than we needed. There were two apartments on each floor, and by chance, the other (a two bedroom) had gone up for sale.

"Do you think we could get the two bedroom for two twenty?" Ben asked Stefan, the words rumbling out slowly behind his thick tongue. At times, I almost liked Ben—he often told Wendy she was beautiful, bought her dresses, courted her even after marriage. He treated Stefan nicely too, his manner formal, glum, almost comically respectful. "Do you think the Iranians will release the hostages?" "Do you think Reagan has a chance?" "Do you think sixteen percent inflation is the peak?" It didn't seem to bother Ben that Stefan had answered no, no, no to the above, nor was his track record any better in predicting the value of Knick draft picks or even recommending doctors. Ben missed the point of Stefan: his ability to empathize, to forgive, and, most of all, to be funny in even the worst extremity. During our first year of marriage, en route to a romantic inn, Stefan skidded out of control while driving on an icy Sawmill River Parkway. It's a tight, curvy road with no margin for error. As we careened toward the divider, possibly to death, Stefan said, "This is going to put me in a bad mood for the whole weekend." The car was totaled; we were merely scratched, saved, I'm convinced, because we were laughing on impact. Stefan was gentle, loving, kind—all heart beneath the encrusted jargon. Ben didn't notice that; instead he paid court to Stefan's brain, turning to him for expert opinion, in the manner of a panel moderator: "Why does that happen? What would make a man do that, Stefan?" So it was no surprise that Ben (despite his own work as a financial analyst) cast Stefan as real estate maven: "What if we made a bid for two twenty? Think they'd take it?"

Of course, this brought out the worst solemnity in Stefan. He pulled on his earlobe and worried over the question, his dark little face thinking with exaggerated effort. "Two twenty . . . hmmm."

"Two dollars and twenty cents, that's what Ben means," Wendy joked. "It's all we can afford."

"No I didn't. I meant two hundred and twenty thousand. We have the money. Stop acting like we don't." Ben's crankiness, his sudden rudeness to Wendy, happened often enough that she was no longer ashamed of it. There would be weeks when he was sweet to her, at least in public; and months when she couldn't make the most innocent remark without suffering abuse. In those phases, I came home from seeing them with throbbing temples: I wanted to smack him, tell him he was lucky beyond calculation to have Wendy. "She likes to poor mouth," Ben said to Stefan.

"No she doesn't," I remonstrated in the gentle and forced politeness of womanhood.

"What do you think, Stefan?" Ben ignored me. "With the baby we're going to need another bedroom, another bathroom. It's perfect. Should we offer two twenty, or is that too low?"

Although Stefan claimed a certain tolerant fondness for Ben, he had discouraged socializing with them as a couple, suggesting Wendy and I have lunch instead, or spend a Saturday afternoon together. When we did meet as a foursome, I would monopolize Wendy, and poor Stefan was stuck with Ben. I knew he was bothered by the thought of Wendy and Ben moving next door. Living two blocks away in New York City can be as forbidding a barrier as the Berlin Wall—a hallway was nothing. Probably even the courtesy of telephoning first would go by the boards. Stefan broached this worry gently: "Aren't you concerned about us living so close?"

"No, I think that would be great," Ben said. "Does it bother you?"

"I think too much contact can put a lot of pressure on friendships."

"In other words, yes." Ben pursed his tiny red lips together, leaned back, and folded his thick arms on top of his belly. He looked out from over the top of his glasses. "Okay, we'll look elsewhere."

There was an uncomfortable pause.

"I say that for both your and Wendy's sake, as well for Molly and me." Stefan used his shrink tone, liltingly reasonable, and his shrink gesture, his hand touching his own chest and then elaborately opening toward Ben, a pantomime of gentle exchange, as if Stefan wished to make a present of his heart.

"Yeah." Ben almost groaned the word. "Thanks a lot. You're a real lifesaver."

I enjoyed Ben's sarcasm. "Do you really have to move?" I asked, smiling at his skeptical remark.

"Where do we put the baby?" Ben snorted this bitterly.

"You could convert the dining room—"

"Where do we eat?" Ben was belligerent.

"In our kitchen," Wendy said. "We can—"

"No. I'm not going to live like some welfare family—all crowded in together." He stood up and paced around our table toward the French doors leading to our small terrace. "I guess we could come here and eat in your dining room. We could sleep in your two extra bedrooms." He opened the doors and stuck his head out, breathing deeply.

"Can you afford a co-op?" I asked Wendy quietly.

"I don't think so. It'll be too tight—"

"Oh come on!" Amazingly, Ben had heard. He wheeled on us, pulled the door closed in the same motion, rattling the frame. Stefan cherished the small panels of lead glass on the door, had claimed its elegance was what sold him on the apartment. He jumped as it banged shut. "You have the money for the down payment," Ben accused Wendy. "Don't pretend you don't. Molly's not a fool. She knows your trust is big enough and you have control of it now."

Surprised, my eyes went to Wendy for confirmation.

"Ah . . ." Ben smirked. "So you don't tell each other everything. Her uncle is a first-rate money manager. She's got enough to buy that two bedroom for cash."

"But then I'd have nothing left," Wendy argued back, and I was pleased to hear the resolve in her tone.

"So you come up with the down and we get a mortgage," Ben persisted. "We can handle the interest—"

"I've said it's all right! Why are you bullying me? I've already said yes."

Ben continued to pace around our table, big feet treading heavily, eyes on the rug. He nodded at her concession, tiny red lips squeezed together in a sour frown, apparently disgusted by the victory. Ben finally stopped in front of Stefan and asked, in an accuser's tone: "Did you like your real-estate broker?"

Stefan answered at length—his opinion of the broker was complicated. I listened for a few familiar sentences and then whispered to Wendy, "What did your uncle do? Make a killing in the market with your money?"

"You really didn't know?" Once again, Ben had overheard, despite his attentive posture toward Stefan.

"No. Wendy and I don't discuss our finances," I told him as haughtily as I could, which seemed to consist of my voice squeaking. "I never discuss people's money. I think it's rude."

"That's okay, I understand that, you're not Jewish." Ben smiled, and narrowed his small eyes gleefully. "But Wendilah? She doesn't tell her best friend about her money? It's goyisha!" Ben only used Yiddish for jokes or belligerence. He leaned over and poked Wendy in the side.

"Stop." She pulled away.

"She's ticklish," he said in a tone of weary despair. He slunk away from her, rejected.

"You have your secrets, too," Wendy said, an unpleasant, teasing smile on her face.

"What!" he demanded nervously.

"What is it?" Stefan smiled happily, his bright teeth shining out from his black beard. "I love secrets."

"No kidding," I said.

"I don't know what you're talking about," Ben said in an officious tone. "But violating my privacy—"

"That's what you did!" Wendy was thrilled by her logic. "That's exactly—"

"No." Ben bowed forward, shaking his great bald head vigorously, "I didn't—"

"That's exactly what you did!" Wendy gripped my chair in her excitement. "Just like I'm going to—did you know Ben was married before?"

Ben was stilled, nervous legs quiescent, head down; his bald skull reflected our overhead light, his delicate fingers curved down over his knees.

"I only found out last week by accident—"

"Because you were spying." Ben spoke in a mumble.

"I was looking in the drawer for our insurance forms, to pay—"

"You were spying!" Ben was on his feet, wide and thick and ugly. His sallow skin, instead of turning red with fury, bled two small pink blotches on each cheek. His glasses slid down almost to the end of his nose, his chin was scrunched up, and his tiny lips made a tiny circle. Though big and loud, he didn't scare me. I almost wanted to laugh. I felt pity for him, that he cared so much about trivialities, that he wanted to live near us, when neither Stefan nor I was really his friend. "Admit it! You were looking—"

"What?" Wendy appealed to me. She faced him. "What was I looking for, Ben?"

"Fuck you!" That hurt. He shot it out violently and watched her, obviously wanting it to be painful.

"Ben," she complained.

"Go fuck yourself! You can live alone in that shithole with your baby!" Ben marched past her and out into the hall.

"Ben!" Wendy pleaded.

"Ben," Stefan said softly, slowly rising from the chair.

The front door squealed open and slammed hard. It seemed to take all noise along with it.

We sat in its vacuum until Stefan, rather stupidly, said, "Ben?" and then went into the hall. "He's gone," he reported a moment later.

Wendy leaned forward, put her face in her lap, covering up, and cried silently. I put my hand on her trembling back. "I'm okay," she said, as if the touch were a question. "Hormones," she mumbled. She was quiet then. Stefan, of course, brought tissues. She sat up, wiped her eyes, and loudly blew her nose.

I waited for her to volunteer, wishing I didn't care, wanting to be concerned only about her feelings, but when she didn't say anything, I couldn't leash my curiosity. "What's the secret?"

Her eyes were clouded with pain when she answered. I felt stupid and mean. "Oh." Her voice droned, played at too slow a speed. "Ben was married once before."

"When he was young?" Stefan asked.

"In his twenties. Right after college."

"That's all?" I said. "That's the secret?"

"She left him for his best friend." Wendy lifted each word out with effort, her sadness settling in. "I guess that's what bothers him about my talking . . ." She couldn't lift anymore.

She loves him, I thought to myself. She's carrying his child, she's bound to him for life: in her eyes, I fancied I saw this tragic knowledge that it was too late, that she had picked wrong and yet had to stick with the selection. I too was committed—because of my love for her—to her choice.

I swore there and then I would be nicer to Ben for Wendy's sake: she was about to become a mother and needed my help.

⚜

You may have gathered that Stefan isn't easily ruffled. Ben managed it, spectacularly, a few weeks later.

"I'm furious," Stefan announced. He stood at the door to the room we had converted into a miniature gym—my arms were pinned to my chest by a Nautilus machine. Stefan's dark skin seemed to be tanned by his anger. He spoke in an even tone, yet his body was strung tight, feet together, stomach in, chest out—on military alert. "I'm in a rage," he said. "I feel totally manipulated."

I pushed my way out of the press. I had overworked the lats

earlier—they stabbed with pain. I knew his upset had nothing to do with me—he never hated me. I waited for his explanation.

"Ben has made an offer on ten B." That was the two bedroom across the hall. "It's been accepted and he and Wendy are supposed to go before the board in two weeks. He's told them we're friends and—I ran into Margaret Hibbing in the elevator"—our co-op president —"and she assumed I'd be delighted—assumed I knew! Assumes we'll recommend—"

He was sputtering. I handled him the way I've seen good cross-examiners manage a hysterical witness, fixing his eyes with mine and asking sharply: "What did you tell her?"

"I didn't know what she was talking about! I covered. Pretended to be ignorant only of the fact that their offer was accepted. I'm tempted to blackball them. I really am."

"Wendy never said anything," I told him.

"Of course not. She probably doesn't know!"

I thought it rather funny, although I put on a stern face. Stefan was accustomed to getting his way with his civilized method—remember his reasonable shrink tone and shrink gestures? Ben had foiled him. Either Stefan could tell Margaret Hibbing that he wouldn't recommend them (which Ben would deduce), or Stefan would have to give in. Ben had forced the issue: Are you friend or foe? Of course Ben wasn't playing fairly. We were Wendy's friends and couldn't answer him directly. He was a coward.

"I don't want to give in to this," Stefan said after a pause, his tone considered. "It may be childish rage, but I don't want him to get away with this. He asked me—"

"All right, I'll talk to Ben," I interrupted. Stefan made a feeble attempt to offer to go with me, but I insisted, got out of my exercise clothes, showered, and then called.

Ben answered. Very cheerfully. "Molly! How are you?" He was ebullient, sounded almost drunk.

"I'm fine. I'd like to come over and talk about the apartment."

"The apartment?" He was quizzical.

"Your offer on ten B."

"Uh-huh." Now he was glum. "Wendy doesn't know. I wanted it to be a surprise. She'll be so grateful to be near you, it'll mean so much to her—"

"I doubt that's why you haven't told her." Silence. "I'm coming over now."

He insisted we meet outside their apartment to give him a chance to explain privately, in case Wendy came home from the clinic while we were still talking. I agreed to go to a coffee shop a block from both of our places. I got there first. The windows were steamed up from the contrast of the baked heat inside against the outer cold. Although it was mid-April and the weather had been mild, that day felt like winter again, reminding me of Maine and its long freeze and dark afternoons. I felt sad.

Ben took over a half hour to arrive: he appeared to have just showered and shaved. "Sorry," he mumbled, calling out to a sullen waiter that he wanted coffee. He wore a black turtleneck and thus his thick-skinned face seemed whiter than usual—glowing in sickly fashion, as big and dully luminous as an old-fashioned school globe. Indeed, he looked a little bit like my former elementary school principal, I realized. Nothing about this seemed amusing anymore.

"Stefan is furious," I said.

"He is?" Ben hunched down, a fearful soldier ducking a shell.

"What did you expect?"

"I . . . uh . . . I know he said he was concerned that it might put pressure on the friendship, but I didn't think that . . . uh—"

"Come on. He was being polite."

At this, Ben was no longer meek. He puffed up. His long legs shuffled under the table. His right knee whacked against my leg. "If he meant he didn't want us to move next to you under any circumstances, he should have said so. You don't leave things like that to people's imagination. I don't have much of an imagination," he sneered. "Never have. Can't be subtle with me."

I thought him disgusting. Ugly, self-conscious, mean, insecure. I experienced his unpleasantness in a concentrated way, watching it beam out from his pugnacious, rhinoceros-hide face, soaking it up, a massive dose of miserable Ben Fliess.

Getting no verbal response from me, Ben waved his hand. "Anyway, if he's angry why doesn't he confront me?"

"I wouldn't let him because Wendy is my friend and this concerns her too. She would be humiliated to know what you've done."

"No." He shook his head from side to side. "I know you think that.

But it's not true. She was crushed that Stefan didn't want us to bid on the apartment."

I smiled. He really wasn't a clever man. "So you admit you understood that Stefan didn't want—"

"Listen to what I'm saying!" he shouted, shoving his thick chest over the Formica tabletop. I leaned back involuntarily. Imagine having him on top, I thought, heaving up and down, with his massive size, rough skin, and thick speech—I couldn't understand Wendy loving him. Ben saw that I was repulsed. He glanced self-consciously at the other patrons, leaned back (he was so strong the entire booth shifted with him), and tightened his small mouth. "Wendy would never admit this to you, but she's scared—"

"Scared?"

"About becoming a mother. She has no family to help her, she's counting on your support."

"What has that got to do with moving next door? There are other buildings in the neighborhood!"

"Not like yours," Ben scolded gently, shaking his finger. "It's easily the best building in the Village. I think it's the only prewar building with three-bedroom apartments. And certainly the only one with formal dining rooms, eat-in kitchens, and maid's rooms."

I suppose in any other American city, Ben's little speech would have been considered the talk of a lunatic. Because he was a New Yorker, I merely considered it faintly ridiculous. Mostly, I wanted to laugh at the discovery of his true motivation and at the exposure of my own self-centeredness: he wasn't a pathetic, lonely man who wanted to be closer to Stefan and me; he was a real-estate snob.

"If we don't get into your building, we'll be forced to move to the Upper West Side. Ugh," he groaned. "Wendy'll be totally isolated up there—all her friends live downtown—and I'll have a terrible commute. I can walk to work now, go on my bike. It's really not fair. Ten B is a perfect apartment for us."

I cocked my head, astonished, unable to formulate my reaction.

Ben sipped his coffee, peeking at me over the rim of the cup. "I don't know what you're worried about—you think we'll have you babysit? That we'll be over all the time? What? What's your worry? I'm sure we can make an arrangement that will alleviate your concern. It's the toughest co-op board in the Village. We're not gonna get past them without a strong recommendation from you and Stefan."

"Does Wendy even care? Does she—"

"Look, don't kid yourself. You're the most important person in the world to her. She loves you. Nothing would make her happier, nothing would calm her more about having the baby. It's not why *I* want to live there—I won't bullshit you about that. Frankly, I could do with a little less of you and Stefan."

He hates us, I realized, shocked. His small eyes darted up and down from me to the coffee, unable to hold my glance, not because he was embarrassed, but because he felt only contempt and dislike for me. I had the reaction of an egomaniac, I'm afraid. I had never liked him, it's true, but I'd assumed he liked me. Strangely, I was hurt. Hadn't I made a great effort with him? I felt I should have been rewarded. "I'm sorry to hear that," I heard myself say, and now everything was crazy, inside out.

"I want to know what possible objection there could be to us moving next to you?"

"Well, you say you see too much of us—"

"We don't have to get together any more often than we already do."

"Isn't that unrealistic?"

"I want that apartment," he said, rubbing behind his glasses furiously. The lenses jiggled. When he stopped, his small eyes were bloodshot, the pink eyes of a huge bald-headed mouse. "I'm not raising my child in a cramped shithole. You and Stefan have rooms coming out of your ass that you don't need and you expect us to huddle together like Puerto Ricans."

Of course I wanted to get up and forget about him. Despite my strong feelings for Wendy, I almost did. And yet, I had to put up with him for her sake. I stared, unable to speak, my emotions churning in a pointless swirl from the opposition of these tides.

"Look," Ben added, after a few moments of silence from me. "If it bothers you both so much, why don't you and Stefan move?" He smiled after this, pleased beyond measure by his logic. Got you there, his look seemed to say.

I gave in and convinced Stefan to write up this experience to the madness of New York real estate and to the anxieties of insecure people facing parenthood. It was presented to Wendy as a surprise cooked up by the three of us—ironically, she told me she was angry at Ben for committing her to spending her money without asking her. She forgave him, she reported, because he said he had done it to please her, so she could be near me.

I thought I learned a lesson from this. Dumb, submissive, and thick-tongued though Ben might appear to be, he was determined to get his way. I fumed for months at having been tricked and cornered. Even Stefan, soft and sweet Stefan, was cold to Ben for a long time.

The night they moved in next door we made dinner for them and listened politely to their excited talk of how they would redecorate. Ben was puffed up. He kept saying, "This is a really classy apartment. You know," he commented to Stefan, "you and us and one other family are the only Jews in the building." Ben had triumphed. He was happy.

I couldn't sleep that night. I'll be honest: I hated him. I didn't suspect anything else about him other than his crude selfishness, but that was enough. I lay in bed and couldn't get my rage out of the way. I got up, went to our little gym, and tried to exhaust myself on the machines. I made herbal tea. I considered starting smoking again.

I hate not being able to sleep. Sleep has always been my consolation, a possession that cannot be stolen. I succeeded in ending my insomnia by promising myself something. I'm ashamed to admit it even now. Even now, when it no longer matters.

I promised myself that once the baby was born I would encourage Wendy to leave him.

⚜

A few months later that anger was overwhelmed when Naomi visited me in New York.

"A very scary thing is happening," she said in her brash voice, a jazzy trumpet, not at all frightened. "They think I may have bone cancer. I'm here for tests at Sloan-Kettering." She told me this in a suite at the Pierre Hotel. She wore a long print dress made by Indian women in New Mexico and her frizzy bush of hair was longer than ever and completely white. With her burned skin and wild hairdo, she could have been mistaken for a medicine man. Her brown eyes, as warm and clear as when she was young, searched my face with concern. You might have thought she was telling me I had the disease. What is she looking for? I wondered.

"I see," I said, sounding cold, although I simply didn't know how to respond. "When are the tests?"

"Tomorrow."

"I'll go with you." And that sounded reluctant, although I meant it as a consolation.

"You don't have to. There's no point. You'd just be waiting outside."

"I want to!" In an effort to get the right emotion out, I shouted this and sounded scared.

"Okay," she answered gently. "Joshua also wants to take me." That was her son. "You can keep each other company."

There's no point in stretching this out. I don't have the heart to remember each wrenching pull: when the doctors did the surgery a week later, they looked inside, and closed her right up. She's riddled with cancer, the internist reported to Joshua and me. The sun had murdered her. Naomi had had skin cancer, he said, which could have been treated if caught early. Once under the skin, it spreads with glee. She was doomed.

Joshua leaned into my arms, crying. The doctor seemed embarrassed by the display. I was numb. I closed my eyes to rest them from the dismal sight of the hospital waiting room. In my head there was Naomi, years and years before: young and beautiful, naked but for the bottom of her bikini, lying on her sandy beach in Maine, her breasts full of life for Josh, her heart big enough to love me and Sam and all her crazy, self-indulgent friends.

Three months later, shriveled and ghastly, she died. There was not only a funeral, but two memorial services, one on each coast, an exhibition of her collection of feminist papers—there were many ripples of her good deeds. I resented them all. I knew what Stefan thought of my reaction, that I was possessive, wanted Naomi all to myself because I thought she was never really mine.

Of course I had a last time with her, in the hospital, when only the core of her still lived, behind those now-hollowed eyes, deep and brown and yet—incredibly—not scared, but busy, busy with the problems of life: "Are you happy?" she asked.

"Yes." I hated that question.

"I'm leaving plenty for Joshy and to the collection. I'm assuming you're okay on that score."

"I am."

"I'm also setting up a women's shelter in Bangor. I want you to run it—"

I resented her for this, for pushing me, even at the end, to be like her. I couldn't be like her. "No," I said, my eyes filling, not with sadness, but frustration.

"It's not just for battered women, but for all kinds of problems. They really—"

"I can't do it." I wanted her to stop. She was forcing me to reject her when all I wanted was to embrace and say good-bye. "I can't leave my life here in New York."

"None of the poverty pimps will be able to do the job you could. To them all the pain is academic. Consider it. I'm willing to emotionally blackmail—"

Damn me, I couldn't hold it in: "I don't give a shit about saving the world. I don't feel guilty that I got lucky and escaped. There's no button for you to press. Quit trying to find it. You saved the wrong girl."

"Don't say that." For the first time since her illness, I saw something that hurt her, not the exhausting agony of death, but a living pain. "It's bullshit." Her voice choked a little. "In the end, I know you'll do the right thing. You need me out of the way. You need to come to it yourself and not have me nag you."

"Okay," I said, lying. "Okay, I will. Soon as you're not looking."

I hope you believed me, Naomi. I'm sorry, sorrier now than ever, that I spurned your last gift, which I mistook to be an obligation, and was really my only hope of rescue.

❧

Wendy had her child twenty-eight days after Naomi's death. One cycle of the moon. One circuit of a soul about the earth, perhaps? In my deepest dreams, she came back to me.

Certainly, Wendy hoped I would feel that way. Stefan forced me to go to Wendy's hospital bed (I hadn't wanted to, I was sick of them) and she put her hand out—banded with the ID bracelet—over the railing, fingers arched, grabbing the air between us. "Moll," she said. "Before they catch us. Come and look."

Newborns don't seem real—they are aliens that become human in our arms. We make them by how we hold them, by what we give them. I was scared of the creature she showed me: a tadpole, unshaped, a challenge. I was very glad I didn't have to spend nine months sensing such a thing inside me.

"They don't let babies stay when there are visitors," Wendy explained to Stefan, who had asked why she was worried about being caught. She glanced over at her husband. Because Ben stood in the corner of the room, dressed in a hospital gown, I briefly mistook him for an orderly. "Ben, are we agreed? Can I ask her?" Wendy asked.

I didn't pay attention to their talk. My eyes were stuck on the alien, feet and arms spastic, eyes blind to the world. My head was drowning in death and the pointlessness of life. I saw nothing worthwhile about birth.

"Moll." Wendy grabbed me so hard it hurt. "Moll, I want to ask you a favor."

I must have said all right. I may not even have looked at her. I was mad, I guess, mad with grief.

"I want to call her Naomi. Because we're Jewish, I can't name her after you, and I hope you don't think it's, I don't know, presumptuous. But I wanted to call her Naomi."

I cried. And I couldn't stop. I cried for so long and so hard, I began to choke. Wendy hugged me. I sobbed more violently. Stefan shook me and urged me to drink water, but I couldn't calm myself sufficiently—I coughed it out. "She's hysterical," I heard Ben say, and I suspect Stefan was tempted to sedate me, but the reminder that I was putting on this exhibition in front of Ben forced me to regain control.

Naomi is a solemn little girl. Sometimes I think that's because she heard so much unhappiness come out of me her first day on earth. It felt as if all the unhappiness I had ever known was wrung out, exorcised.

The next morning, grief was gone. There was life to be cared for.

I helped Ben set up the nursery in the morning and spent a long lazy afternoon with Wendy. We cheated on the hospital rules. I hid in the private bathroom when feeding time came around so that I could see the baby again, in a calmer state, I hoped.

Wendy scooped her out of her see-through bassinet and offered: "Do you want to hold Naomi?"

For a moment, hearing her name, I felt I would cry again.

"Come on," Wendy urged, and shuffled in my direction—the episiotomy caused her to move gingerly. In her mother's arms Naomi seemed more human. Her eyes, though still blind, peered at the movement of my face and her restless movements were quieted.

"Make a basket," Wendy said, and I made a cradle out of my arms. Wendy gave her to me. Scared by her fragility, I tensed up, arms rigid as boards, my neck so tight I was sore until I got home and stretched out the kink on the machines. Wendy laughed at me, delighted by my awkwardness. "She won't break," she assured me. Nevertheless, I was relieved to give Naomi back.

Later, I regretted that I hadn't held her longer. It was odd how persistent my remorse was. All through dinner and the evening, I was sad, disappointed by my reaction. I told Stefan and he said, in his maddening, reasonable tone, "You'll get used to holding her. It's not an automatic knowledge. It's not instinctual. Good mothering can be learned."

"She's not my child," I said.

"Yes . . . ?"

"You made it sound like she's mine."

"How did I do that?"

He was being a shrink. I clammed up. Stefan often complained that I held my emotions in, yet his response to my loud and bitter grief over Naomi's death had been almost panicky, and now his reaction to my yearning for the baby Naomi seemed patronizing, dismissive. He didn't want to explore or live with either of those feelings. Makes sense, I told myself. Why would a man be attracted to an emotionally cool woman and then want her to become volatile? The complaints were phony: he liked my repressed self.

❧

That night the memory of my incompetence with the baby alternated with my disappointment in Stefan: rocking back and forth between the two kept me up, unsettled. Well past midnight, after another session in the gym, I wandered into the kitchen for a drink of water and looked across the courtyard to Ben and Wendy's kitchen. An air conditioner dominated the bottom half of the window (Ben hadn't wanted to spend the money to install it in the wall below) and short curtains covered the top half. Their lights were on. Wanting a better view, I went into what had been our maid's room. We had converted it into a country pantry to match our country kitchen, paying through the nose to install old wood cabinets salvaged from a Vermont farmhouse, and replacing the old frosted-glass window in the bathroom with clear glass. Wendy and Ben had made more modest changes in their maid's room, modifying it into a laundry, but the old-fashioned window had been preserved. Their laundry was improperly vented or maybe too small; always hot, they had to keep the window partly open during the winter, closing it for summer air-conditioning. To my surprise I saw Ben—or rather, his naked legs—below the obscuring frosted glass.

I knelt down to see more. I did so without considering why and I still don't know why.

Ben was naked, except for red panties. Presumably they belonged to Wendy. The fit was grotesquely tight—the panties had rolled themselves into a thin line running up the crack of his buttocks. He was bent over, searching for something in the dryer.

I was thrilled. Embarrassed also, but only at what he was doing, not by my surveillance. He turned sideways—I could see only the lower two-thirds of his body—apparently studying what he had removed from the dryer. I guessed it would be a bra, but I was distracted from my reasoning by his erection.

His penis had gathered all the meager fabric about it, wrapped like a mummy. Wendy's panties had been brutally converted into a soft frilly jockstrap.

He grunted.

That startled me. Worried I would be seen, I shut off the light. For a moment he seemed to have noticed. His legs turned to face me. I ducked below the window line, a soldier peering out from a trench.

Obviously he could see well enough through his frosted glass to notice our light. I had turned it on when his back was to me, but he was sideways when I flipped it off, and he would have noticed the change.

His body lowered. I caught a glimpse of a bra hanging loose at each elbow before I dropped flat on the floor to hide. I could hear nothing. I didn't know how I could determine when it was safe to rise. Finally, I decided to crawl backward until I was out of his line of sight.

From the relative safety of our hall, I peeked around the door—Ben was gone. I was thrilled. My heart pounded, I felt the excited guilt of an adolescent doing mischief. I wanted to laugh. The thought of him in panties rummaging for a bra was hilarious. It was great gossip, the kind of thing I would be eager to tell Wendy, only—

Worry about Ben's weirdness set in slowly, after my bout of glee. What did it mean? Was he gay—no, I knew enough from Stefan's idea of chitchat that cross-dressing was under a different heading in the textbooks. Anyway, I wouldn't have believed in Stefan's explanation. I don't worship Stefan's Freudian gods—that's what they've become for many bright people, a faith sometimes held obstinately in the face of facts. Almost weekly Stefan first argued against, and then was disheartened by, the mounting evidence that everything from autism to migraines was caused chemically. I had no doubt that some people were born bad, just as some were born with an arrhythmic heart. Psychiatrists, as good priests do, can help flatten a hill in the road that's too steep for even good drivers—they cannot cure nature.

I was up until dawn considering my situation. There were many options, more than you might notice at first glance. I imagined all sorts of grand scenarios. Tell Wendy, she confronts Ben, he admits it, she throws him out. Confront Ben myself, he breaks down and willingly leaves. Or Wendy forces him to seek treatment, he becomes a better person, or at least less obnoxious. I guess my poor reasoning was due to lack of rest. I fell asleep for only a few hours before Stefan woke me with a reminder that I had promised to help Ben and Wendy bring the baby home. Bleary-eyed over coffee, the obvious truth hit me: what I had seen was harmless, laughable, probably no odder than the fact that I was spying. Did wearing panties walk ahead of peeping in the perversion parade?

"How weird is it," I croaked at Stefan, despite my lack of faith, "for a married man, presumably heterosexual, to put on his wife's panties and bra?"

Stefan was reading the *Times*. He lowered the paper comically, one semicircular eyebrow raised. "Sometimes your bathrobe when I can't find mine, but never the panties. I swear."

You see, even a professional finds it silly. Silly things are harmless, no? "Come on, you know about this stuff."

"Depends on the context. Does he do it all the time? Is it part of a masturbation ritual? It's only a symptom. Like any doctor, I would have to run some tests, know more about the patient. Why?"

I told Stefan what I had seen. I would have preferred to gossip with Wendy about it, but she was excluded from this one.

Stefan was fascinated, delighted. He took the information from me as if he were selecting a delectable chocolate from a dessert tray— examining the sweet with relish before he popped it in his mouth and pronounced it to be: "Not surprising really. Ben's obviously uncomfortable with himself. Wish I knew more." Stefan raised his brows and stared off, lost in silent inquiry.

"Is it something for me to worry about?" I almost snapped at him.

"Worry about?"

"Wendy and Naomi. They live with him."

"Just be sure to buy them oversized clothes—"

I was tired and disappointed my snooping hadn't been worthwhile. "Sometimes you're a jerk," I told him.

He snapped to attention, the alert charming Disney chipmunk. "Sorry. Of course you're worried. I don't think there's anything to be concerned about. I wouldn't discuss it with Wendy, especially not now—"

"I'd never bring it up to her! Of course not!" I was furious with him.

"Of course you wouldn't," he asserted, and smiled, paws crossed, cheeks puffed with self-satisfaction.

"You haven't said anything about my being a Peeping Tom."

Stefan nodded sagely. "You don't trust Ben. You worry about how he treats Wendy. You don't believe he tells you the whole story, so when the opportunity presented itself to get a glimpse of his private life, you took it."

I must confess that made me feel better. Nevertheless, I hesitated before ringing Ben's doorbell half an hour later when I was supposed to pick him up to drive him to the hospital. Ben answered right away, as if he had been waiting behind the door.

I jumped back.

"I was just about to get you," he said.

"You startled me."

"Sorry." He reached for me, his elegant fingers and long nails wrapping around my wrists. "Listen, I want to say something." His small eyes, alternating between wariness and resentment, darted from the floor to my face and back again. His tongue unraveled slowly to make the words. "I'm very grateful for your helping with everything. Wendy had a rough time in delivery and your visit yesterday really made her feel better. I'm really thankful." He pulled me to him, hugging hard. His body was big, stronger than I had expected. A thick odor, a man's smell, enveloped me. I felt stupid and embarrassed. I hurried to squirm out of his arms and talked brightly of how beautiful his daughter was.

"She's a jewel," he said with great feeling, his slow voice quavering, his eyes shimmering. "I hope I can be a good father to her."

"Of course you will."

He looked at me straight, with those nervous eyes, and they paused. Behind his thick glasses, I noticed how worried he was, his almost childish fear of failure: "I don't know," he whispered. "I want her to be happy."

I liked him. In spite of everything, that morning I liked him.

❧

I t's easy to be the generous aunt. Unruffled, rested, able to break Mommy's rules with a single wink. I was shameless, seized any excuse to indulge little Naomi.

She was an extraordinary child. She had Wendy's big face, only she didn't have her mother's sallow skin or her father's thick rough hide. Presumably smoking, lack of exercise, poor diet, something had corrupted Ben's and Wendy's complexions, because their daughter had bright, smooth white cheeks, soft and sweet as clean linen on pillows. Nor did she have their sluggish bodies. Once she was past the beer belly of the two-year-old, her figure was lean, with slim elegant legs and wide bony shoulders. Even her thick head of reddish brown hair had no origin in what could be seen of Ben's once-black hair or Wendy's dull, party curly, mousy brown. And the oddest trick of genetics topped off her difference from mother and father—her deep blue eyes. Not Wendy's curious pale blue or Ben's small, almost black, suspicious eyes. Nor did they magically resemble the bright, cold, shallow blue in my eyes—my father's heartless eyes. No, Naomi's had the deep life-giving blue of the ocean, populated by feeling and love.

What a lot of love she had to give! She was affectionate to everyone and yet in a distinct and individual manner; she found a private entrance to each of their hearts. She performed as an early through-the-night sleeper, talker, walker, bottle forsaker, toilet trainee, reader, and so on, to the delight of Wendy, who was vain of her intelligence and precocity. She was cuddly and affectionate to Ben, who obviously longed for this feminine attention. She laughed at Stefan's jokes, which made him feel young, and took seriously his sporadic attempts to teach her what science he remembered from his college days, which made him feel wise. With her babysitter, Yolanda, she was imperious until scolded, and then she was as prim and sweet as a novitiate, shaming the other caretakers who could not control their spoiled charges, thus lifting Yolanda to the status of lecturing expert on proper child care. Among her many friends, she had possession of their hearts and minds, the leader of a clique which you and I would have died to get into if we were little and knew her. I like to think she was a beneficent despot, but she ruled, there was no doubt of that.

I don't know how to explain that she filled up all the blanks in my life. Unless you have loved a child, not merely raised one, but cared deeply, you can't understand the complicated and beautiful pattern that fills your head. Watching a child evolve from creaturehood into human being, from expectation into reality, writes a text of memory that can always be read with pleasure, accompanied by the images, a coffee-table book of moments for reminiscence and for encouragement. Naomi, big-eyed, feet flat, stumbling out, hands spread ready to catch the floor should it decide to rush up and whack her, waddling the first steps of her life. Naomi finally letting go of her grip on the park slide, leaning back, her long hair splayed on the metal, her wide-spaced teeth popping out with joy, gravity whisking her into my arms. Naomi wandering between Wendy's and my legs in the clothing store, briefly decapitated as she ducked under and out of the racks, until we took her to the girl's section and made good on our promise that she could pick out a dress for her fifth birthday party. Wendy and I held each other's hand, suffering through the tension, fearful that she would select a fashion nightmare, and watched her imitate us, sternly pushing her way through the hanging garments, thoughtfully pulling them by the hem to hold against herself, finally removing several and solemnly pronouncing: "I'm going to try these on and see which one I like best." They were all in excellent taste. Or Naomi, pale, burning hot, asking Wendy if I would come over on a dreary Sunday and keep her company, saying, "I think Mommy is enervated," a word she had picked up, to his delight, from Stefan. There's no sense to it, no logic: I knew her life, its secrets, its smallest details, better than my own, certainly more honestly. Her flaws and brilliancies were the same to me: all precious.

Her fifth birthday was a festival. It seemed to last a week. I began to expect that our street would be blocked off and all the buildings would empty out to celebrate. It climaxed with a party for her entire nursery school class. I helped Wendy and Ben clean up. They were dead by evening and I took their place for the bedtime ritual. Naomi's legs were still hopping with excitement, pushing at her sheets while I read, eyes nervously taking an account of her presents. Her gifts were lined up in a neat row on her dresser; she couldn't light on one to relish, and her vision skipped frantically. "I'm too happy," she said, her cheeks drawn. "I'm too happy!" she repeated, crying out.

"It's okay." I stroked her forehead and kissed its hot skin, fairly melted from exhaustion.

"Take them away!" She pointed to the presents, horrified, threatened by them.

"I'll cover them up," I suggested, and used a bed sheet from her dresser to do that.

"Please stay with me," she said when I had finished reading the book.

I turned out the light and sat on the edge of her bed.

"Could you pat my back?" she mumbled. Her profile on the pillow relaxed when I put my palm down between the bony wings of her shoulder blades. Her eyelids were swollen, her mouth sagged. I saw the suggestion of adulthood in her face: that's what she had experienced; with all the fuss and greed of her party, she had known how unsatisfying the world can be, even when it gives you everything you want. At that moment I was glad she wasn't my daughter. I would have felt too sad, too sorry to see that sweet face growing old before my eyes.

I waited until the poor child was fast asleep. Even then her chest heaved from time to time, sighing through uneasy dreams. I was reluctant to go. Her room was quiet and peaceful, the dolls and toys idle, waiting for their duties to begin. Her yellow night-light cast a gentle shadow over all: it was safe there in her child's world.

Ben had fallen asleep on the couch in the living room. Wendy sipped coffee, a blank look on her round face, her pale eyes almost completely white. I told her about Naomi's hysteria; we gossiped about the various mothers; I praised her for all her work; reassured her that Naomi wasn't spoiled. "Indulged," I said. "If you say no, she accepts it."

"I never say no," Wendy mumbled.

"Yes, you do."

"There's something I want to ask your permission to do," Wendy said. Ben groaned on the couch and we both looked at him for a moment. He mouthed something with his small red lips, chewing. He could have been a bum on a park bench that we passed, unconcerned. He used to be an enormous roadblock; since Naomi's birth, he was shunted off to the side, a bystander holding a video camera. Not to Wendy, presumably. "I'm sure you'll say yes, but Ben thought I should make sure it's okay with you. We've finally gotten around to writing our wills. It's incredibly irresponsible that we've taken this long—"

"It certainly is!"

"You know me. My uncle's been hocking me every month for five years and I finally gave in. Anyway, I've already had the lawyer—"

"What lawyer did you use?"

"Someone who works for Ben's firm and did it for free."

"You get what you pay for, you know. We could have done it for you. I could have gotten Peter Thompson to do it cheap."

"Well, no big deal. We left everything to each other or to Naomi if we both die, and that's what I want to ask you. We want to name you and Stefan as her guardians."

"Of course," I said casually. I was very pleased. I had never thought about it, and obviously it didn't surprise me that I would be Wendy's choice—still, I was moved and flattered.

"You've been another mother to her anyway, so I took for granted—"

"Yes!" I said emphatically, and there were tears in my eyes. I felt silly about them.

Wendy cocked her head and smiled, her chin up sympathetically. "Thank you. She loves you very much, you know. I wanted to make sure, just in case some cousin of Ben's or my uncle got a crazy notion in their head, I wanted to be sure you would take care of her."

"Okay, okay, stop," I said, and tears rolled out of my eyes and I laughed and she laughed and there were tears in her eyes and we hugged. It was a simple, pure exchange between good friends, one of those ambushes of happiness that life can sometimes spring when you are in the middle of nowhere.

※

Almost two years later, about nine one evening, Ben rang the doorbell. He had been careful of us all those years, always phoning before coming over. Little Naomi, naturally, was the one who knocked without warning and I expected it to be her. "Ben." I greeted him dully, obviously disappointed, blocking the doorway, unable to will myself into a smile.

Ben was dressed in jeans that sagged below his waist, suspended from total collapse by his hips. Impressions made by his knees now puffed out near his shins and the heels dragged, frayed, on the floor. He was barefoot and shirtless. His laurel of hair was darker and sleeker than usual, pressed flat to his skull. There was a towel around his neck. "Sorry for the interruption," he said. "Wendy sent me over. Naomi came home from school today with a note saying she has lice."

The word sickened me, a finger touching the back of my throat. Not me, I thought, remembering the endless dirt of my parents' trailer, the humiliating consciousness of my shabby clothes when the richies drove up to buy lobster—the microscopic, itching discomfort of poverty, too small and too plentiful to get rid of, and still pursuing me.

"Since she was here last night—," Ben began.

"She didn't have it then!" I cried out.

"She's had it for weeks. The nits are halfway down her hairs." Ben showed me two boxes, the words LICE, EGGS, NITS written in black, nauseating letters. "You and Stefan should both shampoo with this." He held up one box. "And all your furniture should be sprayed with this." He showed me the other.

"Ugh." My hands went to my scalp, abruptly on fire with movement, and scratched. "How did this happen? Don't you regularly shampoo her head?"

"Hey!" Ben jerked his head, offended. His glasses slid down his nose. "It's got nothing to do with cleanliness. If one kid at school's got them, they jump onto anything, a coat, furniture, anything—"

"Did she get it from Yolanda?"

"Jesus, Molly, isn't that racist? It has nothing to do with money. Being rich doesn't kill them or stop them. Fucking detergent doesn't stop them. You have to use this."

I took the boxes, leaning on the doorway to stabilize my queasiness. INSECTICIDE was written on the side, cautioning the user not to get it in the eyes. I thought, quite seriously, of walking out of the apartment forever, abandoning all my possessions, moving to a hotel, and starting life over tomorrow with a new apartment, new furniture, new clothes. Behind Ben, their door opened. Wendy, her hair also wet and plastered to her skull, peeked out. "It's a nightmare. I'm sorry. Just remember you love Naomi."

"I'm going to kill her," I mumbled.

"Look, it's a drag, but it can be done," Ben lectured, belly forward, spilling over his wilting jeans. "We've stripped all the beds, sprayed everything. Only took two hours. It's not like it's another Black

Monday. There's no point in whining about it."

"Don't use that tone with me," I said, enraged. Ben had gradually become more familiar and belligerent to me, as if I were another Wendy, part of his family.

"Sorry." He lowered his head, touched me with a hand, and backed away. "You know I love you—I'm tired, that's all. I felt exactly like you when I heard. But really, they say you do this and they're gone. I'll help you do it. Yolanda will wash your things tomorrow—"

"No," I said, only half-joking. "I'm burning the sheets."

Wendy smiled. "Ben, take care of Naomi. I'll help." She came in, babbling, joking, apologizing. "We send her to a six-thousand-dollar-a-year school and they give her lice." Wendy and I got to work, doing, in effect, an extermination job. Stefan took the infestation with good humor, suggesting we get ourselves arrested and let the city hose us down for free. Later on, my own hair slicked and stinking from the insecticide in the shampoo, I held a screaming Naomi's head in my hands while Wendy slowly, painfully, pulled a fine-toothed comb through her hair to pick out the nits. "It's the collapse of Western civilization," I said in the smelly wreckage of my living room at around midnight, pillows airing by the window, sheets in a pile by the hall, the vacuum cleaner and its many parts still not put away. Stefan had gone to sleep. So had Ben and Naomi, of course. Wendy and I were having brandy, giddy from the horror and the work, girlish together, a reminder of the days when we were single.

We had more than one drink and let two o'clock pass, careless of our work schedules. Wendy was in charge of the Special Education Program for all of Queens and had an early meeting with the chancellor. I was supposed to advise whether a major bank should withdraw from the financing of a telecommunications satellite in light of the minor error that had occurred with the latest launch into Earth's orbit—namely, somehow the satellite had been lost. "We're so irresponsible," I mumbled.

Wendy's mood had darkened in the last half hour. She had gone from jokes about the lice to complaints about work. Her mouth settled into a gloomy frown and her shoulders slumped. "I don't care if I never work again," she said. "I wish Ben would come up with some great idea, make a lot of money, and I could sleep late."

"Naomi would wake you up anyway."

"I'm so tired of fighting." She spoke in a hoarse croak, presumably from the cognac and the late hour.

"Fighting?"

"With Ben. It seems like we do nothing but bicker. Or he screams at me. And I feel sick. Sometimes I wish he would just say 'I'm leaving you' and go."

I waited. To make sure she meant it? To replay the words to be sure I understood? "You think he wants to leave you?"

"He's not happy. He yells at me about everything."

"He does? Yells?"

"Throws fits. Temper tantrums."

"I've never seen—"

"Doesn't do it in front of you. He's scared of you. You'd punch him in the mouth." She laughed, straightening a bit, and then slumped into a pathetic pose. "I'm getting a little scared of him."

My face was loose from the brandy, my cheekbones asymmetrical, my jaw heavy. I swallowed hard, trying to sober up. "What are you saying, Wendy? Say it straight out, okay? Is he hitting you? What are you scared of?"

"No, no!" She waved a hand at me. "I knew you'd get overexcited—"

"I am not," I tried to protest loudly, but the words lumbered out, sliding, not exhaled.

"He throws fits. You know. If he weren't so big, it would be funny. He throws things on the floor—"

"What things?"

"He broke an ashtray when I told him about the lice. Threw it on the floor. Or, like last Saturday, he was sweeping up and I teased him about something and he broke the broom. Smashed it on the table, sent the dishes flying, and snapped the handle off."

I was so sleepy and heavy from the cleaning and the drinking that I had to lean on the coffee table and prop my head up. "He wasn't always like this . . . ?"

"Not . . . not, you know"—Wendy also was able to speak only with great effort—"this often. Every once in a while, he'd get frustrated. It's happening a lot now because of the crash."

This was early November 1987, a few weeks after the stock market collapse. Everyone we knew had lost something, but the damage was to their pension funds or savings and would have no effect on their comfort. Ben had told us that he expected there would be layoffs on Wall Street; however, he was a securities analyst, and he thought most of the cuts would be retail brokers. He believed his job was safe. I asked Wendy if that had been a lie.

"No, but—you have to promise not to let Ben know I told you this. And please, don't even mention it to Stefan. Especially Stefan. Ben would be particularly embarrassed if Stefan knew."

"Really? Of course I'll shut up. But why Stefan?"

"Some male pride thing."

"What is it? He lost money in the market?"

"He lost a lot of money. He was buying options, writing them or something. I don't understand it, I've never understood that stuff. He did very well for a long time. That's why we could buy the house. And now it looks like we have to sell it."

The year before they had bought a country house on the New York side of the Berkshires. Wendy thought Naomi should have regular access to nature, with its supposed benefits. You can imagine my feelings about that. Besides, I resented the purchase because it robbed me of my Saturday outings with Naomi; I couldn't take her to the movies, or ice-skating, or just to lunch. Also, along with work, marriage, and children, Wendy's weekend country house was another distraction from our friendship. In addition, Stefan had been concentrating on his book when he wasn't seeing patients. Lately, life had been lonely. I was drifting more and more into my work, making money without need, a kind of work-ethic decadence, puritanism without spirituality. Selfishly, I didn't sympathize with Wendy's tragedy. "I can lend you money," I offered.

"No, no. That's a great way for us to end up not being friends anymore. Anyway, I have money, the money from Uncle Manny." She meant her parents' insurance money, the money that her uncle had managed until his death the previous year. "I don't want to use that—we need the income and it's—" She put her head to one side and paused, her pale eyes sad.

"It's what you have left of your parents," I said.

"You better tell Stefan to watch out," she said. "You might take over his practice."

"Ben wants you to use your money?"

"He's always spending my money in his head. He wanted to put it in the market last year when Uncle Manny died. Thank God I said no." Because the couch's pillows were airing out, we were both seated on the rug, our arms spread on the black marble coffee table, hands supporting our heads. She slid on her elbows in my direction, lowering her voice almost to a whisper: "Do you think Ben might be having an affair?"

I was flabbergasted. Why? Because I thought he was unappealing. I had accepted Wendy's original attraction on the basis that she was desperate for marriage and children, but I couldn't imagine a woman having an illicit romance with him. Ben was hardly a candidate for passion—although there was that night of the red panties, a suggestion he had some sort of appetite. After a moment's reflection, I supposed that there were enough unhappy women in New York to cast even Ben Fliess as Romeo.

"No, I don't. Do you?" I asked.

"His schedule has changed. He stays later at work. An hour later for the past six months."

"Have you asked him why?"

Her face was near. I noticed how much her skin had aged: there were lines everywhere, ghosts of the smiles and frowns of her youth. And of mine too, for that matter. Was Ben so arrogant that he dared to decide he could do better? Was he so greedy that he demanded youth? I had underestimated his acquisitiveness before. He was a man. Such things are commonplace, after all, the day-to-day evils of humanity.

"Something about in-house meetings with the brokers. He says there's a lot of pressure these days because of the crash—it sounds reasonable."

"How's sex?"

"We're parents. Parents don't screw." She tried to laugh, but her shoulders sagged even more and her big round face, lined with worry, took on the exaggerated pathos of a sad clown.

Her pain hurt me and I hesitated to ask, but I was too thirsty, after so many years in the desert, for more about her marriage. "Has it been a long time?"

She was ashamed. "Yeah," she mumbled, and averted her eyes.

I remembered our quarrel so long ago, when I first met Ben. I was scared I had crossed that border again. Wary of her later regrets, of a sudden revocation of my visa, I said nothing, passive, waiting for her to go on. She didn't. She sighed and looked off, giving in to her inward, suppressed hurt. The bottom of her eyes shimmered with water, and a big tear, like the symbolic tear of a clown's makeup, ran down her face.

Damn him, I thought, and all the rage from past offenses woke inside me. My long-buried wish for an end to their marriage was resurrected.

There was a thudding on our front door, a fist pounding steadily, hard, but not furious.

"That's Ben," she said, and scrambled to her feet. She was scared and guilty; her neck retracted, her body became frantic. She dashed toward the foyer, abruptly stopped, turned back, and said, "I'll talk to you tomorrow in the office."

He thudded on the door. I got up, almost ready to tell him off. "Stay," she said, a plea really. "Everything's gonna be okay. Good night."

I heard his rage and disgust from the hallway as soon as she opened the door. "It's almost three! What the fuck's the matter with you!"

She tried to shush him, went out into the hall, and quickly shut our door behind her. I hurried into the foyer and pressed my ear against its cool surface.

"I'm coming home late tomorrow!" he scolded. "You're gonna have to handle Naomi yourself." Their front door squealed open.

"I do that all the time—," she protested, but the anger was sat on, steam squashed under a lid, only wisps escaping.

"What the fuck were you talking to her about, anyway!" he said, full of contempt and fear.

They passed into their apartment and I heard no more.

❧

Did I say no to the client's offer to drop me in his limousine because I hoped to see Ben? Did I choose to walk home, rather than take the subway, and stroll past the entrance to Ben's office, because I thought there was a slight chance, a remote possibility of catching him?

If so, I wasn't conscious of it. I finished my meeting on Water Street, excited by the reassurances about the next satellite launch, and declined the limousine ride, thinking not of Ben, but of the cool fall day, the bright blue sky, the long gray streets, knowing Stefan would be with patients until eight-thirty, and wishing to make practical use of my machine-strengthened muscles—or at least substitute a long walk for that day's session on the Life-Cycle bicycle. However, I chose to walk north up Nassau, which would take me past Ben's office, rather than the obvious choice, Broadway.

The streets were busy with people on their way home at four-thirty—the Exchange closes at four. I felt so good, so grateful for Stefan and for my work. I rather enjoyed helping, if only in a paperwork capacity, to launch something into space, especially if we could manage not to lose this one. I was glad about little Naomi and for my friendship with Wendy. I was also thankful to New York, pleased by its concrete lawn, its brick forests, its curbside gardens of watches and scarfs, its background surf of traffic, its animal kingdom of sidewalk people. Even the city's public misery—wounded and shelterless people—seemed right to remind me that there would always be a challenge to my self-satisfaction: I was confident and felt strong.

I saw Ben, from a block away, exit from the gleaming silver doors of his building, pivot eagerly on his heels, and make for the subway entrance on the corner. The previous night I had overheard Ben say he was going to be working late and yet he was leaving his office at the usual time. I knew something was up and I trotted after him without giving it a second thought.

By the time I reached the subway entrance, he had disappeared down the stairs. I followed cautiously, my token already out. Ben wasn't on line at the booth, or at the turnstiles. I went through and hesitated for only a moment before going down the stairs to the uptown side of the tracks.

Several people took a second glance at me as I descended. I moved in a peculiar way, pausing every few steps, bending down to see if I could spot him before committing myself to a full appearance on the platform. Once I had satisfied myself that Ben was not at the bottom of the steps, I hurried the rest of the way, panicked by the sound of an approaching train. I didn't see him. A train was coming on the express track and I manuevered to peer about the back of the stairs to check the rest of the uptown platform. No Ben. The train now roared in. I looked in its direction and saw him across the way on the downtown platform.

I ducked behind a post and then peeked. Ben was on the opposite side, looking, not at me, but into the tunnel, nervously shifting his weight from one foot to the other, obviously impatient. The arriving train cut off my view of him.

I now felt justified that I was skulking about the station. Ben might have been innocently on his way home if he were on the uptown side of the tracks, but heading downtown he was probably up to mischief. His uneasy manner, running a hand over his bald skull, watching the tracks eagerly, also helped confirm my assumption. I rushed up the steps, attracting a bored look from a Transit Authority cop, and crossed to the other side, selecting a staircase that would put me on Ben's platform but not near him.

I was excited. Discovery, as any lawyer can tell you, is always a thrill when you are convinced it will lead to the truth. This information—where Ben was going—was power. It could arm Wendy against him. You know I hoped it would lead to divorce. But even if not, surely this would stop the fits, the demands for her money, force him to apply cosmetics to his ugliness.

Doubts crept in while I leaned against a post, concealing all of me, except for a sliver of my face so that one eye could have a view of him—doubts born of arrogance. I assumed I would follow him into the arms of a woman. I worried that divorce might harm Naomi. Perhaps I should use the information against Ben, force him into marriage counseling, without informing Wendy? I was full of myself, scheming grandly, making life choices for my friend with the air of a finicky eater at a buffet.

I boarded the downtown local when he did. I rode by the door, stepping out at each stop to see if Ben departed. I assumed we were Brooklyn-bound since there were only a few more stops in Manhattan. I was wrong. He got out at Rector Street and then it hit me. Then I knew where he was going, but didn't know what it meant.

I trailed him to his old building, his bachelor pad in Battery Park City, at the edge and bottom of Manhattan. Stefan and I had been there once, just before he and Wendy were married. We helped him move some books. Wasn't that right? I asked myself. Ben had moved out his possessions, so naturally I assumed he had given up the apartment. That was eight years ago. Could he have kept the place all these years and Wendy knew and had never mentioned it?

I stood on the plaza, the river beside me, surrounded by sightseers, by young parents with strollers, by frowning and depressed Wall Streeters, and looked at the Statue of Liberty, already illuminated for the night. I was disappointed. I didn't like to admit it, but the possibility I had discovered nothing was crushing.

I had to make this find important. I called Wendy.

"Hi." I spoke in a cheerful rush. "A young lawyer here is looking for an apartment and I was suggesting he check out Battery Park City. Does Ben still have the lease on his old apartment? Is he subletting?"

"Wow," Wendy said, hoarse, her speech slow. "Aren't you hung over? Where did you get that energy?"

"I sweated it out."

"No, Ben doesn't —" She seemed to wake up a little. I heard the television on in the background. She had probably plunked Naomi down to watch, too tired to entertain her. "Why would he? You know he moved. You and Stefan helped, didn't you?"

I excused myself and hung up. My senses tingled. The city seemed to glow, highlighted by mysterious twilight pastels. It would be just like greedy Ben to keep that apartment for all these years, calculating that he could someday use it for adultery.

I walked into the lobby, with a hurried step, right up to the doorman. "I'm seeing Ben Fliess. Is that twelve C?"

I had to repeat the name. Obviously the doorman didn't know it. That made me wonder. "No," he said, after a long study of his panel of names and apartment numbers. "Fliess is fourteen D. Your name?"

"My briefcase," I said to him, and tried to look blank.

"What?"

"I forgot my briefcase!" I rushed out and returned to my distant post on the esplanade by the water. For a long time I thought nothing. It was darker and cooler, almost cold, nearly winter. The Statue glowed.

Was the doorman new? No, then Ben would have been obliged to announce himself only a little while ago to get past and the name would have been fresh. It meant that the doormen knew Ben by sight, knew that he lived in the building, yet didn't recognize his name readily because no one ever visited. If Ben didn't have people asking to be rung up, then what? What did he do, alone in that apartment, everyday after work—?

He dressed in women's clothes.

I laughed. The wind picked up off the river and I was pushed a foot or so before regaining my balance. Vividly, I saw thick Ben Fliess, swollen inside a tawdry red dress, and I laughed.

Quickly, it wasn't ridiculous. He had kept an apartment for this activity, for this secret. He had planned elaborately and expensively to satisfy this taste.

And Wendy knew nothing of it?

And he had no need of sex with her?

And he was Naomi's father?

And I was going to keep this secret with him, collaborate in his madness?

No. I caught a cab and went home to tell her. Miserable though it might be, the information belonged to Wendy. Tell her what? I didn't know he was cross-dressing. I only knew about the apartment. I would have to admit that for seven years I had withheld the story of seeing Ben from my pantry window. Besides, even if I did confess to my silence, so what? The only thing I knew for certain was the existence of the apartment.

Then that's what I had to tell her.

I didn't wait for a discussion with Stefan. I didn't wait for a night's sleep to think it over. I didn't wait until Naomi was in bed. I have to admit now that I had no regret I was hurting poor Wendy, hurrying her toward divorce. No, I brimmed over with self-righteousness: Wendy was owed the truth.

Wendy was giving Naomi a bath. She appeared at the door with a towel over her shoulder.

"Molly! Is it Molly?" Naomi called from the tub.

"I have to talk to you privately," I whispered.

Wendy's clothes were damp, splotched with water, her uncertain curly mop of hair wilted, her pale eyes shrunken by dark circles. "Ben's not here. What is it?"

"Ma!" Naomi cried out. "Who is it? What's going on! Will somebody please answer me! I'm not getting any younger here, you know!"

I laughed at Naomi's excellent imitation of her mother when she was exasperated. Wendy said, "One second," went down the hall, and poked her head into the bathroom. "I'll be back in a minute. You can turn the water back on and rinse your hair again. Turn on the cold first. Then—that's right." Wendy returned to me, not eagerly. Perhaps she didn't believe that she was owed anything as grand as the truth.

"I had a meeting downtown this afternoon, near Ben's office. I decided to walk home and I saw him leave ahead of me."

"When?" She squinted at me.

I held up a hand and spoke faster. At least I can report that I didn't enjoy my role and wanted to finish quickly. "At four-thirty. He went into the subway and I followed. I thought we could ride together." This lie embarrassed me and sounded obviously false. Wendy, however, nodded as though that motivation was a matter of course. "When I got onto the platform for the uptown side, he wasn't there. Then I saw he was on the other side, going downtown."

She sagged against the wall. "So he *is* having an affair," she said with calm, almost relief.

"I'm not so sure. I ran over to the other platform and I followed him."

She squinted again, put a hand to her forehead, and massaged. "You called—"

"Because he went to his old building. At least I think it is. Down at Battery Park. Anyway, I asked the doorman and he's listed. Fourteen C. Is that his old apartment number?"

"That's crazy," she said in a hushed tone, looking off with the absent expression of someone searching for a memory. "But he gave it up! Are you sure? You saw him go in?"

I nodded. "I'm sorry. Maybe I shouldn't have told you—"

"Of course you should tell me! I would have killed you if you hadn't. He's using it for affairs," she decided; then her doubts—or perhaps her hopes—crept in: "Right?"

"I don't think so."

"You don't!"

"The doorman had to search for his name, like he wasn't used to announcing visitors for Ben."

"Maybe she has a key, maybe they think she's Mrs. Fliess. Maybe he's married to someone else. Maybe he's got twelve kids with another woman!" She squeezed her eyes together, then opened them very wide, as if she were trying to wake up. "It's been, what . . . eight years since we moved in together? When I think of all his whining about money! He's spent thousands of dollars! I feel like he's laughing at me right now. What a creep."

"Ma! Ma! Ma!" Naomi screamed. We both jumped, our hearts pounding, and hurried down the hall.

"What is it!" Wendy shouted.

Naomi winked at us, silver skinned in the bathwater, her right eye shut tight. "I've got soap in my eyes!"

The jig was up. Naomi had seen me and it took half an hour to convince her that I had to go home and couldn't play. Wendy put on a videotape of the *Wizard of Oz* to distract Naomi and then walked me to the door. "I'm not going to tell Ben how I found out," she whispered. "I think that would make it worse. He's liable to throw such a fit about your following him that I won't get anywhere. Please don't let on you know."

"Sure."

"I think my marriage is . . ." She couldn't finish that thought. "I'm gonna need help—"

"Don't jump to conclusions," I said. There's not one of my deeds or words that I can be proud of, and yet it seemed so logical, so right at the time: "He might be doing something else in there," I hinted.

Wendy didn't hear, she was in a private spiral of worry and unhappiness. "I don't know if I can afford a good lawyer—"

"Don't worry about money or a good lawyer. That'll be taken care of."

She hugged me, suddenly, desperately. Her arms snaked down my back, the way a child does when preparing to climb into your arms. She wanted to be small, to be cared for. I felt her soft mother's belly and smelled on her neck the perfumed shampoo Naomi liked. "I don't know what I'd do without you," she said into my ear.

I've told you before: she was my sister, my only family. I meant to help her. But I didn't do her any good that day.

"Call me any time. Remember, we're right across the hall."

"That I can remember," she said, laughing through tears.

"Don't worry about waking me, okay?" I went out into the hall. Her hand followed, fingers still entwined with mine. "Call," I insisted.

"I'll call you from work in the morning. Tell me it's going to be okay," she said, her clown's face rounder, whiter, sadder than ever.

"It's gonna be okay," I said, nodding my head up and down, exaggerating my confidence.

No, I didn't do her any good that day.

⚜

My excitement at the discovery of Ben's hideaway was drained by the distress in Wendy's face. Listening to my story I fancied she had aged in front of my eyes. I felt mean—a messenger who deserved to be killed for delivering bad news. I lingered in the foyer until I heard Ben arrive in the elevator and enter their apartment. Then I moved into the kitchen near the window that along with the pantry window were the only ones which gave me a view of their apartment. Of course, Wendy would wait until Naomi was asleep to discuss it with him, but I listened anyway for the sounds of a quarrel, although I had every reason to believe that I wouldn't have been able to hear even if they screamed at the top of their lungs. I had never heard anything from their place except when Naomi stuck her head out and deliberately called across the courtyard. Wendy and I didn't copy her for fear the co-op board would accuse us of tenement manners.

When Stefan came home, I told him about my surveillance of Ben in an ashamed pose and voice, a little girl confessing her naughtiness. He expressed some amusement that I had followed Ben, but when I got to the meat of the story, his dark-bearded face looked grim. "That's a pretty elaborate secret life," he commented.

"Is he crazy?" I asked with all the naïveté of an ignorant yellow-haired Maine girl, my years of education and exposure to New York sophistication gone, evaporated by the heat of the moment.

"He's going to react vigorously." Stefan nodded to himself, closed his bright teeth, and pursed his hairy lips, stroking them forward, as if coaxing his mouth off his face.

"Stefan, what the hell does that mean?"

"Just that it's obviously a big secret. He's put a lot of energy into keeping it secret. That energy will be released with its exposure."

"Does that mean he's going to explode or fall apart?"

"I have no idea. He might be happy to let go of it. It can be a relief to be free of that kind of burden. But you were right not to tell her about the cross-dressing. It's better that he decide to give up that secret voluntarily, rather than be caught."

"Should she leave him?"

"Oh I don't think so. They should go into therapy."

We had fun, nervous, concerned, but gossipy fun, deciding what they should do with their lives. Stefan pretended to be only professional, I pretended to be only a good friend, but we were titillated, anxiously waiting for the denouement in tomorrow's episode. We talked and ate in the kitchen in between glances at their dark kitchen and laundry windows.

Later, I lay in bed, expecting the phone to ring. I fell asleep on guard.

And I woke alert, nervous. While I slept my conscience must have reached me through the busy circuits and delivered its message that I had done wrong. After a swallow of coffee, I phoned.

"Hello." Ben's thick voice, hoarse from exhaustion, answered.

"Hi Ben. It's Molly. Hope I didn't wake you."

"No." His tone was angry.

"Wendy and I talked about having lunch. I wanted to—"

He dropped the phone without saying anything. I heard him call out in the background. "It's for you. It's Molly."

"Hi." Wendy's voice was a whisper, soft and beautiful. She had a sweet sound, even when tired.

"I just wanted to make sure you were okay."

"I'm all right. I'll call you later, before we go to the country."

"You're going away this weekend?" I was surprised. I had assumed they wouldn't want to be up there, isolated together. "Oh, yeah. We should. It'll be the best thing. Call you later. I'm fine."

I reported to Stefan. He nodded sagely and spoke with paternal confidence: "I'm sure they'll work it out. Probably get him to open up and deal with some of his problems."

Part of me still tossed, uncomfortable, not at rest. Wendy didn't phone all morning and I tried her right before lunch. She was in a meeting, I was told. She'd call back. When I returned from eating, she had left a message. I tried her. We didn't connect until almost four.

"I'm so exhausted," she said. "I haven't slept in two nights. We were up all night."

"What did he say?"

"I can't really talk about it here."

"Let's meet for a drink."

"I can't. I have to get home, we're leaving in half an hour." She sighed, groaning at the effort of rising. "He's not having an affair. That's the bottom line, I guess. It's something else. I don't really want to talk about it now—"

"That's okay," I reassured her grandly. After all, it's easy to be patient about gossip when you already know it. And I was embarrassed, anyway. I regretted my pleasure at his sickness. I thought of myself as a bully, insensitive and crude. "But he *was* keeping his old apartment?"

"Oh, yeah. I saw it myself. We went there this morning. That's gonna change, believe me." She was firm, in control.

Hearing her strength calmed me. "He didn't get angry, throw a fit?"

"Oh God . . ." She trailed into despair. Then a grunt, an amused sound, but embittered. "We both ran the full gamut of emotions. Can we have a long lunch on Monday?" She laughed. "From my hospital bed. By then, I'll be a wreck. I'll talk to you then, okay?"

"Sure, dear," I said, gladdened by her plucky tone. Maybe I had done no harm, after all. "Get some rest. I'll see you Monday?"

"You will. Take care, Moll." That was her sign-off, from the beginning of our friendship, a constant throughout the changes of the years. A gentle note, sung three times, a soothing farewell: Take care, Moll.

I was lazy that weekend. I can't remember doing one damn thing that was worthwhile: I didn't even enjoy the indolence. I thought about her, naturally, and how it was going, even considered phoning up there—something I never did. Which is why I chose not to. Ben would suspect from my call that I knew they were going through something momentous and supposedly I didn't know.

Early Monday morning, I heard Naomi's voice in the hallway by the elevator. I almost opened the door to say hello. Then I almost rang the bell before I left for work, but decided not to since I was uncertain whether Wendy or Ben would have taken Naomi to school. Wait for lunch, I told myself. In the office, I canceled a meeting scheduled for eleven-thirty, worried that it might impinge on my date with Wendy. When I phoned her office, I got a shock: her assistant reported that Ben had told her Wendy would be out of town for a week because of a family illness.

I was immediately alive with horrible thoughts, which proves part of me knew, knew all along, and should have been more careful. In a panic, I called their apartment, got no answer, and now, frantic, I rang Ben's office. "Where's Wendy?" I said without a hello.

"I don't know." His answer was blunt and uninterested.

"What do you mean? We were supposed to have lunch. She's not at—"

"I told you already. I don't know where she is. She walked out last night. We had a fight. She just walked out. I don't know where the fuck she is. I'm furious at her for dumping everything in my lap. If you hear from her, tell her to call me. Good-bye." He hung up.

It came at me from all sides. Screaming at me, my skin shriveling with horror. If she had walked out, alive and well, she would have called me right away.

I had a million questions, many of them still being asked—unanswered—to this day.

I checked with my secretary to make sure I hadn't missed any messages.

I buzzed Brian Stoppard, one of the leading partners at our firm, our top litigator and criminal lawyer. I told him I was worried about the whereabouts of a friend. He said the police wouldn't accept a report until she was missing for twenty-four hours and I would have trouble getting their attention even then because I wasn't a family member.

But I am, I said in my head.

"If her husband claims he's heard from her, for example, they'll wait," he said. "Might ask him a few questions, but they'd wait a while. You suspect he's hurt her?" Stoppard touches the tenderest spot with the cool curiosity of a dentist. He urged me to tell the particulars and then impatiently cut me off after a few sentences. "Husbands and wives walk out for a few days, weeks, even months, all the time. And they don't call home or their best friend. Believe me, it's common. Don't imagine the worst. If you've heard nothing, and he's heard nothing, after three or four days, let me know and I'll help with the police." From his tone, he obviously thought I was overreacting.

But I knew, and you must know by now, that Wendy would never leave Naomi without a word, would never choose to go on a scary and difficult path by herself.

⁂

I left the office after instructing my secretary to get a number or location from Wendy if she called. I went down to Naomi's school, Riverview Chapel, the best of the private schools downtown. It occupies a trio of five-story buildings on a quiet block east of Fifth Avenue, complete with an outdoor playground, divided into swings and slides on one half, a basketball hoop and an open area for ball games on the other. I knew Naomi's schedule. We often discussed her likes and dislikes, and one of her criticisms was that recess in the yard came right after lunch, at one o'clock: "When I'm sleepy from eating and don't want to run around."

I stood across the street from the playground, far enough away so that Naomi couldn't easily spot me, and watched. She was there, holding her end of a rope and counting the skips of the second best of her five best friends, a brilliant redhead, Sarah. Did I imagine that Naomi seemed concerned? Her smooth face was tight. With worry? Or with concentration on the game? Anyway, I had verified that it *was* her voice I heard in the hall that morning. I walked to our building. The afternoon doorman, Billy, was on duty, He is my favorite of the staff, a tall thin black man with a wandering eye, the left side of his head more gray than the right, as if he had begun a dye job and abandoned it half done. When not covering for one of the others, his hours are from two to ten. But he often arrives early and chats with the morning man, Pablo, and he usually stays until eleven or so arguing sports with the night man, David. I asked him if he was there when Ben and Wendy came home from the country.

He said no, that he had left at eleven-thirty, and they still hadn't come in. "I was surprised," he commented with his usual attention to detail. "They usually get here about nine, nine-thirty. He always carries Naomi in. She acts like she's sleeping, you know, while I hold the elevator, but then she opens her eye and winks, you know, while the door is closing." He smiled. "And I say, 'Caught you!' So I noticed they were late." Billy was too discreet to question why I asked. I got the impression that he didn't like Ben either.

I went upstairs and rang the bell. Yolanda no longer worked for them, but they did have a woman come in twice a week to clean and do laundry. I didn't know her schedule. There was no answer. I took out the spare keys Wendy had given to me for emergencies and entered their apartment.

I went from room to room, opening closet doors with terror for a companion.

Nothing. I found nothing suspicious. I looked for keys to Ben's secret apartment, unsuccessfully.

What was I doing? What did I think I could accomplish?

I don't know. I was her family, you see. I had done her no good. Maybe she was somewhere, needing help. Maybe I could rescue her still.

Downstairs, Billy proved my faith in him. "Mrs. Gray?" He knew I used my maiden name, but I was married, so this was his compromise. "David just called to ask me something, so I asked him your question. He said Mr. Fliess and Naomi came in late, about two in the morning. The little girl was really asleep, he said, no winking."

For a moment I couldn't speak. "Not Wendy? Not Mrs. Fliess?"

"No." Billy studied me, curious. "She wasn't with them."

❧

I must have wandered in a trance for a while. I came to a few blocks from our building, walking aimlessly. I didn't remember saying good-bye to Billy or leaving. The street seemed to rise up and meet my feet, the sky jiggled in my vision. I was seated in my consciousness the way a passenger is seated on a bus, bounced along will-lessly, inside myself without control.

I stopped at a phone booth and called Stefan. He was in a session, he told me, and I had to shout at him that this was an emergency to convince him to interrupt it. He listened, uh-huhing without comment until I was finished. "You sound very upset. I can understand that. But I do think you're jumping to conclusions. She might just want to be by herself for a while. They could have fought—"

I hung up. I knew he was wrong to patronize me. I was angry that I had ever listened to his reasonableness, to his civilized perceptions.

I considered driving up to their country house. But then I would be out of reach for hours.

Then it hit me. Of course. Wendy had stayed behind in the country, that was it.

I called my office. Wendy hadn't left a message. I asked my secretary to find the country house number in my book. I dialed it, desperately, almost happy, sure that I had solved the mystery.

No one answered. I let it ring until I began to tremble and I thought I would faint. "It can't be," I whispered. "Can't be."

I wandered the streets, checking my messages every fifteen minutes, hoping that the next woman I passed would turn out to be her. I arrived across the street from Riverview Chapel School at four forty-five, fifteen minutes before dismissal from the after-school program.

I wasn't sure why I was there until after I arrived. Had Wendy sent me? Certainly I knew she wanted me to: no spirit world was necessary to direct me to this duty.

Besides, she would be there, if anywhere. Wendy would come for her daughter. If she was alive.

But it was Ben who arrived. He went inside the school, and came out with Naomi. They held hands. Naomi skipped all the way; Ben lumbered slowly, dragged by her energy and animation. I followed them, walking half a block behind.

I waited outside our apartment building for only a minute or so before going up. I stood in the hallway, between my front door and theirs, and made my choice. At last I did the right thing.

I greeted Ben with a cheerful smile. "Hear from Wendy?"

He shook his head no, moving his hairless head sullenly, the thick bloodless skin on his face glowing white, immobile and expressionless. He had the look of a sluggish zoo animal, eyes wary, hands closed, defensive, but beaten.

"Thought I'd make you some dinner and help out." I pushed in, bumping him slightly. "Okay?" I smiled into his face, daring him to find anything in my eyes but help.

"All right," he conceded in his slow speech. "Thanks," he added with the slightest suggestion of a sneer.

I knew then, struggle though I might against it. I despaired in my heart, while I pretended to be calm for Naomi's sake, because that was when I knew my friend was gone. I knew because all evening long (even when I probed about their quarrel and he mumbled that she wanted him to change, "and I can't change who I am") Ben never asked, not once, if Wendy had called me. He didn't have to—he knew she couldn't have.

❧

This is how I heard the news.

I ignored Stefan's reassurances about Ben as a parent and went over to help with breakfast and getting Naomi to school. While she dressed, I chatted merrily with Ben, pouring charm and energy over him: thick doughy frowning pancake that he was, I was syrupy sweet. Especially because the night before I had checked with Stoppard: in New York State an indicted murderer, even one accused of killing a spouse, retains custody of any children, unless there is evidence of abuse. Indeed, if Ben were convicted and sent to prison, should he ever achieve parole, under the law he would be entitled to Naomi even then.

"You're really jumping the gun," Stoppard said to me. "He's

probably told you the truth. She walked out of that house into town, got herself a room at the motel—"

"I checked that," I told him. I had phoned the motel that was within walking distance of their house. No woman had taken a room on Sunday or the next day. I cut him off when Stoppard proposed other benign scenarios—I was furious at all the soothing talk. I knew better: I knew better the first time I met Ben Fliess and I should have clung to what I knew.

I told Stoppard about her will, that Wendy had named me as Naomi's guardian.

"That's in the event of both of them dying," he objected.

"But it would apply if he goes to prison," I argued with more hope than sense.

"I don't think so," he said. To make sure—Stoppard always makes sure—he called Jake Prosser, our divorce and child-custody maven, on his other line. No, not if there were willing relatives, Prosser said. They would take precedence, especially if the murderer preferred them. Ben had three first cousins. I asked if cousins qualified. Yes.

So I was sweet and sugary and helpful to Ben. I offered to pick up Naomi from school and start dinner if he needed to work late and I was relieved when he agreed.

Ben explained Wendy's absence to Naomi by saying that she had to visit a sick relative in Florida for a while, he didn't know how long.

Naomi picked at this scabby explanation, peeking under to see the real wound. She didn't ask her father; she worried me with her questions on our way to school.

"I thought Uncle was Mommy's only relative."

I told her this must be a distant cousin her mother hadn't mentioned to either of us.

"But why can't I call her?"

"We don't have a phone number where she is."

"Why doesn't she call us? She called when she went to Washington. She called when I stayed with you."

Naomi had stayed with me for the week Ben and Wendy vacationed in the Caribbean. Wendy had phoned every evening at exactly six-thirty.

Naomi's face lengthened while she waited for me to answer. I remembered Wendy's anxious hello each night, easing only when I told her that Nommy was fine and handed the receiver to her eager daughter, stepping into the hallway, but staying right outside the door to eavesdrop enviously on their mother-daughter love affair.

"I don't know, honey." I caressed her hair with my hand and kissed her good-bye at the school doors. "She'll be home soon."

I ached for her and understood in a physical, almost sickening, way that I would never be able to replace Wendy, that Naomi had been robbed of her mother's blind love, something precious and irreplaceable. And it hammered home the obvious fact that all these stupid men couldn't see—although it was as big and bright as the sun—that Wendy would never leave Naomi in this way, never, never, never. Wendy's heart would break even to think of her little girl's face, that clear brow wrinkled, her deep blue eyes clouded with confusion, saying, "I wish I could talk to Mommy."

Ben knew. At least he understood. He said to me Monday night, "Maybe I should tell her I don't know where her mother is. I can't keep this up. Maybe I should talk to Stefan about what I should say to her."

"Don't bother. Stefan doesn't know, either. Wait as long as you can, then tell her as much of the truth as you can stand," I said, ambiguously I suppose.

He stared at me stupidly, a cow blinking in the sun, and then surprised me with tears, developing slowly in his small eyes: "I think telling her might kill me."

Naomi loved Ben. Before we left for school Naomi rushed from the table to him, burying her face in his belly, squeezing him with her arms, eyes shut in desperate rapture. "Daddy, Daddy, Daddy," she kept saying the word over and over even when he pushed at her and complained that it was enough. A magic chant, I thought crazily, that's what she's doing, wishing for goodness, wishing for beauty: "Daddy, Daddy, Daddy."

In my office I called Wendy's many acquaintances, even old college friends, people who lived in other cities. No one had heard from her. There was nothing. She seemed to be at the other end of a hallway in my head, walking away, waving, leaving me alone with a terrible responsibility, moving farther away with every hour. But I could see her still and thought she might yet, somehow, come back.

At five o'clock I went to the school to pick up Naomi. From two blocks away I noticed the police car. I ran to the entrance. There was a plain sedan with city plates parked alongside a patrol car. I pushed through the double wooden doors and there was Naomi, weeping in the arms of Mrs. Wylie, her kindly, matronly teacher. Behind her, rubbing his chin, frowning with confusion, was the school's headmaster, Mr. Lassiter. I had stood in as Naomi's family on Grandparents' Visiting Day and knew her teachers. Naomi clung to Mrs. Wylie, resisting the coaxing of a thin nervous black-haired woman and a sleepy-eyed balding blond man. Two cops stood awkwardly back at the door, uncomfortable footmen.

"What is it?" I shouted, and they all looked at me as if I were scary. "Come here, Naomi," I yelled, and she ran right to me. That felt so good, when Naomi came to me instantly, relieved at the sight of me, yearning into my arms with absolute trust.

Mrs. Wylie blathered what I had already supposed. "These people are from the Child Protection Agency—"

"Are you a relative?" the blond man demanded.

I looked at the cops. They would check. "I can take care of her. I'm her mother's best friend—"

But it was no use. Mr. Lassiter, the headmaster, backed up my account of myself as a close family friend, but they wouldn't allow it.

"Where are you taking her?" I asked, knowing it was hopeless and worried that a struggle would only frighten Naomi more.

"To a family shelter for the night."

Naomi focused her eyes at me, her deep blue eyes, lifting her sweet smooth face, a face that had never known cruelty or want, and begged: "What do they mean, Molly? Where am I going?"

I grabbed her shoulders and squeezed. "Listen, these people are okay. They'll take you to a good place nearby and keep you company—"

"I don't understand. Where's Daddy?"

"Can I ride with her there?" I grabbed hold of the nervous black-haired woman's arm and willed myself to be pathetic, to be as humble and ashamed and needy as my poor mother. "Just so she feels safe."

"Prolong the agony," the blond man mumbled, his eyes half-closed.

"We don't want a scene here," the woman answered him, indicating Mrs. Wylie, who was aghast, staring at the city people as if they were bums who had urinated on her. The blond man also glanced sleepily at Mr. Lassiter, who stood tall but baffled, his back stiff with indignation, ready to give an order, yet confused that he had no authority.

They let me go with her. I took one of my business cards from my purse and gave it to Mr. Lassiter, instructing him to call Brian Stoppard, tell him what had happened and where I was going.

In the city car, I babbled at Naomi, making promises, promises I would have to keep: "You'll be with me tomorrow. Everything will be all right. It's just for one night. And then I'll take care of you."

"What's wrong?" she shouted, almost angry in her fear. "I don't understand what everyone is doing! I just want to know what's going on!"

The blond man turned to her. "Let me explain, Naomi. Your mother had an accident, a bad accident."

"Did she die?" Naomi said with great courage, her head up, demanding.

"Yes," he said.

"Don't!" I complained, but I had no energy, I couldn't fight. I had known all along, but I hadn't either. Wendy was gone. And I had no time to mourn her.

Naomi turned her head and looked at me for confirmation: her bright skin was now pale, her cheeks drawn, her mouth shattered. Is it true? her ocean blue eyes asked me. I took her face in my hands and kissed her forehead, wishing hard in my head for happiness to come and sweep us all away, back to our expensive co-ops, to our happy dinners, to a past that I had thought was also an inevitable future.

The blond man said in a monotone, without sympathy, without emotion: "Your father is helping the police about the accident. Helping them figure out how it happened. So for tonight, while he's busy, you're going to stay someplace safe, a nice place with other kids and grown-ups who will take care of you."

"We know it's very scary for you," the nervous woman said.

Naomi continued for a moment to look into my eyes wonderingly. The closer I got, the deeper were her blue eyes, fathomless as the ocean. I thought my love for her would drop in and disappear, inadequate. Then I saw she understood the facts: the clear water swirled and was muddied by pain. She pressed her head into me. I expected wailing. I looked for more tears. She merely squeezed tight and kept still, playing possum, I guess, hoping to feel nothing, hoping terror would pass her by.

On arrival, they wanted to separate us, to take her in without me. I glanced at the institutional building through the car's window. It had the look of a police station and in fact they had converted an old precinct house into rooms with cots, brown blankets, and used toys. I stalled, holding on to to her, ignoring their coaxing.

The blond man whispered in my ear: "We have to question her about it. She may have seen something."

"I love you," I said to her over and over. She didn't move or cry. Her arms squeezed my waist with all her strength, her bones without joints, stiff as metal.

"You don't want a scene," he whispered. "It'll scare her." He waited again. "I'll have to ask the cop to drag you out," he threatened.

I let go. Opened my arms and left her vulnerable.

She held on. They pulled her off and then she wailed, crying in terror and frustration. I looked away, couldn't watch her go—I didn't want that picture to haunt my memory.

The cops offered to drive me home, but I waited, searching the windows for a sign of her.

"You don't want to stay here, ma'am," one of the cops said, a reference to the neighborhood.

They gave up and left me. Eventually Stoppard arrived with a police detective, a friend of his, a lieutenant who, although not working on the case, had found out the details. I don't think I'm really in his debt, but I might as well not name him, since he broke rules by leaking information and might get into trouble. The lieutenant went inside to check on Naomi. Stoppard explained that there was no way to get her out until the morning and that I could have her only if Ben and his cousins agreed. Ben was under arrest. The lieutenant returned and claimed that Naomi was okay. The police psychologist had questioned her, given her some food, and she was watching television with the other kids. I was powerless: I had to surrender Naomi to the state and hope she could survive that night—

the worst of her life—without my protection.

I asked the lieutenant to tell me about the case. We drove to a place off Union Square. It was a dark working-class saloon, not gentrified. I sat at a decrepit old-fashioned wooden booth while they ordered food at the bar. I had a drink that had no taste and no effect. Once he had his steak, the lieutenant settled himself and talked. Stoppard kept his eyes on me; his look was evaluating, almost cruel. The lieutenant was a small man, with long thin black hair that he combed straight back, exposing a bulbous forehead. He had a row of small pimples above his eyebrows and spoke with a raspy smoker's voice. "They arrested Fliess this morning when he arrived at work. Joey said everybody there assumed he was being busted by Giuliani for insider trading." The lieutenant smiled, saw nothing on my face but despair, and returned to cutting up his steak.

"What happened? What did he do to her?"

He glanced at Stoppard, who nodded reassuringly. "It's not official, you understand? They want to keep it tight for a couple of days—"

"I just want to know—for me," I explained. "That's all. Tell me, okay?"

The lieutenant put down his knife and fork. He rubbed his pimples, leaned forward over the table, and met my eyes. Not kindly, but with a steady gaze, giving me his full attention and time. "They found her body in a dumpster in the parking lot of a shopping mall in Westchester. She had been bludgeoned. With something heavy, not made of wood, probably metal. There was no sex indicated, no other bruises. They believe he killed her sometime Sunday night, probably outside the house, got the body into a garbage bag, and put her in the trunk of the car. They figure he must have put the girl, who was probably asleep, into the backseat of the car and started driving around. He stopped at a hardware store about fifteen miles away and bought a shovel and a pick."

Stoppard grunted. "They did quick work to find that out."

"He paid for them with a credit card!" the lieutenant said, almost gleefully.

Stoppard shook his head. "He's not a smart man."

"He killed her in a fit—he didn't know what he was doing." The lieutenant caught my eye and lowered his head, embarrassed. "Anyway, he probably stopped somewhere else and got rid of the weapon. He obviously planned to bury her. The mall is under construction, it's deserted, and behind the dumpster there's a field. He may have started to dig there. Probably the little girl woke up, it was late, and he decided to just toss the body into the dumpster. Then he drove into the city."

That was the life choice I had helped make for Wendy: stuffed into a Hefty bag and tossed onto a garbage heap. With my help, that was how life ended for my friend—her brain smashed by her husband, her child a sleeping witness to the disposal.

"When they arrested Fliess today," the lieutenant said, "he was strip-searched. He was wearing a woman's panties and bra. Then they discovered he had another apartment in the city. There they found a whole closet full of women's clothes, and also they found videotapes of him dressed up. He says he made them himself, set up the camera on a tripod."

Both men looked at me—what did I know? The lieutenant had already told me the detective on the case would stop by my apartment later tonight to ask questions. By then I would have to answer them.

"Will he be out on bail?" I asked.

"Sure, he'll make bail." the lieutenant said.

"And then he has custody," I said, not asking. Stoppard nodded. "How long will it take for him to come to trial?"

"That depends—"

"What would be average?" I asked.

"A year," Stoppard said. "Year and a half."

"And until then, for that year and a half, he goes on just as before?"

They nodded. I discussed with Stoppard how we might get Naomi out of the shelter first thing in the morning. He promised he would rouse Jake Prosser to work on that right away and that he would call a friend in the DA's office and ask for any favor that might help. I kept my attention on the details. If I did otherwise, if I allowed myself to feel, I would have collapsed. Stoppard and I talked them out while we walked back to my building, where there had also been excitement—the police had come to search the Fliess apartment.

At home, there was Stefan to deal with—solicitous, offering tranquilizers, chattering away with reassurances about city psychologists and family shelters.

Then the detectives assigned to the case arrived.

"Did he ever hit her in front of you?"

No.

"Did she ever tell you he had hit her?"

No.

"Did you know he liked to dress up in women's clothes?"

No.

Stefan's sweet shocked chipmunk's face was astonished. He covered his mouth as if he had to restrain himself physically from contradicting me. You know that I had no choice—I had to avoid becoming an enemy of my neighbor Ben Fliess. I couldn't be a witness against him. I couldn't be part of the community's outrage or participate in his ostracism.

I had lost my mother, who gave me life. I had lost the first Naomi, my benefactor, who had given me an identity. I had lost Wendy, who gave me happiness. I had one left to preserve.

That night, once I was rid of them—the experts, the maintenance men of civilization—I sat in the bedroom we had converted into a gym and waited for daybreak, fighting off images of poor little Naomi hugging nothing but loneliness in that place. When I pushed that picture away, I saw the rebuke of Wendy's face, moonish and loving, her pale eyes wide with amazement that Ben was about to strike her. I felt with her the terrible fear she must have known. Even if she understood what was happening for only a second, for a wink of consciousness, the agony of that moment would have stretched out forever, covering everything with its pain. She died not living to see her daughter grow up happy and beautiful, but abandoned to a killer's mercy. She died not surrounded by people who loved her, but with blows of hate. She died not satisfied by a life of completed deeds, but unfinished, right in the middle of her story.

I had lost all the women who created me: mother, sister, friend. All gone but for little Naomi, who was now my daughter. I swore I wouldn't lose her.

So I waited in the dark, keeping company with the restless souls of the dead, and prepared myself to play host to the murderer next door.

GRIEF

At seven-thirty the following morning Brian Stoppard and Jake Prosser picked me up in a limousine and we set out to rescue Naomi from the shelter.

The long black car and its driver's somber uniform were reminders that soon there would be a funeral for Wendy. I couldn't get myself to ask Stoppard what was usual in homicides, where they were keeping her body and when she could be buried. Instead I listened to him speak confidently of our mission. He spoke in a soothing voice, patting down his wavy white hair while he assured me that Ben was going to be declared an unfit parent and punished for the murder. Stoppard's skin was evenly tanned, browned out of season not by ultraviolet machines, but due to his frequent vacations to warm climates. He wore a charcoal gray pin-striped suit—he was both elegant and comfortable in his finery. As if for contrast, Jake Prosser sat by the other window like a caged animal, head hunched low, peering outside with suspicion and resentment in his eyes. I took the jumpseat facing them and rode backward against the flow of the world.

My happiest thought—the only one—was that Naomi's terrible night had ended. While Stoppard tried to reassure me I silently rehearsed the lines Stefan had passed on to me from an eminent child psychiatrist, advice as to how I should talk to Naomi. Presumably this was the proper emotional medicine for a traumatized child: embrace her, show your pleasure at being reunited, and say, "I'm here now. I know things have been very scary. It's okay for you to be upset. If you feel like crying, go ahead. If you don't, that's okay too. You don't have to act in any special way." Don't celebrate the reunion and pretend her troubles are over. Be comforting, not gentle. Give her strength, don't ask her to manufacture it.

I didn't know whether I could manage to talk so artificially to Naomi, but I could certainly comfort her, and welcome her tears.

During the ride Stoppard related the morning report from our friend the lieutenant. Last night Ben had remained silent until his attorney arrived. Ben had retained Thomas Varney, a young man partnered with a pair of other lawyers similar in inexperience. Varney had, for the most part, handled small-time mafiosi. That did not mark him as sleazy; gangsters are the likely paying customers of any young criminal attorney. With Varney by his side, Ben told his version of Sunday night to the detectives. He said that he and Wendy had quarreled during the day and evening because she demanded he give up his Battery Park City apartment; Ben refused. Adamant, Wendy finally stormed out, walking away on the country road toward town, and that was the last he saw of her. When questioned in Varney's presence, Ben admitted his secret sexual life, he admitted Wendy had just learned of it, he admitted she threatened to divorce him if he didn't give it up, he admitted losing all his savings in the market, he admitted he had been warned that his work had been unsatisfactory and that he expected to be fired soon. He admitted everything, except he did *not* admit to killing Wendy. Ben explained away his purchase of the pick and shovel with this story: after Wendy left, he had decided to yield to her ultimatum about the apartment, hoping to win her back; but he was determined to keep the women's clothes and he bought the tools in order to bury them behind the house; he could then exhume the garments after she cooled down.

The detectives didn't believe a word of his account. When they told him so, Ben got angry and, much to their surprise, berated them as anti-Semites.

The police hoped to cinch their case with the results of the forensic examination; specifically, proof that Wendy's corpse had been in the trunk of the car. That might seem an easy task, but the lab would need to discover more than merely a hair, or even a microscopic amount of blood—either could have been insinuated into the trunk during normal use. A bone fragment from her shattered skull, significant traces of blood, or bloodied hairs from the scalp—any one would do. They also hoped to match the pick and shovel with the sandy field behind the mall where her body was found. They needed something that could link her body to the car or to Ben himself: any scrap that would place Ben at the dumping site. Just one would convict him.

I knew Ben had killed her. I can't pretend that I had doubt. Remember his willfulness about buying 10B? Or consider his long concealment of the Battery Park City apartment, the expense and elaborate setup, done to satisfy his sexual desires while maintaining his marriage. He was a greedy man and I believed he had struck Wendy out of that selfishness, out of rage that he wasn't going to get his way. Above all, I was scared that one day Naomi would frustrate him. Eventually, as children always do, she would refuse to gratify his pride or his will or perhaps a new twist in his perverted desires and then he might kill her too. That fear obliterated everything else in my head and heart.

We were a pompous processional on arrival at the shelter. Stoppard stepped out of our chariot first, stood tall, and moved toward the drab institutional doors with majesty and the self-assurance of power. Jake Prosser followed, swaying from side to side as he walked, like a menacing wrestler. He brandished our writ of habeas corpus in the air, ready to cut Naomi free of the state's shackles. Last, I emerged, wary, but reassured by the arrogance of my helpers. During the night, Prosser had been at work, a judge was aroused, Stoppard called in a political favor. They worked for a good cause: the rescue of a little girl, a nice middle-class girl to whom such things were not supposed to happen.

I trailed behind Prosser and Stoppard as they entered the shelter. They were immediately confronted in the hall by a grossly fat woman, balancing her big behind on a stool. She listened to them present their credentials and documents, obviously unimpressed, her lips in a sneer, her eyebrows raised. She appeared to be formulating a sarcastic answer to their demands. My eyes searched for Naomi down the hall. I peeked into a dreary room with cots. I listened for her sob. Everything was empty. The kids must be elsewhere, eating breakfast perhaps. It was the look on Stoppard's face that told me something had gone wrong.

"What is it?" I asked.

"She's not here," Prosser said, head hunched low, a champion wrestler frowning that he was deprived of his title defense. "The cousin took her. I blew it. I never thought they'd be that fast."

"We didn't have precedence over the cousin anyway," Stoppard consoled.

"I blew it," Prosser insisted. "Once we got ahold of her, we could have stalled the whole process."

Hours passed before Prosser sorted it out. He insisted I stay with him and make no attempt to find Naomi until we were properly rearmed. We returned to the office. Stoppard went off to attend to other duties. I acted as Prosser's assistant, making calls, reading cases for citation. This was costing the firm a small fortune in billable hours; both men had expended their professional esteem on my behalf. I worried about how far Prosser's and Stoppard's patience would stretch.

We learned that one of Ben's first cousins, Harriet Fliess, had arrived with Tom Varney at dawn. Entitled by virtue of a document Ben had signed which named her as the temporary legal guardian, Harriet took Naomi to her home in Queens. According to the overweight social worker at the shelter, Naomi went happily. "She skipped out of here," she said. I felt a stab of jealousy and disbelief. I had to admit, though, that, after all, Harriet *was* a relative and Naomi did know her—slightly—from the occasional seder and Fliess reunion. I had also met Harriet at Wendy's wedding and maybe a few other times, but I couldn't remember what she looked like. It was even possible that she would make an excellent protector, although the fact that she was Ben's choice spoke against her.

Stefan interrupted our efforts with a well-meaning call. I told him what we knew so far. He must have asked me a dozen times how I was feeling. I had said okay for the first eleven responses. On the twelfth, I said, "Take a guess."

"I understand. I'll give you room," he said, again intending to be kind, not condescending. "There's one thing I do want to insist on, though, Molly."

"What's that?"

"There's going to be a memorial for Wendy tomorrow. Amelia Waxman called to say that since the body wasn't going to be released for a while—"

"Why not?"

Stefan hesitated, surprised to have to tell me: "The autopsy."

Of course. They would take my friend apart and search deep to discover the obvious.

Stefan continued, "Amelia is arranging to have a service tomorrow. It's tentatively set at the West Side Chapel at one-thirty. She wanted to know if you wished to speak."

"God, no." To summarize Wendy, to reminisce in public about her freshly killed life—it seemed obscene to me.

"I want us to go, Molly."

"I'll talk to you about it tonight."

"No—" He began an argument, but I said good-bye and hung up.

By five in the afternoon, Prosser had established that we could do nothing to abrogate Harriet's temporary custody. He said our target would have to be Ben's custody once he was out on bail and the best petitioner would be Harriet. After all, Ben had already stipulated that Harriet was a viable and responsible caretaker. Jake proposed we drive to Harriet's house right away and convince her to allow us to go before family court in order to ask that she be granted permanent custody—with a private understanding that, in effect, Harriet would leave Naomi's upbringing to me after she won. "Basically, you'll have custody," he said.

"I'll let Harriet live in my apartment if I have to," I told Prosser. I wanted to believe we could succeed. Unfortunately, Jake's plan seemed unwieldy to me. And his hope that the cross-dressing could be used to prejudice the court against Ben as a parent also sounded wishful—unless we could show that she had been exposed to it. Nevertheless, I wanted to make the trip to Harriet's so that I could at least see Naomi and hug her and promise that someday, somehow, she would be safe with me.

We were about to leave when Stoppard banged the door open and shouted: "Turn on the TV! Channel four!" We didn't react fast enough for him. He obeyed his own order, opening a wall cabinet and turning on the television set that slid out.

Naomi exploded silently onto the screen. It was a still photograph of her, wavering big, then small, in time with the first thrust of the electric pulse. Once the image had stabilized I saw that she was perched above the anchorwoman's left shoulder, appealingly vulnerable in her navy blue school jumper, her mouth and eyes wearing the cautious formal look of an enforced pose. I didn't know the photograph. Obviously, it had been taken at Riverside School, maybe cropped from the class picture. It wasn't very good; Wendy must have kept it hidden away.

The anchorwoman, although her mouth was set in a grim and serious expression, was otherwise pretty and perky as a girl scout. She spoke in an ominous tone: "A cousin of six-year-old Naomi, Harriet Fliess, says the accused, Benjamin Fliess, should be released on bail so that he can be with his daughter."

The video image jumped. A long face, with great hollows for eyes, hovered in front of a white door. It was Harriet. I recognized her immediately: in my memory I had confused her with a different cousin. Although it must have been years since I had seen her, she looked the same, wasted by poor nerves, her gaunt face surrounded by long black hairs that curled off her scalp, wilted by her brain's hot worries. "I love her. I'm like a second mother to her, poor girl," Harriet said. "But there's no replacement for her daddy. She needs her daddy." The camera pulled out a bit to include the microphone and head of the reporter. The wider angle revealed that Harriet was on the stoop of her home, one of those houses you see when you come in to land at La Guardia, all alike, row after row, made by a giant cookie cutter.

The political favor we had asked was that they stall Ben's arraignment for the maximum allowable, forty-eight hours. Prosser hoped to steal a march on the custody issue while Ben's legal efforts were concentrated on getting bail set and made. Obviously that had failed: Ben hadn't forgotten that he wanted control over Naomi; Harriet was his substitute.

"She's a kook," Wendy used to say about Harriet. Seeing her on television had jogged my memory—now I could place her. I had met her while selecting hors d'oeuvres from Wendy's wedding buffet. She told me all about herself, that she was a brilliant dancer with Martha Graham when young, that her career was cut short by an injury. Later, Wendy said that Harriet liked to exaggerate both her talent and her association with Graham.

I also remembered that from time to time Ben had gossiped about her and his other cousins. I hadn't paid much attention, although I did recall Ben asking Stefan, "Why are my people so crazy?"

Because you have lousy genes, I thought.

"Everyone's relatives are crazy," Stefan told him. "That's why there are so many psychiatrists."

Wendy laughed, threw her head back, her mouth open, showing her small teeth. She touched Stefan on the arm, pleased by his humor, happy to be with us. Watching her, even Ben was relaxed. Thoughts and images and memories like this—meaningless, random, and painful—bothered me all through the tedious day.

We were about to leave for Harriet's when Amelia Waxman phoned. Amelia was Wendy's closest friend from work. She wanted to mourn with me. She cried as soon as she began to tell me about the memorial service. I cut her off, explaining what I was trying to do.

"Oh, that's wonderful of you. When you see Naomi, please give her a hug from me. I was just talking about it with Julie and I think it would be good if Naomi could come to the service tomorrow. What's happened has to be acknowledged and I think being with her mother's friends—"

"I have to go." I begged off, avoiding a commitment to attend myself, much less to take Naomi along.

I was glad to drive to Queens, relieved to take action. Prosser and I arrived at Harriet's house around six. It was already dark. Although I felt comfortable without my overcoat, the air had the clarity of winter, and the sky its gloomy, lowering hue. The house was quiet. There were no lights in the front windows or on the second floor.

Prosser had to ring the bell twice before Harriet answered. Jake told her our names and asked if we could come in to discuss Naomi's welfare. Harriet ignored Jake, obviously recognized me, and asked urgently: "How are you?"

"Upset," I told her.

"Ben thinks you should be kept away from her." Harriet nodded back into the shadows of her house. Behind her I could make out a staircase and a small living room to its left. All the lights were off. Faintly, I heard a television talking upstairs.

"Why?" I asked.

She didn't answer my question. She winced. "You know my condition," she said instead, and put a hand to her hip. She arched inward on contact, as though her touch had been a stabbing wound.

"May we come in?" Jake said. He leaned against the open door and relieved her of its weight.

"I promised his lawyer," she said, tolerating Prosser's occupation of the doorjamb; but she did not budge from her position, which obstructed any further entry.

"Promised *what?*" Jake's sharp tone caused her to look away.

"Don't bully her," I said to him. He was startled by my comment. "To keep me away from Naomi?" I helped Harriet.

She nodded. "Miriam doesn't want to have anything to do with it. She's a coward—"

"I don't know who Miriam is," I said.

"My sister Miriam?" She was surprised. "You don't remember her? Well, she's a colorless person," Harriet conceded. "She doesn't make an impression."

"I'm sorry. Your sister. I remember. So it's all on your shoulders?" I prompted.

Harriet nodded, her eyes uncertain.

"If Mr. Fliess is convicted, he expects you to take care of Naomi?" Prosser asked.

"What do I say to her!" Harriet whispered furiously at me, bony arms spread wide in a plea. "Her mother is dead. What can I say to her about it!" She stepped outside, brushing past Jake, and pointed past my face down the street at one of the other homes. "Mr. Kahn, he lives in the red house over there—"

"On the corner?" I asked.

"Right. He saw his mother shot in front of him at Buchenwald. Lost his whole family. I thought maybe I'd take Naomi to talk with him." She lowered her skeleton's arm slowly, a dramatic gesture. Her skin was sickly white, striped on the forearms by long thin black hairs. She put her narrow face and hollowed eyes right up to me. I could smell the dank cellar odor of her body: she had been stored in a sunless life. "Do you think that's a good idea?"

"No," I said.

"Why?" She was surprised. Her fingers lit on my arm briefly. She pulled back the instant we touched, as if my skin were electrified. "He knows what it must feel like."

"Wendy wasn't killed by Nazis because she was Jewish."

"We don't know." She jumped on my answer with the ready pounce of a hunter who had long expected this prey. "Ben says that area is loaded with anti-Semites. Rednecks who resent the rich city people. Maybe that's why she was killed. Teach everybody a lesson."

The head part of me, my brain, laughed at this portrait of the year-round residents of the Berkshires. It was a vision of America from a simpler time, when the enemy was ugly and ignorant and scary only because they were violent. Harriet imagined the Berkshires were populated with men like my father; what she didn't know was that men like my father would never dream of hurting a rich summer person, even if he were a Hasid. Lobsterman Gray would have sooner killed me than a potential customer. But I was too agitated by her speech to be amused; I had no time for ironies. Obviously, even from the distance of prison, Harriet was listening to Ben's music. He seemed to enchant the will of everyone who encountered him. He had mesmerized Wendy, he had fooled Stefan, he had blunted me. He would have at least a year to work on this pathetic, nervous woman.

"You've spoken with Mr. Fliess?" Jake asked. Every time he opened his mouth Harriet hunched her shoulders and looked pained. I wished I had come without him, or had had him wait in the car.

"No." She seemed offended. "I haven't."

"It's your theory?" Prosser asked.

"It's not a theory—" Harriet began.

"Go to the car and wait," I ordered him.

Prosser faced me with his low square body in an aggressive pose, prepared to level me. "Huh?" he let out with a whoosh.

"I don't need you," I said.

"Thanks a lot!" he said indignantly, and pushed past me, waddling back to the limousine.

Harriet watched him, interested. After Prosser got in and slammed the door behind him, she said, "Men don't like hearing you don't need them."

"He's a big boy."

She laughed forcefully, her skinny body quaking, a hand raised to stop her mouth. She was excited and embarrassed—she must have taken my remark as a sexual innuendo. "I'm sorry," she mumbled.

"I can help with Naomi," I told her, keeping my distance, my voice gentle. "I have money, I'm healthy, I live in her neighborhood, I know her friends, her school—"

"He doesn't trust you. He says you hate him."

We both heard rattling from above. Naomi was trying to raise the window. She had seen me. I thought I heard her muffled voice say, "Molly!"

"Oh God," Harriet groaned.

"She knows I'm here," I pressed her.

"Molly! Molly! Molly!" Now I could definitely hear Naomi's calls, muffled by a door, the flight of stairs, and the hall. "It's not fair!" Harriet complained. I was about to argue when I realized she meant Ben's injunction. "Come in," she said, and stepped aside.

I ran up the stairs—they sounded flimsy, hollow—before she could think better of her offer. One of the three doors leading off the second-floor hallway was shut. I tried it. Harriet had locked Naomi in. "She's locked in," I said. Hearing me, Naomi's young voice escalated: "Molly! I'm in here!" Her keen desperation pierced the wood and made me crazy.

Harriet moved without raising her feet off the floor, in no hurry. She used an old-fashioned latchkey to open the door. "I locked it so she couldn't run downstairs," Harriet explained. I could have hit her. I could have hit anyone at that moment. Everyone, everything, seemed demented and insane. Did that mean I was the lunatic?

In Harriet's bedroom, the television was on, broadcasting the news. If they showed a report about Wendy's murder, she would see it, see the sickening clip I had seen earlier, film of the state police carrying her mother in a body bag from where Ben had parked the car, while Naomi slept in the back, her head on the cold leather. She might have already.

Naomi hugged me so hard I had to drag her a foot or so to reach the power button and turn the set off. Naomi pressed against me all the while, saying, "Molly's here! Molly's here!" over and over in a frantic, almost unintelligible chant.

"She's so glad to see you," Harriet commented without envy, with relief. She lay down on the bed. She took a heating pad from the night table, bandaging her hip with it. She adjusted the dial. "Why did you turn the TV off?" She smiled apologetically. "I'm going to be on, you know."

"Can we go home?" Naomi asked me. She pulled on my arm to get me down to her level. "I want to go home with Molly," she told Harriet.

Her hair was dirty, greasy, dull. That bothered me, reminded me of the lice, seemed symbolic of the shelter, of Harriet's dreary house. "No. Not until your father is . . ." I had to remind myself of the euphemism: ". . . finished helping the police."

"I'm hungry," Naomi whined.

"I gave you soup," Harriet complained.

"I don't like soup!" Naomi was exasperated. At least she wasn't scared of Harriet.

"I don't know what children eat," Harriet said. She groaned. She put a hand under the waist of her skirt and seemed to massage her stomach. "I don't feel well," she whispered. "I don't know if I'm up to making a meal."

"I can make us dinner," I said, forcing cheerfulness, like the mother in a fifties sitcom.

Harriet brightened. "Great," she said. But then she worried, "I don't think there's anything to cook."

I sent Jake for groceries. He howled at this, pretending his objection was to the propriety of my staying with Harriet and Naomi; really, I think he felt shopping was undignified. I answered his legal complaints one by one while writing out a list of what he should buy, pointing out that if we hoped to use Harriet I had to gain her confidence. Meanwhile, I would be taking care of Naomi, giving her a decent meal, shampooing her hair, and warding off Buchenwald anecdotes.

Once Harriet observed that Naomi was calm as long as I was present, and I agreed to become the housekeeper and cook, she allowed me to stay. Naomi and I went downstairs to make dinner. Harriet lay content in bed, soothed by her heating pad, waiting to see herself on the news. Prosser returned with supplies. I dispatched him to Manhattan to begin the paperwork on Harriet's suit for custody. I promised I would plead our case to Harriet after Naomi was asleep.

Naomi helped me boil the spaghetti and heat a jar of sauce—no gourmet treat, but her favorite dish nevertheless. We brought a tray to Harriet. She was thrilled. "A hot meal," she commented, as if it were a luxury. We returned downstairs to our own portions. While we were cooking Naomi had seemed happy; but at the sight of the meal, she sat listlessly. Her shoulders slumped, her blue eyes were rounded by sadness. She held her fork limply, poking the strands of pasta.

"When do I go back to school?" she asked.

"Maybe tomorrow. If you want to. Do you want to go back?"

She let the handle of the fork go; it clattered on Harriet's yellow Formica kitchen table. "To Riverside?"

"Of course it would be Riverside."

"Oh," came out of her, a sound of relief, and her face flushed.

"Were you worried you might have to go to school somewhere else?"

She nodded, her chin quivering. "I thought I wouldn't get to see my friends, you know"—she was crying, her eyes were dripping, her face collapsed—"and I didn't want to have to make a whole new—"

I opened my arms. She slid off her chair and ran into them. Her head shook against my breast. She cried for a long time; obviously this wasn't about losing her friends. I stroked her greasy head of hair and let myself go too. My first few tears felt enormous, stuck in their ducts, encrusted by the fear and horror and rush of the past few days. Letting go of them hurt, but the tears washed everything clean. When we were done, I was lighter, freer—once again able to imagine being happy.

I hadn't wept for Wendy until then, until her daughter cried in my arms. Holding her sorrow, there was solace. That was yet another reason, a selfish one, for taking care of Naomi. Being with her made me feel better.

❧

She woke up screaming. I found her out of bed, rooted in the center of the guest room, dressed in the overlong pink nightie borrowed from Harriet, shoulders bowed, face down into her hands, alone and in terror.

I put my arms around her and felt all bone; the sounds vibrated through her fatless ribs, as if she were hollow inside. For a while the screeches shattered her words. Eventually the sounds were glued together into, "I want my daddy! I want my daddy!" Said over and over, in twos, with a moan, an inward gasp of breath between each set.

"He'll be back," I interjected, and we were soon a duet of hysteria and comfort.

The evening had been a series of failures. Once Naomi was—I thought—asleep for the night, I had called Prosser. Since I sent him back to Manhattan he had done nothing. He was pouting at what he called my high-handedness and wanted thanks for all he had done so far, as well as an apology for my insulting behavior at Harriet's house. I used my grief as an excuse. Although in fact I don't think any of my actions were flighty or irrational, I pretended to Prosser that since Wendy's body was discovered I had been in a daze, that my dismissal of him was due to nerves, to the loss I had suffered. His feathers didn't smooth easily—they were still puffy with indignation even after my apologies. He ended the call in a disdainful tone; he said he would get on it in the morning, once he had taken care of a more urgent case.

Screw you, I thought. If Prosser needed to be stroked for every good deed, then he was too much trouble.

Stoppard confirmed my assumption when he phoned minutes later. He said I was foolish to ignore Prosser's advice against spending the night at Harriet's house. "You're handling Jake clumsily. After all, he's doing you a favor," Stoppard lectured. I realized Stoppard might also be speaking for himself as well as the firm's view of my own billable time. En route to the shelter I had wondered how long their professional goodwill would stretch, vaguely imagining at least a distance of a few weeks. No matter. Although I hoped against hope, already I could see the road ahead, the only real choice open to me.

Still I made the effort. I went into Harriet's bedroom. She was flushed, talking on the phone (to her sister Miriam), drinking cold tea, her eyes, no matter where her head went, tied by invisible strings to the television. She had seen herself on the five o'clock news, the six o'clock, the eight o'clock, and now she awaited the ten o'clock.

I asked if she could interrupt her call with her sister and she complied. Then I botched the pitch of Jake's strategy, stumbling when I got to the main point—that Harriet would have to petition in family court to get custody away from Ben. While she listened, she twisted a few hairs of her dark eyebrows around and around, distracted by each changing image on the set (she had muted the volume), and seemed in a trance when I was done.

"Oh . . ." she said, and paused, staring ahead. Her face seemed to lengthen. "Ben's my family—I can't do that to him. I can't take him to court."

I fancied I heard reluctance, that she was attracted by something in my proposal. The promise of more notoriety? The promise of money? I was unsure and worried that I might offend if I became more explicit.

"Of course, after you get custody, you might want to move into Manhattan and live with my husband and me. We have a large apartment, three bedrooms, and we'll hire a cook. There's plenty of money. Perhaps we could even persuade Ben to sell us his apartment, he'll need the money for his defense, and you and Naomi could live there."

"No." She had made up her mind. She pushed the heating pad off her and sat up in bed. "I can't."

"It's really not a betrayal of Ben. In the end, it's the best thing for him and his daughter."

She shook her head no. "I can't live in Manhattan." She continued to shake her head. "I'm too high-strung for that pace. That's why, even if I had recovered from my injury, I couldn't have rejoined Graham and danced. I can't take that kind of pressure. Makes me unhappy."

Her phone rang. "This is she," Harriet said after a hello. She covered the receiver to tell me in a thrilled whisper, "It's the *New York Times!*" The reporter had only to ask one question and Harriet was off on a marathon. Harriet spoke of her close relationship to Wendy, her history as a virtual second mother to Naomi. Harriet's pale face flushed while the lies grew more fantastic; prudently, she turned her body sideways away from me and my gaze. I pictured grabbing her mass of hair and shaking her rag doll body until I held nothing but the empty fabric of her robe. Witch, I called her silently, and wished I could pour water on her and watch her melt away.

You feel rage, Stefan likes to say to me, when you can't control what's happening.

Who doesn't?

I had spoken to Stefan earlier, called him first, before all the others, while Naomi and I were cooking.

"Did Amelia get you?" he asked.

I quickly launched into a review of recent events, not only to report to him, but to forestall more talk of the memorial service.

"What can I do to help?" he asked, sweetly, although I sensed he didn't approve of my actions. "Should I come out there?"

I asked him if I could offer up our lives, or at least our bedrooms, to Harriet and Naomi.

"You really think that's necessary? There's no other way to get custody?"

"It's a desperate situation, Stefan."

"I know." He hummed, a habit, one of many stalling mannerisms. "Hmmmm." The phone line buzzed from the sound, almost a mantra. "Do what you have to for Naomi. We'll work it out."

That is goodness. *Do what you have to for Naomi.* Stefan doesn't negotiate, doesn't evade with possibilities. From time to time Wendy used to be overcome with admiration for Stefan; she'd jump to her feet, rush to him, pinch his cheeks, and squeal: "You're *so* good! I can't believe how good you are!"

Listening to Harriet give her interview to the *Times,* I regretted that I had told Stefan to stay at home. He might have impressed Harriet, might even know how to deal with her. She could easily be one of his patients, although she couldn't afford his fee.

"I'm surprised," Harriet said when she hung up. The edges of her hair were wet with perspiration, her cheeks were red, and she panted between words, winded—she could have just finished a two-mile run. "You expect the *Times* to have culturally sophisticated people," she commented about her interview. "He hadn't heard of Graham."

"Harriet," I tried again, "in the long run Ben is never going to be able to devote the kind of attention to Naomi that she needs, given what's happened. He has his defense—"

"Look, I don't like all this going behind people's backs—it's ugly. It's not the kind of person I am. I'm not a crafty person. I'm not shrewd. Never have been. I know you're a lawyer, you're a suspicious person. You have to be. But I trust people. I love people. Ordinary people especially. And I find that if you trust them, they'll do right by you. What I'll do is ask Ben straight out. He'll need money, you're right about that; he won't have a lot of time to devote to Naomi, you're right about that too. If we ask him straight out—instead of behind his back—he may say yes."

So my plea had ended in a disastrous ruling. And obviously she would also be a disaster as a surrogate parent. Prosser had said I would stand no chance against her in family court if Ben were found guilty and named her as guardian. Momentarily, I experienced what my favorite law professor at Yale called "Common Sense Silliness," namely, the phenomenon when you assume the court will rectify an obviously unjust condition. I thought, surely a judge would give me Naomi over this nut. Common Sense Silliness. The court neither could, nor would. She was blood, I was water. The same with Ben. More so. Ben was thicker blood.

Again, Harriet's phone rang and this time it was an Associated Press reporter, someone with whom she had apparently already become great friends from a previous conversation. "I have to help him with some fact checking," she whispered to me. "Would you get me another cup of tea? I'm hoarse from all the talking."

I kept her throat lubricated and she continued to give interviews until past midnight. "I'm exhausted," she told me then. "Are you staying up?"

"I'll read for a while."

"If there are more calls, tell them I can't give any interviews until after lunch tomorrow. Don't you think that's right? I can't be at their beck and call." She had become accustomed to my role as her servant in only one evening.

I agreed to everything. Anything to shut her up. "And when you go to sleep, maybe you should take the phone off the hook." That was her last instruction.

I couldn't fall asleep because I was busy thinking murderous thoughts about her. I had just calmed down when Naomi's screams started my heart racing again and brought me, breathless, to her side.

"I want Daddy!" Naomi said in the grip of her night terror. "I want to see my daddy."

"He'll be back soon," I reassured her. I stroked her back and rethought the evening. I was alone, really. Harriet was obviously unreliable and I could already hear, in a few weeks, both Prosser and Stoppard saying, quite reasonably: "There's nothing more we can try. The law is against us. Once he's found guilty we can make another effort." And they would be right. Only it meant that Naomi, longing for her father, needing a parent and a hero, would live with Ben while the world turned against them. And Naomi—as would any loving child—must take his side and see it through his eyes. Through the eyes of her mother's killer.

I got Naomi into bed and patted her back.

"Could you sing to me?" She turned her head and kept one eye on me.

I couldn't think of anything except "Rock-A-Bye Baby." Naomi didn't protest my selection, although she was too old for it. When I sang the verse, "And down will come baby, cradle and all," I was surprised by the lyrics. That was meant to be soothing? "And down will come baby, cradle and all"?

Disturbed, I hummed something else, I didn't know what at first. I recognized it in midhum to be a number from the *Three Penny Opera*, one of Stefan's favorites, and then I remembered the lyrics: "There was a time, but now it's all gone by, when we were poor, but happy, she and I."

I suppose Stefan would think there was significance in my choice—I *know* he would. I didn't seek the words, though. I wanted the melody, music both sad and strong.

Naomi's eyes closed. Her breathing sounded congested. I raised the blankets to her chin and kissed her cheek. "Good night," I whispered.

"Good night, Wonder Woman," she answered.

I shivered, thrilled. Wendy had told Naomi her secret nickname for me. That was a surprise. The indirect contact was almost scary— it was as if my friend were still alive, telling me what to do.

❧

O f course Ben Fliess surprised me. When he phoned Harriet at six-thirty in the morning and found out I was there, instead of blowing up he asked her to put me on.

I had fallen asleep only two hours before, into a sweaty, headachy tunnel of dreams, all filmed in silver colors, dreams of the dead: my sad broken-faced mother; animated Wendy; and my benefactor, Naomi, baked brown on her beach in Maine, smiling from under her huge horn-rimmed sunglasses, singing lullabies.

Harriet's pasty face, looming over me, seemed to be part of the quiet nightmares: "It's Ben. He wants to talk to you."

But he's dead too, I thought, and stumbled after Harriet into her musty bedroom, remembering, as I took the hot receiver (did Harriet sleep with it in her hand?) where I was.

"Hello, Molly." Ben sounded relaxed and warm. "I'm glad you're there. How's Naomi?"

"Scared. She wants to see you."

"I'm gonna be out in a few hours. I'm arranging bail. Could you take her to school this morning? I think it'd be a good idea for her to be there, with her friends."

"Sure, I'll be happy to." My voice came out as gravel, in small rough pieces.

"Also, I don't feel like picking her up. I can't face all the outraged Riverside mothers."

"No problem. I'll bring her home."

"Thanks. Is she up?"

"I'll get her."

Naomi showed little emotion at hearing her father's voice, none of her middle-of-the-night longing. "You're coming home tonight?" was her first remark. Then softly, "Yes. It was okay. I'm okay, Daddy." Finally, almost a whisper: "I love you too." She shoved the receiver at me. "He wants to talk to you."

Ben's voice in my ear was again calm and heartfelt, confident that we were good, good friends. "Thanks, Molly, I really appreciate it."

"No problem," I said. The temptation to add a soothing or encouraging remark, if only as a civility, was hard to resist: a willful pull against a natural tide. I had to remind myself that Ben was more than a man I disliked—he was evil. "Take—" I started to sign off, about to say, "Take care," and then caught myself.

He picked it up, however, saying, "Thanks. You too. See you at five."

I burned for hours. I told myself: No, no *you* are fooling him, don't mind his little tricks. You are playing for something more important.

I used the firm's car service and took Naomi home to get her into fresh clothes for Riverside. If her school uniform (white blouse, navy blue jumper) could ever be considered to look fresh. Why do Episcopalians want girls to appear so formless and asexual? The boys in their blue corduroys and white turtlenecks had a devilish solidity, handsome and mischievous even with their shirttails flapped out, the wales on their knees worn flat, and their collars wilted and soiled. The poor girls looked so drab—blue teardrops with pale faces. The weather was cold enough to chill Naomi's exposed legs; I should have insisted on tights when she declined them. She looked all the more pathetic in the institutional outfit, an orphaned child awaiting the state's whimsy.

While changing at home, obviously relieved to be back among her things, Naomi had been chatty. She told me that day's schedule—Thursday—was her favorite because they had recess and gym *and* dance. "And then we have computer! We've been writing stories in computer," she said happily. "I'm going to finish mine today." But on her way to school she was silent. Was she worried about how she would be received? Or perhaps what she should say to her friends? I wondered myself. Should I advise her? And if I should, what?

Her friend, the redheaded Sarah, saw us coming and ran to meet her. "Naomi, guess what! Guess what!"

"What?"

"Guess what!"

"What, already! What is it?"

"My grandma is gonna take me skiing in Europe!"

"So what," Naomi said with thorough disdain, no envy. "I don't like to ski."

Sarah's mother, a big friendly, ungainly woman—rather like a large cheerful dog—had reached us. "I'm so glad to see you"— she nodded at Naomi—"with her." Her voice was deep and loud, a resonant bark.

"I'm glad to be with Naomi," I said casually, and tried to remember the woman's name. We had been introduced a few times. Wendy often gossiped about her, and I should know it. I started up the stairs to the school doors, following the girls.

Naomi stopped me with her hand. "Where are you going?"

"Yeah," Sarah shouted. "We go in ourselves."

"Very grown-up," Sarah's mother said. "Bye." She bent down, her russet hair meshing briefly with Sarah's scalding red. "Bye," Naomi said to me, holding up her hand in a brief wave and going in. She seemed to have deliberately chosen to be so casual and unemotional. Wendy always knew why her daughter did what she did, or at least was convinced she understood. I should know—better than most— what a girl in Naomi's circumstance might feel, but I was confused.

As soon as the doors shut, Sarah's mother turned to me and woofed in a rush: "Do you have her? I mean, we heard she was in some kind of child—"

"A shelter. One night."

"Hello!" Another woman I had met before, this one also broad shouldered and tall, but topped with a petite head of blond curls, came up holding the hand of Naomi's best best friend (Sarah was only a best friend, Naomi often explained), a haughty solemn-faced girl named Holly. "Is Naomi here today?" the mother asked me hopefully. I couldn't remember her name, either, although I thought it might be Jane.

I nodded.

"Yay!" Holly's mother said. She lifted Holly's hand in the air, declaring her a champion in the ring.

"Can she come to my house after school?" Holly asked me, not celebrating. "I have to talk to her privately," she said gravely.

The two mothers exchanged looks. Holly's mom beamed proudly at her daughter's precocious dignity; Sarah's mom rolled her eyes mockingly. "I'm sorry," I told her, "I promised Naomi's father I'd take her home right after school." I was going to add that we could arrange something for tomorrow, but because of the expression on the two mothers' faces, I didn't. Both women stared at me, parodies of shock: mouths open, eyes glazed, regarding me with horror.

"What are you talking about?" little Holly said, breaking the silence. "Her daddy's in jail."

Holly's remark got Sarah's mother unstuck from gazing at me with amazement. She glared at Holly and then at Holly's mother. "You told her!" Sarah's mom barked. "But we agreed at the meeting—"

"She saw it on television!" Holly's mom defended herself.

"And I can read newspapers, you know," Holly pointed out, her tone reeking with contempt.

"Go on in, Holly," her mother told her.

I decided that fleeing was my best option and so I bluffed a cheerful good-bye, turned, and made for home. I had phoned Stefan from Queens and asked him to wait for me. I was functioning on less than four hours sleep out of the past forty-eight and the nights before that had not been ideally restful either. I was not equipped to handle precarious conversations.

"Wait!" Holly's mother pursued me. She was by my side in seconds. "He's free? She's going back to him?"

"He'll be getting out on bail today." I kept on, but she maintained my pace, walking sideways. Sarah's mother was on my other side, lumbering, but equally persistent.

"You're seeing him? You're—"

"I don't have a choice. If I want to be with—" This was saying too much, relying on the discretion of people I hardly knew. There were no television crews and reporters at the school entrance (that surprised me), but there probably would be in the course of events. If I confided something to these mothers which they repeated and it reached print for Ben to see . . . I simply could not take the risk of explaining my actions. I moved on.

"Wait!" Holly's mother grabbed hold of my elbow and I had to stop. We were only twenty steps beyond the school doors. All around there were mothers paused, watching. For a New York street, the quiet was extraordinary. I fancied they could all hear. "Wendy was a friend of mine," this virtual stranger said, "and you were much closer to her—how could you even look at him! Don't tell me you think he didn't do it?"

"I have to think of Naomi." I rushed off, in a trot. Her question and her tone infuriated me. She was hardly a real friend of Wendy's.

And I've never believed expressions of delicate sensibilities, or the ease with which people feel absolute moral revulsion. How does all the evil in the world happen if merely looking at a murderer is unthinkable? What was more important, my fine feelings or Naomi's life?

That's what I told Stefan, solemn chipmunk Stefan, seated in our bentwood kitchen chair, arms folded, bearded chin lowered gravely to his chest. I recounted my conversation with Holly's mother and ranted about her question. That was my way of explaining to Stefan, preparing him.

He knew it. "So what you're saying is that you have to deal with Ben. That there's no option."

"If I fight him, he'll have Naomi until he's found guilty and then he'll give her to Harriet. If I play along, I can persuade him to give me custody. Once he's in prison, I won't have to deal with him."

"Don't kid yourself. That won't be the end of it." Stefan didn't smile, his tone was hard. "You'll have to bring her for visits, you'll have to help him petition for parole. It'll never end. Are you prepared for that? I don't think you are. I think you're upset, I think you're exhausted; I don't think you know what you're letting yourself in for. I don't believe that you can hide your real feelings from him. Sooner or later, what he's done to Wendy will hit you and you'll feel compelled to call him to account. Otherwise you will hate yourself. And then the sham will have been for nothing." Stefan waited. He let this depressing and reasonable vision of the future hover in my vision. He got up from the chair and embraced me. His thin arms squeezed me tight and he arched back to look me in the face, eyebrows up, bright teeth flashing in the curved frame of his black beard. "Fight him in the courts. You don't know you'll lose. And his cousin, Harriet, she may not be terrific, but she doesn't sound abusive—"

"She's a nut! She'll make the whole thing into a circus, with Naomi as the main attraction." His arms around me were bothersome. I pushed out of them. He was going to be a problem. He was part of the past, of the lost dream—an easy life.

"I want you to get some rest," Stefan said. He wagged a finger at me. "That is my professional opinion: you need sleep." He glanced at his watch. "The memorial is at one-thirty. So there's plenty of time for a nap."

I agreed to rest, if only to avoid a discussion of whether I would go. Stefan preceded me into the bedroom, pulled down the blackout shades, and drew the curtains. We were in our cave, our safe place. He asked if I wanted him to lie with me until I fell asleep. "Yes," I said, regretting that I had pulled away in the kitchen. While my burning eyes cooled on the pillow, I clutched him, my transitional object, my comforting animal, and cried, not for Wendy, or Naomi, or even myself, but for Stefan and me.

❧

Where are you going?" he demanded.

I had tried to sneak out of the apartment, tiptoeing past his study after taking my shower and dressing quietly. I thought I'd take a drive (the armor of a car and the anonymity of the road has always soothed me), but Stefan caught me in the foyer.

"I can't go."

"Molly." Stefan pressed his hands together and brought them to his lips, solemn, almost a priest. "You have to say good-bye to Wendy. You have to acknowledge the passing of people you love."

"It's too soon," I pleaded.

"I'll be with you."

I let him coax me down into a taxi. I was ashamed of my fear, too cowardly to say no and yet too frightened to be glad that I was being dragged to it.

At the sight of the chapel's dark awning, and the mob of familiar faces, most of them alert to my arrival, eager to talk to me, I felt sick.

I was only two steps out of the cab when a man hugged me and said, "What a terrible loss." I hadn't seen him in years. He was a sociologist Wendy had met in school; she had gone out with him a few times. He wasn't ready for commitment, he told Wendy after their first date. Wendy had reported he was lousy in bed. . . . Why am I poking fun at their mourning? It's just that I hate false senti-mentality. He, and the other awkward mumbling sentinels who stood behind him, all claimed to be shattered, to have loved and cherished her. I couldn't help thinking that if Wendy had lived another five years she would have discarded them, as she had discarded the set of people she knew in her twenties. *I* was the one who had suffered a loss that could never be regained.

Amelia Waxman was next: she came running with her arms up, arched in the air, grappling hooks out to capture me. Her mass of blond hair, permed to within a follicle of its life, covered my face. Her perfume made me sneeze on her shoulder. She didn't notice, she was talking the whole time.

"I can't bear this, Molly. I can't believe it's happening. Poor Wendy. I can't think about it. I don't know how to go on! I can't believe it's happening!"

I pushed out of her arms, not shoving, but hard enough for Amelia's eyes to widen and stare at me, fearful and apologetic.

"It's happened!" I insisted at her.

"Molly . . . ," Stefan commented, a gentle rebuke.

Amelia nodded at me and her face wrinkled up. "I know," she gasped the words just ahead of a convulsion of sobs. She bowed her fuzzy head of blond hair and her arms hung loosely. They patted her, the other women from Wendy's office, and the sociologist, and probably everyone else wanted to; they formed a chain of mourning and the more Amelia cried and they stroked her, the less I felt like joining them.

"Let's go in," I said to Stefan. He put his arm around my shoulder as we entered. I shook him off.

So many people die in a city that there is more than one farewell being said in each funeral home. A soft-spoken young man directed us to the Sonnenfeld memorial, one of three currently showing. The room was painted brown, all the way up to its double-height tin ceiling, and very large, so big I wondered if it would be filled. To my shock, it was jammed, some even had to stand at the back. Who were they? Had the old SoHo crowd, now unrecognizably middle-aged, come? Were they from her college life, another lapsed past of hers? Was it morbid New Yorkers, murder victim groupies?

I had been too horrified to go to my mother's funeral and I had to leave Naomi Perlman's memorial after taking only one step inside, but Amelia's histrionics and the mass of strangers made this event seem silly and weird. I twisted on the bench and watched the door, studying the strange faces. Most appeared excited, talking in fast whispers, thrilled to be present. An occasional silent pale mourner went by, usually female, always (in the instances I knew them) a do-gooder like Wendy, thoughtful and empathetic. But their hollow-cheeked looks might be narcissistic fear as much as they were grief. I wasn't moved by them—only the sight of little Naomi suffering an inconsolable loss could touch me. Wendy's body was absent. Without the presence of living grief and physical death, I felt nothing. None of the pangs I was scared of.

Stefan cried during the service and although I didn't, I could tell he was pleased with me, satisfied by my attendance. He held my hand while Amelia talked, and while the sociologist talked, and while a rabbi who knew nothing about Wendy, hadn't even met her, talked. No one said anything real. They listed her good deeds and they sounded banal. They told of how valuable Wendy's friendship was and made themselves sound self-important: "Without dear Wendy I never could have won the Nobel prize." And most of all they enjoyed themselves. They were sad, but they were in public.

Outside, in order for Stefan to help me find a cab to get downtown, we had to elbow past two television camera crews. From the other side of Columbus Avenue, just as I got into a taxi, I noticed that Amelia and the sociologist had stopped in order to be interviewed.

❧

I picked up Naomi from the Riverside School at three, ignoring the curious looks and hellos, and took her home.

Ben greeted us in a bathrobe, still wet from a shower. "Honey," he said to Naomi, embracing her. His long, floppy terry cloth arms completely cloaked her head. After a moment he whispered, "Thank you, Molly. I'll never forget your kindness."

Naomi's face was pressed into his groin area. I couldn't help thinking about the fact that he was naked under the robe, that Naomi shouldn't have only fabric between her face and his private parts. But the contact seemed obscene because of the killing, I reasoned. He was still her father, not a strange man. I followed Naomi into the apartment and thus broke the promise I had made to Stefan before going to pick up Naomi, namely, that I would leave them alone together for the evening.

Ben moved back as I entered. Naomi clung to him. "Honey," he murmured to his daughter, rubbing her hair with his long delicate fingers.

"My daddy," she said, her voice sweet from her open trust and absolute love. It was shattering to witness.

"Did you try to call?" Ben asked. "I've kept the phone off the hook. Been in the shower for hours. Trying to get the smell out. I can't."

"Smell?"

"Of being in . . . there. Not the smell, the feeling. I don't know how I can take this." His small red lips trembled and his nude eyes glistened. He wasn't wearing his glasses. Without them he looked bewildered.

I indicated Naomi with my eyes, signaling him to calm down in front of her. "Why don't you get dressed," I offered. "I'll make us some tea."

I turned on all the lights, opened the windows a crack, and brewed tea while Ben dressed and Naomi completed her two sheets of homework. She accomplished that in minutes. Of course her speed reminded me of Wendy's pride in her, the countless times she . . . well, I've told you before.

Ben talked avidly to Naomi, asking detailed questions about her school day. He knew the routine, that on Thursday she had computer class and that she was due to finish her story. At his urging she took a printout from her backpack and read it to us. I'm not sure what I expected, but I was surprised there was no reference to her mother or to recent events.

Ben and Naomi chatted happily after that, sipping tea, munching on Pepperidge Farm Milano cookies, Naomi filling him in about the shelter and Harriet and her day at school without emotion, as if it were all part of some camp experience or a special day trip. After a while I tuned out Naomi's talk, sadder by the minute, missing Wendy more and more, angry at Naomi for being pleasant to Ben, dismayed she wasn't demanding explanations. Preoccupied by my disapproval, I missed it when she did get around to questioning him.

"Who asked you that!" Ben was furious, without warning it seemed to me.

"Nobody," she mumbled, head down, immediately intimidated.

"Mrs. Wylie?" That was her teacher.

"No! It was one of the kids."

"Oh." Ben relaxed. He sat back, put a hand on his bald forehead, and closed his eyes, sighing.

"Who said what?" I asked. "I didn't hear."

"Nothing!" Naomi reached over and, with her little fist, banged the top of my hand. Because of her sharp bony knuckles, the blow hurt. "I don't wanna talk about it!"

"Ow!" I reacted to the punch, rubbing my hand.

"Sorry, sorry." Naomi was frantic. She stroked my hand and repeated, "Sorry, sorry" with the nervous haste of a savage appeasing an impatient god.

"Some kid at school asked her who she would live with after I was put in jail for good." Ben was disgusted. "Was it a boy?" he demanded of Naomi. "Doesn't sound like a girl's question."

"Leave her alone about it," I told him.

"Forgive me, Molly," he said sharply, sarcastically. "But *I'm* her father. I decide what I ask her."

"It's more important to answer the question first!" I cursed myself after it slipped out, thinking, don't get into unimportant fights, you're only here to protect against the worst.

"What question?" He was genuinely confused.

"I don't want to talk about this anymore!" Naomi screamed, covering her ears.

"What's going to happen if . . ." I trailed off meaningfully.

He understood. "I see what you mean," he mumbled, sluggish. He was slow-tongued unless angry. When he raged at Naomi about who had asked her the question, his speech was rapid and articulate.

"I don't want to talk about it!" Naomi shouted again, her hands still covering her ears. Her face was red.

"Okay!" I shouted to penetrate her muffled hearing. "We're not talking about it!"

We sat there in silence: Naomi breathed hard, her mouth tight; Ben stared at the table, his shoulders sagged by defeat, his jaw slack; I felt dizzy from my odd sleep schedule. I had been up most of the night and then slept most of the day. I yawned and shivered in a spasm. My head was stuffed, I seemed to have caught cold. Naomi's nose was red, she had been sniffling—no doubt she was the cause.

Three days without exercise and vitamins, three days of being responsible for a child, and I was ill.

I thought, I can't do this. I have to go home, forget all of them, just take care of me, the only person I can rely on, the only person I know how to please.

I roused myself and cleared the table. Ben spoke softly to Naomi. She climbed into his lap, rested her head on his shoulder, and they sat that way for a while, quiet.

The doorbell rang and violated the calm, the sad silence. We all looked at each other. I was amazed that the doorman had allowed someone up.

Ben, for all his size and bluster, was beat. He resembled a huddled refugee, waiting for charity to give him a home, reduced to sheltering his daughter with his arms. "I'll get it," I said.

"Thank you." Ben was heartfelt, pathetic.

It was Stefan. Not, as I had feared, a reporter, a cop, a lawyer. It was Stefan, stern and unhappy. "Molly," he said, and opened his hands, asking.

"What?"

"You said you would give them time together, remember?" He kept his head back, out of view of the apartment's interior, obviously hoping to avoid the sight of Ben. I guess he couldn't bear to look at him. What was wrong with me that I could?

"They don't have anything to eat. I've got to make them something. Why don't you come in?" If I could involve Stefan, I thought, it might be easier for me, even for them. He knew how to handle emotional trauma, that was his profession.

Stefan remained still: brown face, black beard, smooth brow, eyes a circle, regarding me dispassionately. His annoyance had sunk beneath a lifeless neutrality. "That would be inappropriate," he said softly. "It implies approval."

"What are you talking about?" I kept my voice to a whisper also, but my irritation was clear.

"Both to Naomi and to the world—a world in which I operate, in which I have a professional standing—for me to come in and help implies approval."

"Bullshit," I spoke so quickly, I wasn't sure if it had come out or merely reverberated in my head.

"I don't think so," Stefan said in a whisper. "You're not standing back from this situation. I understand that it's hard to. But if you gave yourself some space—"

"You're a doctor, you'd be helping them—"

"No, I wouldn't. In this context I would be doing harm!" Stefan said sharply, his volume rising.

"Hey!" Ben's voice came from right behind me and I jumped.

"God!" I exclaimed. "You scared me."

"Sorry," Ben said. Stefan reacted to Ben's presence by becoming a statue again, still and lifeless, his eyes calm pools. Ben, though exhausted, had the energy of his anger: "I don't want this discussion going on around Naomi. You guys have a disagreement, fine—keep it away from her. Thanks for helping out, Molly. You can go home now." He took hold of the door, relieving me, and opened it wider. He pressed his body against the back of mine without backing away, and left no space for me to occupy. The action was typical of Ben, of his ability to polarize. If I broke the contact, that would put me in the hallway, and if I did not, I would be his appendage.

"Let me say good-bye to Naomi," I asked permission testily.

"Sure," Ben said. His tone implied that I didn't have to ask.

Naomi clung to my neck, embracing me from the chair, pulling down when I tried to end our hug. I reminded her I was across the hall, that she could ring the bell anytime; I promised to come by after dinner, that we'd do something special on the weekend, see a movie, go shopping, whatever she wanted. She didn't say any words. Quietly, she hummed, "Mmmmm," to each of my assurances, commenting on their taste, a bit louder for some, perfunctory for others. She locked her fingers together and allowed her weight to drag me down. "Let go," I asked her, first nicely, then sterner, until I had to pry her hands off my neck.

Stefan and Ben watched. They observed us, ignoring each other. "Hi, Naomi," Stefan said to her after I was free. His casual manner seemed cold, even cruel to me.

"I'll call you after dinner," I told Ben, and didn't wait for an answer. I walked past Stefan and into my own apartment, defeated.

"Jake Prosser phoned," Stefan said, following me as I paced from the living room to the dining room and on into the kitchen. "So did Stoppard. They both want you to call them back."

I didn't know where to put myself while I waited. I didn't want to think, I certainly didn't want to feel. And I didn't want to talk.

"Also, three reporters. I have their names written down—"

"I'm not calling them!" My vehemence surprised me.

"Molly," Stefan implored, and said no more.

Now in the kitchen, I lit a burner to heat the coffee. I watched the pot. When Stefan didn't add anything, I finally looked at him.

He seemed small. He stood with his hands folded in front of his groin, his arms forming a V. "What?" I asked him.

"I'm not suggesting you *have* to do anything," he almost whispered. "I'm just giving you your phone messages."

"Thank you." I returned to my surveillance of the coffee.

"When you want to talk, I'm here," he said, and left the room, which made his statement seem false. Was he here?

Stefan is good and Ben is bad—why was I equally angry at Stefan? Because Stefan could help. He had no excuse for not helping. Ben did. He had a good excuse—he was the bad guy.

❧

I made so many mistakes during the week of Wendy's death, I'm embarrassed by the recounting. While waiting for eight o'clock to come—the time I figured would be appropriate for me to resume contact with Ben and Naomi—I told Prosser and then Stoppard not to pursue any hostile legal action against Ben.

"Fine," Prosser said coolly, and hung up.

Stoppard wasn't so easily satisfied. I put him off the scent with pleas of emotional exhaustion, fear of reprisals against Naomi, and pretending to have some faith in Harriet's competence. "Well, there's one good thing about your decision," he said. "You'll be on the job tomorrow, right?"

"Right," I said. For a moment I couldn't remember the office, its look and feel. What was I working on—launching a telecommunications satellite into orbit? Laughable.

Stefan tried me again after an hour had passed from our previous conversation, pretending to want tea, hoping I might break the silence, finally asking, "Would you like to talk now?"

"No," I said.

He went away. Stefan would have to choose without any babble. I would force his hand, just as Ben had forced mine.

I worked out. I had trouble matching my usual repetitions. The scale showed my weight to be up by four pounds. I seemed to be able to feel them all—two on my thighs, one on my belly, and one in my brain. Fat cells blocked my linear thinking; everything detoured back to the beginning. I found circuitous ways to believe that Ben was a better choice for Naomi than Harriet—at least Ben loved her, my cellulite head argued, at least he was a real parent, even if he was a killer.

The really nonlinear idea announced itself when I was done with all the machines, my body limp, the muscles unstrung, damp with exhaustion. My head was finally clear of musty daytime sleeping, pounding alive in my overcooked body.

I could kill him.

I peeled my skin from the leather and checked in again: What did you think?

I could kill him.

What for? That stumped my brain. The thought had seemed to answer everything. I was giddy with the notion. It lit a neon sign in my head, flashing bright: *Kill him.* Blink. *You could kill him.*

But then Naomi would have no parents, and no me, to take care of her.

Silence came for an answer. The neon shut off: the brilliant light of a certain final action went out.

I showered, dressed, and watched the clock progress from 7:53 to 8:00 exactly. I had said I would phone first. Instead I crossed the hall without a warning. Hoping to catch him at something?

"Who the fuck do you think you are!" Ben greeted me. His small mouth pursed as he spit the words; his glasses jiggled, rising off his nose and bumping into his brow. "Harriet told me what you're trying to do! How dare you come here!" He reached out, put his hand between my breasts, and shoved me. A two-year-old fighting in the sandbox wouldn't have done it any differently.

I fell on my behind. The bone at the base of my spine landed on the hard tile hallway floor. Two paralyzing bolts of pain sizzled down my legs. The pain was brief, but overwhelming. He slammed the door.

In moments I realized my legs were all right. I rang the doorbell again.

"Go away!" he shouted from the other side. Again he sounded like a child. Is that how he killed Wendy? I wondered. Striking with the stupidity of a toddler, ignorant that his blows have consequences?

What difference does that make?

I rang again. This time there was nothing, no sound, no answer.

I was frantic. I returned to my apartment and called. An instant deafening busy signal seemed to say fuck you, fuck you. Obviously Ben had the phone off the hook. I was shut out. I tried Harriet. Her line also buzzed frantically.

I banged the receiver against the base. Over and over I smashed it against the cradle. A recording lectured me: "There appears to be a receiver off the hook." A section of plastic splintered off, Stefan appeared and watched, the mechanical voice shut up, the phone base trembled and fell.

I pulled on the curly cord, ironing out its wiggles, dangling the base as if hanging Ben, and kicked, dully ringing the bell inside. I said nothing, although I screamed in my head. I pressed my lips together and concentrated on the destruction. Although I could batter the telephone, I couldn't smash it. I had made a mess. "Throw it out," I told Stefan, dropping the corpse on the floor.

His hands were at his mouth, prayerful, although he probably had placed them there to stop himself from speaking.

"Throw it out!" I screamed after a moment of his silence.

"Okay." He moved in a rush, scurrying, disconnected the wire from the base, and dumped the instrument in our kitchen garbage can.

"I'm sorry," I said, and I was crying again, only this was frustration and defeat as much as it was missing Wendy. "It's my fault," I tried to explain to Stefan. "If I hadn't stuck my nose in—" I couldn't complete the confession.

"You didn't do all this. You're not responsible, Ben is. He killed her. Don't ignore the obvious."

Stefan's words were no consolation. I couldn't accept his view, his love. His poem was tinny, its meaning too clear and simple, sentiments on a Hallmark card, their truth anonymous, and therefore hardly better than a lie.

After a while, Stefan gave me something more effective than his point of view—two Valium.

They pulled the rug out. I collapsed into a stupor, watching television, unable to follow a story, finally stunned by the rapidly changing images and meaningless crushed sounds on one of the music video channels. They were pretty silly, all those kids dressed up in fierce costumes, children for whom evil still meant naughtiness and fun.

I bolted awake. Into a gray-blue, silent New York. No cars, no lights in the buildings, the city at five A.M., a tomb. I must have frightened Stefan pretty badly; he had slept in his study on the fold-out couch and left the bed to me. I touched myself, probed every muscle, and felt nothing, my skin was foreign, numbed. I showered and the water rolled off me, unabsorbed, as though I had been Scotchgarded. Underneath the drops my skin stayed dry. I rubbed hard with the towel and made patches of myself blotchy and red. But it didn't hurt. I felt neither pleasure nor pain—I was dead.

I peered across the courtyard. Their laundry room and kitchen were dark.

Then I remembered: I had keys to Ben's apartment.

I was alive after all. A thrill shivered through me, rippling my skin. I found the keys in the file cabinet, tucked away from the last time I had used them, when Wendy was missing.

At six A.M. I opened our door, excited, silently goading myself to be bold, extending a silver-colored key toward the bottom lock, ready to insert it, wishing my hand had a will of its own that could conquer my doubts.

I held my breath, listening, about to put it in, and then—

Ben opened the door.

I hid the key in my fist as I jumped back. Ben appeared, half bent over, ready to pick up his copies of the *Wall Street Journal* and the *New York Times*, delivered askew on his black rubber doormat. He got stuck in midmotion, peering up at me, confused.

"Let me in, Ben. I'm sorry about the thing with Harriet. I promised Naomi I would—"

Ben resumed his stalled action, gathering the newspapers. He listened for a moment and then calmly stepped back inside and shut the door in my face.

I had apologized to him. Without thinking I had pleaded—no, begged.

I had to quit trying.

I retreated to my apartment with my own delivered copy of the *Times*. I was living a fun-house-mirror life—I read in my morning paper the fruits of the interview I had overheard Harriet give two nights earlier, followed by an account of Wendy's memorial, quoting Amelia and the sociologist at length on Wendy's goodness. What Harriet said was presented at face value, on a par with the others— Harriet sounded loony anyway, or at least full of herself. There was also a quote from the Riverside headmaster that the school was concerned about Naomi's well-being and would welcome her return. It was a mystery how the *Times* missed that she had already gone back—presumably that was old reporting.

I heard Stefan stirring, running a shower.

I didn't want to talk to him. Nor did I want to make the effort *not* to talk.

I went outside. Fifth Avenue was lovely, swept by a cold fall breeze, its low downtown buildings gradually rising toward the Empire State's spire to the north. Its slice of sky was a clear blue section, cloudless and vivid. Washington Square Park to the south might even be mistaken for a bucolic setting—the few remaining leaves were bright red and yellow, the Christmas tree was up under the arch, a jogger or two bobbed around its perimeter, a bicycler bisected its center. There didn't seem to be a single crack dealer. The park appeared quiet and civilized. On Twelfth Street a homeless man was spilled on the church steps. From several feet away I looked to see if he was breathing. I knew him. Those steps were located on a side street, protected from the wind by a low wall. This particular man had made it his sleeping alcove since September and had seemed in pretty good shape so far, although the really cold weather was ahead. But that day his feet were in an odd, worrisome position. It took some squinting until I saw his chest rise and fall.

Wendy, who was a do-gooder, had suggested we help out on the weekends at the soup kitchens in the Bowery. I mused about her instinct for good, whether she really meant her acts of charity, or if she thought she was obliged to make the effort. Was it guilt or true giving?

What's the difference? Wendy would argue.

But to me there's all the difference: guilt tires, guilt gets angry, guilt abandons. That's why liberals had failed—because they wanted social justice only in order to feel good about themselves: it was emotional self-improvement for them, not righting wrongs for the poor. When it got hard, got inconvenient, got scary—they gave up.

Why are you so bitter? I demanded of myself. The world has been kind to you, opened its grand doors, and let you in out of the cold.

But it wasn't bitterness. It was self-criticism. I knew I would quit doing good works as soon as the giving was costly. Look at my actions so far—I helped Naomi until I had to accept the penalty, namely, dealing with her father.

But I couldn't deal with Ben. Already I had apologized to him! I had yet to accuse him with a single word about the killing. Instead, I had asked forgiveness for suggesting that he might not be a fit parent.

I was wandering, in my head and on the street. That bothered me. I should be moving to get somewhere. I guess I wasn't wandering. I was waiting. I found a coffee shop on the far side of the avenue of Riverside School and sat in a booth that gave me a view of its entrance. Again, there were no television cameras, no reporters. Mothers and fathers appeared from the two corners, little people by their side, some holding hands, some independent, some pairs silent, others babbling, but they all troubled my heart. In my overwrought state the sight of such pairings—lone parent and lone child—was sad and compelling. Holly and her mother, Janet, arrived. I had checked with Naomi and learned that Holly's mother was Janet and Sarah's mother, the big-boned redhead, was Pam. Janet lingered after her daughter went in. Soon she was surrounded by two or three other mothers and one father, obviously gossiping. After delivering Sarah inside, Pam joined them and there seemed to be a lively discussion going on.

Ben and Naomi turned the corner and walked slowly toward the school entrance. I saw them before the group of parents noticed. I left the coffee shop. My thought was that if they created a scene, or if Ben did, I could intervene and spare Naomi at least some of the resulting humiliation.

At the curb, a car door opened and Stoppard's friend the lieutenant called to me from inside. "Ms. Gray? Could you get in for a sec?" He slid over to the driver's seat to make room. I did and continued to watch Ben and Naomi. The others parents had finally spotted Ben. They scattered instantly, as if they had something to be ashamed of. Ben—I had to hand it to him—carried himself remarkably well. He would have made an impressive martyr. I didn't know if he had marched against segregation or the Vietnam War; he would have been good at it. Ben came at them head up, holding Naomi's hand, his wide pale face washed out by the sun. Smiling, he nodded at the sole parent who stood her ground, not the big-boned Pam, but the flouncy blond, Janet. She ignored him, instead bending over to talk to Naomi. Ben didn't allow Naomi to pause, however; he led her up the first two steps and then kissed her, right on the lips. He usually did that, but everything had new significance for me. The papers were full of mad fathers assaulting their children. And I knew from Stefan that even the subtlest of gestures has meaning. . . .

But I didn't believe in Stefan's Freudian religion, I had to remind myself. A kiss is a kiss.

The lieutenant's car smelled of take-out coffee and stale cigarettes. He was also quiet while we watched Ben. That didn't take long now that Naomi had gone in. Ben strode off briskly, heading downtown. The expressions on the faces of the parents Ben passed were comical. One woman stopped dead in her tracks until he was by her, then she put a hand on her forehead and bent over, apparently trying to prevent a fainting spell. Her son squatted down and cocked his head to look up at her.

"Going to the office," the lieutenant mumbled about Ben. "He won't be happy there." The lieutenant's brow was still lined by a row of little pimples. He rubbed them with the knuckle of his thumb. "Mr. Stoppard says you're not gonna fight the custody thing." I said that was true. He asked why.

"Because I'd lose. Either to him or to his cousin."

"What have you got to lose by trying?"

"I don't want to put her through unnecessary pain."

He nodded sympathetically. "You gonna try and keep an eye on her?"

"Sure." I shrugged. "I have to get to my office. What about you? Aren't you following him?"

He smiled. "No, I just stopped by. I was curious if he was gonna bring her."

I opened the door and then remembered: "Did the forensic report come in?"

"Yeah, I guess so. Not my case, you know. I'm just kibitzing."

I knew from the impassive look on his face. "Wasn't good enough, was it?"

"They got a strong case. But, uh, it would be helpful if you kept your eyes and ears open. Maybe the girl can remember something. Any detail might be good. . . ."

"They're going to convict him, right?" I demanded. "If the case is weak tell me."

"No, no, take it easy." He tried a smile, but his lips were too thin, his mouth too wide, and he appeared sad and wan. "Not weak. Just . . . you never have enough . . . you never know what it takes to get a verdict. Everything seems simple, until you get in front of a jury."

Nothing seemed simple to me. Does it to you?

It did to Stefan. I was in my office for only a minute, staring at the draft of the prospectus for the satellite, when he called, demanding I discuss what was going on, why I had become angry at him because he didn't approve of my helping Ben take care of Naomi.

I said, "You seem to think it's so easy—"

"No, I don't."

"Tell me. I want to know, what am I supposed to do? Forget that she's across the hall, completely in his hands? I don't know if he's sane anymore, if he's desperate enough to kill her and himself, if he's going to molest—"

"Why do you think he might molest her?" Stefan asked with the shrink's equivalent of a cross-examiner's sharp tone, communicated not with speed, but emphasis. He imbued, "Why . . . ?" with profound curiosity and skepticism.

"I don't know . . . I don't . . . but how do I know!" I was shouting. I had left my door ajar. I moved close enough to kick it shut. "Is that so crazy? I have to *know!* I have to absolutely know that she's safe."

I was freed by saying it. That was the point, that was what I needed. The rest—society's feelings, the long-term, moral questions—had no meaning. Being assured Naomi was taken care of, at peace and safe, was the only justice I believed in.

"I understand." He sighed. "I merely think you should be aware that if you appear in their household as a . . . replacement—"

"I'm not a replacement!" I was disgusted.

"Substitute, then. Choice of word is unimportant. The implication to Naomi is that you have validated whatever Ben says or does—"

"That's nonsense—"

"No, it isn't, Molly. It really isn't. Think about it from her point of view. Her mother is dead, and you, her mother's best friend, take care of her *and* Ben. How could he be truly guilty, truly bad, if you are willing to make him dinner, help him take care of her?"

I wished he would shut up. I wished it was simple.

"On the other hand, if you are vigorously fighting his custody and Harriet's, then she knows that you don't approve, that her father is not a victim, and when you finally win, or at least when she gains independence from him, she can face the truth with less conflict, less ambiguity."

"And less guilt?" He had made a mistake. He was wrong about this part. I knew better, and he knew I knew better. "You're wrong, Stefan. If I challenge Ben, I'm forcing her to pick sides and there's no right choice for her if it's between betrayal of her father and betrayal of her mother's memory. *I* must make the choice for her. The guilt must be mine. Let her grow up to blame me—not herself."

It *was* simple. Stefan *had* helped. After this conversation I was thoroughly convinced he was wrong.

※

They disappeared. I had resolved my doubts, was prepared to molify Ben, and they were gone.

Billy, the afternoon and evening doorman, told me as I entered. "He took her to the weekend house," he said in a worried rush instead of a greeting.

In an attempt to catch up I had worked until seven and brought home a load in my briefcase. Even if I had quit early, I would have been too late to stop them. Riverside School dismissed at noon on Fridays to accommodate teachers and parents with country houses. Billy told me that Ben and Naomi had come into the building shortly after twelve and emerged in an hour with two suitcases. He saw them cross to University Place. "I left the door and went to the corner to watch. He took her into the Budget rental and they got a white Ford."

"How do you know they went to their weekend house?" I hoped he was right, that Ben had no more distant or secret objective.

"I asked. He wouldn't tell me. But Naomi did. He didn't like me asking." Billy laughed nervously. "I don't care. I'm not scared of him," he added a little fearfully.

I called the Berkshire house number, informing Stefan of Ben's departure while I listened to it ring unanswered.

"You're kidding," was his response and I thought him stupidly naïve, although Ben's simply driving away hadn't occurred to me either. "Don't the police have him under surveillance?" The lieutenant had been at the school, but he hadn't followed Ben to work. Stefan was right to wonder—why weren't they tailing him?

There was no answer at the house. If that had been Ben's goal, they would be there already. I called the lieutenant and suffered from Common Sense Silliness again, amazed to learn that Ben was allowed to travel, provided he didn't leave the state. Of course he was obliged to show up for trial, but until then there was no basis to issue a warrant. Since he was entitled to Naomi, naturally there was no reason to object that he had taken her with him. I did learn one useful fact: the police had sealed the country house while they continued to gather evidence. Ironically, the only place Ben was forbidden was his own property. The lieutenant said he would have the local sheriff send a car to make sure that Ben hadn't violated it.

I pulled at my memory, yanking empty files. What places had they visited? What friend of his? What relative?

I tried Harriet and got rudely buzzed by her phone.

I couldn't locate the other two cousins. They were probably married and used their husband's names.

I went to the kitchen drawer where I kept the copies of Ben's apartment keys.

"No," Stefan said on sight, understanding my intention.

I continued through the hallway to our front door while Stefan, the nervous chipmunk, hopped along, rubbing an invisible nut between his paws, white teeth flashing from the center of his black beard, flashing a frantic Morse code of objections.

"You've been wrong about everything!" I stopped to tell him. "You were wrong about Ben from the beginning! You were wrong to tell me to keep quiet about his dressing up! You were wrong to tell me not to worry about her confronting him. You're wrong now!" I shouted into his little dark worried face.

Stefan blinked at my vehemence. His eyes were sad and hurt.

"I'm sorry, Stefan, I love you, but you're a doctor, you think everyone can be cured. You think deep down everyone's good."

"Molly." He was soft-spoken and gentle, although the wound in his eyes had not healed. "I know you've done your best to learn nothing about psychoanalytic theory, but you *should* know that, if anything, just the opposite is true of a Freudian."

Condescension is the worst insult to a yellow-haired lobsterman's daughter. "This isn't an exchange of letters in the *New York Review of Books*, Stefan. These are people's lives. You've had a lot of opinions about all this, and you haven't been right once."

He gave up; turned away and marched to his study in a proud huff.

The Fliess apartment was hot, the air unbreathable. I had been unsuccessful in my many attempts to convince Wendy that she should turn off some of her radiators. You're from the frozen north, she'd answer, normal people get cold in the winter. . . .

You miss odd things about a person you love. I missed nagging her and getting teased back.

What am I doing here? I wondered, waking from a vivid memory of Wendy kidding me. Sometimes I lost the real world, hallucinating her: not bad moments, but odd bits of conversation, slices of casual joy. I had wandered into the master bedroom. I decided to check the dresser drawers and closets. Ben hadn't taken more than you would for a weekend, but that didn't provide much solace. You don't need a lot of clothes for a murder/suicide or an escape to Brazil.

I was deflated by going through Wendy's clothes. Although inanimate, they still had possession of her, her perfume, even her shape. I wondered—without a laugh, without a chill—whether Ben tried on her clothes, now that he was free to do what he liked.

Why did he want to dress up as a woman? He was so much a man, so utterly unfemale—thick, rough, jarring. Or was that why? Were we so different that to him we might be aliens? Was he like a child who is scared of ghosts but loves to wear the costume, becoming the object of his terror in order to possess its power?

Now I was writing a letter to the *New York Review*.

I sagged onto their bed. I wanted to stay. I wished to inhabit my friend's empty apartment, to keep her things company. I should find out about her body, when the coroner would release it—I wanted to bury her in that plot in Jersey, next to her parents. *Cherished Mother & Father.* I could visit her there.

The prospect of a real funeral crushed me. I lay down on their bed, exhausted, wanting to sleep.

I felt something bulky under the bedspread.

The lump was no more than a foot long. I pictured part of a human body under the sheets. I scrambled away, sickened. My heart pounded, my flesh wanted to flee. . . .

I willed myself to stay.

I watched the lump, nestled under the taut red bedspread, afraid it would move. I touched it. It was soft, not a body part.

That made me feel stupid. With my good sense recovered, I fearlessly pulled off the cover.

The lump was a crushed mass of lingerie. Black bra, black panties, black stockings.

I didn't understand. What was it doing under a neatly made bed? I checked the sizes: they were the largest I knew of, not Wendy's. What did he do, wait until Naomi was asleep, then . . . ?

Ben was mad. His was a consuming obsession, not merely a sexual diversion, a kinky variant. It had made him kill. Even with the world watching him, his daughter in the next room, he was compelled to give in.

He scared me. A manipulative, selfish, evil Ben I could negotiate with—a monomaniac couldn't be controlled. Threats and bribes would be useless.

Again I was tempted by what had been my lifelong moral infirmity: the weak muscle of my conscience. I can't lift this weight, I thought. Let the fight happen in the courts. Whatever damage is done to

Naomi's psyche I would pay doctors to heal.

Run back to your apartment, to your comfort. I was ready to give up.

But God wouldn't let me be.

A key was inserted into the front door. The top lock turned.

Terrified, I tried to remake the bed before Ben caught me. I had completed my frantic housekeeping when I heard a woman's voice.

"Hello . . . ? Is somebody here?"

I walked out into the hall. From that vantage point I could see into the foyer. A middle-aged woman peered back at me. Behind her, peering not at me, but off in the other direction toward the living room, was a couple in their late twenties, carrying briefcases, obviously having come from work.

"What is it? Who are you?" I asked.

"Who are *you*? This is ten B, isn't it?" she parried. She was well dressed, a little too well for an office job: her hair had been done, teased, and sprayed to survive a tornado, and her leather briefcase was too thin and too elegant to hold anything substantial. She appeared to be a rich suburban wife. I knew at once that she was a real-estate agent.

"This is the Fliess apartment," I told her. "Are you showing it?"

"Yes, I was told the whole weekend was good. Did I get it wrong?"

Like a joke—there's good news and bad news. The good news is Ben and Naomi are coming back; the bad news is it's only to move. My one consolation, my proximity to Naomi, was in jeopardy.

"No, no, not at all. Sorry. I'll get out of your way," I said, talking as I left, to prevent awkward questions.

I returned to my apartment, hoping Stefan would stay out of my way and continue to sulk in his study, his usual retreat when we fought.

But he poked his head out from the living room as soon as I entered: "Everything okay?"

"There's a broker showing the apartment."

"Really?" Stefan was thoughtful. "Needs the money . . . you think?"

"They probably fired him," I thought out loud, remembering the lieutenant had commented Ben wouldn't be happy when he got to his office.

"Listen, we can make the eight o'clock showing of *Hannah and Her Sisters.*" Stefan's voice trembled a little, although he moved toward the hall closet and pulled out my coat, pretending casual self-assurance. "We'll get a pizza after—"

"At *John's?*" I asked, I admit with heavy irony. In case you—like Stefan—have forgotten, we met Ben for the first time at John's Pizzeria.

"Sure!" He smiled with innocent triumph and pleasure.

I spoke calmly, my body composed, resolute, and rational. I hoped that would impress Stefan. I fancied I was rather shrinklike in my manner: "I need to know that Naomi is safe. I'm going to try Harriet again. If her phone is still busy, I think I'd like to drive out there. It would be a great help to me if you came along."

Stefan had my coat by the collar. It sagged as I spoke, a hopeful flag falling sadly. He shut his eyes and sighed. I think he was fighting anger more than hurt, but I'm not sure. "Would you do me a favor first?" Stefan asked. He became alert, flipping my coat over his arm, his dark face smoothing, his bright eyes curious. "I'd like you to call Jim Reynolds and—"

"No," I cut him off. Dr. Reynolds was the psychiatrist Stefan had referred me to when we first met. "I don't have time to be analyzed—"

"I'm suggesting you have a conversation, not analysis."

"I know what you're suggesting."

Our tones had become openly hostile. He stroked his bearded chin, sighed again, and said, "What's that? What do you think I'm suggesting?"

"You're suggesting a surrogate to argue your position."

"I haven't talked to Jim. I have no idea what he'll—"

"Stefan, that's crap. You don't have to talk to him to know he'll take your side."

"My side? What is my side, Molly?"

"That I should give up, let Prosser do what he can, let them find Ben guilty and hope to take care of Naomi later. You think I'm kidding myself believing that I can deal with Ben."

"Actually, if you want to know the truth"—he tossed my coat on a chair, folded his arms, and talked rapidly, letting go, scornfully, of his angry opinion—"I think you're acting out of guilt, terrible guilt that you've harbored for years, hidden from me, from everyone you know, even from your own awareness. You're trying to make up for abandoning your mother to your father. You hold yourself responsible for the way she died."

I had trouble speaking. I was furious, but it was stuck in my throat, choking me. Stefan's kindness all these years seemed to have been nothing but a lie, a phony manner adopted to disguise his low opinion of my psyche. "That's . . . disgusting," I managed to get out.

Stefan rubbed his eyes. "Jesus . . . ," he mumbled. "That's . . . I . . . didn't mean . . . I'm angry." He had it at last, the appropriate shrink babble. "I'm angry. I feel you're pulling away from me so I resort to attacking you with jargon. I apologize. That's why I think you should talk to Jim. Maybe you're right, maybe you should deal with Ben. I can't trust my own judgment. Jim'll be objective. And I think it would also be helpful for you to be clear about your own feelings."

"You don't think I'm normal." I was insulted. Stefan's love had been my company when I went out alone into the world: his belief in me had been constant and reliable, a better self.

"Molly, what does normal mean? Your best friend has been killed. Anyone would have trouble dealing with that. And you have a special relationship to this kind of event—"

I stopped paying attention. He was a phony again. The truth had oozed out with his anger. Stefan thought I was sick, not in control of my actions. I was insulted and I was scared he was right. Not to have his confidence hurt, hurt more than I understood immediately, but the fright of hearing his tentative diagnosis was worse. After all, Stefan was an eminent psychiatrist who knew me well, knew me best, and his judgment was that my behavior was irrational, an apparition out of the nightmare of my past.

My legs trembled. My head was full of air, but there was no breath in my lungs. I was about to faint and that would have only confirmed Stefan's opinion. "Shut up!" I shouted. I had to get out, out of the building, out of all the bad choices.

I half knew when I took the bankbook and my goose-down jacket. I thought of packing an overnight bag. "I'm taking the car," I shouted into the living room, and let the door bang shut as I left. I feared Stefan would come out and argue while I waited for the elevator, so I took the gray fire stairs, my hand skimming on the red banister, my feet a waterfall of noise as I accelerated down, faster with each landing—a kid fleeing school.

⁂

The geography of Queens almost did make me crazy. I went around and around searching for Harriet's house, infuriated by the Xeroxed streets, misreading the curlicued numbers on the front doors, finally asking directions from a forlorn pedestrian. When I got to her place I realized I had driven past it twice.

A car was parked in front, a visitor, no doubt an interviewer. It wasn't Ben's car. Harriet greeted me casually. "Oh, hello, Molly."

"Do you know where Ben is?" I asked matter-of-factly, hoping that would seduce an answer.

She smiled. A wan, sickly, smug, regretful, infuriating grin. "Molly . . . ," she said with gentle rebuke. "You know he's disappointed. He can't trust you now. You don't expect that he wants you to know his movements."

"Harriet, may I come in and discuss this with you? I've feel I've done everything all wrong. Everyone's misunderstood. I was simply thinking about Naomi. I realize now I was crazy even to think of taking her away from Ben. She needs him." It was truly sickening to speak these words. Not a figure of speech: the lies were abrasive, cold, foreign objects whose texture and size were nauseating to expel.

Harriet enjoyed them. "I told you. Isn't that what I said when you tried to get me to sue Ben?"

"Yes." She wanted praise. I regurgitated more disgusting stuff: "You understood everyone's feelings so well."

"I've always been very sensitive to other people's feelings. I'm very intuitive. Ben was amazed that I was able to understand how a parent would feel, since I don't have children. I told him, I'm a woman, after all. We know. Right?" She leaned back against the door and chuckled, her skinny tense body almost relaxed.

"Yes," I agreed, and pretended to shiver. Actually, in my red goose-down jacket, I was hot. Late November and still New York continued to have mild weather. "It's cold."

"Come in. Have some tea." She stepped back and waved me in, her long arm dipping low and sweeping back, a dancer's gesture. She was in an expansive mood. As I entered, she took hold of my arm, pulled me close to whisper in my ear: "I could use your advice. He wants me to write a book." She nodded toward her living room.

A young man was seated in an armchair of sixties vintage. It was typical of her furniture—every piece was shaped into sharp angles, their fabric a dull green. "Hello!" he called out cheerfully. His young face was red cheeked; his blue three-piece suit almost shined. He looked bright and bold in the faded room, an odd contrast, as if he were a brassy cartoon figure superimposed on a black-and-white film.

"This is the son of a neighbor," Harriet said, introducing us. The young man shook my hand vigorously while she explained. "Robby Tatter. He's just starting at the William Morris Agency—"

"I'm interning there actually," he interjected.

"—and he thinks maybe there's a book in all this. And a movie?" she asked him, rising on her tiptoes, her lips pursed, eyebrows up, a picture of dainty greed. She could express emotion with her entire body—maybe she *was* a talented dancer.

"TV, I think. The important thing is to get in first. Look at the Steinberg case—there are at least three books, probably just as many movie deals, and that's only a month old."

He was a fraud. He had been an unpaid intern during the summer thanks to a famous relative, the novelist Fred Tatter; he was a freshman at City College and hoped someday to work in, as he put it, "the entertainment industry." Harriet loved his jargon. He babbled that her story was "sympathetic. A modern woman who had chosen to devote herself to her career suddenly being given the responsibility of mothering. And not just regular mothering, but to handle a little girl involved in a sensational murder case."

"Won't people think she's exploiting Naomi?" I asked.

"Oh, no!" Harriet covered her mouth as if she had spoken my horrible words.

"No way!" Robby was so eager, he rose from the armchair. He gestured to take in the whole house. "She needs the money for the girl's sake, to raise her right."

"I do," Harriet agreed. "All of Ben's money is going to go to his defense—he's going to sell his apartment and they'll live here. I can't afford to raise a child. Especially not in New York—"

I considered telling her that this boy had no more connection to agents, publishing, television, or movies than a clerk in a video store, but I thought better of giving good advice. Why help her? Let her chase show business red herrings.

When she ushered him out and asked my opinion, I told her there was no harm in letting him "set up some meetings," as he put it. "Thank you. I'm not worldly," she said. Her mood clouded over with the rapidity of time-lapse photography. Clear blue sunny sky. Blink. Cloud on horizon. Blink. Stormy weather. Her shoulders slumped, her face lengthened. She wore a look of profound sadness that you might see painted on a clown. "That's what ruined my career."

"I thought you were injured," I commented, and cursed myself instantly. I didn't want to be stuck there, playing the interviewer.

"It's the old story. Not what you know, but who. I used my back as an alibi. I couldn't make myself, you know, suck up to the right people. All dancers deal with pain—I did for years. I stuck with it. I was stoic. Until they broke my heart."

Has anyone ever failed because they were inadequate to their ambition? I resent excuses: they rob the successful of their due credit. "Harriet." I made a last try. I took her hand—her fingers were cold. I baked them between my palms. "I want to help Ben take care of Naomi. Tell me where they are—"

"I can't—"

"*Please!*" She smiled at my desperation. There were tears in my eyes, my arms shook with fatigue and tension—I craved this simple information. And she smiled. My opinion of her changed. She wasn't pathetic. There was malice in her, pleasure at her power over me. I rubbed her fingers briskly. "You're cold," I said.

"I'm always cold," she answered slyly, and grinned. Her long hollowed face was ghastly in triumph. Her teeth were dull, her gums gray. Harriet was death. A vain, dry, childless woman—like me. She scared me even more than Ben—I couldn't become him.

"Tell me where they are," I whispered, a seduction.

"They'll be back Sunday night. You can see her then. Maybe you can help me!" she added brightly, and withdrew her fingers. They had absorbed my heat. My hands felt raw. "You probably have a lawyer at your firm that handles books and movies, don't you? Someone who specializes in all that?"

"We do entertainment law. I could get you help. *If* you tell me where they are." I wanted to fight back. At least make her admit she was a schemer.

Blink. She winced in pain. "Oh, no!" Blink. She was irritated. "I can't do that." Blink. She was cool. "If you don't want to me help me, that's fine. I thought we had become, you know, maybe not friends, but friendly. I thought you might want to help me make sure the story is told right for Naomi's sake."

"And I thought you might want to tell me where they are for Naomi's sake," I said, coming right back at her. No more babying. It had gotten me nowhere. "You know, so far I have been friendly. Very friendly. I don't have to be. That can change."

Her nerves couldn't conduct that much electricity—she jangled in front of my eyes, twitching, rising from her chair, her answer staccato: "I can't . . . Go . . . I won't stand for . . . I should have . . . Ben was right . . . Get out! Get out of my house!"

I left her. I hated her. I stood outside her house and hated Queens. She lived near the Long Island Expressway. I listened to the cars humming low on the ground. After a few moments, I could hear the jets landing at La Guardia, tearing the sky with their slow descent.

I wanted to go north, where it was clean and cold, bright green or stark white everywhere you looked.

I started my car and drove home to Maine.

THE
MURDERER
NEXT
DOOR

B right green or stark white, and yet there was a lot of sludge too. On the highways and especially in the service stations along Interstate 95. But no people. I looked for them, the way a country girl might search for missing trees in the city. Where was the normal background?

I was glad to be alone. Maybe that's why the drive appealed to me. Reaching my destination was something to be deferred. Being alone, even missing Wendy and Stefan (not the critical Stefan of today, but the loving Stefan of yesterday), was pleasant.

I stopped that night in Augusta. Oddly, I had my first good night's sleep, dead to grief and worry, in a motel room so anonymous I could fantasize that when I opened my curtains in the morning I would see not a white frosted parking lot but a hot tropical paradise.

Back on the road again Saturday morning I was happy to be solitary and in motion. Why not go on forever, like that? If I cashed out of the law firm, insisted Stefan pay me half of what our co-op was worth, what could I realize? Half a million dollars . . . one million? Living on treasury bond income, I could drive back and forth across the United States endlessly. Call me the Phantom of Route 80, heroine of a perverse television series, stopping in each town only long enough to heal the emotional wounds of others, while mine sting, the cuts still glistening red, forever.

But the food would kill me. Between that and the lack of exercise I'd bloat up—at last I would become a Boneless Person.

By midday, when I reached Sargentville, the fantasy was jaded. I was sick of sitting in the car, relieved to arrive at the retirement apartments where I paid for my aged father to live. It's a low complex, fashioned to resemble a string of little New England houses: the gray aluminum siding mimics clapboard, there are dummy chimneys, and the signs for the office, laundry, and dining room pretend to be hand-painted in black script.

I parked in front of a substantial snowbank created by the plowing in the visitor's parking, and braced myself for Sargentville's weather. My bones squeezed together at the blast of cold when I opened the freezer door and walked into my hometown's winter. This cold is sharper than can be measured by numbers. The damp and frozen air ignores layers of clothing, slices through skin, dissolves hollows in your bones, and blows ice into your joints so that you creak and get stuck in place, as if you were the unlubricated Tin Man in *The Wizard of Oz*. Finally, to move a dozen paces toward a building seems an impossible trek. You lunge at entrances, half-convinced you'll die on the steps, legs numbed, too weak to propel you inside. Imagine freezing to death so close to home, so near to rescue.

The door to my father's apartment was open. I found him alone in the living room, erect in a red chair, staring at a game show on a portable black-and-white television. He had nothing beside him. No book, no paper, no snack, no empty coffee cup, no cigarettes, no ashtray. His expression was grave. Watching was a matter of life and death apparently.

The sight of me seemed to scared him. "Molly . . . ?" It was a fearful question, asked of a possible ghost.

"Ayah," I said, unconsciously sinking into Down East lingo. "Wanted to have dinner with you. So I drove up."

"What's going on?" He was suspicious. But he pretended not to be, glancing away from a study of my face after he asked his question, to return his attention to the set.

"Nothing," I told him. "Came to see you," which was, after all, the truth.

"I see," he answered in a tone that implied he did not.

"Going to take you to supper."

He nodded. On the tube contestants squealed with delight at winning furniture. Even Father didn't think the prize was worth a celebration. "Looks regular to me. Nothing special," he commented.

"Expecting someone?" I asked because of his open door.

"No," he said.

We drove into Blue Hill. I took him to the town's fancy restaurant. Its prices are moderate by New York standards, but the atmosphere is pretentious because they cater to the summer traffic and to the retired rich in the winter. At the entrance my father appeared uncomfortable. He pulled on his red-and-white-checked wool shirt to tuck it into his dungarees and wiped his boots feverishly on the mat outside. Whatever dirt he scraped off from their soles, he could do nothing about the stained leather on top. I was fascinated by a large white blotch that covered the toes—it could be a snowman's tear.

"Need a jacket to go in there, I think," he worried.

"Doesn't say that," I dared him, and went in.

He took it, entering behind me. He cleared his throat at the sight of the interior. Probably looked grand to him: tables covered with linen, real china plates, comfortable chairs instead of booths, carpeted floor, stone fireplace burning real logs, waitresses dressed in real clothes, not a uniform. I didn't intend to make him uneasy. The other choices were a fast-food joint in Ellsworth or a pizza restaurant run by former wood hippies. He wouldn't eat pizza and McDonald's wouldn't have allowed me to proceed at the right pace. I wanted more than a fast-food conversation.

"Molly," he asked me over the top of the menu, "do you think they'll give me the steak without any glop on it?"

He meant the wine, shallot, and mustard sauce described in calligraphy on the menu. "I'll ask," I said. He was as intimidated and scared as a little boy would be. I watched his old eyes, dulled and worried, shrinking in their sockets, nervously survey the empty room.

At four o'clock we were hours ahead of the normal dinner traffic. They had warned us the kitchen was idle and we would have a half hour wait for our food. I asked for bread right away. Father's stomach was in agony—he was accustomed to having his supper at three. "Don't say nothing," he decided about the sauce. "I'll shove it off myself."

I daydreamed of taking Father to New York. I pictured him: Jimmy Stewart, gawking and excited, astride Fifth Avenue, arms akimbo, in jeopardy from the onslaught of indifferent traffic. No, wrong actor. Gary Cooper, maybe. Not only awed—also skeptical and scared.

His face was thoroughly wrinkled, grooved and floppy, a beagle's fur. His blond-gray eyebrows appeared to be glued on: how could anything grow out of that tough hide? I ordered a bourbon and encouraged him to do the same.

"You mean it?" he mumbled, sticking his tongue into his cheek and poking, pretending indifference.

I ordered for him.

"What's going on?" he asked crossly. "We celebrating?"

"Want to come back with me to New York? Visit for a while?"

He raised his bushy brows. They had grown around the sides of his eyes, half-formed spectacles. "No, ma'am!" he said, and laughed. Briefly. It was a loud squawk, like a complaining gull.

"You'd like it," I told him.

"No I wouldn't. Can't even take Ellsworth. Too many people at the mall in the summer. Can't find what I want. Place like New York'd make me go blind and deaf."

The drink and the waitress's easy manner relaxed him. He ate a roll with butter and drained his glass. He rattled the ice and cracked cubes between his teeth.

"Want another?" I asked.

"Hmmm?" He had heard. He wanted more; pride made him pretend indifference.

I signaled and asked for another round. When she brought them to the table, he sipped his immediately, he was so thirsty for the stuff. "My father wants a steak," I said, watching Father close his eyes at the taste, savoring the pleasure. "But he doesn't want your sauce."

Father woke from his sensory reverie. "Moll . . . ," he complained, mildly.

"Better to have it the way you want it," I told him.

"So just a plain steak?" the waitress said.

"My stomach's shot," Father lied. "Can't take nothing really good—only the nourishment."

She told us again that there would be a wait, they were starting up the stove or something, I couldn't follow her logic. I didn't care. I hadn't seen Father in five years, studying his face preoccupied me. There were spots on him: liver, skin cancer, dismal freckles—I didn't know. Since the retirement that followed breaking his leg, he no longer spent hours out on the boat exposed to the sun. Though his hide was leathery, a paler color and variation had blotched the surface, like the spots on his worn boots.

"Don't shame me in front of her," he said.

"Nothing to be embarrassed about."

"What are you doing here?" He ran his tongue over his teeth, retasting the bourbon. His blue eyes, whitening with age and cataracts, went gray with bliss, turning inward, blind to the world, seeing only interior pleasure. "Can't pay for me no more? That it?"

So the ugliness had begun after only one drink. "Nothing's changed," I said. "You can stay there. Do you still like it?"

"No liquor there, you know. Don't allow it."

"Not good for you."

"Why you giving it to me?" He leaned forward and brought a smell with him, not fishy or boozy as when I was a girl, and yet it was familiar.

It was *him*, the smell of his sweat, of his body. The odor of a man—dangerous and strange. "A little fun won't kill you," I said, repeating his excuse to my mother from years ago. I could hear it shouted in our kitchen still.

He chuckled, then sipped his drink, an ice cube bobbing against his thin lips, swallowed, and laughed. "True enough!" he said, loud. The waitress glanced our way and smiled. Father scratched his head. The once blond hairs were silver, not polished, but dulled and stiff. His frail skull was visible through the full head of hair, as if it were the cleared floor of a mature forest; all the thickening lower branches were gone.

He was old. Not dangerous.

"Don't know when I'll see you again," I said. My childhood accent had completely reasserted itself: I was an instrument playing the song of my people, brash and bullying and telling stoic lies. "Let's put it behind us, Mr. Gray. We've got nothing but death ahead."

For a moment he was shocked—his whitish pupils were blank. "True enough!" he shouted.

"Shhh," I said. Someone had peeked out from the kitchen.

"By God!" He blew out air from between his numbed lips. The familiar stale smell of booze fogged my nose. "That's true enough! What the fuck is there to worry about now!" The old bright blue lasers burned through his cataracts. Reckless, he looked younger.

"Daddy," I protested, "your language." I hadn't called him Daddy since I was a girl.

"Sorry, dearie," he said. "I'm enjoying myself. Having too good a time."

I allowed him another drink when the food came. He reacted to the steak passionately: "By God that's a good cut of meat! Yessir, worth the wait. Thanks, dearie," he told the waitress. She smiled indulgently—probably had one at home just like him.

He ordered the fourth himself. The waitress glanced at me for an instant, checking. I considered stopping him, but I reasoned that he was as drunk as he could get. Between the second and one hundredth drinks he used to stay evenly sloppy, a cork bobbing, always in apparent danger of submersion, yet surviving crazily.

Father complained of his neighbors at the retirement apartments. He was bothered by the communal intrusions into his privacy. "They keep away now," he bragged, but sadly, as though secretly he missed the invasions. After the plates were cleared, he leaned forward and touched me on the back of my hand. "Dearie, time's running out on you giving me a little devil."

"What are you talking about?"

"Can't have them?"

"You want grandchildren?"

"Why not?" He tapped my head with his index finger, mocking me. He used to do it when I was a child and had disobeyed him. "What's in there? Wood? Didn't know that. By God, that's something I never thought of—course I want a grandkid. Old biddies get out their photos and I got nothing to show." He winked. "Maybe I'd better get a fake one."

This made me ache and want to cry. I kept silent, afraid I would choke up. Why was I moved? Because I didn't think of him as caring about me, except as his financial support. I had long ago given up on family feeling, even simple vanities, such as an old man wishing for a photograph of a grandchild to show off. I had thought Father and I were thoroughly burned out; that only the crusty charcoal of our old hate was left, no flame from its spark of love.

"You got the stuff to give—can get a kid anything it wants," he said, gruffly, no self-pity or appeal. "Kind of a waste not to. Know what I believe? Don't think they ought to allow poor people to have any. Don't know why everybody's got the right to make life. Everybody don't have the right to end it. Not even my own. Can't kill myself. Against the law. Don't have the right to shoot deer all year, can't dig clams wherever I want, but I can make a hundred babies who won't get enough food. They ought to make people get a license. Test them for mental stuff and then prove they have enough money." He exhaled forcefully, vibrating his lips, neighing like a horse. His eyes rolled, unmoored. He swallowed hard. He hadn't had any alcohol in a long time: his limitless capacity might be a thing of the past. I had been too indulgent. But I wanted him vulnerable. I wanted him honest. Booze accomplished that because the next morning he could deny he had meant what he said.

I took his arm on our way out of the restaurant. Other people had come in by then and a pleasant man—obviously a retiree—held the door and steadied Father as we went past.

"I'm all right," Father breathed into the man's face.

"I know you are," the stranger answered with a city smile, brilliant with promise and welcome and, of course, insincere.

The surgical cold sliced through us and sobered Father. Or at least froze his legs into a steady position. "Can you make it?" I asked, referring to the ten paces we had to go to reach the car.

"You feel warm and happy before you die in the cold," he said. The words were blasted into clouds as they left his mouth—each one a silent white explosion.

"Is that what you tell yourself about it?" I asked him. The air blew around my eyes and into my skull. They burned. But I held him with the look and accused him without another word.

"You're a cunt," he said. The insult blew up and the remnants hung in the air. Father moved onto the sidewalk, his feet not raised, skidding a bit, like a novice ice skater. Puff went another blast: "Always been a cunt. And you still are." He slid to my blue Volvo—a darker color than the one Naomi had used to drive me away from him—and finished his theme in a cheerful tone: "Guess you always will be a cunt."

When we began the drive back to his apartment, a twenty-minute journey, it was already dark. Father's head nodded back and forth with the motion of the car. I slowed so that we wouldn't arrive quickly—besides, the road was treacherous—and soon his head pitched forward and stayed there, chin propped up by the puffy collar of his down jacket.

I called to him a few times. Not Daddy. I used his real name, Sherman. Saying it softened me toward him again. He didn't respond. He stayed asleep.

At the crossroad I turned off 176 and got onto the back route, the inland road that would take me past the dump, and eventually to the town cemetery. I had never been to my mother's grave. I had refused to go to the funeral because my father was attending. Now I wanted his company.

He stirred when I stopped. The cemetery was small, only fifty graves. Mother was entitled to burial there because her family, along with five others, was listed in the town charter as one of the founders, and their descendants were given that right in perpetuity. Most did not avail themselves of the privilege since it meant separation from their mates. Besides, the town's fee was high. I paid. Father had no money for anywhere else. Thus I barred him from eternity with her.

"Sherman . . . ?" I whispered. His eyes opened slowly. Covered by the filmy blur of sleep and impaired by the cataracts anyway, they didn't recognize the darkness outside. For a moment, the white circles held me in their sight. But the look was blind. He said nothing. He shifted away from me, shut his eyes, and leaned his head against the window. He wanted the comfort of rest.

Nightfall was complete. What headstones I could make out were visible due to the car's headlights. There was no moon. The woods disappeared in the blackness. I got out and stepped among the generations carefully.

I had lived in the city too long. I was afraid of the outside: of the dark, of the animals, of the beds of the dead. I picked my way with fearful glances, checking behind me, and looking over at the car. Father appeared dead also, slumped against the window, mouth open. Only the Volvo was animate, like a dragon, breathing smoke, eyes burning bright.

Some of the soldiers had miniature flags on their headstones. Besides sorting trash, the dump man was also responsible for maintaining the graves. He had done his duty—none of the flags was tipped over. Two were from World War I, but the others, five in all, were from the Civil War. A lot of Maine boys died in the Great Conflict. While in college I had researched the area's history. Mainers were to the nineteenth century what the blacks were to Vietnam:

a supply of bodies. It's a commonplace of history—the poor die to preserve the principles and the property of the rich.

I admit I had wanted my mother buried alongside the few heroes of my people to steal a little of the honor done them. For her, life had been nasty, brutish, and short. Perhaps it had been no better for the young soldiers, but they had been rewarded with headstones that told of their bravery and reproductions of the Union's flag flying proudly all year.

And, you know, I was right. For once I had done well. I calmed when I found her place. The headstone, by rule, was done in the style of the ancient ones, low to the ground, modest in size, letters carved in a fancy script. Not the minimalism of today, but the illusions of the past:

HERE LIES KATHERINE EATON GRAY
1932–1980
DIRECT DESCENDANT OF TOWN FOUNDER JACOB EATON
BELOVED MOTHER & LOVING WIFE
SHE KNEW NO HOME BUT HERE

I couldn't cry. My eyes ached, but it was too cold to weep. Besides, I was glad to see her there, safe from him, with a place all to herself, pompous and sad, honored and irrelevant.

I found a black stone, weighty and smooth. Of course there were no Jews in that cemetery and so the dump man would knock it off tomorrow, but I put the rock on her headstone.

At last I had done my duty to her memory. That left my duty to her death.

I opened his door and Father fell halfway out, stopped by the angle of his torso. "Wake up," I said.

His white, ghostly eyes stared at me. "What . . . ?" He tried to right himself back into his seat, but couldn't. He peered, uncomprehendingly, at the black world behind me.

"You killed her, didn't you?" I had brass in my voice, cocksure and mischievous, as if I didn't care one way or the other. "You left her outside, passed out—"

"What?"

"Like this." I pulled on his arm, and though he tried to grab hold of the dash and then the door, he tipped out onto the hillock of soiled snow by the edge of the dirt road.

He moaned, "Jesus! I'm hurt—"

I dragged him—to my surprise, it was easy—away from the warmth and safety of the car, down the snowbank by the edge of the road into the beginnings of the wood. We made noise on the crusty snow, crunching it like a breakfast cereal.

"She didn't get drunk!" I had shouted this in my head, on Dr. Reynolds's couch, but never in real life: "You're telling me she was too drunk to walk ten feet into the house! She couldn't call to you! You couldn't hear her!" I kicked him. I don't mean this as an excuse, I know it isn't valid, but I didn't think of him as a seventy-five-year-old man. He was the great blond terror, hands thick and heavy, body impervious to winter wind, eyes blind to my pain. How could I hurt such a creature?

He wheezed at the blow. I swear I heard a bone crack. He wasn't my terrible nemesis anymore: merely a poorly stuffed doll, hollow or soft depending where you touched. "Jesus . . . ," he groaned into the snow, feet pulled up to his belly, hurting.

"Tell me the truth, goddamn you!" I was insane—weepy, in a rage, worried I'd killed him, terrified that he could get up and kill me. "What did you do? Force her to drink until she passed out, and then dump her in the snow?"

"Fuck . . ." I think he meant to curse me, but his voice gave out. He coughed once, groaned, and coughed harder. "Going to be sick," he said.

"I'm leaving you here," I said, and walked away. I had to set my foot in the imprint of my last step down from the road, put my hand in the next to last, gather momentum, and jump to surmount the snowbank. Once up, I still had to fight to keep my balance. He'd never make the road, much less get to the nearest house, more than a quarter mile back.

I'd be caught. They knew at the retirement apartments that I had him with me.

Anyway, I didn't want to kill him. I wanted the truth.

He was vomiting. The sound of his retching boomed in the

tamped-down snow-covered world: a very loud, solitary noise amplified in an empty auditorium.

"Blood," he growled. "Blood!" he roared.

Mine? He wants my blood? I was scared of him. Now that he knew
what I believed, he might kill me if I went to rescue him. Those
hands were still powerful. Once around my neck, he could squeeze
life out of me.

I watched my breath flow, a white flame, in the air. It must be very
cold, but there were no more hollows in my bones for it to freeze.
I was burning.

"You fucking cunt! I'm bleeding. Get me up, you fucking cunt!"

From what I could see he was on his knees, arched forward, face
in the snow. The goose-down jacket came down only to his waist. He
wouldn't last long.

You die happy in the cold. The car was near. I could be in it and
driving south, the Phantom of Route 80, a woman with a tragic past,
doing what she can to make up for it. I wasn't laughing. I wasn't
mocking. I thought it might be the real answer. To go back to New
York meant dealing with Ben, with another one.

"Tell me the truth you bastard!" I hurled the words down at him,
stoning him with my hate, so old and still so new.

"She was . . ." He raised up, although on his knees; he thrust his
chest out and reached toward the black sky. In the half-glare, posi-
tioned away from the headlights, he resembled a wounded soldier,
dying on the battlefield. There was blood on the neck of his jacket
and his face was contorted in pale horror, a ghastly death mask. "She
was . . . ," he repeated, talking not to me, but to the woods, blacker
lines of trees against a black mass, cracking from the ice, branches
shivering in the cold wind. "She was pissed! Thought she was inside,
in the fucking house!" he yelled in a rush, and fell forward, fists out
to punch the ground. They sank into the snow. "She drank. Once
you left us, she drank! Took my stuff! I threw her out. She used to
come back in the kitchen door. She couldn't get to it. I was sick in
bed. But she drank!" he wept into the crusty snow. "Don't tell me
nothing else," he blubbered. "She was a fucking drunk."

No she wasn't. She wanted to be close to him, to be intimate, even
if that meant living in a stupor, too far gone to get up, open a door,

and enter. Even if that meant you died five feet from home and rescue.

What was I going to do? Kill him for a crime he didn't understand? There was no truth to get out of him: he had converted lies into truth. I climbed down the snow to get him.

He hadn't vomited. The blood was from a cut on his chin. I pulled him out of the snow. He'd stopped weeping; his breathing was labored and rapid.

"Come on, Daddy," I urged him, his arm around my shoulder. I pushed to move his body toward the road. Could I get him up the snowbank?

"Let go of me," he mumbled. "Don't want to go back there," he whined like a child. He kicked me in the shin with the hard rubber of his boot and leaned his weight on me.

We toppled. I screamed as we went down. Stuck under him we could both freeze.

He put his bloody chin on my cheek and whispered in my ear: "You hate me?"

"No, Daddy. Get up."

"What do you hate me for?"

The snow burned on my calves and wrists. It crawled, alive, into my sleeves and shoes.

"Don't care anyway," he mumbled.

I pulled hard to get myself out from under him. Abruptly yanked free, I rolled over and over, falling down the snowbank toward the woods. He flipped up, arms spread, crucified, sinking until he was level, imbedded in the white crust.

When I stood over him, his eyes were shut. "Help me, Daddy. I can't get you up myself."

Silence. The trees cracked and moaned. Father began to hum a song.

"Going to leave you here," I warned him.

" 'Ain't nothin' but a hound dog,' " he sang, softly, " 'cryin' all the time.' "

I had to go to the Volvo and get the towing line Stefan stored with the jumper cables. While Father sang Elvis Presley, I tied it around his chest, attached the other end to the trunk lock, and slowly drove on the road, pulling him up the snowbank. He cursed and dragged his heels, digging deep furrows and uncovering a patch of brown frozen earth. Eventually I got him into the car, and finally to the local hospital, where we were both regarded as too drunk and too crazy to be allowed to do anything more for ourselves. They admitted him for observation and a doctor drove me to the nearest motel.

I stopped by the next morning and found Father pale and bandaged in a bed. I told him I was going back to New York. What else could I do? There were no answers in my past.

"Good seeing you, Moll," Father said. "Had a good time last night."

❧

I tried to negotiate with the devil.

Going home on Sunday, I stopped twice for gas and once for a meal—tepid meat at Burger King eaten in twenty minutes. I reached the city in ten hours. New York was miserable, suffering from a winter rain, cold and wet, streetlights smeared on the gutters, pedestrians scurrying from corner to corner as if they were fleeing hunters.

Stefan appeared as I entered. He moved silently, in stocking feet, his little face appealing to me: "Molly, are you all right?"

"I saw my father," I told him. I took off my coat and put it in the closet. The sight of our stored possessions on the upper shelves (a slide projector we never use, a neat pile of scarves, an old humidifier) saddened me.

"I see . . ." He was surprised. "I thought you were looking for Ben."

"Are they back?" I moved through our hall, glancing into the kitchen on one side, the living room on the other, curious about this place where I lived. Everything seemed to belong in an exhibit, the objects deathly still, unused.

"I don't know. I'm not concerned about them—"

I interrupted: "It made no difference."

Stefan beamed his small row of teeth between the neat dark lines of his beard: "What didn't?"

"Seeing my father. Didn't make any difference. I faced it, Stefan.

He is what he is. I left my mother behind, stuck her with him. That doesn't change. I can't make the same mistake again. Now I need to know—you can help me or fight me. Which is it going to be?"

"Help you to do what?"

"I'm going to go over there and make peace with Ben. If I have to I'll pretend—no, I'm kidding myself. I'll help Ben, if that's what I have to do to protect Naomi. Are you on my side or not?"

Stefan lowered his head, shut his eyes, remained still and silent. What was he praying over? Finally he sighed and looked up at me. "I think we can be happy," he said. "I really believe that." He beseeched me with his hazel eyes, their color highlighted by all the black that surrounded them—semicircular eyebrows, finely mown beard, kinky hair. "Don't you, Molly? I really believe maybe this is all for the best, maybe our relationship could even be improved by this. If you've gone and confronted your father—"

"Stefan, what the hell are you talking about!" He was stuck in the past, thinking of our marriage before the murder. Did he really believe that once again I should preserve myself instead of fulfilling my duty to others?

What about my duty to Stefan? you want to know.

But he had lived without me for years.

"I think you have an opportunity here to explore feelings you've locked away—"

"You're against me, Stefan!" I yelled. "That's your—"

"No!" Poor man, he covered his face in pain. "Don't make it into that—"

"Yes, that's your answer! I'll tell you your answer because you can't. You're against me, that's your answer!"

"Please stop saying that." He rocked from side to side, swaying, hands shielding himself. "I beg you! Please don't make this mistake! This is our chance!" he shrieked in panic. He trembled, little creature, dark sweet animal, wishing he were a bright lion whose roar would rule the black jungle of my heart.

My face flushed. My skin tingled, prickly, infected. I was hot, steaming in the damp air. I smelled my mother's blueberry pie. I shut my eyes and saw its soft browned crust breathing on the wiped-clean surface of the trailer's yellow Formica counter. The pie oozed purple fruit, the counter's edge curled up underneath, its glue blackened with age and moisture. I opened my eyes and saw Stefan: "I . . . don't . . . love . . . ," I recited.

"No!" he begged.

". . . you," I finished. I had spoken aloud the terrible secret of our marriage. Shooting him would have been easier and more merciful. You're cold and hateful, I told myself.

I don't know what Stefan did the rest of that night, other than stay away from me. I showered, worked out, drained my body of the little energy I had left, and sat by the pantry window wearing comfortable jeans and a white T-shirt, wrung out.

Staring across the courtyard at Ben's kitchen and laundry windows, I realized my life was erased. The dust of the old assignment was still on the chalkboard, its ghost could be deciphered if you squinted, but any minute a new teacher would stride in and write over the past with tomorrow's homework.

Their lights came on at eleven-thirty. I crossed the hall right away. When Ben opened his front door, I extended my certificate book. "It's a fifty thousand dollar CD," I explained. "Should be more than enough to handle your immediate legal fees. I can turn the money over to you tomorrow."

Ben peered at the green booklet. It was old-fashioned; not a computer statement, a traditional bank passbook. "For doing what?"

"Stay here. Don't sell the place. I want"—and, of all things, I began to cry. I was able to keep talking, yet tears flowed with the words, raining out of my eyes as I pleaded—"to help with Naomi, to take care of her. Please let me."

From behind him, down their hallway, Naomi called: "Daddy . . . ? Who is it?"

"Come in," he said quietly. "Wait here." He disappeared down the hall. "Okay, honey, just go back to sleep," I heard him tell her. "You've got school in the morning."

"I know that!" she said contemptuously. "I thought I heard Molly," she added with, I fancied, a little bit of longing.

"Go to sleep," he evaded. Ben returned to the hall, a finger at his lips warning me to be quiet, and then gestured for me to go into the living room. He veered off to the kitchen and returned carrying two beers.

"No thanks," I said when he held a bottle toward me. He had

crude manners; that was another of his qualities which had clashed with Wendy's character. She was a generous and gracious hostess, able to throw large parties without exposing her own nervousness, clever at prodding strangers into conversations. Ben thrust the beer at me and shrugged when I refused—that was more or less his party style.

"You don't trust me," he said.

I was at a loss for an answer.

Ben began a kind of laugh, mostly silent, mixed with a grumbling noise. He interrupted it to say, "Listen to me: You don't trust me." He broke off to laugh in earnest, mouth open, torso shaking. "Of course you don't!" He smiled broadly. "Pretty stupid thing to say, wasn't it?" He expected an answer.

"Maybe you meant something else," I suggested.

He nodded. "What I meant was, you don't trust me with Nommy."

"Really, it's not that," I lied. "I just figure you'll have your hands full. I know you need money—"

"Okay, okay." He waved me off. "I don't wanna hear the whole crappy speech. I need help. That much is true."

The phone rang.

"God," he moaned. "We've only been here ten minutes."

"Want me to get it?" I offered.

He considered for a moment, while I moved to the phone, my hand hovering, ready to lift the receiver. "Sure," he said with a why-not? look.

It was a reporter. I told him, sharply, that Ben was out of town, and not expected back. He asked for my name. I declined to give it, hung up, then left it off the hook. "I think you should have the number changed tomorrow," I suggested to Ben. "And keep it unlisted. I can take care of that, if you want."

"Good idea," Ben said. I thought I detected a hint of wonder in his tone. He took a long drink out of the bottle, eyes staying on me even while he tilted his head back. "What do you know about my lawyer?" he said.

"Not much. He's young. Supposed to be bright. I don't know any more about criminal law than anybody else."

"But you can find out things. What about your guy, Brian Stoppard? He's supposed to be the best. Shouldn't I get him to defend me?"

I hadn't expected this. Seemed stupid in retrospect—it was a logical use of me. "I guess so."

"But you won't ask him." Ben took another long drag on the bottle and made a dull popping sound as he pulled it away from his lips.

"If you're serious, I'll ask him."

"It's my goddamn life!" Ben was furious. His head jerked forward, pecking out the words. "You better believe I'm serious!"

"I said I'll help"—I raised my voice to match his volume—"but not if you yell at me."

"Fuck you," he answered mildly, with disgust. "Who else can I yell at? Her?" He nodded at the hall, indicating Naomi's bedroom. Was he threatening me with abuse of Naomi if I didn't take it? Is that how he kept Wendy in line? Is that why she didn't complain of his moodiness, his bullying, and his sexual abstraction?

"What makes you think you have a right to yell at anybody?" I asked.

"I got plenty to yell about." He sucked on the bottle; looked as petulant as a baby doing it. "Believe me," his lips smacked off from the suction to say. "I'm fucked. Really fucked. You wanna help? Get me a good lawyer."

"I can ask Brian. That's all I can do. I can't make him agree."

He cleared his throat and finished off the bottle. "Thanks for offering the money. I'll be happy to take it, but I've got to be honest, I don't know if it's really enough for me to afford staying here. They fired me. I don't think I'm going to get another job easily."

"I'll pay the bills."

Ben's eyebrows twitched. His mouth hung open.

I specified the offer: "I'll pay the maintenance, her school, your legal bills."

He cleared his throat again, louder. "Why? What do you want?"

I lowered my head and spoke to the red Oriental rug. "I want to stay."

"Excuse me?" He hadn't heard.

"I'd like to stay, Ben." I trembled—shivered really—after making this naked request. Managing to look at him, I noticed a smudge on his right lens—I've always been amazed that people who wear glasses can be unaware of what's right in front of their eyes, so to speak.

"What do you mean, live here?"

"I can sleep in Naomi's room. Or on the couch."

His face scrunched up, everything moving toward the center, utterly confused: "For tonight or—"

I nodded my agreement at the unspoken phrase, scared to be more explicit.

"You want to live with us?"

I nodded. I was ashamed. My hands shook. I lowered my eyes during the brief but intensely painful silence, waiting for his response as if it were a benediction.

"I think that's going to look really bad, Molly. Don't you? People would think we were . . ." He raised his eyebrows lasciviously. "You know . . . ? That might be just the thing to put me away for good." His tone changed, to suspicion and anger: "Maybe that's exactly what you want."

"No, Ben!" I skidded forward on the edge of the couch. Unconsciously, I grabbed his hand. "I want to be with Naomi, to take care of her."

Ben winced, one eye winking with outrage: "You think I'm gonna hurt her." His thick hot fingers lay loosely in my tight grip.

"No, you need my help!"

"I'm a good father," he said, pulling out of my grasp and pointing to himself. "No," he revised, "I'm a great father. Have you seen those guys, the fancy daddies at Riverside? They don't know a fucking thing about their kids' lives. Brag about them, sure; show them off, sure. Take them to ice-skating on Saturdays, go to the ballet recital, sure, but take care of them when they throw up at three in the morning? Do anything for them that's menial? No." He shook his head, summing up, triumphant and scornful.

He's proud that he cleans up vomit, I noted. The observation was subversive to my mission. I kept quiet, pressed my lips together to ensure my silence.

"I'm not gonna hurt her," he insisted, his eyes misty. "I love her. I would die before hurting her. Do you understand?"

My smart-aleck attitude was wrong. He was no Lobsterman Gray, he cared for his daughter. He spoke the truth; Naomi was more than a component of his vanity. "I understand, Ben. I'm sorry," and I was sorry. "I want to help. That's all. I have confidence in you—"

"That's such bullshit!" He pushed his way out of the chair. "You tried to take her away from me! Did you forget that!"

"Yes," I said.

He had paced away, in his irritation. He stopped in his tracks. "What?"

"I did forget I tried that. Seems like years ago. I was angry at you. I wanted to hurt you. But you're right—you're a good father."

Ben held the empty beer bottle by the neck. He tapped his leg with it, crinkling his broad hairless forehead, puzzled. "You wanted *Harriet* to have custody?" He emphasized Harriet's name comically and broke into a smile. "I mean, she's meshuga. Really meshuga. The word was invented to describe her."

I laughed. He did too. We relaxed. We were at ease.

How strange.

"Why do you want to sleep here?" he wondered. "Obviously you think I'm gonna do something to her. I mean, I don't expect you to believe that I'm innocent, that I didn't do it. That's too much to hope for. But you really think I would hurt her?"

He seemed to have no awareness that I feared sexual abuse: he meant hurt as in brutality. Was that a good sign, or proof that he had those longings? What worried me? That he would beat her to death someday? Fondle her? Rape her?

Stefan had told me—in our famous discussion a hundred years ago last week, after I followed Ben to the Battery Park apartment—that transvestites are not pedophiles.

"Maybe he's a Renaissance pervert," I had said. Punchy, we laughed our heads off. I thought I was so clever, such a good friend to Wendy, sympathetic and yet witty too.

"I don't care what else you think about me," Ben warned, and accused me with his long elegant index finger, "I don't care what you say, I don't care if it means I lose your money—but don't ever think, even for a second, that I would hurt Naomi. I . . . ." The word reverberated, he turned his tapered finger on himself, and his voice quaked with feeling: ". . . love her."

"I know you do—"

"Do you believe me?"

"I do, I do. I really do."

He nodded, satisfied. "All right." He moved toward the kitchen, waving the empty green bottle jauntily as he walked. He halted abruptly, frozen in midstride, twisted his head around to say, "But I can't let you stay here. It would look bad." And then he resumed his pace.

A murderer worried about appearances. Stefan had thought of his image as well. Men.

"You can come here every night if you like, have dinner with us and so on, but if you sleep in, everyone's gonna think the worst." Ben talked from the kitchen. He dropped his bottle into the garbage (it landed with a great thud because of the height of the fall) and returned the one I had refused to the refrigerator. Idiotically, I was annoyed that he didn't save the empty to recover the five-cent deposit. I was excruciatingly tired. I had driven one thousand miles in two days; I had nearly killed my father. I began to regard my situation from a sarcastic distance. I thought: Why should I give him fifty thousand dollars if he's going to toss out nickels like junk mail?

"Can we talk about this tomorrow, after I take Nommy to school?" Ben asked, hands on his back, arching forward, a body yawn.

"Yeah." I got up, resigned. Back to my limbo with Stefan. "I need sleep too."

❧

Stoppard said no. What amazes me, looking back on it, is that all these men were so uncooperative and yet I was convinced it was my fault, that I was the failure. Why didn't I appeal to women for help? You're right to notice. I didn't because none had power in this circumstance. The one woman who seemed to have access to power was me. But its use depended on these men: Brian Stoppard for the law, Stefan for the head, Ben in possession of the fragile property.

"You're out of your mind," Brian said casually. He swiveled in his chair, like a kid on a soda-fountain stool. He smiled, a laughing, mocking flash of teeth. "The approach you're taking to this situation is"—he gestured helplessly—"nutty. I can't think of a better description. It's nutty. He killed your best friend. I'm not going to defend him at your request because right now you think it's better for the girl's sake. That's an emotional whim. What happens if in two weeks—or worse, in a year when it goes to trial—you've changed your mind? Molly"—he stopped the boyish swinging back and forth—"let's fight to get custody of her! For God's sake, we'll make it a feminist issue. Child abuse is a hot topic right now. If you want, I'll lower myself and we'll go on 'Donahue' and 'Geraldo'—and anybody else with their name as the title of a television show." He smiled at his joke, saw I was not amused, and continued: "We'll embarrass the law into changing. It can be done—everything is political. There's nothing inevitable about the current premise that a natural parent is the best guardian under all circumstances. All we have to do is say, 'If Joel Steinberg had killed Hedda first, under the law he would have retained custody of Lisa—' "

"But that's not true, Brian, this situation is different. Ben is Naomi's real father, it's not an illegal adoption, Ben has never hit her—"

"That doesn't matter!" Brian sprang his chair forward and pounded the desk with both fists. "We'll make thunder and scare everybody under their beds. I'm talking public relations, not reality. We don't have to be right, Molly, we just have to win."

Yes, and little Naomi would have her face published daily in the *New York Post*. She could become chums with all the Child Protection people while she shuffled from one hearing to the next, from one psychiatric evaluation to another. You'd thank me for that, wouldn't you, Wendy?

I declined Brian's alternate strategy—disappointed, he sullenly returned to his back-and-forth swivel, perhaps thinking up a different flavor of ice cream to ask for.

Years and years ago, before anything that I have written about so far, a bluebird flew into my first-grade class. Unable to find its way back outside, our schoolroom became its prison; and we also became inmates of the bird's noisy terror. Her wings—the science teacher told us later it was a "girl bird"—slapped sickeningly against the blackboard, the glass door to the hall, the green wall map, the yellowing window shade. I seemed to hear the bird's wild panic as a human plea; and though I ran from her unpredictable swooping flights, what really scared me was her situation, her inability to find the one exit, so cruelly obvious to us, and finally, fatally—when she dashed her tiny skull on the handle of a metal filing cabinet—hidden from her.

I remembered this incident, not as a fanciful metaphor for my situation, but as an analogy so literal as to be a prophesy, an omen. There was no exit. I whacked into Stefan, Stoppard, Harriet, Ben, my heart, my head, my past—with no result but bruises. Perhaps the next obstacle would be that metal filing cabinet.

I decided to calm down. To settle somewhere and get my bearings.

I gave Ben the fifty thousand dollars and told him to pass along any bills he couldn't handle. For two weeks I came and went from our apartment without explanation to Stefan, who, wary of me, asked for none. I went to the office, worked through lunch (billable hours were now important in a way they had never been), got Naomi from school, brought her home to a sullen, rather beery Ben, chatted idly like a housewife while I made dinner, supervised homework, hygiene, and faced the thorny problem of Naomi's social life, in particular her upcoming birthday.

Feeling a bit foolish I bought a paperback on good parental manners and discovered that the rule of thumb is: invite as many children as the number of the birthday. Wendy must have ignored this convention—Naomi was going to be seven and there had been more than six children at her previous celebration.

I raised this question with Ben one night after reading Naomi her bedtime story. She still liked to be read to even though of course she was one of the best readers in her class. I left her finishing the chapter on her own, came out of her room, and found Ben in the kitchen, loading the dishwasher. "Birthday party? Hadn't thought about it," he said. His big head glowed under a harsh neon light shed by an ugly kitchen fixture—periodically Wendy had wished she had the money and time to replace it. In the glare his thick skin seemed smoother and darker. Squinting, I fancied I detected a hint of makeup. He watched my eyes study him. He was ashamed by my observation so I must have been correct. Head down, he slunk away in a slow shuffle, like a scolded dog.

Why didn't Ben tell Wendy about dressing up earlier? I wondered. And why did she insist he surrender the Battery Park apartment with its secret wardrobe? What difference does it make if he wants to put on pancake and blush and lipstick and eyeliner? I argued to myself.

I *did* think him a fool, relinquishing the ease of being a man. After all, because he was a man it didn't matter that he was unattractive, didn't affect his life the way it had . . . But Ben didn't want the oppression of womanhood—only its clothes.

My sole context for dressing up was from when I was a little girl and liked to pretend to be Mommy. Pretending to be my benefactor Naomi was even more fun—naturally, her wardrobe outstripped my mother's. Was parental identification Ben's problem? Did he wish he was his mother instead of his father?

"What were your parents like, Ben?" I settled down in the living room with coffee. We might be husband and wife, sharing intimacies after a long day of work and child care. He had come from the bathroom where he had apparently washed his face—his eyebrows were damp.

"They were pretty typical." He announced a new subject by clearing his throat: "I don't think we can have a birthday party."

"We have to!" I was amazed he could consider doing otherwise.

"We have to celebrate it," he mumbled. "But those—" He was about to curse them; instead, he pursed his lips and continued, "so-called mothers won't let her friends come."

"Sure they will."

"They look right past me. Like I don't exist."

"I'll make the calls, Ben. We'll do something small in a public place—"

"Like what?"

"The circus?" I suggested. He frowned. "Ice-skating?"

"Ice-skating," Ben decided.

"I'll handle it."

Ben huddled into a corner of the couch, eyes glowering resentfully at the thought of all those parents staring through him. I tried to outrage myself: he killed Wendy, he hit her over and over, crushed her skull. But I couldn't infuriate myself and he wasn't scary. He was a confused, small-minded, unhappy man and I didn't fear him. Ben nodded. "Thanks, Molly. It'll be great for Nommy. You're really a big help."

Yes, I was. For once what I was doing was useful. I was actually helping.

Naomi came into the living room, wearing a long pretty night-gown. It was a gift from me and Stefan, very feminine, powder blue with a lacy collar. Naomi's huge eyes were a brighter, more brilliant blue than the fabric, but it still made a good match. She stood in bare feet, regarding us wistfully. She held a mass of her thick brown hair in one hand, pulled forward over her left shoulder. She was beautiful.

"What is it, honey?" Ben asked.

Very softly she said, "Good night," her tone a tragic farewell.

"Want me to tuck you in?" I offered.

She shut her eyes, pained. Slowly, she raised her right hand and pointed to Ben. "Daddy." She spoke her choice in an ominous tone.

Ben moved to her side, offering his hand. Instead, she took his whole arm, clutched it against her chest, and walked with her prize, pulling the rest of Ben in tow.

"Where would I find the phone numbers?" I called to him.

"In that book." He nodded at a desk-size address book beside the phone.

He was gone—and I heard him reading to her again in a moment—before I remembered that I didn't know the last names of most of her classmates. Besides, I had to ask Naomi whom she wanted at the party. I opened the book anyway.

A mimeographed sheet slid out, a class list of home addresses and phone numbers. I was fascinated by it, noting that only three women used their own names, that half had no office phone numbers. Two of the men had no business numbers either. One of them—Tony Winters—I knew to be a successful playwright. I studied all the addresses and determined which were lofts, which were brown-stones, which were prewar apartments, which were white brick plasterboard boxes. I imagined their marriages, their decorations, their attitudes toward Ben.

I couldn't dream up the person who would be sympathetic to his situation.

After a while, I could no longer hear Ben reading to Naomi. I looked for him in the hallway to the bedrooms. The routine was that after Naomi was in bed for good, he lodged a few complaints about his lawyer and kicked me out. I waited at the hallway entrance for several minutes. When there was still no sign of him, I returned to the living room and copied down the class list.

Half an hour passed and still Ben didn't emerge. I whistled and paced and called, softly, into the hallway, "Ben?" No response.

When an hour went by and there was still no sign of him, I got scared. For the first time since becoming the household nanny I feared him.

I pictured Ben, teeth bared, hiding in the dark of his bedroom, armed with a bat, waiting for me to walk in out of curiosity . . . and then striking.

I pictured him, grotesque, squeezed into an evening gown, wearing a huge stiff wig, face painted, masturbating into panties, ready to murder the poor soul—in this case, me, stupid yellow-haired lobster girl Molly Gray—who naïvely interrupts. . . .

I pictured him, one heavy hand silencing little Naomi's mouth, the other roughly spreading her legs, eyes red with rage as I appeared at her door, his dragon's mouth opening to breathe fire. . . .

Stefan was right. Brian was right. To be with Ben was madness.

I got up to flee. Only I was stopped when my mind bounded through the familiar cars of that old train of thought until I reached the logic of its engine: If Ben is too horrible for me to deal with, then how can I justify abandoning Naomi to his mercy?

And what the hell was he doing in her silent and dark room for so long?

I reminded myself that the point of everything I had done was to protect Naomi. Terrified, I walked down the hall, stamping my heels, clattering a warning of my approach.

Peel off that dress, Ben.

I found father and daughter asleep in each other's arms. Ben, huge and hairy everywhere except on top of his head, lay spread-eagle on her bed. She was huddled against his side, head pillowed in the crook of his arm, hair flowing over his thick chest.

I put her completed math sheet—it had slipped off her desk onto the floor—into her backpack, zipping it shut noisily. I hoped that would wake him.

Ben stirred, brought his legs together, and draped an arm over Naomi's slender body. In that position, she seemed hardly longer than his arm.

I tapped him on the hand to rouse him, to get him up and out, talking again, to learn something of his parents, maybe his first marriage.

I had to understand something else about him other than that he was evil.

Ben's eyes, large and vulnerable without his glasses, opened and regarded me with calm interest.

"You fell asleep," I told him.

"Good night Molly," he answered in a sweet whisper, a lover's tone. "Could you lock up on your way out?" His heavy lids shut like a mechanical doll's.

It was frightening to do, but I managed to will myself into shaking him again.

"What!" Although he spoke in a whisper, he sounded furious.

"Sleep in your own bed," I told him. I thought my heart would burst from terror, but once I had announced myself, I felt brave.

Ben's eyebrows merged across the bridge of his nose. "Mind your own—"

"Ugh!" Naomi shifted violently. She must have kicked Ben because he groaned and fell partway out of bed. He caught himself from a complete spill with an outstretched hand. Slowly—comically—he descended the rest of the way and was dumped onto the floor. Apparently Naomi was unconscious, but I doubted that—I sensed she was trying to help me, interrupting Ben from unselfconsciously displaying his anger.

I took his hot thick hand and pulled very gently, coaxing him to rise. He moaned and sat up. He stared at me for a moment, then rubbed his pale face vigorously. When he uncovered, red streaks showed where his fingers had been. They made prison bars; he peered through them, furious. "All right, I'll get up!"

I went ahead of him, waiting in the foyer to make sure he came out. He did, eyes closed, head lowered, feet shuffling. En route to the kitchen, he passed me, saying, "She's just going to climb into my bed in the middle of the night."

"You shouldn't allow that," I said to his retreating sluggish form. "She's too old to be in your bed."

"How the fuck do you know?" he mumbled, and disappeared into the kitchen. "Good night!" he called loudly once out of view. "Thanks for everything!"

I waited to insist on my point.

Again, his absence nurtured fear in my imagination.

I pictured him armed with the scariest of the large Sabatier knives from the cutlery—gunmetal gray, handle thick and black, blade as wide as my hand. He smiled and cut a few practice strokes in the air, ready to slice me up if I was still in the apartment when he exited from the kitchen.

Instead there was the air burst of a beer being opened and the clatter of its top rattling on the counter. He shuffled out, bottle upended and draining into his mouth. His eyes widened at the sight of me. "You're still here?" he said after disengaging from the Heineken.

"You shouldn't allow her to sleep with you. I read in one of the books—"

"Her mother's dead!" Ben's face was a caricature of disgust. "She comes crying into my bed at three in the morning—'I miss Mommy. I'm scared.' " He imitated her high little girl's voice extremely well. "I'm supposed to open Dr. Spock and quote her a passage? Come on. Give me a break."

"Sit with her until she falls back to sleep."

Ben groaned. He put the cool green bottle up to his broad forehead, shutting his eyes at the sensation of its touch. "Go home," he mumbled.

"It doesn't look good—"

"Get the fuck out of here!" Yanking the drink away from his forehead, he sloshed some on the floor. "I took your money, thank you very much, but I don't want your goddamn advice! You don't have any children—what the fuck do you know about it?"

He stung me with this harsh language. I thought I had won a little of his trust over the past few weeks. "Don't talk to me that way!"

"I'll talk to you however the fuck I want to talk to you. If you don't like it, then get out of here! I could care less whether people like the way I talk!" He snorted at me. "I'm beyond all that crap now, don't you think?"

I had to agree with him. He was beyond a lot of things. Was I? How could I deal with him effectively if I tried to hang on to the old manners, the old values? I put my hand on the glass doorknob (not the originals; Wendy had found these on the Lower East Side), turned it, about to retreat, and decided civilized talk, subtle manipulation, was worthless. "Ben," I said to his angry face, fixed on me, jutting forward in a dare. "I'm the only ally you've got. You know why you have me?"

"You think I'm innocent, right?" The sarcasm was hardly played—underscored softly and quickly, easily missed.

"If you touch her I'll destroy you."

His lips buzzed as he exhaled a grunt and a laugh simultaneously. "Don't threaten me," he said wearily.

"I mean it."

"You're like everybody else in this fucking city. You're so unbelievably arrogant. You think you know everything, you think you know what's good for everybody. Go fuck yourself. You think you're my ally? You're not. You're helping her. Cause I love her, I'm grateful. For the rest of it, I don't give a shit. From now on, when dinner's done, I want you to get out."

"I refuse to let—"

"Come on!" Ben put the beer on the floor and made for me.

I put up my hands to block his blows. My heart pounded. At last it had come: he was going to attack.

Ben took my wrist with one hand, the doorknob with the other, opened the door, and flung me out. I stumbled into the hallway. He shouted, "Get out!" and slammed the door on me.

The noise reverberated throughout the whole building, carried and amplified by the stairwell. I felt ashamed. Crazily, I thought he was right, that I had something to apologize for. Exactly what I didn't know. Probably for my fraudulence. He was honest, while I played at being a mother, pretending to saintliness. Ben at least was real.

That night I took out a foam mattress left over from my single days and made up a bed in the gym room. Stefan watched me, silently. He went away as soon as I was done.

Later, I lay awake among the skeletal shadows of the Nautilus equipment and replayed my fight with Ben. My anger glowed in the dark. I didn't give a thought to Stefan, alone in our big bed. Whatever the future held for me, at least I knew that was one lie I would no longer live.

❧

For the remainder of that week Ben refused to talk to me. I was allowed (that's how it felt, a scolded child briefly permitted certain privileges) to continue my caretaking of Naomi. But once she was in bed, Ben's face settled into immobile sternness—angry stone. He simply wouldn't respond to anything. I humiliated myself the first night of this silent treatment: cajoling, teasing, entreating, pleading. . . . Ben stared as if I were a broken television set whose warranty had elapsed the day before. After that ghastly evening I gave up trying to break his sadistic withdrawal. I returned meekly to my apartment, shivering from his hatred.

During the three days of Ben the Mute, I arranged to rent an ice-skating rink for Naomi's birthday. I told her we would keep the party small; Naomi bluntly said no. "I can't only ask my seven best friends," she told me. She hooked my arm with her hands and pulled down for emphasis. "Everyone would hate me."

"It's not that you want twenty-eight gifts instead of seven?"

"Okay. Forget it. I don't want a party." We were on the daily walk to school. She stopped using my forearm as a chin-up bar and skipped ahead to the corner. When I caught up she averted her eyes; her face was flushed. She exaggerated her petulance so that it was almost as laughable as it was effective.

"That's ridiculous," I told her. "Of course you'll have a party. If we invite your closest friends, you can spend more time with each—"

"I have more than seven friends!" she whined. "It's not a party if it's only seven people!" Like Wendy, she wanted the world; she enjoyed everyone.

Friday night Ben pulled another disappearing act with Naomi. No warning. Nothing about where they were going. This time he did it to punish me.

Saturday morning Stefan appeared in the gym and woke me. I had been up most of the night, anguished, unable to fight off terrible thoughts about Naomi's fate. Having finally succeeded in falling asleep, I was unhappy that Stefan didn't let me be. In general I wanted him to give up, to let go.

Stefan tapped me on the shoulder to rouse me. He had brought a cup of coffee. I sipped; he watched. When I was half-done, he said, indicating the mattress with his eyes: "Is this permanent?"

I shrugged.

"What does it mean?"

"I want a divorce," I said.

He shook his head no. He stood up. "Not now," he said, and left the room. I didn't pursue him. Things have to be ground slowly and thoroughly for Stefan: reduced to an easily swallowed size.

That miserable Saturday morning, in Naomi's absence, I gave in to her wish and mailed invitations to her entire class. This isn't the year to teach her self-denial, I reasoned, if you can call what my brain was doing under those conditions reasoning.

Afterward I made myself lunch, but couldn't eat it. I urged myself out to a movie or a museum, but I didn't want to leave the phone, in case there was some word from them or—worse—about them. (Remember: I wasn't sure they would return. For that matter, each morning when I crossed the hall to fetch her for our three-block walk to her school, I wasn't sure they would answer the bell. As soon as they were out of my sight, uncertainty and fear were my companions.)

And someone did call.

"Hello, is this Molly Gray?" she asked. When I said yes, she cleared her throat, as if hoping to get rid of her nervousness. "I'm Joan Franklin." She paused. Waiting for me to recognize her? "Uh, I was given your name by Amelia Waxman. I wanted to talk to you about what happened to Wendy Sonnenfeld. I'm Ben's first wife."

I had been on the verge of hanging up, sure that she was a journalist. Two had already tried me and I told them nothing. Until she announced herself, I had forgotten Ben had a first wife—now I remembered Wendy weeping in our dining room, explaining that Ben's first wife had left him for his best friend.

I guess the memory paralyzed me because her voice said, "Hello? Are you there?"

"Y-yes," I stammered.

"I wondered if we could get together—I don't know, it's strange to ask, but I don't know who else to talk to." She had a sweet tone, a little vague, but still smart. "I really need to talk to someone about him and learn a little bit about what happened since I knew him. I know this must sound nutty. Would you mind? Do you understand?"

"No, I don't mind. I understand." In fact, I was suspicious, but my curiosity was great (ravenous, really) for anything that might help me control Ben, and anyway it would distract me from the anxiety of the vigil. I said I could see her right away. I'm sure it doesn't surprise you that when I found out she lived in the town of East Hampton, I didn't mind the prospect of driving there. In the winter, on a Saturday, there was no traffic. I made it in two hours. En route I had an image in my head that she would live in a trailer or a ramshackle potato farmer's house. A ridiculous notion—probably there isn't a residence in poor condition in all of the Hamptons.

In fact, her house was a magnificent Cape, carefully restored. I lingered outside, nervous about meeting her. Seeing her place I fantasized that it had been a whaling captain's home, picturing its inhabitants during the nineteenth century: delicate women waiting for bearded men, their pale faces staring out of the lead glass windows at the cold ocean, fearful the Atlantic's gray swelling bosom wouldn't deliver home their love, but had instead become a grave. This image was calming. Right before I knocked, admiring the stately exterior, the look of it provoked a wish for something I had once prided myself on not wanting—romantic love. To give up the comfort of Stefan for a great passion—that would have made sense. I had the same sensation making this brief trip as I did driving to Maine: I could travel away, keep going, forget it all.

Half your life is still to be lived, a voice pleaded to me.

Was that Wendy talking to me? Maybe she wouldn't want me to do all this.

The first Mrs. Fliess opened the captain's door. A glance past her revealed elegance; everything inside looked to be early American antiques, meticulously tasteful, and very expensive. Her looks also surprised me: Joan is a sagging Wasp blonde, skin loose and puffy with middle age, her waist exploded by childbirth. Don't misunderstand, I think she's beautiful: hair long and shimmering, eyes bright and keen, complexion ruddy and sweet. It was her Waspiness that startled me. When Ben was married to her she must have been American apple pie incarnate. Like me, a yellow-haired girl. But not like me: in her welcoming smile I saw that she had always been cheerful, rich, and adored.

I also liked her on sight and trusted her pleasing manner. She cocked her head, her weak chin dimpling curiously. "Molly?"

"Yes." I was shy, like my mother at the door of a summer person's home, obliged to make a delivery of lobster, yet afraid to come in.

"Thank you for coming. I feel guilty you had to drive so far." She reached out and urged me in. She told me that she had gotten my number from Amelia Waxman, whom she had seen interviewed on television. "I called her to find out if I could help with the issue of Naomi's custody. She said you were working on that. I didn't even know Ben had her—I had this terrible image of some Dickensian orphanage. I know it's crazy, but I feel responsible somehow. I only met Wendy once. She seemed really nice." Joan had led me to the couch. She fell back herself into a large wing chair, appeared distracted, and almost shouted: "What happened!"

It startled a laugh out of me.

"I'm sorry. I mean, Ben was always unhappy and messed up, but still . . . what happened to him?" Her face was wrinkled with worry and wonder.

This left me stupid, mouth open, not knowing how to answer, and not wanting to volunteer information. I stared at her fireplace. Split wood, kindling, and paper were ready to be lit, presumably for the evening. "You tell me—I don't know," I stammered.

She was upset. Tears had come to her eyes with ease, and she took no notice of them, which made me think they were a frequent occurrence. I became convinced she didn't have a motive in talking to me. I had wondered during the drive out what she might be after and I was momentarily alarmed by her bringing up Naomi's custody, but seeing her think back to her past with Ben and appear so upset, I thought about her situation. She had been married to a man who killed his second wife—it was scary and worrisome. "He used to call me a flake," she said sadly, quietly, to the floor. "I told him: you dress up in women's clothes and gamble away twenty thousand dollars on blackjack, but I'm a flake." She smiled at this memory, as if it were pleasant.

I was stunned by this revelation; I tried to be casual, but I had to hear it again: "You knew about the clothes?"

"Well, he told me he had dressed up alone a couple of times and then he did it one night. Came out of the bathroom all done up, without warning me. I laughed so hard it hurt. He was pissed."

"Did he hit you?"

"No! Ben? Hit me!" She began a full-throated laugh, but she gulped it down: she forced herself to be serious. "Is that what happened?" she demanded. "I couldn't tell from the papers. Did she find out about his dressing up and then he killed her?"

"No!" I said, very insistently.

She almost gasped: "You think he's innocent?"

I hadn't meant that: I meant I didn't know what happened the night Wendy was murdered.

Joan raced past, assuming I had agreed. "It's hard to believe Ben did it. I mean, I haven't seen him in eight years—people change—but I can't picture him killing somebody." She was resting her head on the tall-backed wing chair; now she jerked it forward: "I'm sorry. Do you want something? A drink? Tea? Coffee?"

Her instinct was to take care of me. She was unguarded, friendly, at ease. Like Wendy. How did that creep manage to snare such good women?

"No thanks," I declined, and then set about clearing up things: "You misunderstood me. I didn't mean I thought he was innocent"— Joan listened to me with expression: her full cheerful face puckered, weak chin sucking in, the lines in her forehead multiplying—"I meant I didn't know what happened that night. I have no idea whether he did it or not."

She gazed off toward the floor, at nothing. Her light blue eyes were fragile and sad. Behind her a gawky black-haired teenage boy thumped, passing through to get to the hallway. He walked with his head down, hoping not to be stopped.

"Your son?" I suggested.

She nodded. "Timmy?" she called out. His thudding up the stairs had already begun.

The drumbeat stopped: "What?" His voice was husky.

"Say hello," she said wearily.

"Hello," he droned, and the drum thumped up the remainder of the staircase.

"Sorry," she apologized for him, which meant she was proud of him.

"He's a teenager." I smiled.

"Exactly. He's really so cute and sweet and kind. He hates to think so." I believed her: she would raise sweet children.

"You want Ben to be innocent," I suggested.

"I'm sorry," she said. "Hope that doesn't piss you off."

"No, no—"

"It's been over twenty years, but I *was* married to him. God, we lived together for four years. I almost had his . . . thank God I had an abortion—" She covered her mouth and, I swear, looked about the room as if there might be a nun or a cop or some terrible judge. "Horrible. I don't know what's wrong—I keep saying the most insensitive crap to you."

"You're upset by what happened."

"You're right." She was surprised. "My friends keep asking me if I'm bothered . . . I've been saying no . . . but I am."

"It could have been you," I explained.

"No it couldn't!" She was on the alert now, erect in the chair, her friendly eyes offended. "I left *him,* you know."

I reached across and touched her knee: "I didn't mean it that way. We're all related, that's all. You were his first wife—he killed a cousin of yours."

She agreed. Her lips trembled and her eyes flickered with pain. She shut them and sighed. "Yeah . . . ," she whispered. For several seconds she was off in reverie. When she returned her attention to me, she asked, "You said he killed her—so you think he did do it?"

I shook my head and shrugged. I hoped she might be someone who could understand this difficult situation: Ben's guilt was irrelevant—and threatening. "You said he lost twenty thousand dollars. He gambled?"

"All the time. Played poker, backgammon . . . doesn't he still?" I shook my head. "Really!" After giving that a moment's thought, she went on. "He was more interested in gambling than being with me. Who knows what would have happened if he had continued making love to me? We were really happy that first year. He liked to hang out. You know, we'd smoke some dope and drink wine . . . we were kids, you know." She leaned forward, her eyes trailing nervously upstairs, and whispered: "Did you ever think about people you knew when you were young? I mean, we were all the same, I thought. I never said to myself: she's a lesbian, he's an alcoholic, she's insecure, he's a control freak. I think about them all now, stuff we did, and it's like they were liars or I . . . I don't know . . . or I was a fool."

"And what was Ben lying about? The dressing up?"

She shook her head impatiently: "Ben was a compulsive gambler."

"He was that obsessed?" When Joan first mentioned the gambling I assumed his interest in speculation had been diverted into the stock market, but this seemed as if she were describing someone else.

"When I was married to him, anyway. It hit me one day. I remember I was"—she smiled—"on the toilet, furious at him for being out all night again, losing again, and I thought: he's a compulsive gambler. Made him seem like a character on a soap opera."

I smiled. "I know what you mean—"

"That wasn't Ben to me—the compulsive gambler. Thinking about him like that—objectively—made him unreal. It wasn't the guy I lived with. Even though he fit all the descriptions, did all the same sick things . . ."

"I know exactly what you mean." It had taken me years to say to myself: my father is an alcoholic. Even now I consider it a fact that describes him incompletely. Again I reached across and touched her on the knee briefly—maybe to make sure she was real. I felt close to her, grateful for her candor and warmth. I was happy I had come. At last, for the first time since the murder, I had someone sympathetic to talk to.

"I kept telling myself it was temporary, that if—can't fall for that, you know," she interrupted herself. "That's what we always believe, right?"

"What do we believe?" I smiled at the phrase—I was glad at the prospect that I might be united with the rest of world in some way.

"That we can change a man. We talk it out with them so they'll change. We throw them out so they'll change. We make them soup so they'll change. We do what they want so they'll change."

"But they don't change," I said tediously.

"Don't be fooled. They don't." She smiled at me. "I don't make that mistake anymore. If a man's not perfect right from the start"—she made an umpire's gesture with her thumb—"he's outta there."

I hardly breathed as I took this in, numb to the comedy of her presentation, sensitive only to her truth.

Joan leaned forward, a naughty look in her eye, and whispered:

"When my marriage to my husband—Howard, my second husband, the man I was *really* married to, the father of my children—" She chuckled at the phrase, then stalled out because of some private thought, and had to start up again: "What was I saying? Oh yeah, Howard. When we were falling apart I got so desperate I decided it was because I didn't like to, you know, to give"—she rolled her eyes and abandoned modesty—"blowjobs."

Now all the grief swelled and thickened, shot with novocaine, nerves dead to pain, and I could laugh . . . even though the world might still be drilling in the cavity. I leaned back, a friend in this stranger's home, and laughed.

"So I forced myself," she continued in a whisper, checking with one eye that her sons weren't nearby. The contrast was funny: this respectable, somewhat dowdy middle-aged woman, discussing oral sex. "Gave him one every day: first thing in the morning, instead of lunch, before, after, during dinner—anytime I thought he was shutting me out. Otherwise, I was as honest as hell, screaming at him the second he acted like a pig. I was free, I was open, I was generous, I was selfish. Boy, Howard was one confused puppy. Two weeks later he walked out. I became the kind of woman he wanted and it scared the shit out of him."

"Nothing works," I said. The words were gloomy, but I was smiling, chuckling, nodding. I regained the hopefulness I used to know when I was with Wendy. If others feel what we feel—no matter how sad—it can be borne, right? "I never had the guts," I told her.

"Guts . . . ?"

"To have a real relationship. I watched everyone else do it. I watched Wendy do it. . . ." I allowed the obvious to hang in the air.

"You're married." She nodded at my wedding ring. I wore a plain thin band, presumably because of elegance. Just there to show the information, not to celebrate or brag.

"I don't have to please him," I said. It actually hurt to confess that. I never liked to speak ill of Stefan or my marriage. Even with Wendy I was elliptical, at best, about it.

"That sounds great!" she cheered, sitting forward, leaning her chin on her hand, her eyes shimmering with curiosity.

"It's not real." I had to swallow hard and shut my eyes. I felt a wave of misery, a fever swimming through my muscles, weakening me. I had confided in no one, you see, since Wendy's death. The closest I had come to a real confidence was when I cried and told Ben I needed to take care of Naomi. My talks with Stefan and Brian were about tactics, about improving things (the way men deal with tragedy)—I had said nothing from my heart to a woman, to someone who would understand it with her feelings, and not impatiently toss me a how-to manual.

"Maybe you just feel guilty that things are equal."

"What do you mean?"

"Want some tea?" she asked, getting up. "Say yes. I like to drink tea with people I want to become friends with. Like little boys sticking a pin in their fingers and becoming blood brothers."

I followed her into the kitchen. The room was like her, big and sunny, cabinets painted light blue, counters messy from the random snacking of a happy family—it welcomed you to be casual and nourished.

"I mean that maybe you have a good thing and you can't accept it." She threw this back, over her shoulder, while she went about making tea and offering cookies. "It's easy for us to say we deserve this and we deserve that, but it's hard to take what's ours, especially if we've been raised to give it away."

"I wasn't."

She almost dropped the bag of Chips Ahoy. "Come on. We were all raised that way!"

"Not me." I insisted on my distinction. I told her my story—that is, the part about Naomi Perlman paying for my education and being my mentor. She listened, fascinated—as everyone did—but her interest was especially greedy. She hunched over her tea (she brewed it, kept the pot warm in a cozy, and served it in gaudy cups and saucers made of fine china), but she drank me in, leaving the cup alone. For that matter I poured myself, gratefully, into her. I had forgotten I was there to interview her.

"She did a bad thing to you," she said when I was done. "Don't be offended—I'm always stepping on people's toes without knowing it. I don't take what I say seriously so I don't expect anyone else to. Just tell me to shut up and I will."

"I'm not offended," I said. But I *had* stiffened, alerted at an ancient post, on guard against a lifelong enemy.

"She made you choose between her and all the great stuff she could give you and your parents. I mean, they were poor and they were your parents and they had problems. That's not fair. Too much for a little girl to handle."

I frowned and shook my head. "*I* made the choice."

"Have you done that to yourself?" She pulled her hair back, painfully, exposing a high, broad, intelligent forehead.

"Done what?"

"Taken the responsibility for that decision on yourself?"

"It *was* my decision. I told you: she gave me a chance to go back."

"Honey." Joan stopped torturing her hairline and let her flop of blond hair fall forward. Its return rounded and sweetened her face again, but it subtracted the wisdom of her high brow. She put her warm smooth palm on top of my hand, looked into my eyes, and patted my knuckles firmly, in time with each sentence, her touch making the periods: "You didn't have a prayer. Your father drank. He knocked your mother around. He neglected you. Then this fabulous rich young woman appears, offers to give you the world—and at age eight you're supposed to say, 'Gee I'd rather stay in the trailer until Daddy decides to start beating the crap out of me.' " She rubbed my hand where she had tapped me and her weak chin sucked in sympathetically: "You didn't have a choice."

"No. You don't understand. In fact, there was only one person who really did understand that it was *my* decision. And that was Wendy." Joan must have been sure that her kind speech would be reassuring and pleasant, because my answer startled her. She returned to gathering her hair and stretching it back. Her eyes went back and forth across my face. I had her thinking hard about something. I continued, "Otherwise, you see, it means the only person who voluntarily did something for me is converted into a wrongdoer. I mean, Naomi saved my life. . . . Really. That's what she did. And if I look at it the way you did, it lets me off the hook all right, but it turns the one person who did me a kindness into someone who did me wrong. It makes a joke out of morality: 'Naomi's good, but really she's bad. Father was bad, but he deserved better.' You've turned everything upside down. Don't you see? *I* wanted to get away, to be happy. Naomi made it possible. But *I* wanted it. And *I* took it."

"I don't know . . ." She dropped her head down and the waterfall of hair covered her for a moment. She abruptly flipped it back, a magician revealing the surprise. Her face reappeared with a settled look of conviction: "I still think you're being too hard on yourself."

"I'm not. It's not about being hard or easy—it's about being accurate."

"Mom!" one of her boys shouted. "It's for you!"

Apparently the phone had rung. I hadn't heard it. Our conversation must have been intense—neither had she. Joan glanced at her wristwatch as she moved to the wall phone and exclaimed, "Oh my God," into the receiver without saying hello. "I'm sorry. I'll be right there." She hung up and told me in a rush that she was late for her writing workshop.

I was disappointed I had to go. And I hadn't gotten the full story of her marriage to Ben. "Do you come into the city?" I asked as we hurried outside. "Can we talk some more about Ben?"

She didn't hesitate. She vehemently agreed that we should get together and said she would call tomorrow to set a day when we could meet. We hardly said good-bye.

I returned to my car to go home. This time, driving to the city in the Volvo, skimming soundlessly on the white-gray concrete of the Long Island Expressway, I wanted to go back, to stop traveling. My afternoon tea with Joan had proved I could still make contact with people. She was right: I couldn't change Ben. But if I was accurate and clearheaded while with him, maybe I could steer around his devils and find his real center. It had to be there—it's in all of us—the final doll in a sequence of diminishing nesting dolls: a tiny, indivisible child who wants to be loved.

❧

On Sunday Joan called and we arranged to have lunch in two weeks. The prospect of another talk with her buoyed my spirits while waiting for Ben's return. Stefan's presence didn't.

During the afternoon, the vigil wore me out. I was obsessed, thinking of nothing but Ben and Naomi—off in the unknown—insisting to myself that everything would be okay. Attempts to concentrate on work were hopeless. I paced in the living room, picking up magazines, reading nothing, staring through old movies on television. Ben couldn't kill her, I encouraged myself. Even in a rage, how could he hurt that beautiful little girl? Logic told me he could. Feelings said no. People do, I lost the argument with myself. They often kill the innocent gleefully.

Stefan ignored me for most of the day. Toward evening, he came in and approached the subject of our relationship by way of my anger at him for refusing to deal with Ben. I told him nothing had changed: I would do whatever it took to ensure Naomi's safety.

"All right. I understand your feelings on that score. I was insensitive. You can't just leave it to the law . . . I understand that now." He rubbed his small dark hands together—the fine black hairs curved over to the very white, meaty part of his palm. Stefan was good to hold hands with; they fit nicely in mine; they were warm and dry and calm. "I don't think it means we have to end our relationship."

"I don't want to end our relationship. I want to end our marriage." I pressed my lips together, squashing them, wishing I could stop my mean mouth.

"What does that mean?"

I kept my lips together: no more talking, Molly.

"You said you didn't love me." He nodded in my direction for me to agree. "You meant it?"

I nodded yes, pressing hard to keep my mouth closed. My teeth bit painfully against the inside of my cheeks, but I didn't ease up. I wanted to spare Stefan the ugliness in me.

"My question is, why is it that Wendy's death has caused you to discover you don't love me?"

Anger stepped to the head of the line, demanding to go first. I pushed it aside with the law: "I'd like to keep the apartment, go on living here. We can negotiate the agreement so that I buy you out."

"Goddamn it, Molly!" Stefan's arms shot out awkwardly from his sides, stiffened in the air, and moved up and down. His rage had a comical quality—a childlike miniature of the real thing. "Deal with me! I'm a real person! You're hurting me. You have to deal with that!"

"Let's make love," I suggested. We hadn't since Wendy's death.

It would be nice to be physical for a little while, to forget the brain and the heart. I thought about Stefan's smooth hands. I could press one between my legs and leisurely kiss his red lips, nested in his fine fur. I stretched out and captured his fingers with mine, entwining us. His confused dark face still pantomimed fury.

"No!" He stepped back; my fingers stuck between his. We stood awkwardly apart and united. "That's not the answer to my anger. Pacifying me—"

I walked into him. His body was a wall, no give of welcome. I took hold of him, rising on my toes, gaining height, arching my arms around him, hands taking hold of his small, little boy's behind.

"—isn't the answer," his lips mumbled into my attempt at a kiss. I covered the fur and red mouth with more kisses. He talked into them: "I don't want sex—"

"I do."

"I want—"

"You're excited," I argued—his flat body had topography now. I have long strong fingers and Stefan likes the feel of them on his back, his shoulders, kneading him. He's a sensual man and the release of sex is important to him, yet he fights his urges. Sometimes I think the great preoccupation of his life is to keep his desires in check.

I cracked his icy resistance with my grip, rolling his skin, paying no attention to his words, listening instead to the resonance of his tone, the rhythm of his breathing.

"You can't manipulate me—this is too serious . . . I won't allow you to degrade our relationship, there's more to it—"

"Let's say good-bye right." I kissed him on the eyes, licking the lids shut. He was a perfect doll, an exquisite miniature.

"You're acting out—," he mumbled, but the talk was an obvious prop now. One push and the flat would fall over.

"This is your last chance to enjoy me, Stefan," I whispered, and slipped a hand between us to caress his tangible excitement, his truthful organ.

At last he took hold of me. His hand squeezed the back of my neck, he bumped his pelvis against me, and the fur flew apart. His tongue forced itself into my mouth and wiggled inside.

He withdrew fast and stared intently at me, his brown face concentrated. He spoke honestly, without a whine: "Maybe I'll kill you."

"Sure Stefan." I covered his mouth and exhaled the words into his open throat: "Go ahead and kill me."

That's what orgasm is: a happy death.

Afterward he cried. Without any preliminary talk or warning. I felt fine. My head was clear, relaxed, thinking nothing, troubles forgotten. I floated on the earth, seeing limitless sky, breathing in time with the world. I heard a sniffle, turned my head, and saw the indentations of his tears trailing down, mountain streams disappearing into his black forest. He made almost no sound. His small bird's chest heaved in rapid motion, his little heart breaking.

I felt a pang, but it was obliterated by rage. How dare he put this on me, the responsibility for his impossible desires?

"I love you," he said at last, and then wailed his first sob.

That was too much for me: "You love a fantasy!" I told him, furious. "My blond hair. My *shicksa* body. You don't love me. You don't want me to be real."

"That's not true, Molly," he moaned.

"The minute I'm real you want to send me to doctors, you want to shut me up. If I don't tie down everything I feel—like you do—you want me medicated."

There is no ending to a past that doesn't hurt. Even an evil past is frightening to let go of. Stefan needed to be hurt—he wanted to be shoved away. He wished to blame me.

Why not? It was my fault: I had lived a pretense, choosing comfort over passion, ease ahead of commitment. Many others seemed to get away with that compromise. Not me. Ben Fliess had flushed me from my hiding place.

Stefan took a pill, the only time I had ever seen him prescribe for himself. Once he had calmed down he packed a bag. I asked him to hire a lawyer and get in touch with Prosser.

He nodded, beaten. But he said: "Think about it, okay? I won't do anything for a month. I want you to think about it."

"You can wait a month. I won't change my mind."

He did an uncharacteristic thing: he grabbed me impulsively as I walked him to the front door. He dropped the suitcase and his body jerked at me, almost a leap. Stefan bent me back and kissed me hard, like a slap, on the lips. His arms squeezed me—a desperate clinging child—and he buried his head in my hair, moaning: "Molly . . . Molly . . . Molly . . ."

"Shhhh," I comforted him. "You'll be all right."

"I won't," he croaked.

I know I'm bad: I was glad when he finally left.

I gathered his things—photographs, mementos, a small sculpture—emptied the medicine cabinet of his toiletries and drugs, and put them in his study, closing the door. I rounded up all the stray copies of psychoanalytic journals. I dumped his favorite snacks into the garbage and—

That's when I saw the Fliess kitchen light go on. I phoned. Busy signal. I crossed the hall.

Naomi answered the door.

"Who is it?" Ben shouted from the living room.

"It's Molly," she hollered back.

"Why aren't you in bed?" I asked her.

"I swam across the whole pool!" she announced. "Even the deep end! I wasn't scared."

Ben and Naomi had gone to a hotel in Westchester for the weekend. The attraction was that it had an indoor pool. Naomi loved to swim. Of course Ben paid the bill with my money. I learned all this from her as she undressed, brushed her teeth, argued that she ought to have a bath (losing), and during our talk in the night-light dark, after I had read her a chapter of *The Secret Garden*. Ben talked on the phone through the whole bedtime ritual. He was still at it when I came into the living room.

He hung up after a few more exchanges and mumbled, "He's an incompetent jerk."

"Who is?"

"My so-called lawyer."

"You can't call him on Sunday night and expect that he'll be happy about it," I said, not for the first time.

"I tried him all day Saturday and today! He was skiing! I'm paying him a fucking fortune—"

"No. *I'm* paying him."

"You want your money back—?"

"I don't—"

"I don't have it! You gave it to me without any strings." His lips quivered as he abused me. But he always seemed happiest when he shouted. Quiet, he was sullen and despondent. At least anger brought him to life. "You can't give me—"

I was sick of his bullying. I didn't calculate my response. I let go: "Shut up!"

"I won't shut up!" He kicked the wing chair next to him. Despite its bulk, it skidded three feet. "Don't shout at me!" Ben bellowed.

"Daddy!" Naomi called out, almost in a scream. "Daddy, I'm scared!"

I moved toward the hallway. Ben cut ahead of me. He bumped me back with his hip. "She called for *me!*" he complained.

"Act like a grown-up," I told his back.

"Oh fuck off," he mumbled, disappearing.

I felt good. Pissed off, a green anger, wanting to ripen. A lively feeling. I was eager for him to reappear.

He entered grumbling. His head was down; he rubbed his forehead wearily as he walked, eyes averted. "I told you I don't want you here after she's—"

"I've got something to tell you. I'm divorcing Stefan."

"Oh yeah?" Ben perked up. He flopped down on the couch, legs sagging, but his face was enlivened: "How come?"

"We see our futures differently."

"Come on, Molly. You want to get along with me, tell me the truth."

"Who says I want to get along with you?"

He smiled appreciatively, nodding at the floor. "What do you want from me? I can't read you. Never could. Wendy claimed she knew everything you were thinking—"

"She did."

"Bullshit." Ben rubbed his face, allowed his legs to sag even more, and mumbled: "Excuse me, but I'm tired of sentimental bullshit. Especially from women."

I was amazed. Overloaded, really. I laughed at him—scornfully. "You're really something."

"What the fuck does that mean?"

"You plan on beating all of us to death?"

The world stopped. I had spoken the scariest words in a tough, casual, thoughtless outburst. Ben himself appeared confused. "Shut up," he said in an intense whisper, indicating Naomi's bedroom. "She's still up. She can hear."

"You want me to go and tell her? She hasn't asked. If she does, I'll tell her what I really think."

"Okay. That's it." He rose from the couch ominously. "You're gone."

But he was too slow. Instinct told me he didn't mean it. "You need my help, Ben. Stop pretending you don't. You'll need more money soon. Deal with me, or I swear to God, I'll cut you off. And I'll help them convict you."

"You're nuts. You can't help them." He dismissed me with a disgusted wave. Then he mused: "I don't know what the fuck you want from me. What is your fantasy, Molly, about all this? You want me to give Nommy to you? Forget it. She's the only thing I've got left—"

"She's not a thing."

"Oh, please! Don't give me that crap! Okay?" He stamped his foot, squashing my semantic correction. "Do you really believe all that stuff? No one else does, you know." He came up to me, slow, not scary. He put a long tapering finger in the air, hovering obnoxiously in my face. I wanted to bite it. "Of course she's a thing, a really precious thing—my life. I lose it and I'm dead. I don't care what happens. You can't threaten me with shit in order to get her, cause she's my bottom line."

"That's your excuse for killing Wendy," I said, and I knew what I risked.

Again, for a moment, the world stopped.

Ben transformed. He lowered his lecturing finger. He cocked his head to one side, brought his chin up. His mouth weakened, almost sadly. "I've always liked you. Always wanted to sleep with you." Didn't surprise me. He was greedy. He wanted everything. If he intended to shock me, he failed. I watched him, wondering what was the goal of this manipulation. My money, my silence, or my body? "Wendy knew that. She said everyone wants you. She said you're like a beautiful cat. People want to possess you, she said, because you can't be owned. They want you purring in their laps." He adjusted his glasses, pushing them back, and squinted through them, waiting. "Did Stefan get to have you? That's what I always wanted to know.

I used to tell her I thought you two didn't screw. She said I was crazy. She said she knew everything about you, whether you told her or not."

"She was right."

"Oh yeah?" He smirked and finally straightened his head, curiosity gone. His tone changed: "She said you wanted to sleep with me."

How many times have I underestimated him? He had a punch to throw, after all. I got hit pretty hard, though I pretended not to be fazed. I stumbled for a moment and concentrated on a riposte. "Well . . . ," I mumbled, stepping away, unable to meet his triumphant, gleeful stare. "She was flattering you," I said.

Ben shook his head, gently, so unconvinced he didn't need to disagree out loud. "She didn't mean because of me . . ." He searched my face for a moment and then gave up on what he sought, shrugging his shoulders. "Well, she was full of shit, too, you know. Thought she was a brilliant, wonderful person, the best goddamn mother in the whole world, the most sympathetic friend. . . . Like all women today—just convinced she was morally superior. And everybody buys it, too. It's incredible. Magazines, the TV, books, movies—it's unbelievable. Your sex is even allowed to kill. When one of you gets rid of a husband, she's a victim defending herself."

All I got out of this was his hatred of women, his typical use of self-pity to justify his own evil, and, of course, I felt relief that he had apparently abandoned his attempt at sexual blackmail, if that's what it was. Since Ben's release from jail, his behavior was disorganized and often pointless. He hardly left the apartment, and although he complained about his lawyer, he made no move to replace him. Maybe he was merely crazy, not evil or perverse, but unplugged from the switchboard, incapable of sending and receiving like the rest of us. Perhaps what seemed to be a sadistic carrot-and-stick use of Naomi in his dealings with me was actually random, irrational behavior.

"Look Ben," I appealed to him, "for better or worse let's try and be civil, for Naomi's sake."

"No way!" He was lively again. "The one good thing about all this is"—he smiled and opened his arms, embracing and welcoming everything—"I don't have to pretend anymore. About anything. I'm not going back to that polite shit of the world, to all those lies. I'm not going back to having someone make me feel like a piece of unworthy shit all the time. I'm not gonna be the ugly one, the selfish one, the failure, the pig, the bad boy who has to behave. Forget it. I'll take your money as long as you're stupid enough to give it away, but I won't kiss your ass for it."

"I don't want you to kiss my ass. I simply want respect—"

Ben grunted. It silenced me. The sound he made was arresting: the noise came from a savage animal inside him. He grumbled and roared and shook his head violently from side to side. He appeared to be having a fit. If I didn't know it was anger, I might have mistaken it for epilepsy.

He's really crazy, I thought.

"Shut the fuck up." He hummed the words through his garrulous growl.

"Okay!" I raised my hand, a traffic cop. "Forget it! Okay! Forget I said it!"

Ben grunted once more, took a deep breath, and mumbled. "I won't be talked to that way anymore. Understand? Not only do I not want you to approve of me, if I accidentally do something to make you approve of me, I'll stop doing it. It's great knowing everyone hates you. I've been scared of it my whole life. But I was wrong." Ben stared at me, almost pleaded this point: "Your hatred makes me strong."

This left a silence to live through. A ghastly moment of eye contact while he waited for a response. Ben seemed bigger. His nervous face relaxed. He lifted a long finger to his small, bright red lips, and parted them slightly with his nail. He almost sucked on the tip. He was at peace with himself, the calmest I had ever seen him.

My knees buckled. I put out a hand and leaned on the back of the wing chair he had kicked toward me. "I h-have to go," I stammered.

"I think that's the best thing for you," Ben said. He glanced toward the hallway. "She'll be okay. Kids are strong, you know."

I tried to move. Let go of the chair. Walk out. I lifted my hand a little, but the world began to spin, a carousel starting up, and I grabbed hold of the brake to stop it. "I'll pick her up for school tomorrow."

"No. I want to take her. I want to see their faces. I can't hide forever. Besides, there haven't been any TV cameras, right?"

I shook my head.

"Guess the school's got influence. Amazing. Everything's like that—not what you know, but who." He wasn't talking to me. This was a phrase from some constant internal monologue. When he caught my eye, he dismissed me: "Go home. I've been entertaining the kid all weekend. I want to be alone to relax."

I was sure if I gave up my crutch I would collapse. I really believed I was paralyzed. "Why don't you go out? Take a walk—"

"No—"

"I'll sit for Naomi. You could see a movie."

"No. I don't want to go out." He smiled slowly, insidiously. "There's stuff I want to do here." He paused to grin. "By myself."

He's going to dress up. While she sleeps he'll live his private love affair, his obsession, his only pleasure.

My queasy legs sobered up, heavy with despair, but now able to support me. I walked away from the chair and moved quickly toward the door.

"You can stay," he said softly to my back.

"Good night," I answered breezily, as if I hadn't heard.

❧

On each invitation I had written RSVP MOLLY GRAY, followed by my home and office numbers. The calls came in at work, during lunch hour, hoping to avoid me. On the days I didn't eat, when my secretary offered to put me on, the mothers declined and then also declined attending the party. The typical excuse was that they would be out of town that weekend, or had a family obligation.

There were four exceptions: Naomi's closest friends. I spoke to only one mother directly, Janet, the flouncy blonde with a constant look of worry, mother of self-assured Holly. She surprised me with her boldness. I suspected she had volunteered to talk to me on behalf of the other mothers who had accepted.

"Is the whole party going to be at the rink?"

"Yes," I said. I knew what she was getting at. After all, every offer of a playdate at Naomi's home had been rejected in the past month. "We'll have cake there. No lunch."

"So you're being the host. That's really nice of you."

"Thank you for letting Holly come."

"She wouldn't miss it for anything. She loves Naomi. You know, if you want to bring Naomi over some weekend, or have me pick her up after school, she could have dinner with us, and you could come by for her later."

I had to tell her what could happen; Ben now wanted to confront them. "Her father might want to be the one who picks her up."

Janet paused. "I see." Another pause. "Is he going to be bringing her and picking her up from school from now on? I thought maybe you were out of town or—"

"No. He wants to do it."

"It's not fair to her. Everyone shuns—" She sighed. "You know, because of him."

"Well they shouldn't," I said harshly. "What are they scared of? It's a little girl's feelings they're hurting. They're not doing anything to him."

"Well," she stammered nervously. "What can—I don't . . . how can we act as though he's okay, as though we condone—"

"All Naomi gets out of it is that people don't like her anymore."

"Oh no!" Janet was wounded and surprised. How could she be surprised? "That's terrible! Nobody wants that. Can't you convince him it's bad for her? Doesn't he have any feeling for her?"

With everyone, conversation became an endless looping tape. The finish of one only started it again, around and around, worse than a world falling apart, more like a world with nothing but a center, no pleasant side streets, no meandering diversions.

Nothing I did came out right. Stefan was out of my hair, yet I spent less time over at Ben and Naomi's. I made them dinner, I kissed her good night, and I left quickly. I was a coward again: scared of him.

After a week of this minimal contact, I coaxed Ben into permitting Naomi to spend a Sunday alone with me. He said he needed the day off from child care, anyway. I wanted to treat her to some fun. The rejections to her birthday party invitations (she kept careful track of them) had hurt her as much as any of the terrible events. After all, it contained all of them, a concentrated dose of everything that was changed and lost.

Things began badly. "What do you want to do?" I asked her. "I don't care," she mumbled. But to each suggestion she said no. "Let's take a walk," I said. Naomi shrugged listlessly. I decided to change my tactics: go shopping, behave as though I were her mother involved with our normal routine and she were merely tagging along.

Removing her happiness as the focus relaxed her. She asked if I would let her help find items on my list in the supermarket. En route, we had a long discussion on the virtues of buying family-size items; we discussed why New York supermarkets don't carry them, but they do in New Jersey.

"It's not like the families in New Jersey are bigger, right?" she argued. "I don't suppose they eat more."

I told her that by law every New Jersey family had to consist of at least twelve people. She found this very funny, doubling over on the street. She covered her open mouth with her hand and hissed through the fingers.

With her help, we checked off the list rapidly. She skipped off to other aisles and rushed back with each item, eyes intent, manner eager. "Got it," she said. "What's next?"

We took the groceries back to her apartment. Ben was still out. I decided we should reorganize the kitchen cabinets. Wendy had been a good housekeeper, but a bit haphazard. I didn't say that to Naomi, of course. She was fascinated at the notion of arranging things by kind so that they would be easier to locate. "I could do that in my room," she said. Out loud she detailed a plan. "I might need more shelves," she commented. Her voice was full of energy.

Wendy often spoke of how proud she felt when Naomi copied her in something. Obviously, I had never known that simple pleasure. I hope I gave it to my mother. Probably I did. I don't remember, though.

I convinced Naomi to wait on redoing her room. We went to the movies. The film was more grown-up than I had expected. When she got bored I asked if she wanted to leave. "Can we?" She was surprised.

"Sure," I told her, baffled why that would be amazing.

We went for ice cream. We strolled through Washington Square Park, diminishing our cones, careful not to lose a single drop of pleasure. We were almost done when Naomi said casually, "I wish you were still picking me up from school."

"Me too."

"You want to pick me up?"

"Uh-huh. But your father said he wanted to do it for a while."

"Oh." She was down to the final point of cone, only a tiny well of ice cream. "Why?"

"I don't know. Why don't you tell your father you want—" I stopped myself. That was an extraordinarily bad idea. He might throw a fit at her. He might cut me off again, claiming (correctly) that I was trying to wedge myself between them.

"I'll ask him," she said firmly.

"No. I'll ask him. Don't you. It's not right."

"You know what you should tell Daddy? You should tell him you don't need to stay at work so late. He thinks you have to stay at work until six."

"Oh, no, if I take you to school then I get in earlier, so I can leave earlier."

"He doesn't know," she assured me. She was laboring hard to make everything right. Removing blame from him. From me. And her friends?

"I'm glad you asked me. But why do you prefer that I pick you up?"

"Nothing. I just like it better." She swallowed the last bit of pleasure and skipped ahead. "I want to swing," she called back, running toward the playground.

She would try to remake the world so that no one was at fault. Where would she store all that blame? On whom would she be willing to put it?

Ben answered the door with a smile. "Good timing. Guess who's on the phone? It's Holly," he said, almost as if he had won a private bet.

Naomi broke from me and raced to the phone.

"I want to go back to taking Naomi to school," I whispered.

"No. I feel better—I have a right to take her," he insisted, wagging his long finger with pompous self-righteousness, and not bothering to keep his voice low.

"She asked me."

"She's flattering you. That's something Wendy taught her. It's why she's so fucking popular—she lets everybody walk over her so they'll like her. She's terrified of not being loved."

So he had bronzed his new philosophy, his rewrite of our culture. Like every prophet, he would make his disciple a victim of his narcissistic martyrdom: Naomi was to be stripped of her friends; she was to be taught that to be alone is to be independent.

Naomi returned, saying, "Holly's coming to my party!" She grabbed her father's thick right hand and dragged him. "Come see what we did in the kitchen!" She towed him off.

Dismayed by my failure I opened the front door, prepared to slink off. "Hey!" Ben came out to find me. "Hey, that's great what you—what you and Naomi did. It was always such a mess."

"Yeah," Naomi spoke carelessly. "Mommy just shoved stuff in there."

It was obscene to me: Naomi criticizing her dead mother. "Don't say that," I ordered her.

She was shamed by my criticism. Her hand rose to cover her mouth. Ben spoke. "Perfectly true. Wendy never knew where anything was."

"That's not true," I said, and it wasn't. Wendy's desk at work, the few times I had visited her, was always clear. People who had dealings with her often spoke of how prompt she was. She always got Naomi to school on time, cared for her meticulously, and yet held down a demanding administrative job. From my experience of recent weeks, I knew how much time that took. Only childless, cold, compulsive women like me have the spare hour or surplus energy to put their groceries away by food group.

"Okay," Ben said, but there was no real agreement in his tone. "Listen, before you go, I wanted to ask you—I thought Naomi and I should get away from the city for Christmas. Wish we could go somewhere warm—"

"Why can't we?" Naomi interrupted.

Ben put his arm around her head and nudged: "Remember?"

Her face, already serious from my rebuke, clouded. Most of the time she doesn't think of Ben's fate, I realized. She forgets her situation. I felt my eyes swell. Again, I turned to go, to hide my sadness for her.

"Molly." Ben caught me with his voice.

"Yes . . . ?"

"I was thinking of going to the Catskills. Maybe Nommy could learn how to ski."

"Don't want to," she muttered.

"Probably too late to make reservations," I said.

"I thought I'd give it a shot. What I want to know is, should I get two rooms and you'll come with us?"

"Great!" Naomi cheered.

I stared my fury at him. Naomi grabbed my left arm and jumped happily. "Say yes!" she chanted. "Say yes!" Her shame and sadness were erased, like her Etch A Sketch toy: one shake and your drawing is gone. The bright blue eyes beamed at me: her hair fell under my hand, soft and innocent.

"It'll be okay," Ben soothed me. "I'll behave," he mumbled.

I nodded my compliance. Naomi spun around in celebration. I continued to burn my anger at him, but he behaved as if he had done nothing, won nothing. He scratched his forehead. "I'll try the Nevele," he said. "You don't know anybody who's got influence there?"

"I don't even know what it is."

"Really? I thought you knew everything." He smirked as if that had been truly witty of him. "It's a resort."

"I can't help you get in. If that's why—"

"Come on! Cut it out! That's not why." He offered his hand. "Thanks for saying yes."

Naomi was back to leaning against me, peering up with love. "I can show you how I swim across the whole pool by myself."

I rejected Ben's hand. "That's great, honey," I told Naomi, and kissed the end of her long nose. "I had fun. Thank you for keeping me company today."

She hugged me hard for an answer. I squeezed back. My congested heart cleared when pressed against her. I glanced up at Ben, to shoot him another look of disdain while Naomi couldn't see.

Ben was teary. He had taken off his glasses and he wiped away at both eyes. He wasn't faking. "Thanks, Molly," he said.

"You're welcome," came out of me, quite naturally and quite fast, before I could think better of it.

❧

The lieutenant called the apartment, very late a few days later, only hours after I learned from Ben that he had booked us into the Nevele, a Catskills' resort, for Christmas. I didn't recognize the detective's sluggish voice. He had to introduce himself. I was wary of him. "How can I help you?" I asked in an uncooperative tone.

"Just wondering how things are going with the little girl. You still helping out with her?"

"She's fine."

"You notice anything could be useful for the case?"

"Mmmmm," I mumbled, wanting to be noncommittal. "How is the case going?"

"Well, we're done, really. It's solid, I guess. But you can never have too much of a good thing. You still want to see him convicted, right?"

I wondered if somehow the lieutenant knew I was going away with them. Perhaps Ben's phone was tapped. "My concern is Naomi. That's all. There are plenty of people concentrating on everything else."

"I understand. I'm with you. There's nothing can be done to change your friend's murder. Just punishment. But the little girl— there's something to preserve and protect. Anyways, I was just making sure you're okay. Remember, I'm here if you do nose into anything."

I roused myself to put feeling in this: "Thanks, Lieutenant."

"Okay, then—oh, and I'm sorry nothing could be done about him getting the, you know . . . disposing of the body."

"What are you talking about!" I had understood from Stoppard that Wendy would be kept in the coroner's office until all the medical evidence was gathered. He had promised that he would keep me informed of any change.

"Didn't Mr. Stoppard tell you? Fliess got a court order for the release of her body. He cremated it last Sunday."

While I spent the day with Naomi, Ben had sneaked off and had

Wendy disintegrated. Destroyed the evidence. Not of how she died, of the fact that she had lived.

I hung up on the lieutenant without a good-bye. He was still talking. The phone rang moments later, but I was too crazy and hopeless to answer. I pulled the bed apart, ripping the sheets in my hands—tearing the fabric helped. The mattress wobbled underneath me, a rocky sea, until it slid off the box spring and dropped me onto the floor. Eventually I exhausted my frustration, sprawled there, crying, I guess. I don't really remember.

I had wanted to bury her beside her parents. I know a corpse isn't the person, but Wendy's life ended without warning, without reality: we were interrupted in the middle of a great lifelong heart-to-heart talk and part of me kept expecting to resume our conversation. I needed to see the vacated life—the empty shell—to know in a primitive way that she was lost forever.

At the office I confronted Stoppard and demanded to know why he hadn't informed me. He covered his embarrassment with impatience. Told me he couldn't stop Ben from getting the body and he didn't wish to upset me about something that was beyond my control. I pointed out that this way of finding out hadn't exactly kept me calm.

"I don't know why the fuck"—he named the lieutenant—"is calling you." That Stoppard used an obscenity was atypical. "He's being a smart-ass cop. I don't like what's going on. I think it's inappropriate for him to be giving you information—"

"He didn't tell me anything that was confidential."

"All of this can be made to sound very bad. You know, it doesn't take much to make it seem like you're deeply involved in some extralegal way. I'm calling him." He stormed off.

My lunch with Joan was that day. I looked forward to it, hoping for comfort and relief. We got together in midtown. She had asked if we could meet at my apartment; she wanted to get a look at the building where Ben lived. I said no. I was very concerned that we avoid any place Ben might see us together.

"You think he would be angry that we know each other?" she mused aloud as we settled down at our table.

"Of course," I answered, amazed she didn't know that.

Wishing to appear less self-obsessed than I really was, I asked about her writing workshop. I had assumed that she was trying out a hobby, or a fantasy, but it turned out Joan was the teacher. She had been a free-lance journalist for a long time, placing her articles in various magazines that I don't read—*Good Housekeeping, Cosmopolitan,* and so on—all famous and respectable. She dismissed this as "working for the rent"; however, she was proud of the book she had written. She described it as a kind of memoir, about researching the real details of her distant ancestor's life, the one who had qualified Joan's mother to be a DAR: *Daughter of the American Revolution.* I remembered the title vaguely. It hadn't been a best-seller, she told me, but it had sold out the first edition and gotten good reviews.

After we ordered, I asked her if she planned to write about Ben and the murder.

"I'm glad you asked, because I wanted to get that straight right away, in case you were wondering. I'm not going to be doing any more nonfiction, except for the occasional feature to tide me over. I've been working on a novel for about two years. That's what I'm concentrating on right now. Someday I'll probably use my marriage to Ben in a novel, but it would be, you know, very disguised and not real and it wouldn't have anything to do with this. Anyway, I would never use anything you tell me."

Frankly, I didn't trust this speech. There were too many words, too many vague phrases that could be referred to later as having implied something other than what was really said.

"You're upset," she commented about my silence.

"No." I wasn't. I considered: What was I going to tell her? Nothing. And what if she did write about me? I could sue if it was false—I'm not a public figure, I'm not on trial.

"I'm sorry, I probably shouldn't even have said what I did. I just wanted to be honest about it. I could have said I have no intention of writing about this, but I thought I should be totally open and admit that I might write about Ben—he was my first marriage. He was my first love. What I may use in a novel about Ben has nothing to do with you. Anyway, I have that material already."

"You seem very defensive." This was Stefan's favorite response whenever somebody was trying hard to get his agreement. He had even used it on the man who sold us our Volvo. I thought the

salesman had answered wittily: "Don't let my boss hear you say that
or I'll be out on my ass."

"I am defensive," Joan admitted. "I worry about people being
offended by my work, even if there's nothing that could possibly
bother them. It's a weakness, really. Writers are supposed to be
ruthless. I can't. I think of other people's feelings. What's going on
now belongs to you and to Naomi. I would never steal that."

Joan seemed diminished by the city setting. She had dressed up
for the occasion in a blue-and-white polka-dot dress that made her
look fat, old, and out of fashion, although she had tried to modernize
the dress with shoulder pads. Unfortunately, one of them had slid
forward and she was lopsided and fidgety, wanting to adjust herself,
yet not facing up to that fact and getting the job done. She poked
the loose pad back up; but the descent inevitably resumed as soon
as she moved her arm.

I leaned forward, took a nip of the fabric at her shoulder point,
and raised it. "Get it under the bra strap," I said.

Quickly, ashamed, she reached under the small tent I had made
of her dress and got the pad properly battened down. She blushed,
embarrassed.

"Sorry," I said. "Your fussing with it made me nervous."

"Everybody's wearing them," she apologized.

"Of course." I tapped mine. For a moment I felt we were playing
Simon Says. My head was tired, depressed by this version of Joan,
seemingly very different from the women I had met on the Island.
I didn't pay strict attention while she nervously elaborated about not
writing a book, admitting that there had been offers from magazines
for her to write about Ben. Her agent had said he could get a lot of
money for a book.

"What sort of book? What kind of book could you write about it?"

"Cover the trial and tell the story of the marriage. You know, sort
of alternate between the past and the present."

"Sounds like you've thought about it a lot." I had drunk the whole
glass of white wine I ordered when we sat down. It had a metallic
aftertaste that overwhelmed my half-eaten lunch of grilled sword-
fish. I felt queasy, almost nauseated. Joan's worried plump face, her
ungainly dress, the restaurant, all this irrelevant talk about books she
didn't plan to write made me feel sad and lonely and ill.

"Well, I may fictionalize it someday into that, you know, but it would not be about you and Naomi or him—"

"I don't want to talk about this anymore. I really need to know about Ben, more about his gambling—" I abruptly burped. "I'm sorry," I said, and hiccuped in the middle of the apology. The last syllable skipped up the scale. Made me sound like a honking goose.

"Okay." She nodded sympathetically. When she wanted them to, all her features could completely focus on one emotion: mouth turned down in a worried pout, eyebrows collapsed together, cheeks puckered with concern. "Where should I start? What do you need—?"

"How was he in bed?" I snapped rapidly, hoping to outtalk the next hiccup. I failed: I squealed like a pig on the word *bed*.

"What?" She laughed, surprised.

"I don't understand his dressing up." My voice sounded irritated to my ear, harassed by my loss of muscular control. "I'm worried about Nao—" and the last part was beeped, censored by my spastic stomach.

"No!" At last Joan was herself again, or at least the woman I had met on Long Island. She relaxed her rigid Sunday school posture, she forgot about her shoulder pads, she stopped eating daintily. "He's not a child molester!"

"No?"

"You think he is?

"I don't know! I'm asking!" I spoke in a hush, but in a furious hush, frustrated by the hiccuping which made me skip in the middle of talking.

"Take a drink of water."

"That doesn't wor—" and the needle skipped again.

"Boo!" she said, very mildly, with a sweet smile.

I laughed hard, all of me, quaking down to my toes. I laughed so hard my feet began to itch; I kicked off my shoes and rubbed them together. The sight of Joan's round gentle face, mildly saying, "Boo!" was hilariously contradictory.

It did get rid of the hiccups, after all, and my queasy stomach too, as a bonus. The laughter helped relax Joan as well. She emptied her glass of wine, pushed her hair off her forehead, flushed from laughing and the drink, and exhaled an elaborated, relieved sigh. "Oh,

God . . . I don't know why I talked all that bullshit about the writing. It's just greed. I could make money doing it and my boys are heading into college—"

"What does your husband do?" I interrupted.

"I'm divorced from my husband. I'm not married to the man I'm seeing. And I'm not sure we're together anymore."

She told me about her current lover. I told her about Stefan. Again I had talked about my life instead of learning what I could about Ben. We reached the end of the meal and I still hadn't gotten to it. I urged her to walk me back to my office. New York was cardboard gray, hopelessly sunless, the air wet and cold, like a rebuke, smacking your cheeks with hostility. In spite of the damp, I kept us circling the block around my office building while she told me, to my surprise, that Ben was an extremely attentive lover for the first years of their relationship. After the actual marriage, he withdrew, became hostile, seemed to lose interest; yet Ben complained that Joan was at fault and had continually rejected him sexually. "We always seemed out of synch," was her final judgment. She winced at the wintry wind. "When I was sexy, he wanted to gamble. When he—I always got the feeling he wanted to fuck me, you know? Not make love. He would come home from losing and I was supposed to be his consolation prize. It's the old story—sex was sex to him. I wanted to make love when we were intimate, the dessert course. He just wanted it whenever he felt lousy: just the pure pleasure, that's all."

"Like an animal."

"No," she argued. "Like a male animal."

I nodded. We had reached the entrance to my building yet again. I peered off down the long avenue and tried to calculate whether any of this information was helpful.

So was Joan evidently: "Does that sound like a child molester?"

"I don't know—no. But he wants women to be passive, do as they're told."

"I don't know, maybe this'll offend you, but . . . I think he's fragile."

"No, he's not. He's as stubborn—"

"Oh he's stubborn too"—she took hold of my sleeve and tugged, urgent that I understand her meaning—"but underneath all the selfishness, he's a baby, you know? Not a teenager like most men.

Most of them are still in high school. I mean he's a child. Wants to be babied, reassured, pampered. Did you ever meet his mother? Oh, no, you couldn't have. She died while we were married. Well, I looked forward to seeing them together. You know, I had read *Portnoy's Complaint* and I had a very specific idea of what a Jewish mother was supposed to be like—"

"And she didn't fit the bill," I said, irritated at the line she was taking. An inattentive mother doesn't make a man a killer.

"She did and she didn't. She was suffocating, but she was indifferent too. He had to perform for her to get her attention: he had to be topping somebody else. She'd tell him what great successes or failures all the sons of her friends were, like she was rating him."

"That's true of lots of mothers—"

"I know, but I had the feeling she never babied him the way Jewish mothers do—this sounds anti-Semitic. I just mean it wasn't that she didn't love him, but I got the feeling she wasn't sure she *wanted* to love him. That he was never, not even for a year or two, the adorable creature, the perfect little baby every mother loves."

Ugly from the beginning? Never loved? "You're making me feel sorry for him."

"Sorry for Ben?" We both smiled at the thought. "That's a mistake. That's what we always do. Make excuses for them. But I just don't think he'd molest . . . he loves his daughter, doesn't he?"

"They tell themselves they're loving them when they do it."

"Did it happen to you?" she asked. "Did your father bother you?"

I have no idea why she thought he might have. Oddly, I had to consider for a moment, as though incest was something that might have occurred without my knowledge. No, Daddy had never touched me. Except to hit.

"No," I told her, and said I had to go. We promised to talk often, and meet from time to time. I liked her on the whole.

Later that day I realized her escape had been narrower than she thought. She'd dropped Ben for another lover who was available because . . . well, Joan must have been very attractive when young. Would she have had the will to leave Ben without someone to escape to? We all have trouble (especially after years of struggle against it) admitting that in this society cosmetics, not biology, is destiny.

❧

On my way home that evening I passed the homeless man Wendy and I kept track of, the one who slept on the protected church stairs opposite our building. He was out at the corner to greet the rush-hour pedestrians, begging.

I had a load of groceries in each hand and couldn't easily reach for change.

"What can we do for him?" I once challenged Wendy while she was in a guilt fit about him.

"Give him money!" she snorted.

"If he's an alcoholic it would kill him. Might kill him even if he isn't."

Wendy stared down at him, huddled in his enclave. She squinted through the French doors of our dining room for a long time, thoughtful, while I read Naomi *The Grinch Who Stole Christmas.* Stefan was in a session. Ben was late getting home.

"We could give him food!" Wendy announced proudly.

I mocked her idea, embarrassing her charity with practical arguments: Where would he cook it? Where would he store it? How would he protect it from other, stronger homeless men? What would she buy him? and on and on until our husbands arrived and her notion was lost.

When I reached the homeless man on the corner that night, I handed him my two bags of groceries.

"Huh?" He took them awkwardly. He had to let them drop almost immediately, he was so weak. "You want me to carry them for you?"

"No. They're yours. They come from Wendy Sonnenfeld."

I rushed off before he could ask me more, before the few startled middle-class passersby could comment.

Later I watched him from the window, rooting through the bags. I couldn't bury Wendy. I had despised her memorial. What else could I do to honor her? It was the one tribute I was allowed to make to my best and only friend.

UNREMEMBERED SINS

I decided to say nothing to Ben about the cremation. As far as I knew he hadn't told Naomi. Anyway, I hoped not.

It snowed on the morning of Naomi's birthday. Not much, but enough to cover New York's dirty gray with a light frosting of confectioners' sugar, appropriate to our celebration. Anxious for everything to be right, I got us to the ice-skating rink an hour and a half early. They provided a small room in the back where we could serve cake. Two card tables, shoved together and covered with a bright yellow disposable plastic tablecloth, were already set up. Ben and I supplied the rest—cake, paper plates, cups, milk, and juice. The private room was painted green, the sort of washed-out color found only in institutions—is it surplus paint? Does anyone ever actually choose that shade? The windows were of the factory casement variety, double height, double width; they would have let in plenty of light except they faced another building's wall. The room seemed to me like a coffin. Having a birthday party at this rink had been recommended by several magazines, Naomi had enjoyed a party she attended there, and Janet (Holly's mother) had confirmed it was good. Certainly it was expensive enough. I decided the luxuries of New York child rearing were pretty dismal—a frozen pond and my mother's kitchen would have been better than this East Side palace.

I told Ben to set up the plates and cups and to put the candles in the cake in the back room while I went out to the rink to greet our guests by the entrance. He agreed to this division of duty. He did not seek a confrontation with the parents, as I had feared. Maybe a month of seeing them at school each morning and afternoon had sated his appetite for disapproval. Maybe this kind of drop-off was too personal, too intimate, even for him.

Naomi's four best friends were—remarkably—each accompanied by a pair of parents, mother and father, flanking them like armed guards. Their grim faces—probably concealing fear—eased, even cheered up, at the sight of me beside a bouncing Naomi. She brimmed with feeling that day, eyes glistening tearfully at the slightest provocation, regardless of whether it was a cause for happiness or sorrow. She hugged me and almost cried when she opened my present; she almost cried when I said she couldn't wear her formal dress to skate in; she almost cried when Ben said in the taxi, "You're the best girl in the world," apropos of nothing. All day, she hopped and squealed, too excited for her own peace of mind. It was as if the emotion no longer fit inside her—square-pegged happiness bouncing off the sad round hole of her loss.

With the arrival of her friends, her pleasure was intense and painful. I understood the phrase—she was jumping out of her skin—for the first time. I wasn't a model of relaxation, either, greeting the parents and Naomi's little guests with so wide and fixed a smile that I got an instant headache.

"He didn't come?" Janet whispered while the girls mobbed Naomi, a couple literally clinging to her clothes.

"Ben's here," I answered. Comically, all of the parents leaned in to eavesdrop on my answer. I disliked them intensely for their alloy of skittishness and curiosity about Ben, although it was commonplace, understandable, and utterly human. On principle I wanted to reassure them—yet my heart wished them to remain uneasy.

"Should I stay?" Janet asked.

"There's nothing to worry about."

"Okay . . ."

"Let's rent skates," I announced to the girls. "See you at twelve," I told the doubtful parents, and turned my back on them to lead the girls off to the rental counter.

Getting everyone set and on the ice, helping the two who had little experience (and less natural talent) was exhausting. But the girls, skilled or not, soon found a rhythm, and enjoyed themselves. The parents were gone when I got off the ice; Ben had stayed in hiding. I was about to ask one of the attendants to watch the girls for a minute while I checked on Ben when a handsome man appeared with another of Naomi's classmates. "Hello, I hope we're not too late," his voice boomed theatrically.

Naomi saw the extra guest and immediately glided over; she moved with natural grace, no hint of Ben's lumbering or Wendy's waddle. "Gina!" she called out. "I thought you couldn't come."

"My daddy brought me," Gina said, and they both giggled hilariously.

"Hmmm." The handsome father winked at me. "I think I've been had. I'm Tony Winters." He presented his hand with a slight incline of his head, almost an old-fashioned bow. "I didn't check with my—" He hesitated. "I hope we're not crashing." I took his hand—it was cool and firm. His brown eyes looked at me with an open and lively seductiveness; the gaze was not only greedy, but conscienceless, untroubled by its own lust.

"I'm Molly. Your wife left a message saying Gina couldn't make it."

"Well, it's Gina's day with me." He whispered, "We're separated. My wife probably thinks I ought to spend the day with Gina exclusively."

"Daddy! I need skates." Gina made her request in a nasal whine, quite different from her father's deep melodic voice.

"I'll get them for her," I volunteered.

While I helped Gina get into the skates, I said casually: "Played a trick on your dad?"

"I wanted to come." She folded her arms and set her chin defiantly.

"Good for you," I said, and patted her head; like Naomi's, it was a silky top, smooth and healthful.

My back was to the rink while I fitted her. When I stood up and turned around I got a shock. Ben had come out from the back room. He and Tony Winters were together, having an animated conversation. They watched the girls, commenting and smiling, apparently friendly. I knew a few things about Tony Winters—he was sort of the class parent celebrity. His mother was the famous television actress, he had a comedy running on Broadway, and he wrote movies. Wendy often spoke of him, his wife, and their very expensively furnished town house. She disapproved of their parenting (she disapproved in one way or another of everyone's parenting—and she was right), especially his. According to Wendy, Tony was away from home a lot, supposedly researching movies or seeking isolation to write; she predicted their marriage would end eventually. I hadn't heard anything about a separation, but I had never been that interested in Wendy's school gossip and she might not have bothered to tell me. Or perhaps it was recent. Tony's handsome eyes had unsettled me. I was single again, and if he was really separated, why not flirt? Especially with someone so self-confident: he was completely at ease with Ben.

"I always lose money in the market," Tony was saying to Ben when I reached them. "I even lost money because of when I signed the separation agreement. I signed four days before the crash and I had agreed to pay her half of the stock value on the day of—"

"Wow. You got screwed," Ben said, and laughed with delight.

Tony noted that bit of sadism with a glance—very fast, eyes flashing bright for a moment, and then returned to the duller, somewhat vacant, but still playful look he wore when he shook my hand. It was as if a video camera had turned on, taken some film, and then shut off. "Yes sir. That's the word for it. So what do you think? Is it temporary? Should I wait it out?"

Ben spoke in a rush, unleashed, pleased to be restored to his old stature as market analyst: "Oh no. Get out. It was the first gong. A little warning. Black Monday'll be forgotten soon. Six months, a year. Then wham!" Ben slapped his two hands together. "I think it'll start in Japan next time: kind of a reverse of the twenty-nine world collapse with Japan substituted for Europe."

Tony nodded at Ben's speech, but his mouth was in a puzzled frown. He caught my eye and smiled again, eyes gleaming. "I have no idea what he means," he said to me in a mock-conspiratorial manner, "and I don't want to know. But I'm calling my broker Monday and selling."

Ben didn't like this cleverness. "If you're smart you *will* follow my advice," he grumbled.

Tony straightened defensively. He was tall (Ben's height) but thin, and his gray-black hair was full and long. He brushed it back with one hand; his face smoothed out, pleasant smile evaporating into impassiveness. "I will," he said curtly. I thought him even handsomer like that, offended, embarrassed, and slightly pissed off.

"Ben," I suggested in my cheeriest tone, "weren't you going to do some taping of the girls?"

Ben gestured helplessly to the ceiling with both hands: "Excuse me for relaxing! I'm sorry I had the nerve to enjoy myself for a second." His sarcasm thudded in the rink, amplified by its echoing acoustics.

I glanced at Tony. He looked down at the floor, embarrassed to be caught feeling sorry for me. For a moment I experienced shame, the kind Wendy must have often suffered, until I remembered that I was not Ben's wife and his disrespect was no comment on my life. "You said you wanted tape of them skating." I tried to be casual, but a wife's resentful hurt crept in. "That's all I meant. They'll be done soon."

"Would you like me to do it? What kind of camera do you have?" Tony addressed this to both of us.

"I'll do it," Ben grumbled, and shuffled off.

Tony watched him go (again the light turned on, recorded, and went out), then glanced at the girls. He smiled thinly: "I wish I were young," he said with a wistful pleasure that was almost sinful. "I hope it's okay I'm staying. Since I should be with Gina, I feel better hanging around." He looked at me; again my body tingled with girlish excitement. "Is it okay?" he asked.

I didn't want to chase him away, but fair is fair. I said, "You don't know what's going on, do you?"

He blinked. "I never do." He smiled when I laughed. "Your husband is cranky. Has that got something to do with it?"

"He's not my husband. But his crankiness has something to do with it. Have you been out of town?"

"Yeah. I was working—if you want to call it that—in LA."

I chuckled. "You and your wife are *really* not talking."

He enjoyed this. "You're right. Have I done something fabulously embarrassing?"

Ben was returning, so I mumbled, "You should give your wife a call." Ben arrived, carrying the video camera sluggishly. He seemed especially drab compared to Tony Winters: his skin was white and puffy, Tony's tanned and taut; his clothes sagging, limp with the depression of their owner, Tony's alive with success and animation.

Of course, the differences were superficial—Tony had been sunning in LA, bought expensive clothes, and wasn't indicted for murder—but little things mean a lot. I signaled with my eyes toward Ben, and then shook my head slightly to indicate I couldn't answer freely.

"Get them in a line or something," Ben complained of the scene provided him. "This is boring."

Tony mumbled, "As bad as Hollywood," stepped up to the rail, clapped his hands to get their attention, and called out: "Everybody hold hands and go in a circle for the camera!"

That didn't work—but it did. In the attempt, one girl slipped and all the dominoes collapsed, laughing, unable to get up easily, grabbing at each other, falling down again, giggling the trill of girls, excited, red-faced, and happy. It was a party. Tony was great with them, urging their silliness on, yet controlling it enough for the activity to be useful to Ben's taping and to their own merriment. He even orchestrated a finish; he sobered them with a sharp word, got them on their feet, and, for one decorous moment, they held their balance and skated in a graceful circle—solemn and beautiful little girls sworn to eternal friendship and loyalty.

"Got it!" Ben said. Even he was flushed with pleasure. "That was great!"

I went over to Tony and squeezed his wrist. "Thank you," I whispered. I looked my interest into his eyes.

Although he was uncertain and nervous now, he made the effort to play back the flirting; his language was certainly right: "My pleasure. I love having six pretty girls to direct."

Ben butted my back with the camera, not hard, but unpleasantly, and, I was convinced, intentionally. I groaned, turned, and slapped at the lens.

"Sorry." He backed away. "Accident."

"That hurt," I said. Again I felt ashamed that this was happening in front of Tony. But that was absurd.

"Come on," Ben said, keeping his distance. "We'd better serve the cake."

Things were pretty miserable in that drab green room, as I had feared. "Happy Birthday to You" clattered on the bare walls; the icing washed out under the fluorescent fixture. There was little or no happy babbling later, either, while the girls sat on the folding chairs, dangled their legs, and ate their cake monotonously, as if they were having lunch in a school cafeteria. Tony Winters was gone during all that, presumably phoning his estranged wife. When he returned I knew he had been briefed about his host and stock market advisor, Ben Fliess. His walk announced the change. Tony entered in a soldier's march, back rigid, legs stiff, moving with courage not desire; and though he smiled, his lips remained closed, the teeth reluctant to join in and show themselves.

"I've been bad. I'd better get Gina and spend some one-on-one quality time with her."

Was he flip to conceal real sentiment, or was he flip to conceal real irreverence? I didn't care; I enjoyed his humor. He was sexy and somehow (unlike me and Stefan and everybody) still young. Nevertheless, he was obviously appalled, and probably would have nothing to do with my situation. He moved past me before I could answer, determined to get out quickly. His daughter met him halfway, making some demand as he neared, I couldn't hear what. Tony frowned and shook his head.

Meanwhile Naomi bounced over to me: "Can she, Molly! Can she, Molly! Can Gina and I go to my house and play?" Behind her Tony bent down to keep his voice low while arguing with his daughter.

"We could take them to a movie or something," I said in his direction.

"That's great! We're going to the movies." Naomi closed the deal.

"No, I'm sorry—" He tried to refuse.

Gina interrupted with a painful whine, a police siren revving up: "Why! Why not!"

"Gina. We can't. I've made other plans—"

"Hello." Janet had appeared at the door to the private room. Behind her, a husband skulked. "Come on, Holly." She motioned from the doorway, reluctant to enter the room. "We've got to go to Grandma's."

"I want to skate more!" Holly insisted.

"Me too," said another.

"Could I skate some more?" Naomi asked instantly.

Another pair of parents arrived at this moment and their daughter hurled herself at them, her greeting an argument: "I want to skate! Everybody else is going to!"

Throughout Ben dumped the plastic plates smeared with frosting into a Hefty bag, an occasional fork skiing off and missing, causing him to duck and hunt on the linoleum floor. Normally this would have kept him unobtrusive, but all the adults watched him warily while they lied and insisted and explained to their daughters that they had to leave right now.

In all the confusion I sidled up to Tony. He was bent over, whispering bribes into Gina's ear: "We'll buy a toy, we'll rent your favorite movies, and we'll have *two* bowls of ice cream—"

"Okay, I'll go," I answered.

He had such a good sense of humor, he laughed, turned his head to me, and smiled. "My wife was ready to kill me before this. Now she's actually hiring a hit man."

"I can get rid of him for the day and we can keep the girls together. I promise."

Both Gina and Naomi eavesdropped openly, solemn and interested. What did they understand of all this? "I can't," he pleaded. "Divorces—" He glanced at his daughter. Poor man, when he looked at the victim of his failure, the clever light in his eyes went out and there was unsophisticated pain. "I don't know how it might be used."

"I understand. Another time." I touched Naomi's head.

"No!" came out of her. Her little fists clenched, her mouth set in a pout, and she ducked away from my consolation.

I had prepared myself for Tony's rejection. I put a business card, on which I had scrawled my home number, into his coat pocket. "I'm also separated," I said as he watched me do this.

He nodded, but it was a polite reflex. "We have to go, Gina." He spoke sadly now, without tension. "No more arguing."

"Okay," she conceded.

I reached for Naomi and pulled her to me.

"I hate my birthday!" she said into my stomach.

There had been a pause in the noise as she spoke; everyone appeared to have heard. Parents and children watched us limply, arms sagging, mouths drooping, pictures of helplessness. But I thought, they weren't helpless. I'm sorry: I believe her unhappiness that day was their fault.

"That's done!" Ben called out cheerfully. Busy with the cleaning, he was the only one who hadn't heard Naomi's despair. He twirled the bulging green Hefty bag in the air to make a closure at the neck. With a squeal of plastic friction he tied the loose ends into a knot and showed off the result, a look of self-satisfaction in his bland expression.

"Let's get out of here!" one of the fathers said vehemently, and dragged his daughter out, almost doing violence to her. They all looked horrified. It was a half hour later when I realized why: I had forgotten, but they had not, the other use Ben had once made of a Hefty bag.

❧

Ben and Naomi were both unhappy afterward, utterly silent during the rough no-shocks cab ride home. With a half-eaten cake bouncing on my lap, I talked across their grim profiles. My voice screeched with false cheer. They seemed angry with each other. Every time Ben agreed with one of my suggestions—"Let's go down to Chinatown for dinner"—Naomi said an outraged no to him, as if he were the instigator. "Fine. Then we'll sit home and do nothing," Ben replied.

At the apartment I suggested we watch the videotape Ben had made, hoping to show them their misery was unjustified—the party had been a success.

"I don't wanna." Naomi sulked. "I want my presents!" she demanded.

"Here." Ben held the shopping bag full of her friend's gifts at arm's length, as if it oozed greasy leftover food. She carried them off to her room.

Ben groaned and lay down on the couch. He put his dirty shoes on the armrest. I stared at them, hoping that would alert him to his sloppiness. No result.

"Well . . . ?" I said, grinning like a fool.

"What?"

"The tape. Aren't you going to put it on?"

Ben blinked. A smile quivered on his lips. "No, I'm not."

"Okay," I said in my bouncy 1950s television Mom voice. I beamed with delight at him.

Ben sneered at me. "You liked him, didn't you?"

"Who?" My attempt at casualness was inept.

Ben snorted, laughed, groaned, then shut his eyes and sighed. Turning his body slightly, he nestled into the back of the couch. I waited. He made no move. "Are you taking a nap?"

"I'm tired," he mumbled. His shoes pressed against the fabric. A sliver of gray-black sludge dripped off one heel onto the cushion.

"Lie down in your room," I suggested softly.

He reared up to shout: "Who made you den mother? You're not happy with us—go home!"

"Take it easy. I know it was hard for you."

He paid no attention, he was having a fit: "When I ask you something, a simple question, why do you lie to me? It insults me. You know? Like I'm not worthy of knowing your feelings. But I'm supposed to tell you everything!"

"You don't tell me everything. Don't hand me that." I trembled, my outrage at the cremation, the rage I hoped to kill, coming alive.

Ben fell back onto the couch, defeated. "I don't like him. He was interested in you. I didn't like that." He rolled toward the back of the couch, hibernating again, and grumbled: "Okay? Now you know."

He was jealous? I wanted to laugh, but I was too scared to reject him. What was going on in his head—did he hate me or love me? Or was there any difference? I drifted into a trance, going over this point, standing there without really paying attention to anything. Eventually Ben opened his eyes, noticed I was stuck in place, and rolled onto his back, asking: "What?"

He startled me out of my reverie; I had nothing to say on waking. "I just don't understand," I said.

"I was jealous. What's to understand?" He watched me, decided his glasses were an obstruction, removed them (with a contemptuous toss they skidded on the coffee table), put both palms over his face, and rubbed hard. When he let them down, he had transformed himself. The shelled, embittered animal was red and soft, his eyes worried and naked. "Never occurred to you, huh? You think I'm a dead person? You start living here—practically living here—taking care of me and her, and I'm . . ." His lips trembled. He didn't finish, shutting his mouth, swallowing the emotion along with the words.

He was in love with me. Or at least that's what he was pretending. It was a very good performance, if it was fake. A liar would have announced his feelings: this choked-off confession seemed authentic. I didn't really think any of that at the time. I sagged into a chair, confounded.

"Well . . . anyway," he said, his tone very low. "I hope to be able to pay back the fifty thousand—"

"I don't want the fifty thousand back."

"I want to pay—"

"I won't accept it."

He raised his hands in surrender. We were silent for a while. He shifted his legs onto the floor (I was relieved those shoes were finally off the fabric) and collected his glasses from the table, replacing them. They sobered his appearance, protected and matured him. They made him ugly, too.

"Have you ever gotten contacts?" I asked. Absurd, I know, but that was all I could think of.

He shook his head. "Can't put glass in my eye."

"They're not made of glass."

"No kidding. Whatever they're made of, I don't want to be putting something on my eye. Wendy was always scratching her cornea and writhing in agony."

"You're exaggerating."

"No kidding," he said again, and smiled at me. "You've lost your sense of humor?"

"You should reconsider. Contacts might help."

"Help what?"

"At the trial." I wasn't trying to be elliptical: my advice came out slowly because I was reluctant to give him good council. The notion thrilled him. Abandoning his depression, Ben's mouth dropped open. He bounced off the sofa and dashed over to a small antique mirror hanging on the wall between the windows. Its thick glass and burnished oval wood frame converted any onlooker—even Ben—into a nineteenth-century portrait. Wendy had bought that mirror with me, on a Sunday stroll down to Hudson Street. She had to be talked into the purchase. At first, she turned away, complaining that Ben wasn't handy and it took months to get the super to do anything. Of course, I had helped make traps for my father; I had done plenty of carpentry, even at my fancy boarding school. I told her I could do the job and I teased her for her helplessness about anything mechanical. Daring me, she bought the mirror. We went straight home, got out my electric drill, and hung it. That accomplished, we did all the other posters, paintings, and photographs awaiting the super's pleasure. Ben and Stefan were impressed. Wendy put up the last two by herself. "We are women, hear us drill," she told the men.

In order to study himself without his glasses Ben had to put his face only inches from the mirror. After a few minutes of peering, Ben patted his scalp and smiled to me in the glass. "Why not get a toupee while I'm at it?"

Presumably he had wigs. This didn't seem like much of a joke to me. "That would send a different message. They'd spot it and know you were faking. Contacts aren't that noticeable."

Solemn again, he studied one profile, then the other, still squinting a bit, even though he was so close to his reflection. "I look that much better without them?"

"They can see your eyes better. Your face looks thinner."

He pulled the bottom lids of his eyes down. "My eyes are bloodshot," he mumbled.

"A beard would also help."

"Everybody who's lost their hair grows a beard!"

"Because it looks better. That's why. Soften you. Make you look gentler."

"My beard is reddish," he said. "I tried to grow one when I was just out of college. Came in kind of red."

"Well, that's great." Unbelievably, I felt enthusiastic. "You should definitely grow one, then."

"Really? Maybe it won't be red now."

"Why?"

"I'm older . . . I don't know."

He was like a child. "It might be a little gray, but if it was reddish then, it'll be reddish now."

"Okay," he said, turning to me, stroking his jaw and chin as if he could summon the hairs. "Could you do me a favor? Could you come with me to get the contacts?"

I don't know if the difference was his blindness (his eyebrows squashed together in a squint), but he appeared heartbreakingly worried and childlike. "Sure."

"Thanks," he said, and then chuckled helplessly, scanning the floor. "Where are my glasses?"

I pointed them out (he had put them on the windowsill) and said I thought I should check on Naomi. I wanted to escape from this intimacy with him.

"Leave her alone," he said, not an order. "She wants to be alone. Believe me, if she wanted one of us, she'd be out here." He gestured to a chair. "Sit," he said. "I'll put on the tape." Now he was happy, trotting merrily to where he had left the camera and portable recorder. "I'm gonna heat coffee," he called. "Want some?" I said yes and Ben had to ask me how I liked it. Perhaps I'm making too much of little things, but that seemed to me indicative of his self-involvement—he had known me for eight years, we had had countless meals together, and he didn't know I took it black?

They had no den, so the television and VCR were hidden in a cabinet opposite the couch. When Ben came back, tape under his arm, carrying two coffee cups, he recited his actions as he did each thing, like a NASA lift-off checklist: "Your coffee, my coffee, machine on, tape in, memory on, hit rewind, and go!"

The coffee wasn't hot enough; I wanted to encourage this feeble attempt at graciousness, so I didn't complain. Ben collapsed on the sofa and sipped his while we listened to the tape whirring backward. "Thanks for today," he said. "I couldn't have done it without you."

I nodded toward Naomi's quarters: "But was it worth it?"

"Oh yeah." The machine clicked, thudded, and stopped. "She had as good a time as she could possibly have."

Ben aimed the remote control and the video recorder started.

Wendy appeared on the screen. Behind her was the green lawn of their country house. She was wearing a swimming suit. It was summer. Her face was dotted with suntan lotion. She shouted at the camera: "Ben! For God's sake! Don't take me like this!" She raised a hand to rub in the yellowish white—

The tape went off. I had my eyes focused on the television. I didn't move. My cheeks were hot from shame.

"Sorry," he mumbled. The recorder whirred again. "I see what happened—I've got it now."

"Forget it," I told him, and got up and walked out.

❧

I didn't feel too bad when I reached my place. I didn't cry and I wasn't trembling. But I couldn't fool myself after the rebuke of seeing my dead friend come to life. She had sent a message: I was drifting into aiding Ben, not rescuing Naomi.

My apartment sounded empty: I wished Stefan was there. And I was glad he wasn't. In my kitchen the sink was dry, every cup and plate was put away, the counters stainless, spotless, and cleared.

I felt no one lived there.

So what? Let's mess it up, I decided, and I made myself a sandwich, leaving the cheese, meat, bread, mustard, head of lettuce, bottle of soda all out. I brewed coffee and didn't wipe up the trail of stray grounds spilled by the measuring.

In the middle of eating, the phone rang. It was Naomi.

"Hi . . ." Her voice trailed off.

"Hi honey," I said. "How were the presents? What did you get?"

She babbled about them, asked if I wanted to see the "radical" sweater Holly had given her.

"Sure," I said through a mouthful of messy sandwich. I had an impulse to turn the mustard jar upside down and spread the contents everywhere. "Come over."

"Okay—uh, wait a second. Dad!" she called. "Dad, she wants me to come over." Open like that, the bread would go stale. I twirled the bag closed, remembered the Hefty bag, and dropped the package angrily, blaming it for the memory.

Naomi was back in my ear: "Dad wants to know if you still feel like going to Chinatown."

"I'm eating." That was obvious but she was a child.

"Oh." Crushed. "She's already eaten," Naomi called.

"Forget about your father," I said. "Come over." I could do it, I thought. A year is not long to hide. After that he would be put away.

"What?" She was concentrating on him.

208

THE MURDERER NEXT DOOR

"Tell your father to rest. Come over, we'll go to a movie. Tell him we'll be back around bedtime."

"Dad—what . . . ? Wait," she said, and I heard her moving away from the phone. She must have put it down.

Come on, come on, let her go, I rooted in my head. Arbitrarily—like a godless savage—I was convinced that this choice was an omen and would determine everything.

"Molly?" Ben this time. "I'm sorry."

"I know. Listen, I thought I'd give you the after—" My voice quaked and I never pronounced the rest of the word. "Excuse me," I said about my choking.

"You'll never, ever forgive me." He snorted. "Well, that's dumb. Of course you won't. Okay, I'd really like to come along—"

"You take a nap," I said, idiotically.

"Yeah right. You win. I'll send her across."

"Listen, Ben, I'll bring her back around bedtime, okay? I thought maybe we'd go uptown and look at the Christmas decorations."

"So . . . I'll expect you about eight-thirty."

"Right." I was clumsy. "Maybe even nine. I'll call."

He was dull and suspected nothing.

I jumped for joy after I hung up. Like an athlete celebrating a championship—like someone in a beer commercial. I knew this was the answer, had been the answer all along. How could I have missed it?

There was little time before Naomi arrived to get the things I needed. I couldn't pack anything, of course, but I got the emergency cash (five thousand dollars) I had kept in the apartment since Stefan moved out, as well as my valuable jewels (probably trifling), and the gold coins Stefan had bought at one point when the world was supposed to come to an end and somehow we could endure the death of everything if we had a Krugerrand handy. I didn't know what the South African gilt was worth, or how to reliably and discreetly convert them to cash. I took all my credit cards, the checkbook, and a passbook for another certificate of deposit worth fifty thousand dollars. That left two more which (in consideration of equitable distribution) rightfully belonged to Stefan.

Whether I would be able to make use of the bank stuff was doubtful. The murderer, after all, would call the police by midnight. I couldn't take the chance of staying in the city and trying the bank in the morning. The credit cards would soon be useless. So would the checkbook. Unless Stefan helped. That was the hope I clung to.

Why not wait until the next day? you ask. Get my money, and then Naomi? I didn't trust the endurance of my nerves: a night of consideration and I might weaken.

Naomi wore the "radical" sweater. There were no political slogans: it had a glistening array of rhinestones sewn into leather patches on both shoulders. There was a Western flavor to the look.

Santa Fe, I thought. That's where we'll go. Out west where there's no law and plenty of space. Crazy, right? Although I laughed at myself (Naomi said, "Don't laugh," thinking I ridiculed her sweater) I liked the idea. Warm, inexpensive, and far away—the West was a good choice.

"Let's go to F. A. O. Schwarz and buy you another birthday gift."

She was staggered, her eyes wide. "Really?"

"Yeah, why not? You're seven. I should get you six more gifts. One for each year."

Naomi frowned at me, skeptical but compassionate. She tilted her head doubtfully: "You okay, Molly?"

On the elevator ride down, going out through our lobby (hailed with unusual enthusiasm by our sleepy-eyed weekend doorman, glad to see Naomi without you-know-who) and during our stroll to my garage, I babbled about buying her gifts and wanting to see all the Christmas windows on Fifth Avenue. When I turned into the parking lot, Naomi, not suspiciously, merely curious, questioned why we were taking the Volvo instead of a cab to midtown. "Where are you going to park?" she asked with the pragmatic precocity of a New York kid.

"In a parking lot."

She whistled. "The midtown lots cost a fortune!" she said vehemently, mimicking her mother.

"You know how much they cost?"

"No. But I know they cost a lot. That's why Mommy and I take the bus." She used the present tense unself-consciously. I waited for a realization of that, but none came.

In the car, Naomi dangled her legs, placed her right arm decorously on the rest (their design is perfect for a child's size), chin up, head scanning like a periscope on her long skinny neck. "The snow's all gone," she reported of the outer world.

That was a help. "I have a good idea! Why don't we drive out of the city and see if the snow stuck there?"

"Okay," she said, not enthusiastic.

I puzzled over her lack of excitement. "It'll be fun. We can make a snowman."

"Snow*woman*," she said, and smiled at me. "Remember?" she urged.

I didn't.

"Remember!" She hopped on the seat urgently. "Last winter. It was Mommy's idea. You and me and her, we made a snowwoman at my country house!"

"I've never been to your country house."

Naomi took this hard. Her bright face darkened, overcast by the cloud of mourning. "Mommy put an apron on it. Remember?"

"No, honey."

"Yes!" Tears filled her shining eyes and they were also dimmed. "Yes you wcrc! You showed me how to make snow bunnies!"

"That was in Central Park." She was so little then, her snow bunnies were truly bunny size. "You were four."

She sobbed.

"Honey!" I cried, and almost crashed us into a parked car in my hurry to pull over.

"You were there!" She heaved the accusation with the weeping.

"I remember!" Double-parked now, I reached for her. The seat belt pulled against my embrace—and so did she. "I remember everything I ever did with Mommy!" she yelled at me, furious and heartbroken. "I never forget!"

"Okay, honey."

"I'm right!" she screamed.

"Okay, you're right," I begged her.

"You don't mean it!"

"Yes, I do. You're right. I forgot. We built a snowwoman."

"It had an apron, remember?"

"Yes."

"And what else?" Naomi's face was ruined by tears and anger.

I didn't know what else. Hadn't Wendy told me about it? A feminist snowwoman, that had a familiar ring, suggesting to me that she had. I wouldn't have paid much attention, especially if she told me over the phone while I was at work. Sometimes (well, more than sometimes) I tuned out Wendy's reveries on the happy life of a mother and wife. Envy? Disbelief? Hostility? I don't care why. I just wished, during this painful moment in the car, that I could remember everything. "What else!" Naomi demanded, and banged her fists into the cream-colored leather seats.

"Lipstick . . . ?" I guessed hopelessly.

She laughed. Like a tropical storm breaking in midrain, the sun shone: "We didn't use lipstick." She giggled. "Don't you remember what it was?"

"No," I lied. "Just that it was very red."

"Not so red. Pink lemonade. We poured it into those lip things."

"And froze them in the freezer," I said, not knowing where this came from. Was Wendy with me, after all? Had she come to help me?

"Right. We put them on the next morning."

"I remember. And you ate them for dessert."

"I told you you were there!"

Thank you, Wendy. "Sorry." I hugged her, kissed her sweet cheek.

I got us moving again. Naomi returned to her periscope self, commenting on pedestrians. Stopped at a light on Park Avenue and Fiftieth, she asked: "Where are we going?" in a sharp tone of surprise.

For a nervous second I worried she had figured it out. I tried a bluff: "F. A. O. Schwarz."

"Oh, that's great! I thought you said we were going to the country to build a snowman."

"After F. A. O. Schwarz."

"Oh . . . great!" You would never have guessed she had been in pieces fifteen minutes before. That's the cruelest and strongest muscle people have—the forgetful heart—and I hate us for it, even if Naomi and I needed one desperately.

What an amazing place F. A. O. Schwarz is: a child's pyramid of Cheops, a death sentence for the adult will. I stood beneath the gay display of gigantic stuffed animals, listening to a Disney theme I faintly recognized playing through a fifteen-foot-high music box.

Faces passed me in a processional dance: frozen looks of happiness on the inanimate jungle; ironic dismay on the parents; children stunned, awed by the prospect of achieving perfect fulfillment. It's greed, I thought at first, that dazed look on the little faces. No, I decided while riding the escalator to the second floor, not greed—appetite. I was happy. I felt free. In that store everyone was naked.

I charged three hundred and forty-six dollars on my American Express card, buying Naomi's preoccupation and tranquility for the first hour of driving. While we left the city she disemboweled the plastic bubble packaging, and looked to be a very modern girl, surrounded by Barbie's hot new denim outfit and her black girlfriend. Later, Naomi groaned or cheered, chin tight, eyes fixed on a beeping hand-held video game, her task to save someone or something (not Fay Wray) from a gigantic ape.

I sealed our windows and ran the heater on low, almost off. Only a hum from the spinning wheels penetrated from outside and just a slight bump from the concrete's seams could be felt. Naomi read the Barbie comic which accompanied the toy. Her eyes lingered on the illustration. Barbie may be a hip girl now, but her body is still establishment perfect. No, not perfect—unattainable. Cosmetics will bury you, Raisa Gorbachev.

My fingers gripped the wheel tightly, elbows locked, arms rigid. I waited for Naomi to put down her toys and question my nonstop pace out of the city. About five, exhausted by celebration, sorrow, and cake, Naomi passed out, slumping forward into the sling of her seat belt. I relaxed and drove her away even faster, pitilessly, from her father.

❧

At night all highways look alike. I drove in a tunnel of light, flowing in a red river, passing a white one.

I heard her voice first, deep and calm and knowing: "Where are we going, Molly?"

I gasped. "You scared me." A glance at the passenger seat revealed her in the passing headlights as a cat—aloof, puffy cheeks ominously shut, eyes glowing. Her head had flopped back onto the seat a while ago; she rested it sideways on the leather, studying me with her profile.

She yawned. "Where are we?" she said, squinting at the glare and the dark.

"I don't know. I can't tell."

"It's night." She yawned again. "What time—?" She leaned forward to get a view of the dashboard clock. "Daddy expects me to be home," she commented on seeing the hour—7:00.

"I called and told him we'd be late," I lied.

"You stopped?"

I nodded. "Want something to eat?" I asked.

"Are we going home? Did we make a snowman?"

"Snow*woman,*" I joked.

"Okay," she grumbled, unaccountably irritated to be reminded of her own distinction. "Who cares whether it's a man or a woman? It's just snow."

"Sorry." I made allowances for her response. It was normal for her to wake up crabby from naps; probably she felt wrinkled from sleeping in a car, she didn't know where we were going, and her head no doubt throbbed, hung over from the birthday's excitement.

"We didn't make one, right?" she said, and yawned mightily. She collapsed against the seat after it was done, cat's eyes glowing at me.

"You were tired."

"No," she argued mildly, unable to lift her head.

"Want to eat?"

She groaned, still not ready for the things of the world. I touched her head. Her skin was baked and swollen. Did she have a fever? What if she became ill? I would have to take her to doctors, to a hospital, give her name, explain who I am. How long could we live on the money and coins I had taken? No trouble to get a job (as a legal secretary; as a waitress if everything else failed) but what about Social Security numbers and so on?

After another fifteen minutes awake, Naomi came to life. She resumed playing her video game, but was disgusted with it quickly (in the dark I didn't know how she could see anyhow), and equally revolted, after a minute, by the Barbie things. This time, when I asked if she was hungry, I got a vehement yes, followed by an irrational complaint: "I thought we were stopping an hour ago."

We were deep in Pennsylvania. I pulled into a combination Burger King and gas station, set by the turnpike's shoulder for the sole purpose of servicing the traveler. I hoped its anonymity would prevent her from being alerted to our distance from home, almost two hundred miles by now.

"Where are we?" she said the instant we got out of the car.

I looked around with her at the dark mass of trees behind the Burger King, then at the dreary highway, and up at the overcast night sky, black and gray, no stars decorating its gloom. "We're in the country," I said.

"Looks more like we're on a highway," she snorted.

"We're on a country highway."

"Let's go," she said. They had newspaper vending machines at the entrance. I took Naomi's hand and pulled her past them.

Burger King was a third full. Ahead of us in the line were a woman and two men, Boneless People, remarkably fat. Their arms bowed outward from bowling-pin hips, hanging lifelessly, too wide to be contained by the chains of the ordering line. Its chaffing contact with their forearms didn't trouble them; nor did the bemused looks they provoked. I was fascinated. The woman had no beauty, not even an exaggerated kind. Her face was squeezed together vertically, and expanded horizontally; consequently, her thick glasses were pushed forward, bobbing on the end of her nose, hopping to the tip, rescued at the last inch by a swollen finger and pushed back to the top of the slope to resume their descent. She had a bold manner with the two men, whacking them with her hand and wheezing laughter when she made a joke. Her two gross companions were her age, apparently not any relation.

Who were they? How did they survive in a world hostile to their species?

"Aren't they the fattest people you—" Naomi whispered this, but I was horrified they might hear.

"Shhh!" I overwhelmed her.

"I was talking in a whisper!" she protested loudly.

One of the fat men slowly turned his head to look at us.

I was mortified. "Just be quiet right now," I mumbled. The man studied us. He was the more attractive of the two, mostly because he seemed to be less than three hundred pounds—the others were well over that. He had a young pleasant face too, gentle brown eyes, puffy red cheeks, and a compassionate, regretful smile.

"Hi," Naomi said to him.

"Hello." He spoke in almost a female's high pitch. He smiled at her, then slowly swiveled his massive head back to his friends.

I was surprised that their order was modest, no extra fries, no second burgers; chocolate shakes, to be sure, but they didn't get to be whales eating those portions. We followed them to booths by the window. Although they managed to squeeze in, they really didn't fit; their behinds, housed in mutant blue jeans that appeared to be two sewn together, overflowed the sharp edges of Burger King's plastic molded seats. I thought: in Manhattan it's against the law for people that fat to be seen in public.

"Molly!" Naomi leaned across at me, speaking sharply. "We're in Pennsylvania!" She pointed to a large highway exit sign, visible from our scenic booth.

Hearing her, the slimmer of the fat men again looked at us with his pleasant but careful deliberation.

"Uh-huh," I said.

"Does Daddy know we drove that far?"

"Uh-huh. How's your burger?" I asked lamely.

"Isn't that very far from New York?"

She had completely captured the thinner fat man's attention. He ignored his friend's conversation, held his burger in midair, waiting to hear my answer. His eavesdropping was undisguised, almost demanding. "Don't worry." I couldn't think of anything better.

"We're going home, right?" Naomi was more than suspicious, she already seemed to be arguing against my plan. She pulled a leg under her, rising up in the booth, leaning toward me, intent and worried. "I have school tomorrow."

The man put his burger down. His smile was gone. His hairless mouth pursed, concerned.

"Let's eat now—"

"Just tell me what's going on!" Naomi demanded.

The fat woman whacked her pleasant companion and wheezed a joke at him. He shushed her, indicating with his eyes that he was interested in me and Naomi. There was no doubt about that. Was he a cop? Absurd. Why was he so nosy? He met my furtive glance with his friendly brown eyes, still amicable, but insistent.

I felt guilty. You're a kidnapper, I told myself, and my throat closed up.

Stupid for a lawyer, you're thinking, surely I must have realized what I risked. But I hadn't. Never occurred to me to judge myself as I would be judged by the law. I was a kidnapper and Naomi was my victim. I would be pursued by the FBI for having taken her across state lines . . . and I expected Stefan to help me?

"I want to go home," Naomi said. No panic, no plea: a fact.

The Boneless People definitely overheard that—at least the woman and the thinner man did, since they were the two who faced us. "Excuse me," the man called to me. He pretended innocent concern: "Are you lost? Can we help you with directions?"

I couldn't speak. I shook my head at him. My throat had closed—a lump of gray burger meat was stuck partway down. "Fine," I mumbled to Naomi. "We'll eat and go home." I sipped my soda and beamed at her; at him; even at the grotesque, unsmiling fat woman. But my brain revolted: Go back and face Ben?

Naomi skidded around on the plastic seat and addressed the Boneless People. I tried to interrupt her, but she spoke over me: "Which way back to New York City?"

"Route Eighty, honey," the fat woman said.

"Just turn around and go back the other way." The pleasant fat man daintily wiped off ketchup from a stuffed index finger and pointed out the window. "You can get off about a mile . . ." He looked a question at the fatter man.

"Mile and a half," his friend grumbled. His voice was low, bearish, especially compared to the thinner man's castrato timbre.

"Mile and a half," he sang to us happily. He whirled his frankfurter finger in a circle. "Just get off, swing round, and get back on the other way. What's your name, dear?"

"Naomi. What's yours?"

"She's cute," the fat woman said, commenting as if no one could hear her.

"I'm Larry. How old are you?"

"I'm seven years old today!" Naomi may have thought them the fattest people she had ever seen, but she wasn't repelled.

"Happy Birthday!" He patted his hands together like an infant; against his massive chest, although bursting out of their skin, they looked tiny.

"Birthday at Burger King?" the gruff man said. I couldn't see his face; his tone was disapproving.

"You seem so smart and grown-up for a seven-year-old," Larry said. He spoke in a slow lilt, head moving rhythmically from side to side, like a giant doll. He could be put on display at F. A. O. Schwarz, he was so massive and kindly.

"I'm from Manhattan," she said.

"Oh . . . ?" Larry nodded, but he was puzzled.

"City kids are precocious," Naomi elaborated, egoless, passing along routine information.

The fat lady wheezed and her glasses slid all the way to the end of her nose; Larry's small mouth opened into an O shape and his chest jiggled, but his laughter made no sound.

"I'm serious," Naomi said.

"Okay, honey." The lady wheezed.

"Can I buy you dessert?" Larry said. He looked at me innocently: "Is that all right? Is she done? Can she have dessert? A little birthday Burger King cherry pie?" He twisted his lips into a red splash of helplessness. "That's all there is."

"Piss poor," said the disgruntled one sharply. He turned in the booth, shaking the whole restaurant. His massive arm oozed onto the backrest of Naomi's chair. He made this maneuver to shoot me a fat-cheeked, small-eyed look of disdain. "What kind of a birthday dinner is this?"

"It's okay," Naomi told him.

"Aw . . . ," Larry said, his great head tilted sideways.

"She's cute," the fat lady said.

"This isn't her birthday dinner," I told them. "We had a party, a birthday lunch. We took her friends ice-skating, we had chocolate cake—"

"And I got six extra presents!" she told them.

"That's great, honey," droned the fat woman. Larry's pencil-thin eyebrows went way up and he nodded with slow, astonished appreciation. The gruff man glared at me, unimpressed.

He made me nervous. I kept talking: "I thought we'd go for a drive in the country and build a snowman."

"Snow*woman!*" Naomi said.

"Snowwoman!" the fat lady wheezed. She banged her plastic cup down in appreciation. "That's funny!"

"Here . . . ?" Larry said, pointing daintily down.

"She fell asleep in the car. I just kept driving."

"Did you build your snowman—I mean woman?" the big one asked.

"No . . ." Naomi spoke in a tone of wistful despair.

"Well there's snow out there. Let's do it!" Larry put his half a burger in his mouth and seemed to swallow it whole.

"Hey Larry!" the bigger male yelled.

"I forgot," Larry apologized through half-chewed food.

"He's not supposed to eat fast. That's what makes you fat," the fat lady said. "Not tasting your food."

"I thought eating too much makes you fat," Naomi said, not innocently. She smiled.

The fat lady didn't wheeze, she honked. Larry applauded, gulped down what was in his mouth, and shouted: "That's right!"

The gruff one patted her head. His hand was as large as her skull. "You know something?" he said to her sadly, pleading his case. "Even if I don't eat a lot I'm fat."

"How much do you weigh?" she asked.

"What do you think?"

Naomi shrugged. "I don't know. A lot. I don't know what's a lot."

"Good," he said. "I like that you don't know. Let's make a snow-woman." He stuck his legs out and skimmed out of the booth, like a kid going down a slide.

"That's neat," Naomi commented.

He offered his hand. She took it willingly, after a glance to make sure I came along. Forcing a grin I nodded, gathered the fast-food containers, and got up.

"I'm B.J.," he said to her, waiting for me. Larry and the fat lady manuevered themselves out of the booth less gracefully than their friend; they twisted from side to side, oozing forward gradually until they popped free, sighing with relief at the expanse of the open air.

"I'm Naomi Fliess," she told B.J. Wendy had taught her that she should say her full name, in case she ever got lost. Even at two and a half years old, when introduced to a grown-up, she answered in her babyish accent, mouth full of words, saying: "I'm Nommy Fliess," and then rattled off her address and phone number, sounding like a POW under interrogation. I did not introduce myself. I was very unhappy. Because of this contact, I doubted we could escape without being traced. They would certainly remember her.

"I'm Maggie, honey," the fat lady told her. We waddled with our trays, dumped the garbage, and went outside, walking past the parking lot to a cleared bit of land before the line of trees. There the snow was untouched.

Naomi hung on to her Beast all the way, a very proud Beauty; she stood by him while he gathered (with bare hands) armfuls of snow and started a base. Dainty Larry produced huge red mittens for his hands: big stiff flags flashing signals against the white earth.

Maggie mostly kibitzed, wheezing with laughter at any stumble or gracelessness of B.J.'s or Larry's. "Don't fall," she warned B.J. when he skidded to one knee. "Get covered with snow and they'll think you're the Michelin man. Put you out at the pumps and sell you at half price." She was very cruel about their weight; they said nothing about hers.

Larry quit long before B.J. He stood next to me and said, "She's great." He was short of breath.

"You're gonna die of a heart attack," Maggie said, and called out to B.J.: "Feel a stroke coming on, B.J.? You're turning red." He wasn't, actually. He seemed peaceful.

Larry whispered to me: "Everything okay? If you're in any trouble, we can help."

"We're fine. I just wanted to go for a drive."

"You know my father used to beat me up." The baggy outer moons of his cheeks were tinged bright red from the cold. He looked even more artificial that way, like a clown or a cartoon. "My mom was too scared to stop him. Maggie was abused too." He nodded in her direction. "Her mother used to beat her with an electric cord. She's got scars all over her back."

"Uh-huh," I said. How do you make conversation like this? Confess back? I'm Molly. My father is an alcoholic, he hit me all the time, he killed my mother, I'm sure he would have raped me if I'd stayed around, but I didn't and . . . what's the point? Sympathy? Everybody has troubles. The people who don't, like Stefan, invent some for themselves, and those fictions are just as real. Stefan himself told me this tenet of Freudianism: if the patient believes something happened, then it has to be treated as if it did. The heart can't be put on trial: facts are meaningless and no court has jurisdiction.

"There are places now you can go and they'll help," Larry insisted. "It's not like when we were kids."

"We're okay," I begged him.

"We belong to Overeaters Anonymous," Larry talked on cheerfully; like a public service ad on television, broadcast when time is cheap or worthless, pedaling agony instead of cars, relief instead of aspirin. "We came from a meeting."

"They let you eat at Burger King?"

"It's not a diet," he said, eager to disgorge himself of himself: "It's about sharing your feelings and experiences. It's a disease—"

"Life is a disease," I interrupted.

"What?"

"Life is a disease. A bug. A flu."

Maggie had overheard my last comment. She nodded at me and wheezed her laughing agreement. "That's right." She grinned, her face expanding sideways, a gargoyle. "We all got bad fevers."

Did her mother hit her because she was so ugly? Or did the hitting make her ugly? I know what you think—I'm heartless, I'm perverted. But chances are you've never had to deal with evil; never had to live with it, to love it, or to forgive it; never had to face the fact that to choose to be evil, just like choosing to be good, is a rare and difficult decision. But I shouldn't state that to you flat out. Saying that truth, even hearing it, is too hard a choice to make.

"B.J.'s father raped him," Larry said in a breezy tone.

B.J. made a massive middle for the snowwoman: his bare fingers were bright red from the cold. Naomi adored his effort. She told him: "You're great at this." He showed no pleasure at her praise, except to bend down and work even harder.

"Raped him more than once, I mean," Larry continued thoughtfully.

"Uh-huh," I answered. He *is* eager to please, I thought, horrible me, cruel me.

"He used to drink."

"B.J. was in Vietnam!" Maggie added, impressed by this part of his history. She coughed, also in a wheezing fashion. "Killed a lot of Vietcong." She choked on the words. "Now they're moving here," she said, clearing her throat.

"We have a Vietnamese in Overeaters," Larry said.

"A fat Vietnamese." Maggie chuckled. "Now that's loneliness!"

"B.J.'s got a great heart," Larry said about Naomi's Beast.

The monster has feelings; even Tyrannosaurus rex sometimes wept. "We have to go," I said. "We have a long drive back to New York."

"There's a battered women's shelter near here," Larry said. "They can help."

We didn't need a shelter—we needed an Underground Railroad. "Is Naomi Perlman the sponsor?" I asked.

"Who?" Larry said in his woman's voice.

"Who?" Maggie wheezed.

"Naomi!" I called, not to repeat myself, but to her namesake, the little girl making a snowwoman with Big Foot. "We have to start back. It's a long drive to the city."

"We're not finished," B.J. growled at me.

"We have to make the head!" Naomi spoke enthusiastically, not making a demand.

"Okay," I said. "I'll call your father"—that was an error; should have said home. I rushed on—"and tell him we're heading back."

Only when I got inside the first bank of doors and located a phone right next to the newspaper vending machine did I realize: I've left Naomi with three strangers. Strangers? They were barely human.

Would Ben have done such a thing? Wendy certainly wouldn't. No matter how many times I had cared for Naomi successfully—even after I had had charge of her for weekends, even after the week she spent with me while they traveled to Europe—each time Wendy recited a long list of instructions, as if I was new to the job. Whenever Wendy had to hire an unfamiliar babysitter she checked whether I was going to be home; to make sure that if needed I would be next door to help, as well as in the hope that I would volunteer to eaves-drop via a phony phone call to her apartment an hour after she left. And I would, uselessly listening for sounds of unhappiness from Naomi or the noise of an orgy in the background—feeling stupid because obviously a wrongdoer would have the brains to quiet things down before answering the phone. My point is that Wendy released her precious girl with sticky fingers.

In the beginning I judged Wendy's mothering to be suffocating, encouraging dependence, lack of initiative, and fearfulness. Except Naomi grew up with none of those traits; I had long since admitted I was wrong . . . and yet you see what I did? Just walked away.

I was right not to become a mother, despite what everyone says or thinks.

And I didn't correct my mistake—even after I knew it was a mistake. I watched through the window (made oval by crescents of frost at the corners), saw that B.J. and she were preoccupied by shaping the snowwoman's head, and decided I could risk a continua-tion of the error and make a quick call to Stefan.

I was stunned: Stefan blew up at me.

"Are you crazy! Listen to me: I won't help you. And I'm not going to indulge this episode any longer."

"What episode? What do you mean by *episode!*"

"You're having a breakdown—"

"Oh God, Stefan!"

"Molly, this is a very objective judgment! I've consulted with Jim—"

"What do you plan to do—have me committed because I don't want to be married to you?"

"You're a kidnapper! I don't have to do a thing!" He screamed this and then stopped. He panted, breathing more angry words, but (like always) he gave them no voice until their passion was exhaled. "I've tried to be patient, I've tried to be understanding. But I can't any-more, not in good conscience. If you don't return by morning, I'll inform Ben and the police of this call."

"Thank you so much, Stefan." I had known in my heart (always, even when I thought I was safe) that he would fail me if truly needed. Ours was a fair-weather marriage.

"You're angry with me now." Stefan had rehearsed this part, it had no spark of feeling. "Maybe you'll stay angry forever. But I have to prevent you from doing yourself harm."

"Stefan." I should have pleaded with him, yet it came out irritated—impatient patron to incompetent waiter: "Don't you understand? If I go back I have to do anything Ben wants. He can hold this over my head—"

"You're going to stop seeing Ben, Molly. I'll give you no choice about that." He was furious. He spoke in a slow cadence, but the rhythm was artificial. He was the one who was angry and might never forgive me.

"That's ridiculous," I answered. They were done with the snow-woman. Naomi talked to B.J., her hands gesturing with animation, raised with excitement, sideways for doubt, up and down as she reasoned between the two. I leaned my head on the frozen glass. The top of my forehead melted an inner film of ice. I shut my eyes. "Just be straight with me, Stefan. Tell me you're hurt, don't threaten me."

"Molly, I am going to proceed with whatever I can to stop you. I won't agree to a divorce—I'll go for a competency hearing if I have to."

This made me crazy. I twisted in the booth, blindly staring at the Burger King neon: "How dare you threaten me! I'll make you a laughingstock, Stefan! You won't have a patient left!" Somewhere I heard a scream. Not a real scream. Very faint. Not from outside, but in me, from a buried soul. What was she screaming?

"I don't care about the damage to me!" Stefan squeaked. A lie—he did. I could hear the fear: he wasn't *that* much in love with me. He wouldn't really risk his professional standing. Even on his side, our marriage was no grand passion, not worth throwing everything away.

Molly, she warned me, something is wrong! I was melting the frost; a cold drop ran down the side of my face. Where is Naomi? Wendy asked me in a panic.

Stefan's voice receded as I turned and looked out into the white-and-gray gloom of the Burger King parking lot. Larry's odd position attracted my attention first: he was slumped against a van, one of his mittens clinging to its side mirror as he slid down to the ground. Maggie waddled at me, making horrible faces through the glass like a gigantic fish in a tank.

You stupid bitch, I told myself, as I saw it—B.J. was kidnapping Naomi. He hustled her across the parking lot, carrying her sideways, thick arm across her middle, her feet and head flopping like a doll.

I went through the booth and doors, invisible. I ran on the cold earth without feet, flying from fear.

I shouted after him. Maggie wheezed at me.

I heard Naomi shrieking: "Let me go!"

I had a very clear, sickening image of B.J. raping her. B.J. stopped at a pickup, all black except for white bolts of lightning on the fenders. He went to the driver's side, opened the door, and mounted, tossing little Naomi in. I got to the door as he made it inside.

Then I was on the ground looking up at a black sky.

I had trouble raising my head off the pavement. B.J. had knocked me down with the door. Maggie's blue jeans appeared next to me. The back of my skull hurt. They were yelling, all of them, even Naomi. No one sounded frightened: only frustrated.

Larry's mittens rescued me from drowning on the concrete. As I surfaced I could breathe again.

"We'll take them to the shelter!" B.J. said.

Naomi shouted at me: "Take me home, Molly!" No tears, just fury.

"Who is she?" B.J. yelled down at me. He was immense, as tall as a building, a true giant. No—he was seated in the truck and I was still on the ground.

"She says you're not her mother," Larry's mincing woman's voice scolded me.

"B.J. just wants to make sure she's safe," Maggie croaked.

"I was lying! She *is* my mother!" Naomi whacked B.J. with her hand. Although she struck him on the cheek, he didn't blink. "Let me go!"

"I'm taking her to the shelter. Pauline'll figure it out." B.J. reached for the driver's door.

Larry interposed himself so it couldn't be shut. "Why did you hit me, B.J.?"

"I just shoved you—"

"No! You hit me." Larry wagged his red mitten. "It really hurt."

"You tried to stop me. I had to hit you." B.J. again reached to shut his door. Larry kept his bulk in the way. "It proves you had nothing to do with this. You tried to stop me."

"That's crap, B.J. Don't give me that. You really hit me. I know your daddy beat you, but that—"

"Shut the fuck up!" B.J. screamed into the steering wheel and banged his head on it in frustration. "I'm tired of your sensitive bullshit!" The whole truck seemed to shake.

I was on my feet now, wobbling like a first-time ice-skater. I touched the back of my skull expecting to discover blood. Only wet snow. I stumbled to the front of the truck and tried to shout, although I sounded feeble.

"Over my dead body! You drive her out of here over my dead body! Over my dead body you fat disgusting pig! Over my dead body!" I went hoarse; my threats were pitifully weak. I felt sick and faint.

The passenger door opened and Naomi dropped down in a hurry, falling to her knees, then scrambling toward me.

"Can you drive, honey?" Maggie had me in her arms. I hung on to the wobbling underbelly of her triceps. Maybe I had a concussion.

"I'm following you!" B.J. shouted from the truck. "All the way back to New York. She told me her address and phone number! She lives on Fifth Avenue! I'm following you there!"

A knight in shining pickup truck. Naomi pulled on me. I slid down and felt her small sweet lips kiss me: "Let's go home, Molly," she whispered.

"I'm sorry, honey." I grabbed her, squeezed her against me, and wept with relief. What a fool I was. Poor Wendy, that you had an idiot like me to take your place.

We got into the Volvo. Trembling, grateful, and terrified, I returned to the highway. The brilliant white lights of B.J.'s truck filled the back of our car, a demanding, scolding presence. I got out at the next exit, swung underneath the highway and reentered, heading back to New York.

Poor Wendy. You were right not to trust anyone with your baby, not even me.

❧

After an hour of driving I had to stop for gas. B.J. followed me into a highway station; he tanked up at the self-service pump parallel to my spot at the credit-card island. I wanted to phone Ben and tell him we were coming, hoping I could cover up my aborted flight with a story about getting lost in Jersey, but I was afraid to leave Naomi in the car. B.J. finished quickly; he returned to his truck and peered at me, full of resentment. For what? What had I done to him? I returned his stare with equal hostility; bleached by the station's neon lights, he looked like an unhealthy ghost. I wished I had a car phone.

"Is he going to follow us the whole way?" Naomi asked as we pulled out and resumed driving. She had been quiet until then. I hadn't made any conversational gambits either. What could I say— attack her for talking to strangers? She was right to seek help. I was the kidnapper.

"He wants to make sure I take you home."

"That's crazy," she mumbled.

"Well, you told him I wasn't your mother."

"He asked me—"

"That's okay, honey. But he wondered if I'm not your mother, then who am I?"

"I told him you're Mommy's best friend."

"Did you tell him your mommy is dead?" That blunt (and horrible) remark was a first for me. Since Wendy's murder I had never acknowledged this fact to Naomi.

She didn't answer. I glanced at her: she was backlit by the interrogating glare of B.J.'s truck. He stayed on our heels, pushing me to drive faster, switching lanes when I did, attached to me no matter how empty the stretch of highway.

"Well . . . ?"

Naomi hung her head.

"Why not?" Again, no answer. "You see, he must have thought I had taken you away from your mommy and daddy. He didn't know that I'm—" and I got stuck. How to describe my role? I'm not her mother, not her guardian, not her aunt, not even her friend. I'm the genius who let her play with abuse victims at Burger King. I was disgusted and repelled by everything I had done. I resolved to be direct: Naomi and I were heading back to the war; it was time for us to make a treaty and become allies. "How could he know that I'm taking care of you now?"

"I'm sorry," she mumbled, and she was crying.

"Damn it," I said to the road, and my eyes filled too. "I don't mean it that way. Don't cry. I'm not criticizing you. I'm only explaining . . ."

"I'm sorry," she said again, and put her face into my side, sobbing.

"It's okay, honey." I stroked her amazing hair, smooth and rich, so incredibly alive and young. I ached for her—and to be her. What's worse: never to have a loving mother or to have one torn away?

B.J.'s lights were exhausting, a marathon for my eyes. Tears didn't refresh them—they continued to sting from the glare. "Do you know what a will is, Nommy?" This was the first time I had used Ben and Wendy's nickname for her.

"Yes." Her crying was over, but the answer had a solemn weepy tone.

"You do?"

"It's how you leave things to people after you die."

"Every grown-up has a will. Your mommy's asks that I take care of you. I would take care of you anyway, even if she had forgotten to make a will—I want to. But it's also what she wanted."

Naomi sat up. I let go of the comfort of her hair. Her face was long and beautiful in the harsh white light. "What did she leave to me?" she asked of the road.

"Well . . . when you're older, you'll get everything of hers."

"Didn't she leave anything to Daddy?"

"Your daddy has things they bought together."

"Like what?"

"Like your apartment. Like your country house."

"Daddy says we'll have to sell those things." She spoke in an enervated monotone.

"Maybe not. We'll see." I waited, to give her a chance.

She broke the silence: "Why did Mommy have to say in her will that you would take care of me?"

"I don't understand. What do you mean 'have to say'?"

"Well, there's Daddy. So why . . . ?" She put out her hands, asking for help.

"I'm sorry, I didn't mean to confuse you. She doesn't have to say unless both your daddy and mommy couldn't take care of you. That's what her will says. I'm your guardian if they can't, if they—"

"Die," she said again in that lifeless, terrible voice.

"Right." What had I just resolved? To be open and direct. Wendy would; she churned emotions needlessly, I used to believe, but had I done better with all my goddamned restraint and control? No more easy lies. I would be Naomi's companion in this horror. "And also if your daddy can't for some other reason."

"Like what?" This brought her out of numbness. Her eyes glowed, the light cutting deep into them; like a prism, they made rainbows all the way to the back of her skull. "What other reason?"

"Has anyone told you about the trial? Has your daddy told you?" She shouted: "He told me they think he did something bad to her!"

"Did he say what might happen?"

She continued in a loud angry tone: "He said no matter what I heard, he was going to take care of me forever. He told me if anybody says anything else it's a lie." She dared me to tell her otherwise. Her head was a periscope again, only this time she scanned me, not the blank concrete.

"That's not true, Nommy. Your daddy might have to go away for a while. If he does, I'll take care of you."

"You're lying!" She lifted a hand and swiped at me. I intercepted her little fist, steering with one hand. The car swerved halfway into the deserted lane beside mine; B.J.'s brakes squealed as he slowed.

I shouted at her: "Don't hit! People don't hit each other! That's not how you solve things!" I released her—she whimpered and turned toward her door. I got the car back in lane and speeded up, checking in the rearview, hoping I hadn't alarmed B.J.

He closed up the gap, searchlights on my back, accusatory and unforgiving. Why not slam on the brakes and end it? Let the stupid Beast crush his Beauty.

"I'm sorry, honey. I didn't mean to scare you. But hitting is wrong."

"I wasn't going to hit you."

"That's not true."

"I wasn't!"

"Okay . . . forget it." It took a while before I could organize myself. I was in pieces: rage, fear, guilt—a kaleidoscope of feelings, merging and twisting one into another. I wanted to feel nothing—is that so wrong?

We passed a sign that said it was seventy-five miles to New York. "Is it much longer?" Naomi asked, forlorn, wanting to be there.

"A little more than an hour. I'm going to tell your father we got a little lost driving around and that's why we're so late. He might get angry, but don't worry about it."

"Okay," she said. I had no idea whether she knew I was lying.

After that I tried to ask the next logical question, something I had wanted to know for a long time. But it stuck in my throat. Literally, I could feel it there; I couldn't swallow or speak it. We drove in silence for miles. B.J.'s moronic lights harassed me. They allowed no rest or calm. At last, despite the great risk, I unblocked my throat: "What did your daddy tell you happened to your mommy?"

No answer. The silence and lack of movement made me think she had gone to sleep.

"Nommy?" I prompted.

"What . . . ?" She crouched below the line of B.J.'s headlights.

"What did your daddy tell you happened to your mommy?"

"He said she had an accident." She spoke with heavy irritation, repeating an answer to a dim-witted bureaucrat.

I glanced at her huddled figure. A slant of light caught one eye: the blue gleam was hostile. "Has anyone said anything else to you about it?"

"Yes." That came out as a moan.

"Who?" No answer. "What did they say?"

"I don't want to talk about it." She turned her face into the seat's leather. Her hair was bleached by the truck's angry glare.

"The police think your daddy hurt your mommy," I said. My hands were shaking; I felt I was killing her. For one second I died. My heart fluttered, skipped a whole beat. I considered pulling over in case I passed out.

Go on, Molly, Wendy encouraged.

You don't believe me, but it *was* Wendy, egging me on tell the truth: "They say—"

"I know!" Naomi cut me off, screaming into the dashboard. "Shut up! I don't want to talk!" She covered her ears and shut her eyes.

Did she know?

I hated myself. I don't mean self-disgust. I mean despair: What was the point of my life? What was I doing? What had I ever done that was worthwhile? Not so long ago I was stuffed with me—my grand job, my wonderful brain, my taut body, my successful husband. But they were accidents: Naomi Perlman's impulse to do good, genetics, our society's structure. This was my real achievement, my personal choice: to break an innocent heart.

Let me go, Wendy.

No, she answered.

"I'd like us to live somewhere else. Start new. Maybe go somewhere warm."

"I want to go home." Monotone, dead. "I want to see my daddy." *My*, she called him with special emphasis. She had that too, a father who loved her. I was sorry for her; and I wanted to be her.

"I'm going to do exactly what you want. Okay? Don't worry about that. I know you love your daddy."

"I love Mommy too." Said resentfully, an argument.

"And your mommy too."

"I can't go away."

"You can't?"

"No! I can't!" she screamed.

"Okay." B.J.'s lights burned on my neck, my shoulders. I was enraged by his intrusion. On the Volvo there are rear fog lamps that brighten the back lights. Flip them on and it appears as if the driver has hit the brakes. Stefan had used this feature on tailgaters to give them a scare, a taste of what a sudden stop might do to them. While we continued on safely they would skid, almost losing control. The lesson always worked; after that they would keep their distance. But Stefan had never played that trick at this speed. We were doing eighty on the empty highway; if B.J. slammed on the brakes going this fast he might really lose control and crash.

I wanted to punish him, to be rid of him. Maybe he wouldn't crash, maybe he would get the message and give me some room. I concentrated on this plan for a while, searching for flat stretches of road with even shoulders. But when we were joined by some traffic, I decided it was too dangerous.

You're weak, that's all, I chided myself. You're making up excuses for being a do-nothing.

"Molly . . . ?" Naomi's tone was soft, but urgent. She sat with her legs underneath her, resting her head sideways against the seat, watching me wistfully. "Did you see Mommy?"

"See . . . ?" Her question scared me: what did she mean?

"You know . . . after. Did you see her . . . ?"

I couldn't think. B.J.'s lights were blinding me everywhere, even in my head. "Go away," I said to the rearview.

"Who?" Naomi said.

"He's still following us."

"I know," she said. "Well . . . ?"

"What?"

"Did you see her? Where is she?"

I couldn't tell her that Ben had incinerated Wendy, couldn't say it—my heart would have stopped forever. The traffic had thinned out, the highway's shoulders looked flat, the road was straight. The fog light switch was just to the left of the steering wheel. I put my finger on it and glanced in the rearview: the white light was impenetrable. My eyes hurt.

"Molly!" Naomi whined.

"I don't know," I answered, blinking at the road, finger ready. I slowed a bit, hoping to get us down to seventy or sixty-five. B.J. was insane—he seemed to ride up the Volvo's trunk, refusing to ease up. "Give me some room!" I said to the rearview, and got a slap of brilliant light for an answer. "I think he's got his brights on."

"How do you know Mommy is dead?"

This shocked me. I looked at Naomi to check whether it was really her. She was unnaturally calm.

"You didn't see her," she argued.

"Did your daddy tell—"

"No!" she shouted.

"Okay—"

"He says she's not alive anymore. He says I can't see her. But I think he's lying. He doesn't know. He didn't see her either."

But he did. He identified the body. They had checked, there was no question. What was I thinking? He killed her. "What do you mean, Nommy?"

"Nothing." She folded her arms, a portrait of childlike stubbornness.

B.J. honked at me.

"What?" I shouted at him. "I can't keep going this fast!"

"He can't hear you," Naomi said.

I put my finger on the switch. The road was empty and flat. Even if he lost control there was nothing to hit.

"How do you know she's really dead?" someone asked.

"What!" I yelled at Naomi. "Who said that!" I peered into the rear seat—B.J.'s lights were two huge eyes glaring at me.

"I said it!" Naomi screamed, grabbing on to my arm and burying her head. "I said it. I'm sorry."

I lifted my foot off the accelerator. "You don't think your mother is dead?"

B.J. honked. His brights flared on and off, taunting. I accelerated. He speeded up too, right on my back, hounding me.

"Maybe she's lost." Naomi spoke into my body, scared of my reaction. No tears. Her tone was awed, ardently wishful: "Maybe she got lost. Maybe it's somebody else they found. Maybe she'll remember who she is, and she'll come back."

I flipped the switch.

❧

Naomi heard the squeals (desperate, dying) of his tires, and, of course, the silverware clatter of smashing metal as B.J.'s truck rolled over and over on the dark concrete.

And she noticed his lights were gone. For all my horror at his fate (I felt it, believe me, and remorse too), I sighed with pleasure at the return of soft comforting darkness behind me. The back of my head was no longer seared: I could think again.

"What happened to him?" Naomi wondered, struggling to turn in her seatbelt, and then to get her head above the level of the headrest. By the time she managed it the accident had diminished to a speck. "Did he hit something?"

"I don't know," I said. I guess I didn't really. Was he alive? His lights had swerved wildly across the road, he had turned sideways and then seemed to flip over without cause, as if his truck did tricks . . . only the smashing sounds proved it was no stunt.

We drove back the rest of the way in silence. Naomi did not fall asleep, although it was past one-thirty when we arrived. I was happy, after all, to see New York's lights. How bright and beautiful the city is when its people want to sleep. She forced herself to stay up. I guess she wanted to make sure I took her home. That was what I had accomplished: losing her trust.

I made a judgment of myself (I hear your sarcasm: finally!)—I was bad. I had tried hard all my life not to be, but the evidence was pretty conclusive. Bad people raised me and I was one too, despite Naomi Perlman's charity.

Know thyself, the Lord tells me. Thanks a lot.

"Home!" She applauded as we drove past our building en route to the garage. I did not feel like celebrating. Among other reasons, I noticed the lieutenant's smelly car was parked out front.

He was in the apartment with Ben. It was weird. Naomi ran into her father's arms. I dropped her shopping bag of toys on the floor and started making excuses while, to my surprise, I noticed that Ben seemed to have been crying, the lieutenant seemed to have made himself at home (there were two cups of coffee and a half-empty box of doughnuts on the table), and that both men regarded me with cold looks of suspicion and hostility.

"Mr. Fliess called in a missing-person report. I'm—" The lieutenant cut off my bumbling story of getting lost in Jersey and introduced himself as if we had never met, which, as far as Ben was concerned, we shouldn't have. "He thought you didn't intend to return."

"Everything's okay," I said to Ben. His face was devastated—drawn, eyes red, arms clutching Naomi. A pathetic figure: Depression-era father holding waif; concentration-camp survivor liberated and reunited with daughter; social-service victim protecting her against a cruel bureaucrat.

I had become the villain.

"It was fun, Daddy." Naomi lied so well. She had already learned not to provoke his anger. "We made a snowwoman. Remember?"

Ben frowned at the memory.

"We made pink lips—"

"Oh yeah," Ben said. "Come on. It's practically morning. Let's get into bed."

"Well, if it's practically morning I should stay up," Naomi the sophist said; but she looked pale, ill with fatigue.

"You're going to sleep. Molly, wait here, I have to talk to you," Ben said sharply, in complete command. "Good night," he dismissed the lieutenant. "Thanks for your concern." Ben opened the door, offering an exit.

The lieutenant hesitated, raising a knuckle to the tiny pimples lined across his forehead. He touched each one, testing them, lost in thought. "Don't you think I should ask some questions?" he mused.

"No," Ben said. "I don't. I got panicky. That's understandable. Good night."

The lieutenant departed sideways, showing me a look of worry and doubt, then turning a bland face to Ben.

I thought about having a cigarette while waiting for Ben to emerge from Naomi's bedroom. Hadn't had one in four years. Hadn't wanted one since the first few months after quitting. I could no longer vividly recall its evils—cancer, stale mouth, smoky clothes, sore throats, long drawn-out congestion. Instead I remembered its masturbatory pleasure, inhaling the tangy air, filling me up, a moment's relief, a private thrill done in public, another dose only a gesture away. "Why did you come back?" Ben's voice came from behind, deep and commanding.

I couldn't see him. I was seated in the armchair facing the windows, looking at that same damn antique mirror Wendy and I had hung. It showed the empty hallway leading to Naomi's room.

"She wants to be here," I answered.

"She loves me," the voice at my back said.

"Don't be so impressed. Children are loyal. Even to the worst parents."

That caused a silence. Perhaps a blow to my head would be next. Did he kill Wendy from behind? Or was it an act of rage, a smash across the face, slamming her into something? That would be so close to an accident, why conceal it? No, he must have come up from behind, like now. Can't you see him approach me with a hammer, or one of Naomi's blocks, and batter my skull? "I could get her to tell me what really happened." He had moved closer. He was right behind me. His belt buckle touched my head. At least I hoped it was that: something small and metal and cool.

"Okay, Ben, what do you want?"

He touched my hair. Gently, the way I had stroked Naomi's. His fingers lightly brushed from the top to the back. He caressed both sides, holding the body of my hair in the air, as if carrying a bride's train. "So beautiful," he said.

What did this rapture represent? I wondered. Desire for me, or envy of my hair? Is this foreplay or window-shopping?

"I want—" His voice was hoarse with desire. He dropped down so that his mouth was at my ear: "I want to fuck you," he whispered.

I wanted to tell him I had killed someone. At least I might have, and that was the important part. Not that I thought—not for a second—my flipping a fog light switch on a Volvo was the equivalent of Ben battering Wendy to death. We had nothing in common in that sense. Perhaps I wanted to warn him. He was the kind of man who hated women, but didn't really think us dangerous, not that way. It would be pleasant to shake him up.

"You don't really have anything to threaten me with, Ben."

"Come on, Molly," he whispered into my ear. "Why are you here? Why are you helping me?"

"I'm helping Nommy."

"That's bullshit. If you wanted to run away with her, you would have kept going. You wouldn't have paid attention—"

"Like you, right? Say or do anything to get my way."

His hand came down my shoulder and covered my right breast. He put no pressure; touching, in possession and control, yet lightly, prepared to flee. "Wonderful," his hoarse voice spoke. "I wanted to for so many years. . . ." Now there a gentle pressure all around my breast. "It's so wonderful to touch you."

"Honestly," I said in a loud clear tone. "I really don't want to. I find you sexless."

Ben searched for my nipple with his index finger and thumb. He tweaked the tip, apparently hoping to arouse it. Men like all kinds of erections, I thought coldly. His touch was compelling because it had so much tension and grace and passion, but he couldn't excite me. I was glad and relieved.

"That hurts," I lied.

"It does?" His fingers opened, his hand withdrew in horror. "I'm sorry," he mumbled.

"You'd better start working out," I said. I kept my head facing forward.

His breathing bellowed out, hot, panting, on my neck. "You want me to have big muscles?" he whispered.

"Build yourself up. Maybe you should take karate. You'll have to defend yourself in prison." I allowed this to sink in, with all its horrifying imagery. "They'll know about the clothes," I added quietly.

"I won't be going to prison." His tone was deep and resolute. He walked away from me: no murder tonight. Soon I heard the refrigerator and the whoosh of a bottle being opened. Ben reappeared with a beer. He passed me, heading for the couch, and mumbled, "Molly, Molly, Molly. Good girl, Molly. I think you're full of shit," he told me mildly, and collapsed onto the couch; I winced at its agonized plea for mercy. "Why don't you tell me exactly what you want me to do? You want to live here, right? Everybody's gonna think we're having sex. Doesn't that bother you?"

"I thought you don't care what people think."

"I don't. But I thought you did."

"No, I don't," I said. "Not anymore."

He brought the green funnel of the beer to his small red lips and half kissed its opening, about to raise the bottle. "Good for you," he praised me, and drank.

"Is she asleep?" I asked, thinking I should have kissed her good night and thanked her for not betraying me.

"Yeah, she passed out while I read to her. Hasn't done that since she was two." He sneered at me, toasting me sarcastically with his beer. "You certainly made her birthday exciting."

"Did you cry while the lieutenant was here?"

He stared at me, found no answer, peered at the bottle as if it could talk, then came back to ask, "How did you know that?"

"You look like you were crying."

He got up and went to the mirror and studied himself. "I don't see how you could tell," he wondered.

"Was the lieutenant impressed? Did he feel sorry for you?"

Ben groaned. "Give me a break, okay? You're pissed off, then go home."

"I don't want to go home."

"Then don't be such a pain in the ass about everything. I thought you had kidnapped my daughter. I thought he was going to accuse me of killing her and you. I was sure that was your plan."

Not a bad idea. I wished I had thought of it: maybe I should have kept going, in spite of Naomi's desires.

"So I cried," Ben continued, strutting, lecturing with his beer bottle. "Doesn't Stefan cry? I bet he cries all the time."

"No, it was Wendy who cried all the time."

"Whoa!" Ben chuckled. He clutched the bottle by its neck and pointed to me. "You're ahead, one–nothing. I like this. You give as good as you get. I really admire that."

"Really?" I challenged.

"Yeah, really," he said, but he paused in his swagger, bottle clutched modestly at his waist, like a prayer book. He waited for my benediction.

"I'd like to see you dressed up." I said it easily enough, confident and calm. Unfortunately, my throat walled up after it was gone; I wouldn't be able to say another thing. My heart pounded as I watched him react.

Ben was amazed. He blinked, he swallowed, his shoulders fell; the bottle sagged below his stomach to his groin, a green sweating penis. "Are you serious?" he squeaked in a high voice, scared.

I nodded, forcing a smug smile. I concentrated on clearing my throat.

"I don't trust you," he said.

"You're chicken," I grumbled, forcing the words out.

He shook his head, scorning my accusation. "Why? Why do you want to?"

"I think it's sexy," I said, and my heart went wild, aching in my breast, squeezing itself frantically. The blood throbbed in my neck, choking me.

"You're sick," Ben said with a kind of wonder and happiness in his tone. "You're a sick person. Wendy and I used to try to figure you out all the time. We talked about you a lot, especially after sex. You know why? I was thinking about it while you were gone. You know why we talked about you so much? Because we were both in love with you."

"That's ridiculous," I whispered, hoarse. Blood pulsed violently in my neck, in my arms; my spongy heart was squeezing itself dry.

"Wendy was no lesbian, but she would have gone to bed with you."

"It won't work, Ben. You'll never convince me Wendy was the person you say she was—I'll never believe you were right to kill her."

"Did I say that!" He put the beer down with a clink on the coffee table and inhaled, revving up his rage: "Fuck you!" He shot out the obscenity. The anger was staged. Frightening, to be sure, with that big body arched toward me, his head snapping words like a gigantic malevolent turtle. But the rage was unauthentic; a tactic, not passion.

"Are you scared to show me?" My blood coursed thickly again, swelling in me. "Is that why you're pretending to be angry?"

"Jesus," he said, and turned away, embarrassed.

Such delicacy of feeling: he gambles, he dresses up like a woman, he kills his wife, but he blushes.

"Why do you want to?" he asked, his back still to me.

"I want to understand," I told him, and that was the truth. Believe it or not. I wanted to know why he had kept so complete a secret, what had been so precious he would kill to preserve it.

"It's not what you think," his voice quavered pathetically.

"Okay," I soothed him. "I want to know what's really going on. I want to understand." I meant these words. I couldn't destroy him; I couldn't ignore him; perhaps I could know him, know him in a way no one else had, not Wendy, not Joan, not his mother—certainly not Naomi, the one person who loved him.

Ben turned and evaluated me for while. He stood still, hands in front, an attentive schoolboy at assembly, studying my face.

"I came back, Ben," I told him. I had no trouble with my blood anymore: I was calm. "I didn't have to. Let me in."

"If you laugh I'll kill you," he said at last.

"I won't laugh," I answered without irony.

He said nothing more, but walked purposefully toward the bedrooms. He paused at the hallway, inviting me to follow. I got up and my heart squeezed again.

No turning back now, girlie, I heard in my people's voice, sarcastic and sad, daring and afraid.

Ben paused at Naomi's room and walked in. I entered a step or two. She breathed heavily, audible even at that distance, panting in her rest, her face sagging with exhaustion. Ben kissed her brow.

I thought of B.J. splattered somewhere on the highway. Was he cursing me?

We went into his bedroom, Wendy's old bedroom, unchanged except for its care. The dresser top was dull and dusty; the rug looked as if it could use a vacuuming. He had fired the cleaning woman, doing a good job with the rest of the apartment. Here, he had given up except to make the bed. Ben went into the closet, pulled on the chain to light the old-fashioned bare bulb, opened a stepladder, and rummaged about on the top shelf. He came down with a large box.

"Wait here," he told me sharply. Before carrying it into the bathroom and locking himself in, he turned off the ceiling fixture. That left Wendy's bedside lamp as the only illumination. Its pink shade cast a demure, flattering light.

He was busy in there for more than half an hour. It was funny thinking about what was going on inside; I smiled at how long he took. I heard some noises—the sharp clatter of glass bottles on porcelain, presumably cosmetics; Ben grunting along with the swishing sound of fabric. It was silly and it was worrisome.

Tired of my vigil, I sat down in armchair by the window. That placed me on the other side of the bathroom. Seated, I was back on the highway, feeling the subtle rhythmic thumping of the road. . . .

I may have fallen asleep. In any event, I was startled by the distinct click of the bathroom lock untumbling. I sat up suddenly, heart pounding, vision concentrated.

The bathroom door opened cautiously. I made no movement, I couldn't breathe.

She came out of the bathroom with her back to me, looking in the wrong direction. She wore a raven black wig, its tresses curling down her back. She was huge, of course, but not crude, wearing a simple black dress that softened her big hips. I could see from where I sat that the breasts were an appropriate size and they had a softened realistic appearance, not a plastic cone shape. The great surprise were the legs—long and quite beautiful, no bulging thighs, the calfs and ankles delicate, womanly.

"Molly . . . ?" he whispered, confused at my apparent absence.

"I'm here, Ben."

I couldn't see her face yet. She turned to me, swiveling easily on her high heels: I gasped at her face. There were no glasses, no sullen shadow of a beard, no bald skull. The cheeks were high and strong, the eyes deep-set and vulnerable, the small lips now full and red. I had never noticed before that Ben's nose was aquiline and striking, ennobling her face. She was too thick to be considered pretty, but this Ben had grace and dignity.

She lowered her head. "Thank you," he mumbled softly, humble and gentle. "Thank you for not laughing."

I got to my feet and circled her. He had spoken in his voice, only mellowed, its tones as pink as the lamp's light.

"Why didn't you tell Wendy?"

She didn't like her hands: they were too big and thick. She hid them behind her back, brought them forward, tried to diminish their size by holding them together in front, was dissatisfied and put them behind her again.

"She would have been disgusted," he said.

I reached for her breast without thinking—and caught myself in midair. She noticed my hand. "You can touch," he said.

"I just want to know what the material is."

"Foam." She took my hand and cupped it over her right breast. The spongy feel had some resilience. Still holding her, I cupped my own breast with my free hand.

"It's the same."

She nodded with a pleased smile. "They're very good," he said.

I let go of her breast and stroked her cheek. "You're pretty," I told him.

She shut her eyes and swallowed, moved. "Thank you," he whispered.

"Did you want to make love like this with Wendy?"

"No," he said. She leaned her cheek on my hand, with the sad tender longing of a child. "I masturbate," he whispered.

"Standing here like this?"

"In front of a mirror."

"You look at yourself as a woman?"

She lifted her head from my palm to kiss it and then rested again. The eyes stayed closed, rapturously. "I'm beautiful like this," he told me.

"You want to be beautiful?"

"I want people to want me," he said. "Women are wanted. Even if it's just for sex, every woman is wanted. Nobody's ever wanted me."

"Do you have an erection now?"

She squeezed her eyes together in pain and nodded against my hand. "Yes . . . ," he whispered.

I was excited, wet and loose, my limbs unstrung, my belly warm. His confession thrilled me; her ungainly look won my pity.

I kissed her forehead. He opened his eyes, foggy with longing. I kissed them shut: there was a powdery taste of makeup and I noticed the perfume she wore. I expected Wendy's scent—but it was mine.

"You're beautiful," I told her. "I want to make love to you."

❧

I slept in my own bed that night, after we were done. Ben was very passionate and I'm ashamed to say I enjoyed myself as much as—even more than—I ever have. But that pleasure was sustained only so long as she was there. Once she disappeared into the bathroom and returned as Ben, I had to get away.

I would like to report that I felt guilty; that I was racked with sorrow and shame at all the sins I committed that awful day. Instead I fell fast asleep, exhausted and satisfied.

I woke up late and fully attentive, no slow transition. I came to consciousness with a clear realization whose obviousness you will laugh at: There's no going back now, Molly.

Oddly, I was glad and full of energy. I called in sick to the office, exercised vigorously on the machines, phoned a law school friend who had become quite prominent as a divorce lawyer, especially for battered women. I no longer trusted Jake Prosser enough to give him the job, especially if Stefan stuck to his new line and was difficult.

"You're kidding!" was her response. "Molly, I can't believe it! Why?"

You'd think she had never heard of divorce, instead of making a living from it. Only after I was stern with her did she reluctantly accept that neither I nor Stefan was having an affair. (Yes, I hear your sarcasm; but, you see, I didn't think of what happened as an affair.)

The lieutenant called. I lied to him: pretended Naomi and I had really been lost; pretended that Ben had been behaving docilely. He knew I was lying. He tried to goad me into the truth: "Mr. Fliess doesn't seem to feel any remorse. He thinks everyone should feel sorry for him. Cried like a baby about how miserable he is. And he'll try anything. He even hinted maybe you knew something about what happened to Wendy."

"He's fighting for his life, Lieutenant. Nothing he says or does would surprise me."

"You're making excuses for him."

"No, I'm not. I'm being realistic."

"You're not beginning to feel sympathy for him, are you?"

"Of course not. The case is solid, right?"

"You can never have enough," he insisted, prodding me.

When I called Ben, it was past eleven.

"Hi, Molly." His tone was relieved and happy. "I was scared you would never speak to me again."

"That's ridiculous, Ben."

"I feel really good today," he stammered.

"I'm taking the day off. Let's get you contact lenses," I suggested.

"Really?" he wondered nervously, like a kid scared to believe he had been offered the best present in the world.

I watched a huge version of Ben's face in the ophthalmologist's mirror and realized it was also the makeup that had improved him, enlarging his brown eyes, stretching the distance between his harassed mouth and nose and worried brow. Nevertheless, getting rid of the glasses would be a big improvement; a beard would also help, especially if it came in reddish.

After he had been examined and got his first lesson at inserting the lenses (he was a baby about it: timid and squeamish), we ducked into a luncheonette in midtown, jammed with people, and thick, not very delicious smells. I praised him for ordering the contacts and urged him to make other beautifying gestures, including exercises, although I had discovered last night that he had a leaner and stronger body than I suspected. I mentioned how terrific he would look with a reddish beard.

"I can't grow a beard," he said.

"Why?" I was a simpleton, indeed.

"You know—," and he glanced about at the nearby tables shyly.

He meant, if he grew a beard the transformation into her would become impossible—or ridiculous.

We discussed that choice, to his surprise.

"I can't believe we're talking about it"—he glanced at the customers holding plastic menus, wolfing french fries—"in public, like it's nothing . . ."

"It is nothing, Ben. Is that what you felt when Wendy found out? Did you think it was so shameful?"

But you thought him sick, remember Molly? You waved it under Wendy's nose and discussed it smugly with Stefan.

"No!" He banged the table, water quivering in the glasses, attracting looks from our neighbors. Tears came into his eyes. "You don't know what she was like."

"Yes, I do." He was easy to confront—why had Wendy feared arguing with him? Talk right back and he accepts it.

"I mean to me! She wanted a divorce, she was gonna use it against me anytime she wanted to. And I'd have to stop—" He looked off. "She convinced me I was sick, that I'd have—" He sucked in his lips to keep his emotions in check. "It was my only pleasure. She was a lousy lay."

"Ben!" I warned him.

"She was."

"I don't care—I can't hear that."

"You asked me. I didn't bring it up. I would never have brought it up. But you asked."

"I asked. You're right. Forget it."

He looked away from me, petulant, sniffed slightly and sighed heavily—an overacted performance of hurt feelings.

"What about the beard?"

"No," he mumbled.

"I think it'll make a big difference for the jury."

"They're not gonna find me innocent cause of how I look."

"It'll help."

"But then we won't be able to . . ." He finished his complaint with a shy glance, a demure smile.

"You'll look great without glasses, with the beard, and we'll make sure you're tan, get you running and on the machines. Show off your height. You should stand up straight like you do when you're dressing up. Gives you elegance."

"What are you saying? That I can give it up if I look great as a man?"

"No . . ." Was I? I didn't know if there was a deeper meaning, a hidden wish.

"I thought you liked it. You—"

"I did. What do you think that means?" I asked him. I had been moved by his fantasy, his vision of himself as beautiful. I discovered his penis under all that fabric and had a wild, almost painful orgasm not long after he was in me. Was I gay? Or did I want men to be women with cocks? Or did I need to heal people when I made love to them? Or was I just nuts?

"I think there's a lot of forgiveness in you," he said. "You're not like Wendy—you're not sentimental and you're not self-righteous. You accept people as they are."

"What happened, Ben? Why did you kill her?" I asked this in a new tone, as if it had never been asked before: naïvely, without judgment or guile, merely wanting to know.

"Are you serious?"

"Yes," I told him, earnest and gentle. "Tell me."

"If I tell you, it means I trust you with my life."

"I know, Ben." I touched his hand. "I won't betray you."

He sighed, his brow rippling with pain. "I try not to think about it." He swallowed and shut his eyes. "She kept at me, nagging and crying all night, all day, for the whole weekend. Either she attacked me or she sat there with that look, you know that look."

"What look?" I thought of Wendy as playful and sympathetic, never recriminating.

"Like a lizard. Those narrow eyes, turning green. And when I called her on it, she burst into tears and pretended I was attacking her. She looked at me as if I was shit, a piece of shit on the street, shit she stepped in—but I was the one attacking her. She was going to have that look on her face for the rest of my life. I couldn't take it. Anytime she wanted something, she'd bring it up. And one day"—Ben was full of energy now, eyes boldly talking to me, his face flushed with outrage—"one day she'd tell Naomi about—"

"No," I argued involuntarily.

"Oh yes, she would. She was very jealous that Naomi loved me more than her—"

I felt myself rebel: Naomi didn't love Ben more than Wendy. I wanted to argue, but I stopped myself.

"—and someday she would have told her. Just to humiliate me in her eyes."

Naomi's still going to know, I thought, as if this were a rational matter.

"She would never forgive me. Can't you understand? I begged her to forgive me. To accept me, like you have." Tears had formed in his eyes and now trailed down his face as his voice broke and he whispered: "She started up one more time about what she would do if I didn't get rid of the clothes, if I didn't go to a shrink, if I didn't do every fucking thing exactly the way she wanted it done. I hit her to shut her up. She hated me and she was going to hate me forever and I couldn't stand it, I couldn't listen to it. I didn't mean to kill her, I just wanted to shut her up." He checked on the effect of this: a nervous glance and then modestly lowered his eyes.

I was straight, but not challenging. "Ben, you didn't just hit her, you bludgeoned her."

"I hit her and I hit her and she smashed her head into the table and she was bleeding and I knew she was dying . . . and I . . ." He shut his eyes again and lowered his head even more, prayerfully. He whispered something I couldn't hear.

"What?" I asked.

"I didn't want her to live," he whispered. "I got one of the logs and I looked away and hit her one more time."

"You knew you were killing her. You chose to kill her." I glanced around us to see if anyone was eavesdropping: New Yorkers on a lunch break, discussing vacation plans, tax planning, office politics; out-of-towners on a pause from Christmas shopping, bags under their feet, panting from the breakneck pace of their spending.

"Why are you saying that? Why are—"

"I just want the truth, I don't want any lies. Like last night. We stopped lying last night, we stopped hiding."

"Yes." He nodded.

"I don't want any more of all that"—I nodded at the restaurant of people—"all that routine posing." I mocked them: " 'We're not all good or all bad, we're just people.' " I touched his chin. "Don't lie anymore."

He nodded. "I could have saved her. Maybe she would have been damaged or something, but sure, if I got her to a hospital right away she would have lived, she might have been totally fine. But it would have been the end of me. No one would hire me. I would never see Nommy again—"

I took hold of his chin and urged him to look me in the eye: "But that's not why, Ben. That's not why you picked up the log."

"Why?" His mouth drooped, stupid and beaten. "Tell me why I did it?"

"Because you wanted her dead. If she was dead then you got everything: Nommy and the dressing up and her money—"

"But it's ruined me! My life is over. How could I want that?"

"Tell me the truth, Ben."

Tears welled at his lower lids again. His chin trembled. "I'm sorry. I really am bad, that's what you're saying."

Gentle, but insistent, I reached for his chin again: "Tell me the truth, Ben."

"I did." He leaned back, away from the touch of my hand. He refused, shaking his head.

"No. Those were facts. I want the truth."

"I don't want to grow the beard," he bargained.

"It may cost you your freedom."

"I don't care."

I nodded my agreement and waited for him to speak.

"I wanted her dead." Once that was out, he breathed in deeply, through his nose. "I was sick and tired of her, of her disappointment in me, her disapproval, her competitiveness. For Wendy to be happy, everyone in the world, even my little girl, had to think she was better than me. I was the schmuck and she was wonderful for marrying me. I was the asshole she put up with—she was a fucking saint. I wanted her dead."

That was the truth. As I heard it, I felt relief—not horror or grief. Even though I had known it all along, I was relaxed—saved really— by hearing its simplicity and its coherence. He had told the truth, both about her and about him, and about the rest of us too. And I was pardoned by this truth. It took away the silly worries of my guilt: if only I hadn't told Wendy about the secret apartment; if only I had insisted they spend the weekend in New York; if only I had driven up and surprised them with a visit. There were thousands of them and they had buzzed me like gnats; they were stupid and maddening and now I knew for sure they were nonsense. Sooner or later Ben would have killed her. To do otherwise would have meant he had accepted her judgment of him.

"But she won anyway," he said. "Now I'm the monster she wanted me to be. And she's a martyr."

"*You* won. She's dead, Ben. And you're alive. Don't start lying again."

He winced, picked up the check, and reached for his wallet. "You hate me now." He was paying me off, ending us.

"I used to hate you."

He paused. "You did?" He was actually surprised.

"Just as you said: she was wonderful, you were beneath her. I don't hate you now."

"But I'm bad." He spoke clearheadedly, no self-pity or inverted righteousness. "Turns out I'm bad. I'm a bad man."

"I know."

"What are you saying? You don't care?" He counted out money and paid. He was ready to rise and go; he had hardened his tone, he was prepared to hear the worst. We must have looked casual to the others, shoppers and workers, as if we were discussing what to do next, a movie or more shopping?

"I care. Of course I care. I'm just saying I don't kid myself about it."

"You don't?" He sneered, turned his head in disgust, then whipped it back at me, an interrogator catching me in a lie: "How about your money? You care about your money, don't you?"

"What are you talking about?"

Ben stuck his face at me and growled: "Your money! You care about that, don't you?"

"What about my money?"

"I lost everything you gave me." He waited. When I didn't explode, he continued: "I had a genius idea—go short the Japanese stock market. I bought thirty thousand dollars' worth of options. Guess what? Instead, the Japs made a new record high last week. The options expired worthless last Friday." That said, he got up and walked out of the restaurant.

When I caught up to him outside on the mobbed street, bumped by sharp-edged Christmas presents and angry elbows, I said: "Am I supposed to be shocked? Is that the game you played with Wendy? How far can I go? How bad a boy can I be?"

"Fuck you," he said into my face, his breath warm in the cold, smelling of the onion he had eaten with his hamburger. He turned his back and walked away.

I chased after him. I had no pride about it; I ran and grabbed him.

"Leave me alone!" He tried to shake me off.

We startled the intent self-absorbed New Yorkers out of their privacy. Several stood and watched for a moment, their packages drooping, their breath flowing toward us. I pleaded with him shamelessly: "Please, Ben, you just trusted me—"

"Go ahead, tell the cops. Put me away. You can't scare me."

"I don't want to!" I stamped my foot like a girl. "I just want to be honest."

"I'm such a fucking idiot!" He smashed his hand against his forehead. He hit himself so hard his head was whiplashed and the blow left a red welt, an impression of the palm of his hand.

"Ben!" Appalled, I grabbed his wrist to stop him from doing it again.

"I can't believe what a fucking loser I am," he moaned. The pedestrians had moved on—our current dramatics weren't entertaining enough. Apparently a woman chasing a man was a superior show to a whining male failure.

"The money's not important. Why did you want to make money, anyway—what use is it?"

He shook his head from side to side, wildly, as if trying to escape from the pursuit of this fact: "I killed her mother." That seemed to be news to him.

"Yes," I agreed to the obvious because he didn't appear to know it was obvious.

"What have I got to give her? I took away her mother and . . ." His hands, in agony, grabbed at nothing. His face wrinkled, his mouth opened soundlessly and then he sobbed, knees sagging, shoulders slumped, his chest quaking. He stood rooted to the spot, but his torso jerked with unhappiness. I approached him with open arms. His head fell on my shoulder; he cried into my neck. I held him and gently rocked his big body, whispering soothing words.

People walked around us, as if we were a misplaced streetlight. After a while he quieted. One woman smiled at me over his shoulder: she thought us tender. We were.

Finally, when he leaned away and looked shyly into my eyes, I told him: "You can give Naomi your self. Your real self. And you can give her the truth."

"I can't tell her!" He was horrified.

"You can admit what you've done and get yourself free of all this as soon as possible. You can guarantee that she'll know you and see you while you're in prison, and that she'll have you when you're out. But if you go on lying and fighting, she has to lie and fight with you, or grow to hate you."

"I can't."

"You have to, Ben. For all of us. You have to save us by telling the truth."

He grabbed my bare hand, fingers red from the winter air, and kissed it frantically, tears running down his face. "I don't want to lose you . . . I don't want to grow a beard . . ."

I smiled. "If you tell the truth you don't have to worry about any of that."

He repels you, doesn't he? At that moment, I think I loved him. This tenderness, this neediness, that was what Wendy had seen, had wanted to care for. I had been wrong, terribly wrong, to think she married him merely out of desperation to procreate. She had wanted to save him, to satisfy his great longing. Ben pressed my hands on his eyes, using them like a handkerchief to soak up his tears. "I'll do whatever you say, Molly."

"We'll go to your lawyer and tell him you want to confess and bargain for a short sentence. I think we might get a psychiatric evaluation, Ben. Maybe you'll never have to go to prison."

"I don't want to go now."

"Let's get it over with."

"Now?" he complained in a pained whine. "It's happening so fast. I won't even see Nommy one more time. . . ."

"Just to Varney. We don't have to go to the police right away—"

"Let's spend this week together. Okay? We'll go next Monday."

He pleaded like a boy wanting more dessert; I was a firm, kindly mother: "No, Ben."

"Let's go away for a couple days. Just the three of us. Please? Let me be with you and Nommy for two more days, okay?"

"We can talk to your lawyer today and agree to go to the police next week—"

"Molly!" he moaned, and pressed his face pathetically into my hands. "Please . . . please . . . please . . ."

I gave in. Partly to his vision: us three together, happy in our solitude, storing up courage to face our future.

The ride downtown was quick, no more than fifteen minutes. I was thrilled. Everything had been lifted off me, all the weights of sorrow. I could breathe deeply, inhale the world without fear, because all the worries had answers. It would be hard and it would cost the three of us a great deal, but we could be saved, Ben and Naomi and I. We could be saved.

We went in together to the Riverside School and stood side by side in the lobby, surrounded by looks of amazement and disgust until Naomi came downstairs. Pam and Janet didn't greet me, averting their eyes, pretending to be so absorbed in conversation with each other that they didn't see me.

Naomi ran into Ben's arms, swaying from side to side, mumbling, "Daddy, Daddy, Daddy." Parents and children passed us quickly, in a hurry to get out. They were all gone by the time Naomi released her father. I didn't care. I was happy and free, my conscience clear for the first time since Wendy's death.

As soon as Naomi had untangled from Ben, I bent down for my hug. Naomi stepped back, away from me, and frowned.

"What are *you* doing here?" she asked coldly.

❧

My fantasy that the three of us would be happy together, pardoned and redeemed, died quickly during that walk. Quickly—but it was agony.

I tried to catch her eye—she looked only at him. I tried to take her hand—she pulled away and moved to the far side of Ben, interposing him between us. I moved to her free flank—she changed position again.

Naomi had sensed the new situation, although she couldn't know in her conscious mind. Naïve, you think, that I didn't anticipate her reaction to peace between me and Ben. It meant I was becoming her mother, I decided; naturally she resented my presumption.

At home Ben said to her, "How about we go to the country for a couple days?"

"Now?" She put her hands on her hips, a scold: "Daddy, you're teasing."

"No I'm not."

"It's not the weekend."

"I know. So what? We'll go to a hotel for tonight and tomorrow. We'll tell your teacher you were sick."

Naomi jumped with pleasure. "A hotel?"

"Sure."

Another leap. "With an indoor pool?"

"No. Only an outdoor pool."

She loved his joke. "We're polar bears," she said, and sprang into the air again.

Her excitement lasted while she figured out what toys to take and I picked out her clothes. My longing for happiness, it turns out, is pathetically simpleminded: once more I was foolish enough to think that everything would be okay. Instead, when Naomi found out I was coming along, her disgust returned.

"I'll go and pack," I told Ben when I finished getting her things.

He had been in his bedroom, presumably doing the same.

"What for?" she said.

"Molly's coming with us." Ben was gentle.

"You *are?*" Her skepticism had no delight in it.

Ben wasn't surprised that she didn't want me along. Had I been kidding myself from the beginning? Was I merely an intruder to her?

"You wanted me to come for Christmas," I argued.

"But that's a vacation. I thought you have to work on Saturdays."

"Don't you want me to come?" I begged Naomi.

"Of course she—," Ben began.

"You can come," she interrupted with a magnificent indifference. I left to pack.

My apartment seemed so dreary. I used to be pleased to leave Wendy's stuffy messy place for my spare elegance. Now the leather and steel of the Nautilus resembled a medieval torture device and our kitchen was a mockery of the bright, loud country homes it emulated. Even my mother's trailer—hot and sweet with the baking of blueberry pies—had more true elegance than this sterile environment.

While packing I was angrier and angrier with Naomi. I had an evil thought: maybe she had made things worse between Ben and Wendy. How else could I make sense of the change in her attitude? Naomi liked me as long as Ben and I were hostile; she didn't like me when we were friendly. Was she jealous? Had she been divisive with Wendy and Ben? Played them off each other to win special attention and love through competitive bidding?

I wanted to smack her. I had given up so much, I had risked everything to save her. I had even forced myself to love her disgusting father. . . .

The phone interrupted this pain. By then I was so worked up that if Ben was the caller, I planned to say I wouldn't go. Let them have this last trip to themselves—see if I care.

It was Jake Prosser. He spoke without pauses for me to answer, as if I were a phone machine. "Molly, I've just received a letter from Stefan's lawyer, Judith Liverwright—"

Stefan had hired a feminist lawyer, famous for defending battered women, a bizarre selection, only it wasn't, it was his way of sending a message.

Jake was still talking: "—and they're going for the jugular. I've just flipped through it—it's nine pages—and they're leaving nothing out. I thought this was going to be civilized, what the hell's—?"

I interrupted and told him I had retained someone else to handle my divorce.

"Fine." He cut off the possibility of an explanation. "Tell Amy"—his secretary—"who it is and I'll fax this over." He hung up without a good-bye, not even bothering to transfer me to Amy.

I wasted no time, dialing Stefan's private line at his office. "Hello," he answered in a confidential whisper. I was interrupting him in midsession with a patient. I had only done this twice in our marriage, once when his father was hospitalized with the stroke that eventually killed him, and recently when I learned that Wendy was missing.

"Stefan, Prosser's gotten the letter. I know what you're trying to do—"

"I can't talk. I'm with a patient. But I have a suggestion to make before your lawyer responds. Call Harriet Fliess."

"Don't play games. Tell me why I should call her."

"She's willing to file in family court to petition for custody of Naomi." He hung up.

I slumped next to the phone, pressing my temples, struggling to understand this legal quiz, as if I were back at school faced with a test for which I had neglected to study.

I'm embarrassed that I required more than a few minutes before I got it: as long as Ben remained single (and if Stefan tied me up in a complicated divorce I could not marry Ben in time), then a cousin's challenge to Ben's custody of Naomi had a reasonable chance. Stefan must have talked Harriet out of her devotion to Ben. How, I didn't know, but after all, Stefan is paid well to talk people in and out of all kinds of madness.

Stefan was no fool: he had deduced why I wanted our divorce. But that was before, before Ben had confessed to me. Now Naomi was only part of the reason for my desire to be with Ben.

When the phone rang again I answered wearily, woozy from the earlier blows, still in a fog, unsure of how I could counterpunch.

"Hello?" The half-female voice was demanding and nervous. "Is this Molly Gray?"

I recognized Larry's voice immediately. "Yes," I said gloomily, nodding my head. I wasn't surprised to hear from him: God was obviously against me, massing His forces. Or maybe it was Satan. Can you tell the difference?

"My name is Lawrence Brady."

I felt no shame—I still couldn't stand him. "Yes . . . ?"

"I was given your number by a Mr. Fliess. Were you and his daughter driving . . . ?" and Larry went on to describe our encounter at Burger King, including the fact that his friend B.J. had left to follow me and the little girl back to New York. "He had an accident. He was killed," Larry said at the end of this speech. He moaned on the word *killed*. "The police say he lost control . . . they don't know why. Do you—?"

I said: "No."

"No what?" he demanded. "It wasn't you or you don't know?"

"I wasn't there." This time I was the one to hang up. I trembled. There seemed to be nothing in me but hate: my heart was dirty and crumbling, as black and as fragile as charred wood.

The phone rang again within seconds. I didn't answer. I stood a few feet away, trembling. Larry wouldn't quit. B.J. was his friend and he wouldn't leave me alone any more than I had let Ben be.

I heard the crash again, saw the truck roll over, bouncing off the concrete. I covered my face and screamed to shout out the noise, to stop the remembering.

The phone stopped.

There was no reason to stay in my empty apartment or my empty life: after all, I belonged with Ben and Naomi.

❧

I packed frantically and crossed the hall.

"Where were you?" Ben greeted me. "I just called you. Someone phoned—I don't know how he got the new number—"

"I told him," I heard Naomi say, but I talked over her, asking Ben: "What did he tell you?"

"He asked me if you and—"

"Was it B.J.?" Naomi was perched on the large suitcase Ben had packed for himself. From its size I had to assume he had brought along his secret wardrobe. His presumptuousness irritated me; his desire to repeat our lovemaking, although predictable and natural (if such a thing can be natural), sickened me.

"It was Larry," I answered her. "Calling to say B.J. is okay." I told Ben a simplified and dishonest account of our meeting with them. Naomi cooperated, although I think for her it was the truth. She talked about making the snowwoman as if that had been great fun; in her version B.J. didn't carry her to the truck, he was merely curious about why we were driving so late and then wanted to help us find our way home.

"What happened to him?" she asked. She seemed to be less annoyed with me, although still distant.

"He had a blowout. He had to stop and change his tire. By the time he was done we were too far ahead."

Ben was suspicious. On the way to the Westchester hotel where he had succeeded in booking rooms he went over it: our location, why we had stopped to eat, why they had been friendly, why B.J. followed us so far. . . .

"I'll explain later," I whispered sternly.

The hotel in Westchester was modern, intended solely for conferences, I think; but desperate New Yorkers who couldn't afford weekend houses used it for getaways, playing tennis in air-filled bubbles, swimming indoors, and skiing cross-country on its snow-covered golf course. The hotel had come to accommodate this business by arranging special events for kids, even a kind of supervised play for a few hours each afternoon. But that was on weekends—we had arrived in the midst of a convention of American Honda dealers. Two of them passed us as we registered, one-upping each other with the cost of their new homes.

"If the world made any sense I would have their money," Ben mumbled to me.

The options he had held against Japanese stocks were bought with my money I reminded him.

"Thanks for the memories," he answered. I thought his joke was a good sign.

We ordered room service. That made a mess. Naomi complained, justifiably, about her tasteless spaghetti, left it gelling on her plate, and demanded Ben take her for a nighttime swim. She whined when

Ben refused. Because he didn't say no cleanly, Naomi tried to coax him into changing his mind. They did a slow, passive dance of demand and refusal which made my teeth ache. Finally, Ben became so exasperated he shouted no (brutally, right into her big eyes) and told her to leave him alone. I was sorry I had come. I was sick of both of them.

Naomi sidled up to me and whispered seductively, "I want to show you I can swim across the pool by myself." Her message was clear: if I indulged her, she would like me again. I found her behavior manipulative and depressing. "You promised, Molly. You promised you would watch me swim across the pool."

"Tomorrow," I grumbled.

"Anyway, it's time for you to go to sleep," Ben said. They got into another long hassle, only this time Ben was very insistent. Even when she was tucked in bed in the other room, quietly reading, he wasn't satisfied. He nagged her, turning off her light (something he never did at home), his tone stern. She asked him to lie with her for a while. He refused bluntly. She then asked if I could lie with her. He said no.

What was his rush? Why did he want her unconscious?

He wants to dress up, I realized.

I was kidding myself. This would never work. They were both greedy, tapeworms of need: they would consume me.

"I'll lie with her!" I half screamed, interrupting their nauseating argument, and walked toward her room.

Ben grabbed me at the doorway in full view of Naomi. "No. I told her no and that's it."

"You don't tell me what I can and cannot do," I said, jerking my arm free.

Naomi yelled: "It's okay! I don't want you to!" She dove under the covers.

"Okay," Ben said. "You heard her."

She was just a baby: What was wrong with me? Her longing for attention and love had no likeness to his thwarted needs. What was the matter with me? How could I judge her so harshly?

I went over to the mass huddled under the hotel's scratchy bedspread.

"Molly!" Ben whispered sharply.

"Leave me alone," I said. "I'm giving her a kiss good night."

I uncovered her. She hooked my neck with her skinny arms and pulled my face to hers. "I love you, Molly," she whispered in my ear. The hairs at her temples were wet with perspiration. It was too hot in the room.

"I love you too, honey," I said. On my way out of the room I lowered the heater. "Go to sleep," I told her. That was the best thing for her—unknowing rest.

I reminded myself as I left her: caring for Naomi is pure and good—remember that, Molly. Caring for Ben is necessary and evil. Don't get the two mixed up.

Only a few more nights, I thought.

No, it would be more than that, it would be months, even with a confession. There would be psychiatric evaluations and if Ben told (of course he would tell) what we had done and were continuing to do, then Stefan would know—psychiatrists are as gossipy and clubby and political as anyone and he had a lot of muscle. They could use it against me to take Naomi away, give her to Harriet.

What had I done?

Ben gathered our foodstuffs, stacking it all on the trays. I sat, stunned and ill, in an armchair facing the television. There was something showing on the screen; my eyes didn't see the images.

Ben's put his hand on my thigh and rubbed. "Do you think Nommy knows?" he whispered. He crouched next to the chair, watching the connecting door, which wasn't completely shut.

I hardly breathed. I shook my head.

"I want you so much. I wish I had seen you naked last night." He hadn't because I had quickly stripped off my jeans in the dark and replaced them just as rapidly once we were done. I never removed my top. In the pink light he wouldn't have seen well anyway. Our encounter was mad, fast, and mixed up; woman to man, man to man, woman to woman—we had no distinct identities.

I said nothing. His hand covered my crotch, not hard, but possessive. "You're blond, aren't you?" he whispered.

I didn't answer.

"I wish I was," he said. "You know I'm shaved."

Of course I knew. I had enjoyed the feel of his hairless large boy's penis, uncorrupted by age and lust.

"Stop it," I said like a dumb heroine in a pornographic film, pushing his hand away. Only I was sincere. I moved out of the chair. I pretended to be interested in the television, switching channels, seeing nothing. Big faces talked at me; cars smashed into each other; a giant deodorant was launched into space. Time passed. The boxed voices were comforting, especially the laugh track of sitcoms.

"So what's the story with this Larry?" Ben's tone was the old one: harassed, suspicious, unpleasant.

"They suspected I was kidnapping her," I told the television. "She told them I wasn't her mother and they wanted to make sure she got home safely."

"You're lying." His tone was matter-of-fact. "Why are you lying to me, Molly? I thought we told each other the truth about everything."

I didn't answer him. My heart thumped and blood choked me. What did he know? Having confessed and been forgiven, why was he so malevolent? Had he fooled me at the restaurant? Or was he right, should I have told him about B.J.?

"Well . . . ?" he asked very quietly.

"They didn't believe I was her mother. One of them wanted to take her to a shelter."

"Come on, Molly. It must have been you who wanted to take her to a shelter. And when they found out you weren't her mother, they forced you to bring her home."

Relieved, I turned away from the television and walked over to him. "No, Ben. They thought I was running away with her and they wanted me to go to a shelter. Then they found out I wasn't her mother and they got very suspicious. One of them followed us most of the way back to make sure I took her home. He disappeared somewhere—evidently he got into an accident. I didn't want to say anything in front of Naomi, but his friend called to say that his truck turned over on the highway and he's dead. He wanted to know if I'd seen it happen." I stood over Ben—he was slouched in the easy chair—triumphant in my array of lying facts.

You see, there is no truth in facts. And if you're busy making judgments, remember there is no risk to all your fine opinions of the way people should live. Imagine a gun is at your head the next time you make a judgment: imagine that you will be shot for what you believe. Do you still believe it?

"I want to fuck straight," Ben said without any indication that this was a non sequitur, that he had changed the subject. Maybe, as far as he was concerned, he hadn't. Perhaps to him all conversations were really about sex. "I'll take off my glasses." He smiled as if this were witty. He waited for a response. When I didn't make one, he took off his glasses and squinted at me. "Can't grow a beard tonight—I could paint one on."

I looked at the door to Naomi's room and shook my head.

"She's asleep," he answered my silent objection. "I looked in while you were inspecting the television screen for scratches." Again, he smiled at his own joke. "I knew she was exhausted from yesterday, that's why I insisted she go to sleep."

I shook my head.

"We'll lock the connecting door. I really want to see your blond pussy." He reached around to the back of my skirt for the zipper. "I love talking about sex without bullshit. Wendy couldn't stand to just say it and hear it. She thought sex was dirty."

My skirt fell to the floor. He peered at my panties and took a deep breath.

"Look at your stomach. It's beautiful."

"Ben, you're treating me like I'm a prostitute."

He lifted his face and I was shocked by what I saw: he was devastated by my comment. His eyes—wide with blindness anyway—floated, lost in their sockets; his cheeks sagged with hurt and his mouth drooped petulantly. "Molly," he complained.

"I didn't mean to hurt you," I said, idiotically.

"I'm just loving your body. I never got to be with someone so beautiful in my life. I'm really grateful." He pleaded this to me—that is, to my face—but his eyes trailed down, glistening with greed, skimming over my stomach, pelvis, and thighs.

On a visit to my mother when I was seventeen I dressed in tight white shorts and a black Polo top, also very tight. I was very proud of my tall figure and what one prep school boy called my "arrogant tits," which had finally blossomed after a worrisome delay. I looked great and I enjoyed it. In fact, I would have considered becoming a model if not for fidelity to Naomi's feminism. I entered their trailer full of myself. Mother kissed me and made no comment except that I had color in my cheeks. My father took one look at nubile me and said, "Sorry, dearie, it's against the law for me to fuck ya. I'll get Gordie to come over if you want." He laughed hoarsely at his joke. Gordie was, as they called it, "slow," and a slob covered with oil; he had dirt from before the dinosaurs under his nails. After that I tried not to arouse men even though Dr. Reynolds pointed out why this episode was traumatic and its consequence crippling. But I did go back to exercising and dressing well and was civil to the men I took to bed, actually having breakfast with a few of them. Then I married Stefan and killed that issue, I thought.

"I want to love normally. I want to be human again," Ben said, looking meek. "I thought that's what you promised if I told the truth." There was no implied threat in his words or tone; I wish there had been: I could have resisted threats.

We locked the connecting door. He asked me to take off my clothes. I did and moved to get in the bed.

"No, please," he moaned. "Stand up."

He inspected me as if I were cattle—no, a slave ready for auction. He practically checked my gums for disease. He pushed me onto the bed. I fell over stiffly, like a mannequin. He lost himself in my neck, my shoulders, my underarms, my stomach, my thighs, my calves, my feet, and finally my genitals—he licked and bit and sucked and I felt nothing. Eventually his hairless cock plunged in.

But he didn't ejaculate. He stopped humping after a while and it was still hard.

"Something wrong?" I asked.

"You aren't responding," he said.

"I'm sorry. I'm having a good time," I lied, wanting to be polite.

"That doesn't make sense. If you're having a good time you'd respond. You feel almost dry."

"Go ahead," I said, and bucked a little, sliding his penis in and out. I was dry, it hurt.

He tried again. No orgasm. Eventually, he got soft.

He lay next to me staring at the ceiling for a long time. I dressed, covered him up, opened the connecting door (Naomi was sound asleep; her breathing was so deep she almost hummed), and put our food tray outside the door. When I returned to his side, he said, in a choked, hoarse, sad voice: "I guess I'd better not grow a beard."

When I didn't respond to that he said, "Do you hate me?"

"No," I said.

"Do you love me?" When I didn't answer right away, he said, "I love you, Molly."

I felt the pressure rolling over from his side, a heavy rock of sadness, crushing me.

"I love you too, Ben," I said.

⁂

I insisted Ben sleep in the other room with Naomi. Strange, looking back on it, that I didn't go myself, since I worried about him turning to her for sex. I guess I was so desperate for solitude. It may be a damning judgment of my marriage to Stefan, but I had never felt the lack of being alone. Stefan was small in my bed, like a stuffed animal that happened to move occasionally. Yes, you're right, I really am a bad person. All those years Wendy must have buoyed me above the depths. I made many protestations of sisterhood and love, and yet I needed her more than I knew. Without her I was drowning.

Anyway, they slept soundly—I know because I stayed awake until five, once again going around and around all these events in a hopeless search for a way out.

Ben's sexual disappointment in me had an immediate consequence: beginning with breakfast he was hostile to Naomi.

Naomi took one look at the hotel's buffet and was dismayed by the long row of heated trays of pancakes, French toast, scrambled eggs, sausages, bacon; beyond that was another row of cold cereals, fruits, juices, bagels, sliced salmon. The killed and displayed food beckoned like a dare: eat me and see if you survive. "I don't know what to have," she said.

"Don't go in for a big production, Nommy. Just pick something out," Ben grumbled. "You don't like what you pick, get something else." He stalked off toward the bagels.

I helped her: she was sweet and docile and hungry. I was delighted by her appetite. Her vitality encouraged me.

262

We sat and ate and chatted for more than forty minutes; we left him alone. Ben said nothing. He scooped clumps of cream cheese on two bagels, slapping on red slabs of salmon, devouring them with wide toothful bites. Bits of the stayed wedged between his teeth and they looked like bloody fangs.

"Can we go swimming after breakfast?" she asked.

"For God's sake, I said we could." Ben's tone was low, but the words scraped against each other with irritation. "Stop bothering me or I won't take you at all."

"Ben!" I complained, and turned to Naomi, my tone excessively sweet. "I'll take you swimming now."

"Okay," she said happily, tossed her napkin down, and got to her feet, bouncing on tiptoes.

I had an awful memory, a sickening memory: Wendy doing the same thing, a plaintive scolding to her husband, a compensating indulgence to her daughter.

The water was tepid and chlorinated. I longed for the cold transparency of Maine's waters—shatter your bones, sure, but it wakens you from the boredom of comfort.

Naomi's skinny body undulated through the water, a swimming snake. Her head, narrowed by wet hair, pushed up in front of me, eyes puffy and red from the chemical.

"See?" she said.

"You're terrific," I praised her, and I remembered vividly how that triumph had felt for me. Maybe such moments are our happiest—commonplace achievements done for the first time. How thrilling it must have been for Wendy to see Naomi do them, knowing that she had made Naomi out of herself, nurtured her from a speck to this full-blown creature of skills and desire.

Ben had robbed my friend of that pleasure.

Because she wouldn't allow him his pleasure.

We were still in the water when Ben appeared. Naomi broke off from our tag game to ask her father to watch her swim across the pool.

"This one is even longer," she gave as an incentive.

"Sure, honey." He seemed to have cheered up.

She performed for him, thrilled with herself.

"That's good, honey. But you're bending your knees. They should be locked." He pantomimed with his arms. "You kick with your hips."

She swam again.

He wasn't satisfied. When she got the hips right, he fussed over her breathing, that she lifted her head out of the water too much. She tried again; he found more faults. The cycle ended with Naomi in tears.

Ben, affecting innocence, opened his hands and pleaded: "What did I do? I'm just trying to help you learn how to swim."

"I know how!" She stamped her foot and stood by the side of the pool, wet and weeping.

"Okay," I said, gesturing for him to move away. "Cut it out."

"She doesn't know how to take criticism," he said as if this were very unfortunate. He spoke loud enough for her to hear, but said it to me—adult to adult—and that made it seem more grave and damning, a heartless judgment.

"You spoiled her fun," I said. "That's what you did."

"Molly!" Ben came up to me. He squeezed my arm and whispered furiously in my ear. "Don't undermine me. She's my daughter. Do you understand?"

There were plenty of people around us—mostly wives of Honda dealers, I assumed—lying in sun chairs even though there was nothing but pale blue light coming through the panels in the ceiling. They all seemed to look at us (what other view did they have?), intrigued by our quarreling. I was humiliated. This too, Wendy. I remembered this also happening to you.

"Let go of me." I squeezed the words out through my rage, though shame kept my volume low.

He did let go, instead shaking a thick finger in my face. "Don't ever do that again." He waved at Naomi, miserable in a towel now, head down, staring at the wet tiles. "Come on, you're shivering. We're going to the room."

We trailed him. Naomi trembled in her towel all the way. I tried to rub her, but he wouldn't stop his pace.

"Hurry up," he snapped.

He entered our rooms ahead of us, walked up to the coffee table, and kicked it over. "I can't do anything right with you two! I'm always in the wrong!"

"Okay, that's it!" I shouted, my heart pounding, rushing past him going toward Naomi's room. "We're going home!" I got my suitcase from the closet, opened it on the bed, pulled the dresser drawers free, and dumped their contents in. We're going home? Where's home? I thought to myself.

Ravaging the room helped: my breathing slowed, my thumping heart calmed. I became aware of Naomi and Ben, both in the doorway, watching. When I had filled the suitcase I shut it and looked up at them.

Ben's hand rested on Naomi's head, thoughtlessly, propping himself up. She was downcast; Ben seemed curious.

"What are you doing?" he asked.

"Looks to me like I'm packing," I said.

"If you want to go, that's fine. Nommy and I are staying. So don't pack our clothes." He had strength in him—where had it come from? He was determined, he was resolved, he was unafraid.

And he should fear me: I could go to the lieutenant and repeat Ben's confession, including the detail about what he used to strike the fatal blow. Along with everything else that would certainly convict him. And then I could lie and say he told me he has sexual desires for Naomi—maybe that would be enough to obtain custody.

Instead I asked: "How will you get home?"

"What do you mean?" Ben asked.

"If I take the car," I spoke slowly, exasperated, "How will you get home?"

"We'll rent one, asshole."

"Don't you dare talk to me that way!" I pushed the suitcase off the bed. It slumped to the floor. I kicked it.

"Okay," he said, and laughed, his hands up in surrender. He bent down and said in Naomi's ear, "Tough lady, huh?"

She shrugged him off and ran off into the other room.

"What the fuck is the matter with you?" I whispered to him in a fury.

"Don't boss me around," he said mildly. "I'm doing what you want. What's your problem?"

"I want you to talk to Varney right now." That was the answer. I couldn't stand things being so unresolved. I even picked up the phone, a visual aide, and said: "Here. Call Varney now and tell him.

Let's get some idea of the legal consequences, what he thinks he can bargain for."

Ben shook his head. "That's not what we agreed," he said quietly. He stepped back into the other room and began to shut the door behind him. Before he was obscured, he said: "When you're fit for human company let us know."

It was almost as if I had been sent to my room for being bad.

I wanted to kill him. No, I don't mean revenge. I mean kill him for himself, for his endless selfishness, for which he had so many faces, so many voices, so many threats, and—worst of all—so many talented lawyers, the firm of Fliess & Fliess & Fliess & Sons, all making pitiful pleas. Even when he admitted he was wrong, he somehow ended up a winner. How could he have failed in business? He must have destroyed himself—no one could defeat him.

I admitted to my vanity that I had never won an argument with him. Despite my superior brain, despite my moral high ground, despite any advantage you can name, he got his way, always, and then somehow managed to make me apologize to him for his victory, which he then quickly transformed into a burden.

Well, I would kill him. That's what I decided. If he did not—for whatever reason, even if he whined and begged and cried—if he did not confess when we returned to New York, then I would kill him.

No, nothing less would do. You might still think there is another solution, but I had finally learned my lesson. If he wriggled free once more, he was dead.

I fixed the room, replacing clothes and drawers, remaking the bed, and rejoined them in the other room.

Naomi, dried off and wearing clothes, was on the couch watching a cartoon show. She didn't turn her head.

Ben was on the phone.

My heart leaped—for a second. But after a moment or two, I could hear he was talking about the stock market, not to Varney. I sat next to Naomi and put my arm around her shoulder. She slid easily into the crook, a perfect fit. I kissed the top of her head.

"I love you," I whispered.

"Hmmm," she hummed, and snuggled in.

"Everything's going to be okay," I said.

"Great." Ben's volume went up a notch, just enough to be clearly heard. His tone had a bluffer's bravado: "Buy one hundred Index Puts at the market. I'll get the money transferred tomorrow. Call me back with the price so I'll—Yeah—I'll give it to you in cash, you stupid fuck—"

"Ben!" I scolded, nodding at Naomi.

"Sorry." He rung off. I could feel his eyes on me. The tension of his wants, his dissatisfactions, was palpable. How had we failed Ben Fliess that day? Let me count the ways:

I failed him in bed.

Naomi failed him at breakfast.

I failed as a swimming instructor.

She failed as a swimmer.

I failed to show public loyalty.

She failed to take criticism well.

I failed to take criticism well.

She failed to walk quickly.

I failed to keep my temper.

Now I was about to fail again.

"Uh, Molly." Ben cleared his throat awkwardly. "Molly, I need your advice about business. I want to show you some figures. Could you come over?"

Naomi raised her body with a weary sigh and a groan that seemed to suggest my departure was a mistake. I had learned the code to her noises—she understood another quarrel was coming.

He pretended to show me some notes on the hotel stationery (I guess for Naomi's benefit) while he whispered his mad idea.

"I think the Index Puts look to be a good buy here. The Japanese market took a big hit their last two sessions. I believe that's a signal it's coming, that it'll crash our market again. Bigger this time."

"Ben, I have no idea what you're talking about."

"Let me explain," he began pompously, adjusting his glasses, a brilliant professor lecturing his student's unripened mind.

"No. Don't explain. Just tell me what you want. Is it money?"

Oh, but that was too naked for him. He flinched, was wounded (I could feel myself ready to apologize), settling finally on outrage. "Okay," he said in a tone that was anything but okay. "If that's the way you feel. You don't want to help, I don't see why—" He shut his mouth and didn't finish.

It was like some stupid reflex. I knew I shouldn't ask, but I did: "You don't see why what?"

"Nothing." He lifted off the chair, ready to walk away, but then turned back, hands on the table, talking down at me. "Then why should I do what you want?"

"You shouldn't, Ben," I said to his face, not bothering to conceal my dislike. "You shouldn't do a goddamn thing for me."

Naomi's head glanced in our direction. Although I was quiet, she had heard a new music in the familiar duet of husband and wife: a woman's anger. Her mother had never played that note. Tearful rage, perhaps, but not this cold fury, this Maine woods ice.

He reacted (and I noted it, understood its implication for the first time) like an actor presented with an unfamiliar cue. His emotions stopped—his eyes scanned one way and another, trying to remember—and then he revved up again, feeling back in his face, his tone and manner whole again, game for improvisation.

"Fine," he said, concealing hurt beneath coolness. He turned and called out to Naomi, the indulgent father, "Want to play some video games?" It was all strategy, all a performance.

"Okay," she moaned sluggishly, half rolling off the couch.

Ben hadn't understood the formation I presented, so he retreated. Later, scouts would appear and attempt to discover my weakness, or simply hope that my will to win would weaken and he would get his way. That was his strongest muscle after all, vigilant and inexhaustible.

"Come on." Ben pulled at Naomi, who remained limp, slumped at the foot of the couch. "What's the matter with you? Are you sick?"

"No," she answered too quickly, springing up. I tried to get a view of her as they left: she was pale.

Alone, I had another collapse of faith. I gave up all my schemes, from Ben confessing (which I knew in my heart would never happen) to cohabiting with him throughout the trial (which I knew would end in death for one of us). I felt my will go, abandon me. I had to let civilization take over, inept and unfair though it was.

I searched for the number the lieutenant had given me—tucked away behind a fold in my Filofax—and called it. I told the male who answered my name and asked for him.

"Well," the lieutenant came on without a hello, "how did he react?"

"React?"

"To the magazine article."

"What magazine article?"

"You haven't seen it? In *Town?* His first wife has written an article, *'Men Who Kill and the Women Who Love Them.'*" He chuckled, unable to resist, then cleared his throat to sound grave. "You're mentioned—"

"Is it out?"

"On the stands—"

I hung up without having told him my information and left the room. There was a shop in the lobby. I found it immediately. Joan's story wasn't on the cover, thank God, but there was a headline along the bottom announcing its presence inside. I carried it off to the women's room in the lobby and read it in a stall.

It was tasteless and stupid and factless and a little dull. Joan gave a sanitized and brief account of her marriage to Ben, told the alleged facts of the murder, and quoted anonymous parents at the school. She mentioned that I was Wendy's closest friend and had maintained contact with Ben and Naomi.

"My main concern is the little girl," she quoted me as saying. The magazine hadn't checked this with me (obviously), but I guess they assumed no one would or could sue for that remark, although I can't believe I actually said it, certainly not the way it came out, a bureaucrat announcing a departmental policy.

Amelia Waxman and a coterie of Wendy's colleagues were also quoted, saying good things, nice things, impossible and untrue things.

Harriet was a featured player, contemplating legal action to get custody of Naomi. She had two long quotes and was portrayed as worried and warmhearted. None of her eccentricity or vanity or lack of fitness was detailed.

What bothered me most was that Joan had managed to prettify Ben. Although the article's point of view was that women are victimized by men, she left out his gambling, his intellectual arrogance, his selfishness, his award-winning combination of manipulativeness, self-pity, and self-deception, and instead portrayed him as sexually tormented, somehow also a victim of "society's rigid role models." Then, having stripped Ben of what made him compelling, her portrait of Wendy was absent the depth of my friend's passions and ambitions, her greed to get what she wanted out of life, including a model husband and father, whether or not one existed. Ben had understood that much about my poor dead friend, that she wanted to win also, wanted life to be lived her way and would have used his cross-dressing against him. Joan wound up claiming we all had kinship with Ben and Wendy, that they were "reflections of ourselves, no matter how distorted or dimmed by their special circumstances."

Obviously I am not as smart as I thought I was before Wendy's murder, and there is a great deal I do not know, but I do have this expertise: we may all be killers and victims, but we kill and die very differently, each one of us, and evil is still evil and good is still good, no matter how thoroughly you understand motivation. On that I will allow no disagreement. Perhaps all men have Ben in them: all men do not kill. Perhaps all woman have Wendy in them: all woman are not murdered.

❧

Naomi complained of a sore throat before dinner and she had no appetite. She allowed her smooth scoop of chocolate ice cream to melt untasted. I touched her forehead; it warmed my palm like an open fire.

"She's got a fever," I said to Ben.

"I don't!" Naomi whined, and ducked away from his probing hand.

"Stay still!" Ben shouted. All day he had used an irritated tone with her, a subtle (not so subtle) blackmail for me to give him what he wanted. I couldn't figure out which one he wanted more—sex or money. Given that it was Ben, probably both. He felt her brow. "We'll go home. Take her to the doctor in the morning."

In the nineteenth century, before antibiotics, people died of heartbreak. She *should* die, I thought, of some beautiful illness, while she was still good, only good, with no adult vengeance or guilt to taint her. Instead, with our medicines, she would have to live to fill therapist's waiting rooms, appear on talk shows, and found groups. Children of Murderers Anonymous.

I had said nothing about Joan's article, although I didn't fear his reaction. My quote was so innocuous I doubt even Ben could have made anything out of it. Besides, none of that mattered now. At long last I had come to the inevitable decision, the one you knew I was sure to make.

I would kill him.

My problem was how. Not the difficulty in concealing that I did it, but to make sure that I succeeded, and that Naomi wasn't exposed to the event.

"I don't want to go home," Naomi croaked at the table. She held her neck and swallowed deliberately, pained. "I want to stay." She was reduced to a whisper.

We ignored her. Back in the room, she continued to moan, "I don't want to go home." She sounded almost delirious. We gave her Tylenol and parked her in front of the television while packing up. Within a minute she passed out, breathing heavily through her nose.

Ben sat down beside her prone figure and stroked her hair. "Maybe we should let her sleep here until the morning. Then drive straight to the doctor." He went to the telephone. "I'll see if I can reach him now and make an appointment."

Shooting Ben would be the surest thing. He could fight off a knife attack; poison was grotesque; setting him on fire, all of that, was part of his madness, the desire to hurt, confusing passion with death. I couldn't trust the justice of the world. I couldn't even trust the judgment of the world: people either wanted to make Ben into an alien or embrace him as a brother. I wanted him eliminated because I couldn't defeat him. I was no victim. I had hoped to redeem him through love, but love was power to him. Like Wendy, perhaps like all women (I hesitate to claim wide kinship), I lose power when I feel: only through action can I regain it. Do you understand?

Doesn't matter.

I didn't hate him; really, once I decided he had to die, I felt sorry for him. I listened to Ben fight his way through the answering service, demanding they reach her pediatrician immediately; he paced while waiting for the return call and then dealt coolly and competently with the doctor. Ben liked actions and decisions. He was efficient, concerned, and sensible. If only the world had appointed him dictator then he would have been a happy man.

"It's probably strep throat," Ben reported to me. "The spiking fever, painful throat. We can bring her in at seven-thirty and he'll take a culture."

"Then we can't leave in the morning," I said. I wanted to go back right away. I had to plan the killing; I could think better at home alone.

"I need to relax," Ben snapped at me in that harassed tone, as if I had been personally responsible for everything that had contributed to his tension.

He carried Naomi into the other room and put her to bed, still clothed. I packed her clothes and mine.

"You'll pack your things?" I asked him.

"I'm not a baby," was his response. He unlocked his huge suitcase (barred from casual entry because of the women's things still inside) and dumped his clothes from the drawer in.

I stared at the box which contained the cross-dressing outfit. He noticed my glance.

He lifted his eyebrows lasciviously. "When we get back home tonight, okay? She'll sleep soundly."

I looked blank, pretending I didn't know what he meant.

"Okay?" he prodded.

If I said no then there would be more ugly moods, probably more talk about the money for the options.

He whispered: "You enjoyed it that way, remember?"

"I might be tired," I said lamely.

"I'll drive," he said grandly, as if that answered any possible objection. He shut his bag and locked it again. "I'll go downstairs and check out so we can leave anytime."

"It's on my credit card," I reminded him.

"I still have one that works," he said in a bratty way, competing with me. "I'll have them switch it." He came over and gave me an awkward buss on the mouth. "I love you," he said.

I nodded noncommittally (I hoped); he smiled back, implying I had shown reciprocation, and blew me another kiss as he went out.

I checked on Naomi. She panted in her sleep like an exhausted dog. Her eyelids fluttered from the activity of her dreams. Could she be dying? I wondered. Waiting until the morning to have her checked suddenly seemed too casual.

I had an uneasy feeling—give me that much credit. While Ben was gone, I walked about the two rooms, convinced I had forgotten something (I certainly had) but unable to figure out what. You must remember I was not myself, otherwise I would never have made such a mistake.

Ben returned very quietly, ominously. I knew something had changed. But I still hadn't realized my error.

He focused on me immediately. He leaned against the wall and asked, "What do you think Varney can bargain for?"

"I don't know, Ben, I'm not a criminal lawyer." I was nervous: I sensed he was prowling for something. "But maybe, depending on the psychiatrists, it won't amount to jail."

"I bet Stefan would help. He'd be glad to say I'm nuts."

I relaxed. So that was it. He had cooked up a conspiracy between me and Stefan. "He 'sn't going to help." I smiled at the thought. "Believe me—he's furious at me."

Ben nodded thoughtfully. He shoved off from the wall and came toward me. "Sit down," he said, and nudged me onto the couch. He faced me, a knee on the cushion to prop him up, an arm against the backrest barring exit. He had me cornered. "Let's say we get that. I'm in a booby hatch—"

"It won't be bad—"

"It'll be great. The vacation I always dreamed of." Ben put his face right up to mine and roared: "What happens to Nommy?"

I tried to remain calm. I swallowed with difficulty. I attempted to shift away from his blocking presence, but he caught my head in his hand. I jerked it free. "Ben!"

"Answer me!"

"I'll take care of her!" I squeaked. "What do you think?"

He nodded, not at me, to himself. "That's what you're after," he muttered. "I'm a fucking idiot," he whispered harshly, his eyes glowing with tears. He shut them for a moment. When they opened, I saw something amazing, something I had never seen before in my life, something that robbed me of breath.

Hate. Pure hate.

He hit me. The back of his hand—knuckles hard and sharp as thick nails—punctured my cheek. I fell over, my face slid on the scratchy fabric. I tasted blood. I wanted to rub myself in it: I wanted to stay down, loathed and hated.

"You called the fucking cops. Are they coming now! Answer me!" He gathered my hair and pulled relentlessly. If he didn't stop my scalp was going to come off any second, my brains were going to spill out.

"Let go!" I begged. I kicked at his legs to get free.

He hit me in the stomach. I couldn't breathe. I tried to inhale, but my belly was gone, I couldn't work my mouth.

I was dying.

"Are they coming!"

I tried to tell him no. But I had no voice. I shook my head.

"You think I'm a fucking idiot, don't you? It's on the goddamn hotel bill! You called the cops! What for? What the fuck for?"

I wanted to tell him anything he liked—that was what all my bravery and strength and courage and hate amounted to: pitiful submission. But I couldn't talk, couldn't even breathe.

He hit me again. Across the mouth.

I would be black-and-blue for weeks. Everyone would know. There could be permanent scars on my face.

He hit me again.

Please stop! I begged him in my head because I couldn't talk. I wanted to tell him anything, anything at all to save myself.

"You faked it! You just want to put me away so you can have her! You're a fucking monster!"

He punched me in my vagina. I couldn't make the moans of my pain. My sex went numb, my legs radiated with hurt. He wasn't satisfied. He aimed very deliberately, lining up the target with his big fist (I remembered how she had tried to hide her hands), and then he smashed my groin again.

My pelvis cracked. It was broken: I was a cripple.

I was dying.

I didn't want to live anymore, not after how he had ruined me, proud me, proud stupid vain me.

And he was right. I had lied: all along, all I had wanted was to care for Nommy, to fulfill my duty to Wendy. My pleasure at our sex was a fluke. He was evil and he was killing me, but you see, don't you, that he was right.

I was his enemy.

He took my throat in his hands. I wriggled in his fingers to free my face, to lift my consciousness up. He squeezed my throat like a butcher grabbing hold of a chicken. I squirmed in the grip of slaughter.

This is it, Molly. This is the moment of your death.

Please let me go, let me escape! I asked the Lord and tried to wriggle out of the murderer's hands, to rescue my mind, my soul, the shrunken part that is free of the body, of all the selfish wants of living, the sexless essence of me yearning not to die. But I crashed down into myself, dying.

I spoke into his eyes, since I couldn't give it voice: Please Ben, let me go. I'll leave you to your daughter. Let me go: I want to live.

You see, I am not good. I am bad, so terribly, terribly bad. And the worst thing was I was dying that way, cornered in my worst self, the one that cared only for me, the evil Molly.

Wendy appeared. The fact is her daughter appeared, like a ghost herself, delirious, hair soaked, speaking in a cracked noise from her red throat.

"Daddy! You're hurting her!"

I didn't see Naomi: I saw her mother, because that's who summoned her from unconsciousness to rescue me.

I was almost dead. In fact, I thought my head had burst with blood, flowing out of my eyes.

There was no room for me in my brain. I was in Ben's head now, hoping to live on through my killer. I heard his thoughts: *She's almost dead—finish. Just one more squeeze and she's dead.*

Ben wanted to kill me: he was happy controlling my existence, as happy as I had ever seen him.

He let go. And disappeared. I saw nothing . . . still couldn't breathe.

Nommy's voice croaked from somewhere: "She's bleeding." It was an old woman's sound: my mother's before she died, mine in another twenty years.

"She's fighting with me. Get back into bed. She's okay."

He would come back and kill me. I struggled to clear the broken bones in my throat. . . .

I gasped for air and fell off the couch. I watched my fingers crawl through the artificial grass of the carpet. Blood dripped from my face.

I crawled away from him, and fool that I am, I kept thinking that I was ruined, that now my ugliness was obvious, all the world could see how selfish and untrustworthy I am.

I heard Naomi talk and talk and talk in her hoarse voice, delaying Ben from returning to kill me. In the notes of her complaints ("My throat hurts." "I'm too hot.") there were warnings: Get out Molly. Save yourself.

That's how I know Wendy still lived in her: she couldn't have understood by herself.

My legs worked after all. I reached the door, pulled myself up by the knob, opened it, and fell into the hall. A well-dressed couple, Honda dealer and his wife, stopped in their tracks. She gasped. He looked embarrassed.

Ben returned at that moment. He stayed at the connecting door, ignoring the couple, and stared at me, half-in, half-out.

"Hurry up," he told me. "Or I'll kill you."

You know what I said?

"I'm sorry," I mumbled through my bloody lips.

Remembering

O f course I'm better now. Is that what worried you?
Perhaps you've noticed that I love clichés for their forgotten terrible truths. I have become proof of one of them: Time heals all wounds.

Ben's attack on me finished him. Besides the assault charge, which cost him custody of Naomi, a pattern of violence against women was established, and I supplied the coup de grace with my testimony that he had confessed to Wendy's murder.

Indirectly the prosecutor made it clear I should forget about the log Ben had told me he used to strike the fatal blow. "Are you sure about the log?" he asked over and over. Eventually, I understood the hint: they had no fragments of wood in her skull to confirm it. I erased the log from my account. I think Ben made up that part for my benefit, anyway. Just another lie from a man for whom lies are truth.

Remember, I saw into his soul as he strangled me: he liked watching my life depart; he had enjoyed taking Wendy's.

I believe that's why Wendy haunted me until I understood. She knew that I blamed her, in some way, for what had happened, that I was smug and superior about her marriage and her death. She forced me to live her life, to suffer, and then she saved me. I don't believe Dr. Reynolds's explanation, his pat answers that I was paying for imagined past sins. Those are Freudian bedtime stories created to soothe Stefan's feelings.

Would I have killed Ben? Yes. We are not all the same. I am not good like Wendy. That is why I am alive and she is dead. Had she not haunted me I would have turned my back and claimed there was nothing that could be done. Just about everyone else did.

No thanks to Ben, Naomi lives with Stefan in our apartment, next door to her sad, former home, which was sold to pay Ben's lawyers. In a last attempt to hurt me, Ben gave Harriet custody of Naomi. Stefan, however, convinced Harriet to leave Naomi unofficially in his care. Although Ben's lawyers howled, their challenge to this arrangement was dismissed because of Ben's status as a convicted murderer. When I asked Stefan (he visits me, in hope, twice a week) how he persuaded Harriet, he explained with a smile of pride at his cleverness. A movie producer wanted to buy the rights to Harriet's story, or rather the story she invented, a sentimental fiction about her close relationship with Ben from their childhood in Queens to their fascinating Manhattan careers. Stefan convinced Harriet that she owed it to herself to concentrate on this opportunity to explain, among other things, what happened to her brilliant promise as a dancer and that the drudgery (and expense) of raising a little girl would only hold her back. After all my struggles and worries with the legalities, Stefan just talked his way around the rules and got Naomi. Of course, Harriet had one condition: that I not live with Stefan and Naomi until it could be proved to her satisfaction that I had recovered from my psychological problems. Telling me of his triumph Stefan was as proud as a victorious warrior. I was glad for Naomi, but I know his charity is aimed at my heart, not hers. Poor Stefan, he dreams that one day I will overcome Harriet's disapproval, he and I will reconcile and together supervise Nommy's life.

As part of my therapy I work at the shelter with Larry and Maggie and all the other freaks. I rent a room from Pauline, the woman who runs it. She disagrees with Stefan's vision of my future. She has suggested that after I'm cured—they speak of cures here—I ought to take the money from Naomi Perlman's estate, still held in escrow, and open a shelter in Maine. I'm willing, except that living so far from New York would deprive me of my one remaining joy, which I must ask you not to talk about to anyone. I am afraid my psychiatrist might think it bad and stop me.

I have Fridays off and my private therapy is in the morning. After the session I drive into the city (not in that Volvo, I couldn't bear to use it anymore) and park across the street from the gray Riverside School.

I follow Naomi and the woman Stefan has hired to help him on their walk home.

Naomi is taller and more beautiful than ever. It hurts to watch her and not be able to speak to her or touch her. It hurts too much.

Last week, on a beautiful spring day, I couldn't bear the separation anymore. I followed them into Washington Square Park. Naomi's caretaker sat on one of the benches and read the newspaper while Naomi went off to the swings and solemnly began a swooping ride up and down.

I had promised my psychiatrist and Pauline and Stefan that I wouldn't make any attempt to speak to Naomi until they felt she was ready, but I was ready that day.

I entered the enclosed children's playground and sneaked behind the benches (I didn't know if the caretaker could recognize me) on my way into the swing area.

Naomi spotted me when I was only a few feet off. She stuck out her feet to brake herself and opened her mouth to shout a greeting.

I put a finger to my lips to silence her and gestured that she should keep going. There are benches right behind the swings; I sat down a few feet away from her slot so that an onlooker would believe I was attached to one of the other swinging children.

"I'm not supposed to talk to you." I spoke into the wind of her movements, not in a whisper, but in the low tones of conspiracy.

"Why?" Her voice was still clear and loud and brave.

"I don't really know. They think it'll bother us. Make us upset."

"That's crazy," she decided.

"I love you," I told her.

"I know," she said softly.

"I just wanted to tell you because I haven't been around, and I didn't want you think that I didn't want to see you."

"I love you," she answered. The words caught in her throat; she slowed her pendulum and stared at me with her wide sad eyes.

Her caretaker looked up from her paper and seemed to notice me. Anyway, she peered in our direction.

"Keep swinging high," I told Naomi.

She pumped and gained velocity.

"You look all better," she said.

That made my tears come. "Thank you," I mumbled, and tried to swallow and brush them away.

"Will you come home soon?" she asked.

"I'm going to try. Is everything okay with you?"

Tears filled her eyes but did not spill. She nodded.

"Stefan's a good man."

She nodded an eager yes, her blue eyes wavering from the tears that wouldn't let go and escape down her smooth white cheeks. "He'd make a good daddy," she told me, echoing her mother's old nagging.

"I have to go." I was nervous. Her caretaker had glanced our way again.

"When will I see you?"

"Keep coming to the park."

She nodded. Her lips were pressed together as if she were holding something back besides the tears.

"What is it, Nommy? Is there something you want to tell me? Are they treating you okay? Is she nice?" I indicated her caretaker.

Naomi nodded again, but her lips quaked. She slowed her pace on the swing, almost stopped. "They don't . . ." She choked and didn't continue.

"What?" I had gotten to my feet. Her caretaker was folding her newspaper and seemed to be about to rise. "Hurry. I have to go."

"They don't . . ." Again she didn't finish.

The hopefulness I had felt talking to her sagged: I suspected she wanted to complain about the prohibition against visiting her father in prison. I didn't want her to see Ben either, but if she resented it I had to know. "Tell me quickly," I urged her. "I've got to go."

"They don't talk about my mommy." She stammered it out and at last her tears flowed: "I'm going to forget her. . . ."

She wanted to remember the heroine of her life, not the villain: she was good.

"We'll talk about your mommy," I promised. I took a risk and hugged her hard—but quickly. "We'll remember," I whispered, and ran.

So far no one has said anything about my transgression. I'm going to sneak off again next week so you mustn't tell either. You can't blame me for needing to see her. Someday—I believe it now—she and I will be together. Someday I will explain everything to her.

Someday, like young Naomi, I will be good. Now, more than anything, I want to be good.